Camille's Bread

Amanda Lohrey was born in Tasmania in 1947.
Her previous novels are *The Morality of
Gentlemen* and *The Reading Group*. She was a
lecturer in writing at the University of
Technology, Sydney, until recently and is now
writing full-time.

Camille's Bread was shortlisted for the Miles
Franklin Award, the Colin Roderick Award, the
New South Wales Premier's Prize for Fiction,
the 3M Talking Books Award, and the
Commonwealth Writer's Award Regional Prize.
It is winner of the ALS Gold Medal and the
Victorian Premier's Literary Awards Vance
Palmer Prize for Fiction.

*C*amille's Bread

AMANDA **L**OHREY

🔥 *flamingo*
An imprint of HarperCollins*Publishers*

Flamingo

An imprint of HarperCollins*Publishers,* Australia

First published in Australia in 1995
First paperback edition 1996
This Flamingo paperback edition 1996
Reprinted in 1997, 1998 (twice)
by HarperCollins*Publishers* Pty Limited
ACN 009 913 517
A member of the HarperCollins*Publishers* (Australia) Pty Limited Group
http://www.harpercollins.com.au

Copyright © Amanda Lohrey 1995

HarperCollins*Publishers*

25 Ryde Road, Pymble, Sydney, NSW 2073, Australia
31 View Road, Glenfield, Auckland 10, New Zealand
77-85 Fulham Palace Road, London W6 8JB, United Kingdom
Hazelton Lanes, 55 Avenue Road, Suite 2900, Toronto, Ontario M5R 3L2
and 1995 Markham Road, Scarborough, Ontario M1B 5M8, Canada
10 East 53rd Street, New York NY 10032, USA

National Library of Australia Cataloguing-in-Publication data:

Lohrey, Amanda.
Camille's bread.
ISBN 0 7322 5873 1 (pbk.)
I. Title.
A823.3

Printed in Australia by Griffin Press Pty Ltd on 80gsm Econoprint

10 9 8 7 6 5   98 99 00 01

The child's first decision, noted Freud,
is whether to swallow it or spit it out.

Contents

Acknowledgments

A part of this book was written with the assistance of
a Fellowship from the Literature Board of the Australia Council
and a residency at Varuna Writers' Centre,
granted by the Eleanor Dark Foundation.

Prologue

In the kitchen of a small house in Leichhardt, a young woman is dancing with her eight-year-old daughter. It's winter, and dark outside. A dish of lentil burgers sits warming on the hotplate and the strains of some exotic Latin tango strum insistently from a large black tape deck that stands on top of the fridge. Mother is clasping daughter in a parody of adult coupledom, each awkward and jolting with laughter as they stride, with exaggerated poise, up and down the skillion kitchen, sweeping across the black and white chequerboard tiles, heads tilted back, arms outstretched stiffly in the arch and demonic thrust of the tango. Dum dum, da da! da-da-da-da dah, dum dum da da! The mother is chanting time, pouting with mock seriousness, her cropped black hair standing upright in silky spikes of dishevelment and impatience. In her arms, her slight, fey, fair-haired daughter, hair drawn back in a French plait, her thin legs in dark green stockings and black lace-up school shoes, alternately mimicking the fierce concentration of her mother and erupting into loud, raucous schoolgirl laughter. For a moment, she breaks away to perform a dizzy pirouette on her own. 'See this step,' she says. 'You go, one two three four . . . and then you go . . .'

The telephone rings.

'Don't answer it,' says her mother. 'I'm sick of the phone. It's no-one we want to talk to. People shouldn't ring at mealtime. Mealtimes are for dancing.' But on these last words she is drowned out by a loud droning thunder as a low-flying 747 roars directly over the kitchen roof, its blinking tail lights creating a flash of momentary illumination in the small courtyard outside. The windows shudder and rattle in their frames but the two figures go on dancing, breaking off now into an improvised jive before the mother falls, feigning exhaustion, into a chair.

'I'm puffed,' she says, looking at her watch, 'and besides, it's past six.'

'No, try this. Look. You go . . .' and the child persists, executing a balletic turn on one foot, all loose limbs and fine ankles. But this time mother is insistent. 'No,' she says, 'that's it. I'm famished.' She gets up out of the chair and moves purposefully across to the stove, raising one finger in the air and pronouncing with melodramatic irony: 'Enough dancing. Time to eat.' At the stove she pauses, and stares into the iron whorls of the hotplate, still a little heady. These are the most blissful moments of her day. Just the two of them, gambolling in a playful embrace, like lovers; the feminine principle triumphant, ecstatic, cut loose in its own dream.

PART ONE

HIM

1

clerk: a person able to read and write; a person who keeps records or accounts; in mediaeval times, a person apprenticed in learning to a priest.

This morning I came to work and once again I found I was holding my breath.

In this purple and pink space with the wide-frame windows and the panoramic views of other office workers I cite myself, here, now, in this ambience of bright sunlight and false calm. The manager of this floor, Joel, is a very short man with a club foot. We call him The Dwarf. He is dark and surly. He doesn't like anyone. He struggles to be fair, in a repressive, Puritan vein. The work ethic: silence, time-and-motion, no visitors on the floor. The bureaucracy has taken him on when the private sector wouldn't and he's going to show them that dwarfs work harder than anyone else. Crack the whip. Snarl.

As for me, I could say that I am an ordinary clerk but there is no such thing as an ordinary clerk. On this floor we are all more or less demented, the only important difference being this: how close we are to panic. With some of us it's hard to tell; with others, all too clear. In my head I have a spectrum: at one end panic, at the other end, poise. I am working my way from left to right.

Next to me, mumbling to herself, is Shirley. Shirley lives with her older brother who's a dentist. Shirley used to drive a bus in the city until she had her nervous breakdown. Her doctor sent her to a psychiatrist who admitted her to hospital where eventually they sent her to the CES who sent her up here to be a clerk in the Treasury Office. Floor Nine: Internal Check. Most days, Shirley wears a dark, formal double-breasted suit, slightly shabby, and a black beret. Underneath the beret she wears her black hair slicked back like a pre-war lowlife. In her heart she is nourishing some secret scenario. Despite this, she is fast enough with the forms. Every now and then she sighs, swivels on her chair, and begins to tell me, again, about her manic-depression. As the union delegate I feel it's my duty to nod sympathetically.

On manic days Shirl goes into the Ladies every ten minutes to smooth her hair. There she stands, feet apart and with intense concentration she stares into the mirror, bringing her hands up with great deliberation to sweep them along the sides of her very neat head. I know, because when it's unbearable on the floor I too go into the lavatory for respite, to do a soothing ten minutes of Shao-lin exercise. The Swooping Butterfly. The Tiger in Repose. The Long Bow. And one day, there in the Mens, was Shirl. And without shifting her gaze from the mirror, without even blinking she spoke, as if to a servant: 'Good morning, Stephen.'

In my sociology course we did a lot on Weber. Weber said that modern bureaucracy is the essence of the new rationalism. Weber didn't know about Shirl.

Or me. I'm working on altering the vibes of this place, sending beams of the irrational out from the heart of Internal Check to permeate all floors. If I concentrate hard enough one day the computers will break down. All records deleted, including mine. I left school, drifted around, drove a pie truck, played football for money in Darwin because it was a recession and I couldn't get a job anywhere and — well, did a few other things I have no plans to mention here. One day, in the CES, this woman gives me an IQ test and sends me off to Tech to do HSC. At twenty-nine I've got an Arts Degree and I've progressed to the magnificent position of Graduate Clerk ASOC1, Treasury Office, Floor Nine, Internal Check. This is called upward mobility and self-fulfilment through learning. But it's better than driving a pie truck. Just.

'Just' is a word that sustains me. This is just a job. This is just a phase of life I'm passing through. What I have to find is my spiritual path.

Yesterday Shirl changed her name. Now we have to call her Freda.

Don't think that I mock Freda. In her own way she has achieved a kind of poise. Which, I begin to think, is all that any of us can aspire to.

Meanwhile I keep an eye out for panic. When the panic coils in Freda she adjourns to the lavatory. It's a banal strategy, not to be compared with my own.

It's 10.25 and I've entered seventy-two of these bank interest statements. Time for a natter. I spot Sanjay over at the water cooler.

*How is the man of tranquil wisdom, who abides in divine
contemplation? What are his words? What is his silence?
What is his work?*

BHAGAVAD GITA

Sanjay is sixty-one and he's been in Internal Check for eleven months. He left
Malaysia two years ago to be with his daughter who'd married 'one of you
Australians'. In Kuala Lumpur, he says, he'd been a relatively wealthy man but
he'd come to Sydney with almost nothing, leaving behind a large house in
KL. He's Hindu, though not so orthodox as his wife; she's strict vegetarian.
Sanjay had been a senior officer in the civil service. During the Emergency in
1956 he'd been a major in the Army and seen action against communist
guerillas in the hills. Raids on small towns and villages. A nasty mess. He is
small, with smoky red lips and his greying hair is combed straight back from a
square face. Sanjay is very quiet in his manners, is a philosopher, knows Plato
and the *Bhagavad Gita* and the Bible and the Koran. He talks to me across the
narrow aisle that separates our desks. 'The Bible is a very interesting book,
Stephen, a very interesting book. The Koran is not so interesting. I spent
many months searching for a copy of the Koran in English and when I found
one, truly it was very dull. Just a long list of do's and don'ts, and not at all
profound.'

I wonder if this is true. I make a note to read the Koran.

Sometimes I ask him about the insurgency. Though he likes to talk, to
lecture me with his quiet courtesy, he is reticent on the subject of war. 'It
changes you, Stephen, once you see terrible things.' Though one day, when he
is relaxed, he tells me a funny story, chuckling and beaming at me. 'One time,
you see, we find the body of a young soldier who has been blown up by a crude
landmine. There is not much left of him, his body is torn in half, with only
the top half intact. The villagers find a coffin for him and fill it up with stones
to balance it out, so that for the pallbearers it feels like a real body. As it
happens this boy's mother lives in the next village, some miles away. When
she hears the news she comes to the commanding officer at the camp and asks
to see her son's body . . .' The Dwarf looks over, frowning, and motions
abruptly at us to get back to work. As union delegate for the floor I feel it's my

duty to ignore him and I look to Sanjay to continue his story. He just smiles, graciously. 'Another time, Stephen,' he says. 'I would not want to get you into trouble.'

Sanjay acknowledges me as a fellow pilgrim. He is impressed by the fact that I spend four nights a week attending to my spiritual path; two nights learning Zen Shiatsu massage and two on the Chinese meditative art of Chi Kung. Both the Japanese *and* the Chinese? he asks. You need as much help as you can get, I say. Anyway, I'm working on a personal synthesis.

'Now tell me, Stephen,' he asks, 'how do you reconcile all this with your very combative work as union delegate for the floor? With your, let us say, rationalist traditions, the dualism of *them* and *us*?'

'I am in a period of transition,' I reply.

When Sanjay applies for a promotion from ASOC1 to ASOC2 he is interviewed, and to his disappointment, not chosen. He asks for his interview report and it says that Sanjay lacks assertiveness. We talk over the water cooler. I commiserate. 'You must realise, Stephen,' he says, 'that these people have a very peculiar notion of assertiveness, do they not?' I agree with him. They are ignorant rationalists, I say. Their intuitive faculties are stuffed. I ask him for a good eggplant curry recipe from his wife. 'Cumin seeds and fennel,' he says, waving his hand in a gesture affectionate but dismissive. 'That is all you need to know.'

●

I find it difficult to sleep at night. My mind goes on and on, turns over and over. Sometimes I dread the start of the next day, dread going into work. This job. The soulless quarter-acre. I sit up in my dark green armchair reading my book on Chinese medicine. I am heartened to learn that any excess of feeling turns into its opposite; that excess sadness is the yin of excess joy. I am working on it.

I talk to my friend, Nathalie. Nathalie likes to talk to me about my job. She thinks it's fascinating, all these clerks, these people — she calls them 'unlikely' — working in the Treasury Office. She says she'd like, one day, to write a short story about it. All these people, enmeshed in the system, computing in the codes of money; and in their hearts, dreaming other codes, other mysteries. I say the use of the word 'heart' is sentimental, that unless you have a hole in it and are up for a transplant the heart means nothing now. That it belongs to a romantic nineteenth century discourse. I say that dreams belong not to the heart but to another part of the brain that's always working, that dreams come in the day as well as at night, that this part of the brain is sometimes confused and speaks out of turn, that Internal Check is never wholly in check. She says this is meaningless talk; that when she has a Zen Shiatsu massage and the masseur, at the end, squats on the floor and encompasses her body in his arms and arches her back over his knees, then, at that moment, she feels her heart expand.

●

At night I sometimes watch television, though I am trying to give it up. There's something about sitting slumped in the spotlight of the cathode-ray tube that makes me feel like a rat in a maze. Tonight, however, I settle back on the couch to watch a late-night repeat in the series *A Question of Survival*. Gazing at panoramas of wilderness reduced to the size of a technicolour tea tray can sometimes bring on a mind-numbing prelude to sleep. I live in hope. The TV says: *Tonight we take a look at the question of origins. We talk to men and women out there in the field who are searching for clues.* Something that looks like an Aboriginal rock painting fills the screen. The TV says: *A new method of dating paint residues shows these to be the oldest paint traces in human history.* Oh, God. I look at my watch: it's 12.05. Should I turn it over to the breakfast programme now being relayed by satellite from New York? No. Too much snow quiver on the screen. The TV says: *And that's not all. The global spotlight is shifting to Australia as the place where the Earth's first four-legged animals emerged from the sea. As well, fossil evidence is rapidly amassing that points to Australia as the origin of important advances such as the four-chambered heart, paired limbs and brain development. And we ask: could it be that Australia, not Africa, was the primal scene of evolution, the original garden of Eden?*

What does he mean 'original'? Were there copies?

I cannot convey to you my impatience with this obsession, this obsession with origins. Who cares where the Garden of Eden was? What matters is the state of the body, here, now. Every nine months the body replaces every cell, completely reconstitutes itself; every six weeks, a new liver; every three days, a new stomach lining. So why should History matter? History is a constellation of thoughts, planted like noxious weeds in the brain as a way of controlling us, distracting us from the material moment and its proper nurture. It's where you're going that's important, not where you come from; not origins, but destination. Transformation. Transcendence. The TV whines on: . . . *tetrapods in East Gondwana . . . spectacular evolutionary radiation . . . giant lobe-finned air-breathing osteolepiforme Canowindra grossi . . .* Blah, blah, blah, blah.

No, this isn't working. It's not soporific. I'm answering back. That's my problem: I'm always answering back. The TV persists in its implacable, portentous tones. I thumb the remote control. Over and out.

It's spring. I rise at six and walk uphill to the park to do half an hour of Chi Kung. On the brow of the hill the brash new green and gold swings are like giant canary perches. The grey lavatory block is daubed in red paint: F U C K C R O A T I A. Plastic syringes spike the dry grass. I walk to the far corner, beneath the smoky blue gums, and breathe deeply. Soon, in a moment, when I move into the first phase of the Butterfly, I will see only the bed of purple and white crocuses that sweep across my eye in a delirious and unsteady blur.

Back in the bright, glassed-in kitchen I prepare breakfast: miso soup and rice porridge that I grind myself in the blender, simmer for three minutes and serve with soy milk and rice malt. So much creamier than commercial oats which have had the life force steamrollered out of them. I try to eat slowly, to empty my head of thoughts, but I look into my white bowl and I see the blurred face of an unknown woman.

I'm jaunty on my walk to the bus stop, past the flaking terraces and the fluorescent graffiti. The little man is at the bus stop again, brandishing his sawn-off broom, sweeping with great concentration, oblivious to the 8.35 commuters. Sweeping over their shoes if they stand in his way. The regulars know his path and concede territory.

The bus pulls in, an old one. I push my way through to a back seat, lean into the window, inhale the fumes and open my book. Robert Musil, *The Man Without Qualities*. Volume Three. When I first started reading this novel I got excited; it seemed full of the density of Europe. A place I've never been but one that I've known in my imagination since I was a child. The Eiffel Tower, the Colosseum, the 1958 blue and white Peugeot, Hitler, the Bridge of Sighs, Hegel, the croissant, Attila the Hun, castles on the Rhine, Woden, the woodcutter and the wolf, Italian tenors, white leather shoes, Sigmund Freud, the Viennese waltz, Auschwitz, Tolstoy, the samovar, Napoleon in the snow, Russian tanks in Prague. History, the dialectic, the unconscious; the continent of philosophy, the continent of answers.

Curious, isn't it, how Musil could write three volumes and nine-hundred-and-eighty-six pages and never tell you once what his characters eat. These people are ethereal sprites; they speak the poverty of a philosophy that is not grounded in the body. Their world is a series of pale dreams.

8.49 and I clock on. Sanjay is at his desk, already nursing his polystyrene cup of caffeine poisoning.

'I thought you were giving up tea, Sanjay.'

'How can an Indian give up tea, Stephen?'

I have to grant Sanjay this. Even though he's wrong at least he understands the cultural significance of food.

At 9.01 I take the lift to the twenty-third floor for the monthly meeting of union delegates. I sit next to Frank, who's already coughing with the chain-smoker's cough; the attacking buzzsaw. He's the most senior officer amongst us and unlike most senior officers is still very pro-union. He tells us there is a recruitment day coming up at the Parramatta branch and asks for volunteers. The idea is to cruise around the offices in pairs, speaking to clerks and persuading them of the righteousness of joining the union. I put my name down. Wednesday the nineteenth. I plan my strategy in the lift on the way down to the ninth floor. I'll take a soft line, soft because everything must be consonant with my spiritual path. This is the Chinese way: unleash the forces and let them take their own path. Never raise the voice. Never push. Not that

I don't appreciate a good lair. Danny, for instance, the delegate from Tax. He strolls into management in his striped red shorts and gym boots and when they patiently explain about government cutbacks he explodes. 'Don't piss me around,' he says, 'I read the papers. That's your problem. Our award is clear and non-negotiable until the next hearing.' In Zen Shiatsu terms Danny is a classic gall bladder case. Lots of anger.

I know all about anger.

Union class dismissed. I take the lift to the lobby, shoot across to Wynyard Station and ring Nathalie on the red phone.

'What about tonight?' I ask her. 'I'll come over at ten,' I say, 'after class.'

It's good to hear her voice. I could ring her from the office, of course, but I just want to get out of the building for a while.

On the way back I run into Gareth in the lift.

'Armed?' I ask.

'To the teeth,' he replies.

I follow Gareth into the Mens and he gives me some dope.

He's a little dejected, even for Gareth: he's just been to an interview for promotion and they asked him what he understood by the word 'initiative'.

'Once it was facts, now it's semantics,' he says, softly.

'It's the trend,' I say.

I'm the union delegate. It's my function to console.

For Gareth I have a special regard. For Gareth, life is absurd. Gareth is a master of the ironic reading which is a great consolation in this world of the literal-minded.

Gareth is estranged from his spiritual path by a perverse response to the cruelty of fate: he drinks. A drop-out from Philosophy at Sydney University, he got to the end of his third year and just before his final exams, at the age of twenty-one he had, he explained to me, not a panic attack, no, it was more a futility attack, he said; his sense of the absurd, hitherto held in check by steady daytime drinking, crept up and ambushed him. In order to cram for his exams he had reduced his daily intake of Guinness to only a few pints and suddenly, dangerously, his mind cleared. The ruminations of his teachers and his own (quote) 'blatherings' on paper struck him as comically absurd, fundamentally frivolous. All assessments were a sham and he ought not to collude in them. As he sat on the ferry one morning (he lived at home with his mother in Narrabeen) and gazed out over the sunlit water, an overwhelming sense of the bogus character of institutionalised knowledge made him laugh out loud, like an idiot, and he felt himself on the verge of doing something crazy, so much that when the ferry docked at Circular Quay he hastened to one of the dockside pubs that open at six a.m. for the wharfies coming off the nightshift, and had a steadying schooner of Guinness to moderate this epiphany. It wasn't panic, he said, it was insight tantamount to a sudden excess of joy, and it was joy, not sadness, that was unmanageable and threatening to every other man and woman's efforts to continually re-invent a sensible day. This was why he was able, unlike me, to accept his work in Treasury. It was an unpretentious and socially useful way of living a life of modest expectation: small gains made in an orderly fashion.

When he talks like this Gareth is completely deadpan, so that I'm unable to tell whether he truly has made some kind of accommodation to deadening routine or doesn't believe a word of it. Irony can be a smokescreen, a baffling camouflage. I told him that I was desperate to pass my exams, that I shook with nerves every day for a month, that I had a point to prove and that I knew this: until I had proved it I would be unable to move on. 'Exactly,' he replied, in his offhand way, and left it at that.

Today Gareth is thin and pale and does not look well. Do I imagine it or is his sensitive head becoming more austere in outline? Of course, he doesn't eat; his lunches with me consist entirely of lager and Guinness. Gareth is Welsh, descended, he says, from the Clan Morgan, betrayed by an incompetent king in the ninth century who sent them out to die in a hopeless battle. That's why he drinks. It's the Celtic fatalism in him, he says. Doomed to defeat and emaciation. Gareth was born in Wales and since his father's death has become obsessed with his own Welshness. That origins gig again. I say it is time we Australians left the Celtic influence behind. He says I'm a deluded Orientalist, a traitor to my race.

He mocks me. I am fond of him.

Sometimes we have a drink after work at the Criterion. Primed, he recites his favourite lines from his favourite poet, W. B. Yeats.

Turning and turning in the widening gyre
The falcon cannot hear the falconer;
Things fall apart; the centre cannot hold;
Mere anarchy is loosed upon the world,
The blood-dimmed tide is loosed, and everywhere
The ceremony of innocence is drowned.

I like to listen to him because he declaims well but privately I think these lines are a bit tired. Some of us have moved on. And where is this centre? The only centre that counts is in the *hara,* in your guts, the solar plexus. The Celtic nationalists worry too much about the body politic and not enough about the body. I sense that on some level of being Gareth knows this, which is why he drinks. He proffers another explanation. 'In the end, all that matters is the song,' he argues, but the problem is that often it's hard to sing, the air won't move in his windpipe, the breath gets stuck in his chest, and that's why he needs to drink, to expand the songways. You could laugh at this, if his voice were not so mesmerising. It makes the back of my head go cold.

Once I accompanied Gareth up to the Cross, a back lane off William Street where we waited for some pale, starved-looking type to deliver the goods. She was little and thin with long hennaed hair and she stared at me as if she knew me (and maybe she did) so I looked away. Afterwards, on the way back to the station, Gareth gave me some hashish. He sometimes makes me a gift because as his union rep I handled his appeal for unpaid higher duties and got him six hundred dollars in back pay. He wouldn't fight it of course. Fatalistic. Quietist. I had to push him, talk him up for days, prepare the case, put on my tie and leather jacket and do the port and cigars routine with the management. I'd been soft but persistent, and in the end they'd agreed. I'd do this for anyone, even the most weak, spineless bastards, but especially for Gareth. He's bright, he's a poet; he's wasting away.

We stroll back to our desks, mute now, anticipating the wrath of The Dwarf. Gareth glances in his direction and hisses at me, sotto voce, '*The mouse that has but one hole is quickly taken* — Proverb.' I know what this is; it's one of Gareth's takes from his desk calendar. Like a modern-day Dadaist he is apt to quote the most perverse of these at any moment. This one is so absurd that I begin to crack up.

the desk-calendar riff

Gareth just loves his desk calendar. You know, those little quotes at the bottom of each flip-over page, inscribed below the date, in pale blue print. How does he remember them? Little one and two-line gems from the Bible, the Koran, the Tao and miscellaneous other sources: everyone from Jesus to Nelson A. Rockefeller. Detached from their origins, free-floating, they come at you, their unsuspecting prey. 'Five thousand years of civilisation condensed into an office accessory,' says Gareth. 'The economy of it is breathtaking.'

'Wisdom lies at our fingertips,' he intones, 'we should make the most of it.' Quite often he sends a note over to me with some laconic witticism on the theme of that day's proverb. Or, when I'm moaning about something over the tea-break or at lunch in the pub, he'll spring one on me that has a kind of loopy application. Like when I was complaining about the union meeting and he said solemnly: *'Never give advice in a crowd* — Arabian proverb.'

Some of them, he says, should be enlarged and hung from the office, like the AIDS warnings on buses. *Neither the front nor the back entrance of the Custom-House opens on the road to Paradise* — Nathaniel Hawthorne. This, he says, should go up in the ground floor foyer of the Taxation Office. Or how about this for the Inquiries desk: *No single principle can answer all life's complexities* — Felix Frankfurter. Or this in Compliance: *It is vain to look for yesterday's fish in the house of the otter* — Hindoo proverb.

Once, he got agitated about the question of authenticity, citing this one: *Laughter is the tonic, the relief, the surcease for pain* — Charles Chaplin. Chaplin, said Gareth, would never have used a word like 'surcease'. 'My faith is shaken in the authenticity of these,' he groaned, and ordered another schooner. 'Chaplin was English,' I said, 'they tend to have better vocabularies than the Americans.' But he just stared gloomily ahead.

Lately he claims to have discerned the personality of the compiler. It's all tongue in cheek, and some of it even faked, he says, citing, *Positive procrastination is a valuable management technique in this rapidly changing world* — Doug Gettingby. 'This has to be a joke,' he said. 'Gettingby — getting by— get it?'

Most of all he loves the way everything is jumbled in with everything else, the way Jesus Christ (*Blessed are the meek*) is followed with equal solemnity by Bill Cosby (*Every closed eye is not sleeping, and every open eye is not seeing*).

He is delighted with the absurdity of this on March 1, the cessation of daylight saving: *Earth's crammed with heaven and every common bush afire with God* — E. B. Browning. Surely, says Gareth, we are about to get less not more light from God's burning bush. Another sign, he says, of a mocking intelligence behind the scenes?

When I first told him about my conversion to macrobiotics he passed me a swift note via the tea trolley. *One should eat to live, not live to eat* — Benjamin Franklin.

After some flicking backwards and forwards on my desk calendar I replied: *Your body is the harp of your soul* — Kahlil Gibran.

Gareth was quick on the return volley: *The mystic tries to rid himself of self, and in the process usually becomes obsessed with it* — Nehru.

But I was ready for him: *Cruelty is more cruel if we defer the pain* — Proverb.

Later, when he complained about the banality of the Christian quotes, I seized my chance. You wait, I said, in the future we'll have macrobiotic ones. '*Brown rice is the manure of the life force,*' I ventured.

'That's a bit weak,' he said.

'Give me time.'

Sometimes, when he's ill, hungover or just dejected I try and rouse him with a favourite quote. *The poet can reach where the sun cannot* — Hindi proverb.

He smiles, wanly.

We are almost at our desks when we're buttonholed by Doug. 'Warm, today,' he says.

'Yeah,' says Gareth, who is not in the mood for the weather.

'Quite a high humidity reading.'

Gareth keeps on walking, but with my usual weakness for humouring the mad, I stop and pass the time of day. Doug is a weather fiend. Doug likes to keep a barometer on his desk. Made in Germany, it says:

FAIR   MILD   STORMY

This is Doug's litany, a magic spell to ward off the panic. Doug especially likes to monitor the air-conditioning. 'It's twenty-five degrees today,' he says. 'That's as hot as it gets in mid-winter. It shouldn't get as hot as that in mid-September. In mid-September it should be — ' he pauses for accurate recollection, 'twenty degrees precisely. Conducive to the wearing of a light jacket, say.'

Doug is a fanatic on efficiency; his desk is always neat and tidy, his passion for measurement undiminished, his meteorological icon always in place.

Every day he reads the charts in the local papers and builds his own comparisons so that on each day he can predict what is going to happen. He discovered that if you approached the Bureau of Meteorology you could get microfiche of the last hundred years of weather, of temperature in any specific spot. Over the years he's spent a small fortune on acquiring Sydney's weather statistics and now we have to endure these lugubrious bits of trivia at morning tea: 'Did you know that in 1979 it rained seventeen inches in August, a world record not counting monsoonal rains in designated countries?' And so on. As an obsessive myself I have a certain respect for other zealots but Doug is painful — I can see no point in obsessing over something you can't control. I remarked on this to Sanjay. 'The weather is not like the body,' I said. 'You can't control it.' But Sanjay rebuked me. 'Obsessions are always about what you *cannot* control, that is the nature of obsession. And besides, what is happening here? What do we know? Like you I am sometimes bemused when I read about this man, this man builds Spanish galleons out of matchsticks; this or that woman collects beer coasters from around the world. This is a curious zeal, yes. But is there not, also, an accumulation of energy, such that you wonder whether, on some level, if we are all patient, it may prove to be true that no obsession is ever wasted?'

I said nothing. What could I do but defer to such immense spiritual tact?

Once I kept a journal, or two actually, one at home and one at work, and every now and then I'd write in them surreptitiously.

I wrote my last entry just four months ago, before I took up Shiatsu and changed my diet.

> *I've just about had enough! I can feel a primordial scream lurking in my body, trying desperately to escape my bowels and make its long-awaited journey upwards.*

> *Being a public servant at the base-grade level is, if anything, a slow death. Or like waiting to be born. A quarter-acre of office littered with desks. Life here is unbearably light. I feel myself floating out of my chair and drifting around the office. This is my soul looking to escape.*

> *As I clock on I breathe in and upon clocking out I breathe out. It's a long time to hold your breath as the clock ticks mindlessly on. Tick, tick, tick fucking tock.*

This is how I used to be. A quality of desperation. Since then I've learned that sooner or later desperate people discover where they need to go.

Look at Freda, now. She has pushed her chair back and begun to prowl in a restless circle around her desk. Her heavy black shoes squeak insistently against the lino tiles . . . *squeak, squeak, squeak* . . . unsettling the rest of us. We avert our eyes, and wait for the Supervisor, Isobel, to come and pacify her.

Yes, some things I leave to Isobel. Although mostly I try to avoid her because, on the pretence of being motherly, she likes to stand a little too close (and anyway I hate motherly women).

Yesterday Bob came to me with a complaint. The Dwarf was giving him a hard time about his sick leave, demanding an exact account of his symptoms, needling him. 'Listen,' I told him, 'you have five days of sick-leave entitlement — you don't have to say what's wrong with you. You just have to say you were sick. You're the best judge of your own health, not some textbook checklist of symptoms. Next time,' I tell him, 'when you or your wife ring in sick, refuse to discuss it. Ditto when you come back to work.' I glance over in the direction of The Dwarf. 'He's an officious little prick.'

Isobel had been eavesdropping on this conversation, as usual. 'Steve,' she said (I wish she wouldn't call me Steve), 'that man [The Dwarf] loves his job. People who love their jobs, like Joel [The Dwarf], it's an affront to them that everyone else doesn't feel the same way. They feel personally let down.'

I just shrugged. I didn't want to get into empathic conversation with Isobel.

Yesterday we had a row over productivity sheets. She came over to Don's desk and started berating him for taking fifteen minutes to fill out his productivity sheet.

'You don't expect me to believe that it took you fifteen minutes to fill out a simple form!'

'It's not a simple form, that's the problem!'

'You only had to count up the number of returns you've done today, Don, that's all.'

'It's not that straightforward. Item Three, it's not clear . . .' and he broke off and gestured across at me with a baffled shrug.

Don is a bit of a goose who spends a lot of time daydreaming about his greyhounds, Dancer's Treat and Radiant Supremacy, but that's not the point.

I addressed myself to Isobel. 'There is nothing that specifies how long a clerk may or may not take to fill out his productivity sheet. They're a stupid idea anyway.'

She gave me that *oh no, not the emissary of the workers* look and wound up to a tantrum. 'There *is* something, Stephen,' she said, 'there is common sense and reasonable expectations. Which tell me that fifteen minutes is an *unreasonable* amount of time — ' her chest heaved and sighed histrionically, 'to take in filling out a productivity sheet!'

We were both aware that The Dwarf was looking our way and that any moment he might shuffle over. She doesn't like that, she doesn't like him invading her patch. 'I think it's time we all returned to our work,' she said icily, and walked back to her desk on fine stiletto heels. I could almost see the arches in her feet taut with the dignity of her stride.

At morning tea I propped by the noticeboard and Sanjay joined me for another one of our recipe consultations. I was telling him that I have never quite grasped the subtleties of cooking with cloves. Meanwhile I was vaguely aware of Isobel hovering by the filing shelves. 'You should always fry them in hot oil first,' explained Sanjay, 'but only for a minute or two or they burn. My wife likes six cloves in the frying, I two. We compromise with four which gives a sweet but not cloying flavour . . .' Isobel must have been eavesdropping again because at this point she can't resist sticking her nose between us. 'Geez you two are precious. *Try cooking for a bunch of kids!*' she hissed, and flounced back to her desk. Sanjay gazed at me with an expression of comical affront, and although I know it's cruel, I looked in her direction and laughed out loud.

Back at my desk I contemplated a new approach to union negotiations. I would go direct to the FAS. I would offer him a Shiatsu massage. I would unfurl my futon massage mat on his office floor and invite him to lie prone, then I would diagnose a *jitsu* gall bladder (obsession with order, with structure; too much meat, cheese and alcohol) and *kyo* spleen (blocked creativity, too much sugar). His gall bladder is afire with irritability; tongues of flame leap up at me. I would trace the invisible meridians of energy, waiting for his body to drift into a state of ease. And then, as I gently pressed my elbow into his back, into the deepest point of his life force, as I heard him sigh with release, I would whisper into his ear: *'What about abolishing productivity sheets?'*

●

12.50. I work through to my lunch hour. Get the avocado out of the fridge, spread it on rice crackers and sprinkle them with the gemasio I keep in the top drawer of my desk (gemasio: fourteen parts seasame seeds to one part sea salt roasted in a hot pan and crushed in a suribachi). Ralph comes over to me.

'What little delicacy have we got today?' he sniggers. 'Scrambled bean curd and seaweed?'

I ignore him.

'What? No chopsticks?'

Everyone else has given up commenting on my diet — there's only so many jokes you can make about macrobiotics — except Ralph. Tedious Ralph.

Ralph is tracing his family tree. He's also writing a local history of his suburb, Stanmore. This is Ralph's way of trying to stave off the panic. It's a dubious genealogy of corrupt rum colonels, mad Jewish mistresses, dull and treacherous offspring and somewhere in there, Ralph's ancestors. As if he doesn't see enough forms during the day he spends his nights inscribing search forms for the archives: birth certificates, marriage certificates, death certificates, shipping records; all in search of some ineffable connexion. Connexion to what? A mere borough of the Marrickville Council, that's what. A stop on the train line between Newtown and Petersham. The Annals of Stanmore. I've learnt a lot about Stanmore in this job, more than I ever wanted to know. I tell Ralph he'll end up one of those people who spend their holidays roaming around graveyards looking for their own name inscribed in stone. He says he's hoping to do exactly that if he can just persuade his wife to spend his annual leave in Tasmania instead of the Gold Coast. Not many historic graveyards on the Gold Coast. He showed me a book he keeps in his drawer called *History and You*, written by a woman he saw on the Midday Show one day while at home on a sickie. Something clicked, he said. And you have to wonder what. The desire to know what has gone before — this, says Ralph, is what separates us from the beasts. Records. Evidence. Documentation. So this, says Gareth, is civilisation: The Stanmore Chronicle. Notated by the Venerable Ralph, functionary of the Abbeye de Finance.

Poor deluded clerks. Reading and writing are not body skills. Keeping accounts will not save you from annihilation; from degradation; from insignificance.

Three o'clock, mid-afternoon, and I'm deep in the grey pit of boredom. Furtively I lift *The Man Without Qualities* from my drawer, hoping the mere sight of it will spark me. Perhaps I can write a novel in which the hero, who works in Internal Check, becomes the first person in the world to die of boredom. I could call it *The Annals of Boredom*.

1993 Joined Treasury Office. Bored.

1994 Still in Treasury. Bored.

1996 Plague, death and famine. Still in Treasury. Very bored.

1997 King Charles III crowned. Boredom rife.

1998 A new supervisor in Internal Check. Boredom unrelieved.

1999 Promoted to ASOC2. Boredom intense.

*2000 Presented with gold bundy card for processing my one millionth
Bank Interest Statement. Overcome by hysteria. Go home. Consult
Natural Remedies book. It says: 'Drink bedstraw tea and rest . . .'
Book of Life says: 'Working in Treasury is not your spiritual path.'*

3.37 in the long, dead day. 3.37 on the soulless quarter-acre. Is this what my life amounts to? Forty years of this, forty years of the clock stopped at 3.37 in the fluorescent, air-conditioned afternoon?

3.45. Gareth looks over from his desk by the window, as if sensing my disquiet.

Sometimes we take our tea-break there (me bancha with roasted barley, him, Nescafé, the black brew of granular poison) and he mocks my interest in matters Zen, mocks me in his gentle, diffident way. He likes to stare out the window at the building opposite, a small bank from the Victorian era. In the last month it has been gutted until all that remains is its elegant, ornate facade; a wall of sandstone fol-de-rol; urns and scrolls and neoclassical pediments, Italian balustrades, all that sort of thing; and at either corner, standing on recessed ledges and gazing vacantly out into the smog of the CBD, six sculpted figures in Grecian dress with their names carved into stone: *Labour, Industry* and *Commerce*; and on the other corner, *Mercy, Justice* and *Wisdom*. Gareth's favourite is *Wisdom* who, with her hand to her forehead, gazes soulfully down at her sandalled feet. 'Looks like she's nursing a hangover,' he said once, wistfully.

In a hot, gusting wind the facade trembles. Gareth says he is waiting for it to fall down. A small, manageable apocalypse.

I join him now at the window and we stand for a minute in silence. 'Cheer up,' he says. 'Look.' From the wristband of his watch he removes a familiar piece of folded paper. A leaf from the desk calendar. 'Here's one for you.'

I take the small white sheet and read: *In the face of eternity the mountains are as transient as the clouds*.

'Hardly seems applicable to this place,' I say.

'Oh, I don't know,' he says, 'I think we could arrive at a synthesis. Rule No. Thirty-eight of the Sales Tax Manual states: Goods can be conditionally exempt or unconditionally exempt, and,' he intones ponderously, 'in the face of eternity the mountains are as transient as the clouds.'

I don't know why this seems funny but suddenly it does. I laugh. He grins.

'We are the confluence of rivers,' says Gareth.

'Granules in the paper cup of the bureaucracy,' say I.

We are pulses in the heart of the universe; with our pens we compile a mountain of paper, on our video consoles we inscribe the air. And as we look out on the stony figure of *Labour*, bare-breasted and barefoot, her arms resting on a long-handled scythe, a gust of wind sweeps down Hunter Street, and for a moment there, I could swear the facade trembled. And we lean forward, waiting for the pediments to topple. But no, the wind gusts on, and everything is as it was.

2

Chinatown

I work until five-thirty. Press the bundy, note my flextime is up to four and a half hours. I've passed the halfway mark into another day's respite. I walk through the pedestrian subway from Railway Square to the Haymarket, then along Pitt Street to the Chinese grocery on the corner. It's the late winter sunset of Sydney, the dark skyline lit from behind by an orange glow. In the seedy, generous cluster of Chinatown, above the Aurora Cooking School, is the Wang Dun Shu Academy. Another station on the spiritual path.

Up the narrow white staircase, two floors and into the enormous room with the high ceiling, like a church hall. Bare polished boards and Chinese scrolls hanging from the walls. Large awesome swords, unsheathed, rest across thick nails; ceremonial dragons' heads jut at a height of four metres; red, black and yellow with fierce, glaring eyes, glaring out at no-one, certainly not at me, glaring out over our heads into some unseeable time of clash and thunder. In the corner, large ceremonial drums with a deep, hollow *brummmmmmmmm* (I patted one, in a respectful way, the first night I came). A high counter at the head of the stairs where two Chinese, whose names I still don't know, keep the books and collect the money and disappear in and out of the little office at the rear.

Most of the others are already there. We are fourteen, nine men and five women, all between twenty-five and thirty-five. It must be the age when the question of the spiritual path becomes pressing. Begins to nag. We're in our leotards, leg warmers, tracksuit pants, T-shirts, socks, bare feet, headbands and a lone tattoo. We are waiting for our teacher, for the master, Dr Cho Yuan Shen. So small and slight in his white pyjamas with black belt. He, too, looks about thirty-five but he's probably the other side of forty.

Yuan Shen. Master. Keeper of the Style. I like that phrase. It comes to me sometimes in my dreams. The Keeper of the Style. Raised since childhood to master, guard and pass on the meditative arts of Lohan Kung and Chi Kung and the martial art of Kung Fu. Why is the master here in Sydney? Why not in Los Angeles or Texas? Is this my fate, my destiny, Sydney's fate, the new Asian city of the Pacific rim? Whispers are that his friend, Dominic, a Chinese-Australian dentist, persuaded him to come here and make some money. Or was it political, I wonder, this emigration? We are not accustomed to masters choosing to settle at the bottom of the world. Yuan Shen could be interested in money. He is certainly not pure. We hear him coughing in the rear, and talking harshly and rapidly in Chinese. Nick, who has been coming here since Yuan Shen set up the Academy, says that Yuan Shen is a chain-smoker. Perhaps he's a gambler, I say; perhaps he has all the Chinese vices. I laugh. Nick doesn't. He's too intense. Too ascetic. He can do meditative exercise until the cows come home but unless he loosens up and likes the world a bit it won't do him any good.

Yuan Shen comes out. Smiles at us. Cough, cough. Dominic is here tonight to translate. He is bigger than Yuan Shen, stocky, genial, a marvel at Tai Chi: like an awe-inspiring sculpture he seems able to strike a pose and suspend himself within it, beyond time; perfect balance, perfect symmetry. Like carved rock. But Yuan Shen is another thing altogether. Yuan Shen is process, motion; the smooth, unending glide of arms and legs and torso. In Kung Fu he is so fast he is the stream flowing, in Chi Kung the wind sighing. We follow, as always, his movements. He holds his arms out, high and relaxed and curved, his palms curving back in. 'Up, now,' he begins. His English is not good, a few phrases. 'More little bit,' he says (Yuan Shen would never use a word like 'hard') and we arch our backs. And then lower the arms: 'soooffft'. These are his two phrases, repeated over and over like mantras. 'More little bit' and 'sooofft'. Yin must flow into yang into yin into yang into yin into yang. The neck arching back, the pain of stretching, 'more little bit': the arms loose and gathering, 'sooffft'.

Some nights he's discouraged. He stops, shakes his head. 'No good, all no good,' he says, despondently. Last week, he stunned me with his approval. He patted my shoulder, casually. 'Arms good. Back not so good.' This is high praise from Yuan Shen.

I slide into the Butterfly, the Archer, the Waterfall, the Ant, I feel that my arms push back the world, that the air is heavy with invisible resistance, the stretching is agony, my muscles are tired, stiff, heavy with boredom, with resistance, with tax, a tax on the brain, a tax on the heart. I watch Yuan Shen in a blur, the small white legs of his pyjamas moving with a strange grace, the small black head floating with an indescribable poise, the poise of a ripe fruit on the bough.

Yuan Shen.

Master.

Keeper of the Style.

Yuan Shen stops. We sit on the floor, like good disciples. Dominic joins him out front to translate Yuan Shen's mid-session talk on Chinese medicine and bodily health. Tonight we discuss the tongue. The tongue, you know, is the body's opening to the heart. Think about that: I do. Yuan Shen brings forward a large wooden box and stands it on its base. He then opens the metal clasp and the two inside halves of the box are almost shockingly revealed, hung with neat rows of wooden tongues. There must be forty of them, each about ten centimetres long. Bizarre, these red painted tongues on metal hooks. Dominic steps forward and begins to explain the various states they represent in diagnosis. Some are bright red, some coated, some spotted. He sticks out his own tongue, engagingly — probably coated, he says, smiling. I eat the wrong foods lately, harass the liver.

I meditate on the tongues. Mesmerised. The language of tongues: *red, thick yellow moss, thin white moss, greasy yellow moss, moist white moss, tip of tongue is red, dark purple, pimples on the surface, pasty, greasy, peeled, dry, pale, swollen, red spots, reddish, scarlet, red tip, yellow tip, darkish, red and purple spots, red, scarlet and shrivelled.*

His brief lecture concluded Yuan Shen asks us to stand and stick out our own tongues. He happens to look first at mine. 'Ah!' he says, 'you are very angry. This, angry tongue. Too much fire. You come into the room, you are like this —' and he waves his arms melodramatically around his head like an actor from some fierce traditional Chinese drama. What is an angry tongue? I wonder, still standing there, with mine stuck out, while the others look, wary of coming too close, not because they're worried about catching my anger but because peering closely at other people's tongues is not a practice they're comfortable with yet in Leichhardt or Maroubra. Is it glistening and red, or furry, or bright and purplish? This is not what they mean in the Bible by speaking in tongues.

We resume our exercise, gazing into the eight-foot mirrors on either wall. Monitoring our style. Watching our hunched shoulders, the shoulders that say we have been waiting, since childhood, for the invisible blow from behind; our armoured chests, our stiff pelvises, our taut thighs and knotty calves, our stiff elongation of the arms, our frozen, awkward hands, our strained foreheads, our dull, serious eyes. Our defiant beauty. The whole, ever greater than the parts. Yuan Shen, gliding. 'Here, in arms, soft now.' I concentrate hard on the breathing. The movements aren't so difficult, the breathing simple, but putting them together . . . If I get my breathing right the rest will follow. Arching my back, and now my neck, way, way back, stiff and sore. And hold. 'More little bit . . .' My yang muscle, my yin flesh.

Out in the lights of Chinatown it's warm and still. No wind. How I love the humid air, the feeling of walking bare-armed through the dark. I say goodnight to the others. Some walk towards the buses and trains at Central, others to the Apple Carpark. The high brick arches of the old market facade are in shadow. Behind them is a demolition site; brick, rubble, tufted grass, a flat, scrappy rubbish site extending the whole block, a hole in the western end of the city awaiting the construction of some vast new shopping mall. I walk toward the arches, in the direction of the expressway, a white arc of steady traffic almost overhead, the constant Sydney traffic of day and night, any hour.

My body is loose, my limbs make their easy way oblivious of the head. The office is an empty, moon-lit room, far away. I look up at the ghostly white scar of the freeway, the sharp headlights of the night stream. I look up and see Yuan Shen, in his little red Honda, gliding along the trajectory of the freeway, disappearing into the skyline. I finger the roll of hashish in my pocket and make a note to pass it on to Nathalie as a present. I'm giving it up. It's time to go for it. It's time to get pure. I catch the lights at the perilous George Street intersection and a silver Toyota swoops around my flank, forcing me back and throwing me off balance; a semitrailer roars through the tunnel, the lights of the freeway unsight me; I'm at the point of losing my poise. Almost, but not quite. It's okay, I tell myself: it's cool. The moment passes. *In the face of eternity the mountains are as transient as the clouds.*

3

Glebe

Loose and light-headed I walk home through the leafy streets of Glebe. Home to my sister's house, an opulent Edwardian terrace high on the Toxteth Estate. My sister is big on antiques, solemn pieces with a high polish, heavy velvet drapes that droop in a musty swathe, fussy gilt frames; all of that. Some houses are like temples, and this is one of them; a shrine to my sister's passion for collecting. All the sacred objects are in their carefully chosen place; the French glass, a tall Lalique vase of milky blue translucence with sculptured glass fish at the base, opaquely erotic; the Belgian porcelain (my favourite), a long Limoges dish with a rich yellow rim; the English pewter, so subtle in its matte palette of greys. Everything, as always, powerfully undisturbed. My sister is in love with symmetry; with regularity, with proportion, with the predictable. Perfect glass spheres; perfectly thrown ceramic bowls; tall Doulton vases, one on either side of the mantelpiece, and in each case the distance from the edge measured precisely. Pictures hung perfectly straight; drapes caught in matching swathes; geometric grace and precision. No-one could love a house as my sister loves this one; it's the elegant salon of her childhood dreams, so far from the scrawny bungalow out west that she ran away from. This is her palace of art. This is where all her money goes. None of which impresses the fat black cockroaches that scurry erratically across the polished floor. Meanwhile I am squatting here, minding this shrine, while my sister and her husband are in Europe for six months, trying to work out whether or not they want to stay married.

I open the glass panelled front door and switch off the alarm. In the hallway is an ornate gilt mirror. I look at my tongue; red with whitish streaks on either side. At the back are raised red spots. Is this the angry bit? On the floor is a pile of mail, including, I see, a letter from my mother and two cards, one from my sister, Helen, and another from my brother-in-law, Ric. My sister wouldn't send me anything so ordinary as a postcard; no, this is an expensive looking greeting card with a glossy print of Michelangelo's *David*.

Florence, November 6

Dearest Stephen, How is the house? How far away it seems, at times I have trouble remembering what it looks like. And yet I dream about it quite often and always that burglars have broken in. I think our dreams are always some months behind and our brains slow to catch up.

And how are you? Are you still growing thinner and thinner on that diet? Will there be anything left of you when I get back? Yesterday Ric and I visited the Uffizi. We were standing in front of Raphael's Madonna when a German man next to Ric fainted. After he'd been carried out the guide told us, with complete solemnity, that once a month a tourist is rushed to the psychiatric ward of the Santa Maria Nuova Hospital suffering from Art Fatigue. These people, said the guide, are apparently healthy when they arrive in Florence but gradually, overwhelmed by the city's art treasures they lose their equilibrium. 'It would never happen to an Australian,' muttered Ric. But seriously, Florence is almost too beautiful, a shrine to human potential. Please do continue to check the security alarm. Love, Helen

Typically, the postcard from my brother-in-law reads as follows.

November 9

Dear Steve, Mate, you should see Rome. Unreal! You think Sydney traffic is bad. Here they drive straight up your bum, any time, day or night. You're in some narrow street and suddenly you find yourself pressed flat against the historic walls while eight little Fiats race their personal Grand Prix inches away from your crown jewels. The river is muddy, just like the Yarra. The art treasures pall after the first day. A museum is a museum is a museum — dead air, dead artists, dead-head Americans worshipping at the shrine. Frankly the place is over-rated. Can't wait to get to Bangkok.Cheers, Ric
P.S. For Christ's sake, check the burglar alarm. I'll never hear the last of it if it's not all there when we get back.

The alarm. Always the alarm. Beside the front door is the infra-red and microwave security alarm module. Beneath the stairs is a yellow metal box. Under the floor runs a tangle of black wires, a fretwork of dread and alarmist vibrations. It couldn't be more complicated. Two alarm zones: downstairs where a keypad is encased in plexiglass by the front door and a second module upstairs on the landing beside the master bedroom, so that if you get up in the middle of the night you have six seconds to de-activate the upstairs alarm and three seconds to de-activate the downstairs. And always, the little red eye follows you around. Blinking. Do I keep this thing alive? Unfortunately I do, as part of my agreement with my sister. If it were up to me I would leave it permanently switched off. It should be enough that I am here. I try to follow the advice of Eva, my Shiatsu teacher: trust in Nature to be supportive and no harm will come to you. My sister does not trust in anything. That's her problem.

Small things disturb her; a fine crack in the living room wall, a dead sparrow in the garden. I would describe her as over-tuned, which explains some of her nervous reaction to me. When I first came to live here she used to accuse me, in her normal undertone of hysteria, of living by the knife. This was her way of objecting to my practice of cooking late at night, after classes, when I would prepare my food for the next day. In the morning she would complain of insomnia, of lying in her bed listening to the steady thud of the cleaver as it hit the chopping board (this while I made my miso soup). Thud, thud, thud, thud.

'Don't forget to switch on the alarm before you go to bed, Stephen,' she would call down the stairs.

Thud, thud, thud.

'Oh, and please don't get up in the middle of the night for a pee, you'll activate the infra-red.'

Thud, thud, thud. *Thud.*

One night when I was out late, she left me a note. 'If you rise early to meditate please don't forget to de-activate the switch.'

In the mornings I fed her the miso soup for breakfast. She ate it silently but she ate it all. Miso, I explained to her, is one of the keys to Zen cooking. In the processing of miso several types of energy have been wisely combined: soybeans; representing autumn energy; salt representing winter energy; and barley, representing spring energy. Traditionally the fermentation process in wood, representing tree energy, passes through at least four seasons. In this way an energetically balanced food is created which can be used at all times of the year and in any weather.

Here is my own recipe for miso soup. Chop seasonal vegetables into small pieces — ginger, carrot, celery, onion, leek, pumpkin, sweet potato and any greens — and saute in small amount of toasted sesame oil. Cover with filtered water and add one strip of washed kombu seaweed and three shiitake mushrooms soaked on their backs. Simmer for twenty minutes then add miso paste mixed with a little warm water. Garnish with something fresh just before serving— chopped spring onions, parsley, grated daikon radish. This will activate the salt and the enzymes. To make a meal add diced tofu or tempeh, a handful of cooked brown rice or soba noodles.

I eat a bowl of this standing by the sink and thus fortified I am ready to read my mother's letter. Well, almost. First I take a shower, put on my white kimono and walk barefoot out onto the front verandah which is dusty and warm beneath my feet. Here I sit and contemplate the rush of humid vine that twines itself around the wrought-iron lace; its dark purple tendrils have a smoky seductive tinge and the bottle-green leaves a hint of flesh in their tiny pink veins . . . Gazing at them now I become aware of my breathing, the breath in my chest, deeper and deeper, down into the *hara*. Trust in Nature to be supportive, I tell myself. Then I open my mother's letter.

My dear boy, she begins. *I can understand why you are studying meditation and massage. You were such an intense child, you always did need to relax.*

Relax! What an ugly, detestable word that is! How characteristic her opening sortie! I put the letter aside on the dusty step.

My mother writes to me once a week. She writes on a battered old typewriter on which the 't' jumps half a line above the other letters giving her writing the look of a prolonged stammer. Her letters are full of irritating 't's — symptomatic, in my view, of panic. With every letter there are clippings; she is shameless in summoning up any dubious authority to contest my diet. The daily tabloids are treated like gospel and we have entered into a war of citations, of chapter and verse, which began, as I recall, with this: MACROBIOTIC DIET IS DANGEROUS *says Head Nutritionist at the Royal Prince Alfred Hospital.* (*Sun Herald*, 7 October).

I'll spare you the tabloid rush on this one, the gist of which was that some bird-brained girl had died from living on a diet of rice and seaweed and *nothing else*. Couldn't be bothered cooking, probably. Missing the point, which is to invest your food with your own good energy. The preparation is vital; it should be slow, meditative, a pleasure, almost a ritual. As Sanjay says, to cook the rice you must respect the rice. Don't just throw it in a pot; first wash it in a strainer under the tap, in warm water, running your fingers through the grains to loosen the dust, then set it aside to drain while carefully measuring out the cooking water.

I tried to explain this in a letter, only to receive the following. NOT ENOUGH OIL IN YOUR DIET CAN MAKE YOU INFERTILE. (*The Age*, 14 November). *You know*, she wrote, in the accompanying letter full of jumpy, stuttering 't's, *how much I look forward to having grandchildren. I read once that models who go on prolonged slimming diets can develop shrivelled ovaries from lack of Vitamin E.*

As time goes on she sends me more and more clippings: I have come to recognise the familiar self-seal envelope, grey-white and stuffed fat with folded newsprint; small missives of war. Once, manically, there was a telegram, brought on, I assume, by an attack of panic.

YOUR SISTER SAYS YOU ARE FASTING STOP PLEASE RING ME TONIGHT

'A healthy person carries a little extra weight,' she had urged that evening, 'something in reserve.'

'That is a famine mentality,' I told her. 'We suffer now from a glut.'

But she was not persuaded.

She wrote: September 20, *Launceston Examiner*. ARSENIC LEVELS IN SEAWEED TOO HIGH SAY CSIRO.

I replied: October 3, *Telegraph*. CHEESE BAD FOR THE HEART.

She wrote: October 25, *The Advertiser*. VEGETARIANS RISK IRON DEFICIENCY.

I replied: November 10, *Los Angeles Times*. HOLLYWOOD STAR SAYS SUGAR AGES.

This, then, is how my mother and I conduct our relationship: we exchange warnings.

When last I went home she plied me with chocolate cake and scones and pavlova and roasts and braised liver ('for iron'). I declined them and she was affronted. 'You are so thin,' she snapped, '*so thin!*' Like all mothers she has a control problem.

Mother: border guard of the body.

It's just before twelve when I deadlock the front and back doors and climb the stairs to the master bedroom. Outside it's still warm and the balmy smell of jasmine wafts into the room, that and the sound of someone shouting in the lane. It's a man's voice. 'Not here!' it shouts. 'Not here, not here!' And then silence. And I turn out the light and lie in my sister's absurd four-poster bed and think of her postcard. Of the white marbled figure of David. Of the German tourist stricken with the loss of his equilibrium. Of Yuan Shen who seems to possess some depthless source of it. And I begin to compose a letter in my head.

Dear Mum, it begins, *I am not, as you put it, learning to 'relax'. I am embarked on something infinitely more profound— an existential inquiry into the meaning of the word poise . . .*

What *is* poise, Mother? Do you know the origin of the word? *Poise: to weigh, to balance.* Can you imagine a set of scales in which you weigh one handful of sand against another, counting out one grain of sand at a time? In a sense, this is the way I spend my days, each day a grain of sand on the scales. I am learning to concentrate on small things, to take nothing for granted, to examine everything anew: what we eat for breakfast; the way we clean our teeth; whether we sleep on wool or feathers, facing the sun or away from it? For each day there are a hundred questions to be asked.

Does this thought tire you? It revives me. I see a way of releasing myself from the past, from bad law and false education.

Is poise a form of stillness, the opposite of restless agitation? Can restless movement be itself a form of poise, a driven fluency, a prancing poise, as in, say, Mick Jagger? Can a single gesture of doubt, of self-reassurance — Freda's compulsive smoothing of her hair — be elevated, through ritual repetition, into a gesture of grace?

I observe that poise takes many forms. That each of us must search to find the way in which our poise can express itself, and accept, if necessary, that it may be in one sphere only that it is able to emerge. I think of Linda, a girlfriend I once had who played piano in a band. While playing she was loose, warm, molten in her rhythm, indefinably erotic; in bed she was remote and wooden. It was clear that music was the medium of her poise; she seemed unwilling or unable to manifest it on any other occasion.

Which leads me to ask myself: can poise be willed? Is the stillness of the mannequin a willed poise or merely affected poise, that is, not poise, unreal poise, a poise of the surface, not the centre? Is this not poise but affectation? I've known people who were unaffected, complacently themselves but gauche. They could not be said to have poise which must, then, consist in or have as a vital element, grace. And grace is inextricably a part of the body, the tone and set of the musculature, the carriage of the skeleton, the shoulders, neck and head, and all of this is determined of course, by food. The *Vogue* poise of the mannequin, glamour poise, is like the food in glossy photographs — half raw and sprayed to look fresh and appetising. True style is respect for the inner body, feeding it with good energy, aestheticising the inner body, not the outer show, not just skin, muscle and bone but every cell, every membrane.

But I hesitate here. The use of this word 'grace' troubles me. When we were children we learned scripture and scripture preached to us of 'grace', but this grace was a static thing that spoke of the body as an empty bucket, a mundane receptacle that could be filled with some ethereal white substance, like mystical cotton wool. Jesus turned water into wine; likewise can he turn shit into grace. And this grace entered the body and was stored in the repository of the soul, a mysterious slate that hovered behind the heart and bore the marks of good deeds and bad deeds until God's agents swooped in, like tax auditors, to keep a reckoning, a fatal account.

And where did this soul, this bucket of grace, sit? In the chest, of course, because in the West we live from our hearts and lock our energy into our chests. But in Yuan Shen the centre of being is in the *hara*, in the stomach;

the centre is where it should be to achieve balance, halfway between the head and the feet. Did you know that the stomach is a more complicated network of energy than the brain, that the walls of the intestines have a greater number of nerve endings?

In Yuan Shen poise is a dynamic process that cannot be computed, an energy that flows through the body like lightning that no page, no calculus, no clerk can inscribe with marks.

And so at night, after work, in Chinatown, in the tall mirrors, I watch my own body strive to achieve some stiff poise. And wonder about Yuan Shen? He smokes, eats routinely. Does he derive his remarkable poise from training? A lifetime of educated reflexes; will translated into habit?

Does personality have a texture? Sanjay as polished cedar; Gareth a scarred white marble; Freda a dusky charcoal . . .

My thoughts here are crude, inchoate. Yesterday, in an effort to refine them, I looked up the entry for 'poise' in Websters Dictionary. 'A balancing,' it said. 'Self-possession during stress; composure.' And then this: 'To sustain equilibrium; to hover; to be prepared for a change of state; as in a bird poised for flight.'

I have always desired the other, the foreign, the exotic; in Sydney I've always felt most at home in Chinatown. I remember the time I went to a Buddhist prayer meeting in Randwick. After two years of eating at the Chinese Buddhist restaurant in Ultimo Road, I asked Li, the owner, if I could attend a Buddhist ceremony. Li consulted with the family and generously they said yes. But the ceremony itself was a disappointment. When I arrived at the given address it was just an ordinary red-brick bungalow, so suburban. There was the usual dull furniture except for a wooden altar covered with coloured glass dragons; a sort of Chinese kitsch, the Buddhist equivalent of those Pellegrini statues of the Virgin and the Sacred Heart that as a schoolboy I'd seen in the home of Catholic friends. I was careful to show respect, to hold my candle with due deliberation, to bow in all the right places, but I was unmoved. The spirit did not here manifest itself in a superior style, unlike the movements of Yuan Shen. This whole excursion into ritual proved to be a dead-end, far too reminiscent, despite the dragons, of the stodgy wool tweed of my mother's living room. But from this encounter in Randwick I learned one thing — I learned not to look too hard. I was too speedy, too avid, too strenuous. I had to learn to await the unexpected.

It's true, I was a little mad then. But it was a necessary madness: it took me where I wanted to go. The dictionary defines madness as 'disordered in intellect', and yes I will admit to disorder, a necessary mess. And I remembered the old truism about omelettes and breaking eggs.

And recalled also that definition of poise: 'to be prepared for a change of state'. Took special note of that phrase in particular. This was the time when panic was most likely to strike. There are times, even now, when I could panic about my diet. Four months after I started on it I went on a seven-day rice fast. On the night of the fourth day I dreamed of eating chocolate cake. It was a brown oval mound and when I bit into it, it was dark and congealed and gluey, and my teeth stuck together so that I couldn't speak. The sickliness of it made me cringe. The next day I began to get diarrhoea. A persistent loosening in the bowels, pain in the upper abdomen, a rippling movement of wind that sometimes was visible on the surface of my skin. After eight days of this I began to feel a tightness in my chest, a nagging anxiety. I could have panicked and modified the diet but I knew that this was my body purging its past. I shat three and four times a day. My shit was yellow and too yin. It floated, broke up, dispersed. At night I felt wave upon wave, the sinewy serpent in my gut, until one Friday evening I began to gasp from the pain in my abdomen and I drove in a rush to the Medical Centre. I remember an Elvis video was playing in the waiting room: the marriage scene from *Blue Hawaii* with Elvis completely in white except for a blood red cummerbund with huge red tassels that hung down to his white shoes. The receptionist stared up at the lurid screen with a vacant gaze while the doctor beckoned me in. The first thing I noticed was that his office walls were covered in framed photographs of Elvis. Above the door was an Elvis clock with the hands permanently at a quarter to three so that they blacked out his eyes and made him look like a vampire. It was crazy, I began to laugh, and the pain gripped my gut.

'What can I do for you?' asked the doctor.

I looked at Elvis, those sad and sinister eyes stopped at a quarter to three. 'Nothing,' I said. 'Nothing.'

And left.

On the way home I stopped off at the all-night chemist for some pain-killers, something to block the panic, and over the next few days the pain began to ease.

Somewhere around that time I wrote in the back of my journal: 'I see the pieces of me being broken up and rearranged: I will examine them and discard the bits I don't want. I won't lose my nerve. I am re-inventing myself.'

After this brief episode of panic I continued on as before, my will intact. My nerve held. And as if divining this my mother's letters ceased. Until one day, out of the blue, I received this.

> My dear boy,
>
> I am sorry that I have not written for so long but six weeks ago I enrolled in the University of the Third Age and goodness, how time flies when you have to do all that reading. My friend from the Golf Club, Ruth, put me on to this and we go together. There are a lot of courses on offer and at first I thought, heck, I'll never be able to make up my mind. I could have chosen a course called A History of World Cuisines but decided against it as I know everything I need to know about food and I wanted to broaden my horizons. I have enrolled in three classes but by far the most interesting is the one taken by Dr Collingwood. He's a retired Professor of Ancient Greek and his course is called Greek Civilization: the Foundation of Modern Man. Yesterday we went to a performance by the University Players of the Oresteia by Euripides. It was very cheap, only five dollars a ticket, and our class made up a sizeable portion of the audience. The play was interesting but too long and after a while I got impatient, particularly towards the end. Orestes went on and on, beating his breast, wailing, calling on the Gods and so forth and telling us how much he suffered. Frankly, I got sick of him.

But as Ruth pointed out afterwards, it was a necessary part of the plot, and I suppose I have to agree with her. He had to show some remorse. He had to pay a price. The killing off of a mother, however you go about it, is no small thing.

Love,

Mum

P.S. I enclose a recipe for sweet and sour Chinese liver.

PART TWO

HER

1

Bright Street

Tonight I sit up in bed, thinking about my daughter, Camille. It's too hot for sleep. And noisy. Every few minutes a low-flying 747 drones overhead. Sirens scream along Parramatta Road. Through the window I watch the moon and the still trees, trying to blot from my sight the black power pole with its ugly network of cables, its scorched ceramic nodes.

Camille. On some level or other I am always thinking about Camille. Did my mother think this often about me?

It's January, and the nights are sultry. Before undressing I drew back the covers and sprinkled the sheets with cold water but now the damp sheet beneath me is as warm and moist as my body. This is not entirely unpleasant. I feel enlarged in the warm air, my pores opening out into the humid night, blurring the boundaries, immersing me in a kind of continuous present. Which is what I desire most. Once I used to worry about having a sense of life's direction. Now, for the moment, all I want is to stand still and get the small things right. Like eating. And breathing.

And so I have given up work for a year. Taken leave. Resolved to live carefully on my savings so that I can attend to my neglected house. And give Camille more of my attention. Last year Camille was unwell: for much of the time she slept in my bed and each night I awoke intermittently to the sound of her light but insistent cough. Even now her appetite is poor; she has cravings for junk food; her breathing suffers in the humidity; she becomes listless and wooden in front of the perpetual television.

When I told the doctor of my decision to give up work, she warned me against over-reacting. 'Camille is only a moderate asthmatic,' she said, 'there are thousands of children like her in this city.'

'I know this,' I said, 'but there are other reasons.' And we left it at that. Like most doctors she did not want to pry into the personal.

These other reasons: I am not entirely sure that I could sensibly enumerate them, fan them out on a grid or itemise them neatly, as in a shopping list. Somehow they're clotted and interwoven in my unconscious, like knotty roots in a dark soil. It's more of a yearning; a blind instinct. And I *am* tired; tired of meetings, committees, rule books, reports. And especially tired of a certain kind of logic.

I have raised my daughter, alone, for eight years, and spent most of that time in an office. I need a rest. I tried to explain this to my friend, Zoe. 'Watch out,' she laughed. 'Soon, you'll get bored. You'll lose touch. You'll become obsessed with trivia.'

What, I ask myself, is trivia?

●

Sometimes I can get a fix on what it is that I desire only by being in the company of my mother. I won't say 'talking to Mother' — this is rarely a satisfactory exercise — but simply by being around her.

This morning I called in to see her. It had been some time since I visited; too long, I knew, for us to be comfortable with one another.

The house was exactly as it always is, flooded with light. Mother, or Ros as I sometimes call her, was barefoot, in a see-through dress of apricot muslin with a princess bodice. As usual she wore heavy make-up and underneath her wide-brimmed straw hat she'd tied her long dark hair back with a ribbon. Though barefoot and bare-legged she wore her double choker of pearls.

'How are you, darling?' she said, but didn't offer her cheek for a kiss.

I always feel older than Mother. Even though she is much taller than I and very slim. It's the way she sits, on the edge of her chair, legs apart and braced on her toes, her hands loosely between her thighs; coltish, ready to frolic. A fifty-eight year old girl. She skips around the dusty floors and sometimes clasps her hands in a girlish, if dated, attitude. Beneath her bare feet are polished boards and old Persian carpets which are rarely cleaned as she is averse to housework. The house is full of family portraits. It has a musty smell and there is flaking paint on the walls, high up near the cornices, and it's crammed with antiques; unpolished, casually used and functional antiques that say Old Family, always had them, take them for granted, just furniture. That's one thing I like about my mother, that she would think it a complete waste of time to polish her furniture, that she is so uncaring about its cachet that she wouldn't even begin to formulate a disapproving remark about *nouveaux riches* and how they wax up their chiffoniers and dining tables until you can see your face, or pearls, in them. She just wouldn't notice. She'd notice whether or not they had books. She herself has many. She reads. And she keeps a journal.

I can't remember at what age she began to read her journal aloud to me. I might have been ten. Perhaps I was older. Father was always away on trips. He too came from an old family, but one recent enough for him to still take a pride in how old it was. Mother's family dated back to the early days of the colony. In others this might have been a source of snobbery, or even pride. In her it simply seemed to liberate her from ever having to worry about what anyone thought — to please herself. She would read to me from her journal, often over the dinner table, where we'd be eating some hastily thrown together and oddly assorted meal. Mother didn't spend much time cooking. She neither loved to cook, nor hated to cook; it just wasn't worth having an attitude to, one way or the other. We might have frizzled lamb chops with chopped raw carrot, bread and butter, cheddar cheese (she called it 'mousetrap'), olives and dill pickle — anything she could find in the fridge at the last minute. This might be followed by an elegant creation that she'd spied in the window of the local patisserie while driving past; *crème anglaise* in a choux casing topped with glazed strawberries. 'How pretty it looked!' she'd say, while whisking it on to the table still in its box and stuck to the delicate tracery of its white paper doily. 'I couldn't resist it!' She was, I think, capricious, although this word is often used censoriously and censoriousness seems an attitude inappropriate to my mother.

Mother was more interested in words than in food. She liked to write about the landscape, the exotica she'd observed on trips with Father to Africa or the Solomon Islands or Portugal. I remember her once going on and on about something in Peru. She was an enthusiast, though always herself; never transformed by her enthusiasms. Are people ever transformed by their enthusiasms? With Mother it was the reverse, she seemed to bestow on her enthusiasms something of her own character. Ask me about Peru or Portugal or Nairobi and I'll think of Mother, clasping her hands and twirling around, barefoot, in an exclamation of enthusiasm. This makes her sound naive. Naive she was not. She was guileless (when had she ever needed guile?) but astute. Astute but absent-minded. I would go for weeks with holes in the soles of my school shoes and come home one afternoon to find that Mother had bought me an opera cloak. Of course, we never went to the opera.

When I arrived home from school she would come up out of the garden which overlooked the harbour, or from downstairs where she had been working at her table, to say hello and perhaps, absent-mindedly, to pour me a glass of milk. She didn't like me to go upstairs with her, though in the mornings I was welcome in her bed. She'd sit, propped up on large white lace-trimmed pillows (family linen) and read the paper with her glasses on. She managed to look girlish even in her reading glasses. On her bedside table she kept her favourite portrait, a photograph of herself as a child standing beside Albert Einstein in his Washington garden. Her writing table was against one wall by the French doors, always a mess of articles and books and stray pieces of paper. It was an eighteenth century *escritoire* and at first I used to call it the 'excretoire' which made Mother laugh and say, 'No darling, what mother does at that table isn't quite that bad!' She was fond of this table, she liked its curly legs, but she treated it with the same degree of reverence she might have shown for chrome and laminex. Her papers somehow spilled into the kitchen where they occupied more room than kitchen things. The kitchen had few kitchen things, but because of the books and papers strewn around it didn't look bare or cheerless. Just disorganised. It could take Mother forever to find someone's phone number.

I remember one particular evening when she read aloud her work for the day. 'The hills were aflame with trees . . .' she began, and I can't recall the rest, only the feeling that she was the child, not I, and I was listening to her homework.

She wrote and spoke wildly of her trip to Africa: on her many travels she has made a study of the male shaman, or witchdoctor. She feels that she and primitive peoples have a rapport, that they are both saturated with the scent of nature, like fine animals (I am using Mother's phrasing here), that they are both in touch with some special knowledge and that here, in Sydney, we are slaves to the mechanical. One evening she put aside her journal to tell me of my grandmother's friend, Belle, laid up with gangrene after a fall. 'The doctors have tried everything,' she said, 'but no dice! They should bring in the maggots! In Africa they would bring in the maggots, cover the gangrenous leg in hundreds and hundreds of little white worms.' She said 'little white worms' as if they were a delicacy, positively delicious. 'Maggots eat only dead flesh, you see, and when they've finished, eaten the wound splendidly bare, they hose the leg out with sterilised water. What you're left with is a clean wound!'

A clean wound.

That night I woke, dreaming that a big brown dog had chased me down a never-ending lane. I woke without fear, but was ill at ease, and got out of bed. I could hear low noises coming from Mother's room. I looked through the gap in the door. In the bright light I could see her clearly, naked, slim except for her loose belly, sitting on the knee of a large, swarthy man, also naked. I remember the black tufted hair on his large toes.

In the morning I wasn't sure whether I had seen this man or whether he and my naked mother had been part of my dream, and that when I peered through the door she was in fact seated at her *escritoire*, naked and in her pearls, writing in her journal.

If I could then have changed one thing about my mother it was this: I wanted her to be a good cook. Somehow what Mother fed me was never quite what I wanted: she was altogether too casual in her approach to food. Often I would come home from school hungry and ransack the cupboards, eager to prepare something myself. I'd open Mother's half-empty pantry and peer along the shelves looking for simple recipes on the backs of packets but some ingredient or other was always missing — dates, cooking chocolate, chocolate drops, shredded coconut, icing sugar, rice crispies, copha butter, golden syrup . . . the list goes on. One weekend, staying at a friend's place on the north shore, I copied recipes out of a book. My friend's mother had an original copy of Mrs Beeton that was something of a family heirloom. I remember one cake recipe that was such an act of excess it was almost a poem: *¹/₃ of a gill of brandy, 12 eggs (separated), the weight of the eggs in plain flour, baking powder, ³/₄ lb of pounded loaf sugar, almond meal, 3 tbsp orange-flower water and a decoration of mauve sugar violets with slivers of pale green angelica* . . . Reading Mrs Beeton that day was a kind of revelation; thereafter the making of cake took on the character of some special mystery; I felt I had been given a glimpse of a religious rite. A few years later I confessed this to a friend who came from a small country town and shared a room with me in college. I expected her to scoff but no, not at all, she seemed instantly to know what I meant. 'In the country towns,' she said, 'women are judged by the delicacy of their sponge cakes. My mother says it's changing and she blames technology, and especially television. When Mum was a girl a woman wasn't a woman if she couldn't bake a decent Victoria Sandwich, put together with homemade raspberry jam.'

Someone neglected to tell Mother this. If they had she would simply have looked wide-eyed and warmly indifferent. She would consider it ungracious to make catty remarks about women who are judged by their sponges and if some ill-advised visitor insisted on belabouring the topic — even if they were to look at it dispassionately from a quasi-scientific or anthropologicial point of view — she would offer them a dry biscuit with their tea, make her excuses and retire upstairs to her *escritoire*.

Last week, when she had a cold, she rang and asked me to come over. This morning, when she opened the door, I looked into her eyes for signs of attrition, but in her bright, girlish eyes she looked as well as ever.

'Marita, darling,' she complained, 'it appears that you no longer answer your phone after dark.'

'Yes, I do. I just don't answer it after ten.' Mother always rings late.

'Was it as late as that? I must have lost track of time.' We sat in the sun-filled living room, she on the dusty leather couch, me on the uncomfortable chaise. It was midday. Outside there was a high, gusting wind. I switched on the television, something Mother hates. 'Not the Olympic Games, darling,' she sighed, 'anything but that.'

'This is special,' I said. 'I want to watch the women's marathon.'

She sniffled.

The bright screen reflected the brighter sunshine outside and I drew the curtains to blot out all reflection.

Mother leaned back into the cushions, her white handkerchief hanging loosely in her hands. 'Must we sit in the dark?' she sighed.

'Yes,' I replied. 'You need to sit in the dark to see clearly.'

Mother didn't reply. For a while we both just sat there and stared at the screen.

The screen framed a long bitumen road.

Out front a band of four women ran in a clump, blank-faced, distracted, herding together, almost at times tripping over one another, each running as if she were alone, as if the others weren't there.

Behind, a hundred metres back, a Chinese girl, looking slower and fresher, strode rhythmically along the white line, her red and yellow silk vest flashing; less creased, less sweated than the others. In the distance, an exotic northern landscape; water and a long, low bridge; a serene hillside, pale green and luminous; a mystical landscape where shamans, magic women, once whirled their red and gold scarves and stood — the ritual knife between their teeth — awaiting the pink sacrificial pig.

The shoulders and arms of the runners glistened with sweat.

There were sporadic claps from the margins. A line of policemen and policewomen applauded politely.

What a great day! the three commentators kept saying, over and over, their disembodied voices shouting above the silence. *What a great day! What a great day!*

'They're like warriors,' said mother. 'Amazons.' She reflected on this. 'No, perhaps a little skinny for Amazons. I always think of Amazons as statuesque, not sinewy . . .'

'Shut up, Mother,' I said, 'I'm watching the marathon.' She can't bear rudeness; it disarms her. At that moment I felt I was going to cry. There is something special about long-distance running, the marathon especially: these women seemed so heroic, in an ordinary, exhausted way, and now almost there, almost to the roaring stadium and the bright white tape of the finishing line. What must it be like to enter at last into that dark tunnel, suddenly to emerge into the blinding light of that vast arena and the sudden roar of affirmation thundering in the eardrums, like a rush of love . . . ?

'I used to love to run,' said Mother. 'I just adored it. At picnics . . .'

'This is no picnic,' I said. I shut off and concentrated on those hipless women on the screen. I thought: this might turn into a good moment, a moment when Mother and I bathe in warm fellow-feeling and share a pride in our own sex. Those non-mothers, yet-to-be mothers, their faces a blank stare of agony, their sinewy calves pounding the hot asphalt; the bitumen road shimmering like a mirage.

When the race was over I felt elated. I couldn't speak.

'Marita,' she said, 'when are you going to bring Camille to see me?'

Uh-oh. She comes at me when I least expect it. 'Camille's at school.'

'Yes, I know she's at school today, but there are other days, weekends for example.'

'Next weekend we're going to Bondi, with Kurt.'

'Kurt?'

'Kurt's a friend.' It's easy to deflect Mother. If I am evasive for even a few moments I know that already she will be on to some other exotic train of thought and making a mental note to write it up in her journal when I go.

But today she is uncharacteristically persistent. 'How is Camille's chest?' she asks.

'Her asthma came back with the humidity.'

'I'm not surprised, living in all that smog. Why don't you come and live here, with me, by the water? The air would be good for her. You could have the run of the house. You know I work in my room for much of the day.'

But this thought is unbearable. To return to that house where the cupboard is always half-bare? Camille and I must find some other way.

'I'll bring her soon,' I say, 'and you can tell her the story of the maggots.'

2

tapes

Sometimes when I visit Mother I take my tape-recorder, the small purse-sized one, nothing obtrusive or ugly, no ghetto-blaster that will antagonise her. I tell her I'm collecting stories and prompt her into telling a favourite anecdote. Soon she is lost in the telling; the dangerous moment has passed and it's time for me to go.

I listen. I let my mother tell her story. In this way I keep her at bay; under a kind of control. There may be better ways but I have yet to discover them.

Under my bed I keep a store of tapes. The usual thing. SONY Type I Normal Bias 120 UsEQ BHF 90. These are my voices.

When I have a problem with someone I tape them.

To sleep at night above a box of tapes, of plasticised voices imprisoned on tiny reels, is a consoling practice. Mother is there, along with many others. Either the voices are in the head, in the white spaces of the unconscious and free to roam and speak the night — and script my dreams— or they are packaged, overlaid with dust, a contained archive, not dignified with the covers of a book but somehow always in process, scrappy, unformed, untransmogrified by the art of the dream. This is the value of technology; everything there but unthreatening, contained, reeled in; in its place.

Mind you, this doesn't always work. Sometimes the mere tape isn't enough. Then, later, I play back the tape and transcribe it; someone else's voice, someone else's words. And as I write down the words (I might rework them a little) I take possession of them, and they, of course, of me. It's like being the member of some highland tribe and eating the heart of your enemy; their strength enters into you, and also, if you're not careful, their madness. It's a symbiosis. No, really, I don't seriously believe this. It's just a habit, a resource, a tic I developed in an oral history project I undertook in my last year at a progressive girls' school. Interview someone you like and someone you don't like, the teacher said. I interviewed Mother; that took care of both categories.

I found the whole process strangely satisfying.

I've been taping ambivalent voices ever since.

I don't mention this to Mother. Mother is not one of the world's great listeners: the idea of transcribing *other* voices would perplex her (*perplexing* is one of Mother's favourite words — I prefer *baffled*, myself.) But for Mother, tapes would be, well, too derivative, a vulgar rent in the seamless meditative fabric of her journal. Mother is a romantic, she aspires to be 'original'. All I am able to do is *re-*write, which is why I prefer to tape people. First, you type up the transcript, a process both tedious and soothing. Then, if you feel moved, if some atom in your brain quivers — and this occurs rarely — you tamper with it, you *re*story it, so that it belongs to no one person but is a kind of bonded, collective effort, like the conception of a child. When I was twelve I began to re-write the endings of favourite stories. My favourite story of all was that of Charlotte Brönte's *Jane Eyre*, but I was too young, then, to take liberties with it. It wasn't until I bought my little terrace in Leichhardt, and set up house with Camille, that I turned to it again.

Though Mother thinks that narrative is inferior to philosophical speculation, it was she who taught me the potency of stories. She taught me in a dream. I think of it as the knife dream and it was my worst nightmare. I was nine years old and I dreamed that Mother and I were in the kitchen. A big man, powerfully built, was chasing Mother around and around the kitchen table with a cleaver in his right hand. The cleaver was raised high and dominated the air and I was terrified and screaming and Mother was terrified and screaming but while running and screaming she paused in her circuit around the table (she was wearing her pearls, I remember), and she said to me, very calmly: 'It's alright, Marita, don't be upset, it's only a dream. It's only a dream. It's only a story.' At that moment I woke, crying, and looked up into the dark ceiling and I could still see the cleaver there, the blade poised behind her head. And I kept telling myself, over and over: Yes, yes, it's only a dream, Mummy. *It's only a story.*

After a time I drifted back into sleep, and dreamed again. This time Mother and I were alone in the kitchen and when she opened the kitchen cupboard, there on an oval roasting plate was the head of a big brown dog. And she cooked the dog for breakfast: 'Look, darling,' she said, 'I couldn't resist him!' And we sat at the table to eat the dog together, and everything was alright. And in the morning, when I woke, I knew that the dog was the man who had been chasing Mother. And this is the really frightening part: at some level of the unconscious, the message: *eat or be eaten*.

The third option is to do neither; the third option is to speak.

Sometimes I speak. I speak into the tape, myself. It's surprising what comes out. It's difficult for me to capture my own voice, to talk about my body, to be honest about the flux, the brilliance and the mire. Often, without thinking, I displace myself on to him, the male. Not the father, no, this is too problematical; instead, the lover, the morbid other. I made a series of tapes once, describing all the lovers I have had. I thought that in this way I would discover the secret of my weakness; the tapes would reveal common traits that in turn would map the current of my need, but no, they were all astonishingly different, just a mess, a babble.

And then there are all those other tapes; some women, but mostly men. I have always taped my boyfriends. It's easy. Either their vanity or their curiosity seduces them. Sometimes I make it playful, sometimes serious. If playful, I point out how phallic the microphone is; if serious, I say I'm making a study of the male voice. I was unable ever to tape my father since he died before this stratagem presented itself to me. All I have of him is a collection of little notes. Always 'at the office', day and night, he would often send home notes with cab drivers. 'Is my little peach doing her homework tonight?' And so on. Father had many little peaches and dined on them in the city. Mother simply absented herself, as it were, from the table. The table is not my domain, she would say.

My father was a complete mystery to me, as was his mother, my grandmother: they seemed to belong to another tribe. They cared about money, in a way that neither Mother nor I care. They were contained, worldly; guardians of a mundane mystery.

When my grandmother died, my mother drove me to the house. 'I want you to see something,' she said. She led me up the stairs to the master bedroom, a vast, brightly lit room that opened out through two sets of French doors on to a white, wrought-iron verandah. Everything in that room was in pastels and kept immaculate by the Filipino housekeeper who lived in the small flat at the rear of the house. It was exactly thirty days after my grandmother's death. Mother took a small gold key from her pocket, unlocked the door to the dressing room and threw open the closets. And there it all was, my grandmother's hoarded bounty! The dressing room, large by any standards, was completely lined with custom-built cedar shelves. On the lower shelves, neatly classified into 'Day Formal', 'Day Informal' and 'Evening' were over a hundred pairs of shoes. But this was not surprising in a woman of her class — it was the middle and upper shelves that my mother had brought me here to see, and these made me gasp, wide-eyed. Here was a veritable bank hoard of elegant white boxes. Boxes of lingerie. Boxes and boxes, stacked one on top of the other with the labels facing outward. New, unopened. Mother stood on the small cedar step-ladder. 'Look,' she said, and selected a box. From beneath its crisp white lid she unfolded a white satin negligee, dated in style. 'Some of these have been here for years,' she said, 'and never worn.' Together we began to open boxes at random. There were boxes of pure white bras, untouched; boxes of prim white corsets, still nestling in undisturbed tissue paper; wide, slim, delicate boxes of silk petticoats trimmed with Belgian lace, fine lawn nightdresses, Swiss cotton, cambric; satin peignoirs and white satin panties in the loose pre-war or bloomer style. All meticulously shelved; the plenitude — in waiting — of my grandmother's body. Mother wasn't fazed: she laughed. 'I didn't realise she had *this* much!' she exclaimed, adding: 'She would only ever wear white and couldn't bear the faintest discolouration. As soon as things lost their brightness she passed them on to her cleaning woman or the gardener's wife.' I stood there, breathing in the faint odour of my grandmother's perfume and an odourless aura of remote sex, fascinated by this display; white box after white box, column after column, like a wholesaler's cupboard or the piles on the top shelf of the patisserie; pristine, homogenised, sterile. At that moment Mother distracted me, calling me over to a vast bureau by the French doors. 'Look,' she said, sliding open each exquisitely carved drawer. The entire bureau was crammed with expensive costume jewellery; beads and earrings, pins and bracelets, sweater clips and belt buckles collected over forty years. 'Take what you want,' said Mother, 'and give the rest to Camille.' At first I rummaged through it with excitement, but then the sheer excess of it overwhelmed me. I felt sick, as if fed on too many sweets. In the end I took only a green glass necklace, a cat's eye bracelet and some amber earrings.

Was this a simple-minded narcissism? Or did it reveal some other obsession? I didn't know my grandmother well enough even to guess at her pleasures. I wasn't close to her. My father was her only child. She took no great interest in me, influenced, perhaps, by the antipathy between her and Mother. And so, by the end, I had little affection for her. Her interest flared, briefly, some time after my tenth birthday when she took it on herself to teach me how to play bridge. I can't remember much, I wasn't an apt pupil. Unlike her I had no card sense; my mind wasn't orderly enough, I kept forgetting the rules and wanting to invent new ones. The only thing I recall is the way in which she placed particular emphasis on learning to deploy the pre-emptive bid. 'Attack is the best means of defence,' she would say. 'An eight club opening can set you up for all sorts of interesting things.' Perhaps I'd have been more motivated if these sessions had been accompanied by treats but Grandmother kept a very plain table. Pork sausages, cold roast beef, traditional English meats, unadorned. What sat in her stomach was not of interest to her, only what lay against her skin. Sometimes when Mother and I visited she would lay out her dresses on the bed to impress me. 'I think the lilac, don't you?' she'd say, inviting me into a maid's complicity that, looking back, I think must have been her idea of intimacy. She thought my mother eccentric because Mother grew tired and impatient with shopping. For my grandmother, shopping was a holy ritual, a sanctified rite. And always one brought home (or had delivered from David Jones) the sacred object, deliciously tissue-wrapped in its simple white box.

Eventually my mother disposed of all those white boxes. She gave some of them to friends and acquaintances and delivered the rest to the doorstep of the City Mission. I helped her load up the back of her station wagon with boxes and watched her drive off in her reckless way, barefoot and in her pearls, to dump the surplus at the warehouse door of the Mission. I cannot believe that any of those satin peignoirs or lace slips or embroidered boned corsets ever found their way to the poor, though the boxes themselves were no doubt put to good use for storing buttons, displaying badges and collecting loose change.

●

Under my bed there is just one box, my collection of tapes. They are labelled, in a slapdash way, but rarely dated. They simply say, Richard, Annie, Sergio, Colin, Paula, Lisa, Adrian, Kurt. Chronology is not important; this is not meant to be a filing system; it's meant to be random, a morass; like the unconscious. Dark matter, under the bed.

And sometimes at night, when I can't sleep, I play them, and the effect is soporific, infinitely more soothing than the conversations I am forever having with myself, the ones that go around and around and around in my head. I lean over the side of the bed, grope blindly in the box, and slip a tape, any tape, into the deck that sits on a steel trolley by my pillow. In the dark I am unable to read the label on the tape— to make a choice, this voice or that — but it's immaterial; in the dark all voices, in the end, are the same.

But not tonight. Tonight my focus is on Camille. Tonight has been one of those blessed evenings when we put aside our routine and do something special. Rummaging in her school bag for her music sheets Camille had belatedly discovered a notice requesting a cake for the school stall. We consulted a recent gift from Zoe, *Classic Australian Cakes*, and Camille chose a recipe for jelly cake. After dinner we laid out the various cake tins and with much indecision Cam finally chose the large round tin with the collapsible bottom. Affecting the role of casual observer I looked on as she performed almost every task herself, and when finally the cake emerged from the oven, looking more or less as a cake should, she was happy to go off to bed, for once without argument, and with a self-satisfied glow of contentment.

In my bed now I reflect on this bonded relationship between women and cakes. When I complain to Zoe of my over-worked and over-crowded brain, and my desire simply to rest, and occasionally to daydream, I am quick to remark that, on the other hand, I do not want to become airy like my mother. I want to be earthy, grounded; a woman who knows how to bake a proper cake. Though Ros could, in her absent-minded way, cook most things (when pressed, when it was absolutely essential, when it could not be avoided), I do not remember her ever making a cake. That had to be my first task when I moved into my own house with Camille. And as I soon discovered, to my relief and satisfaction, cakes are easy, but only the beginning. Cake alone could not nurture Camille and I have recently come to suspect that there are esoteric cuisines out there that feed the life force in ways I hadn't dreamed of. Unfathomed mysteries of the kitchen. And so it is that I have enrolled, on impulse and at the last minute, in a macrobiotic cooking class. Last night I told Zoe of this and she winced. 'Don't turn New Age on me, Marita.' But I laughed. 'Change is always good,' I said, wanting this to be true though only half-believing it. I repeat this to myself now, aloud, in bed: 'Change is always good.' Tomorrow morning I will catch the ferry over to Mosman to begin my modest one-day apprenticeship. Beside me I have the flier which I picked up in Newtown: *Use Your Noodle: A New Approach to Summer Cooking for Vegetarians*. These very words, *summer cooking* . . . white-clothed tables . . . outdoors under clear blue skies . . . laden with purifying feasts . . . as if all this could be conjured up in my dark little house and the hot acrid air of the inner city. No matter. Camille is fond of noodles. And there is something about the look of the flier and the ring of its blithely confident prose that seems full of promise.

3

the cooking class

At the door of the Luna Healing Centre I can smell something. Can it be? Yes, it is. *Incense*. It seems, at 9.15 in the morning, too early for incense.

It's warm, here. On the ferry the floorboards smelled of damp wood and the wind blew cold off the water. I held my collar to my throat and began to doubt my motives in making the crossing.

This house in Mosman is vast, this house is like a ship, an ocean liner built in the thirties with sweeping curves and portholes and pipe railings. The former home of a respectable banker, it has that unstylish, almost indifferent grandeur of commerce. Through an open door I can see the grand salon where, beneath the moulded art deco ceiling and the geometric light fittings, the masseurs have spread their futon mats. Partitioned from one another by waist-high rice-paper screens, inscribed with Japanese calligraphy, they kneel over prone bodies lying face down on the floor. The curtains are drawn, the light is dim.

I begin to wonder if I have come to the right place; the longer I am here the more certain I am that beneath the incense this house smells of meat; meat and gristle, blood and bone. And then I look up at the vertiginous spiral staircase and I remember. Of course. I came to this house in my childhood. Mother brought me here, to visit the mistress of the house, her old school friend. It was, then, a new palace of the fifties but Mother was unimpressed. 'So staid, these suburbs,' she had murmured. 'So sedated. An awful calm. I couldn't bear to live here.'

In this house a banker violated his daughter, who shot him, from behind, in the coccyx. After the bullets were removed he had them encased in a perspex mould which he used thereafter for an ashtray. This was purely an affectation since he didn't smoke. Of course, he didn't walk again. According to Mother, who knew him well, he consoled himself with a passion for roasted pork which he ate at every meal until the fat began to ooze from his earlobes. (This is one of Mother's little jokes.)

Outside in the wide circular foyer there are ten of us sitting on the circular window seats, rifling through *Good Living* magazines or staring at our socks (shoes left at the door), waiting to be summoned. But in this house no-one seems ever to announce the beginning of anything and after a while we just wander down the grand hallway and into the large room at the back where an enormous scrubbed pine table is laid with ten sets of implements; large knife, small knife and chopping board. We stand politely around the table, looking one another over, until a woman with frizzy red hair and a baby on her hip beckons us through into the kitchen proper. Obediently we shuffle in, and cluster around the marble-topped bench.

And there is Johanna Beech, presiding at the bench, waiting, arms outstretched on the white marble. Here then is our sibyl, our witch for the day, and I am willing to be entranced by her: she has a blazing physical charm, a lustrous muscularity that cooks rarely possess, a hint of playful arrogance. Her hair is almost a white blonde, cut very short and covered by a green and white silk Tibetan hat. Ornate silver and green earrings, the size of florins, hang from her small ears. She wears a red silk singlet and her arms are brown and strong, each one graced with a wide gold bracelet. Below the waist she wears black and yellow striped pants, white socks and chunky black Doc Martens. I notice the way she stands with her feet apart; solid, relaxed. She has a wide, sharp, mischievous smile that seems to go with the hat. Here is something clownish but commanding, European yet Asiatic, mystical but grounded; here is something unorthodox but sure of itself.

I observe her square, practical hands. Like all good cooks, she is unhurried. On the large industrial gas range next to her, three saucepans of water simmer in readiness. I know I could never be this calm, this in control.

As she talks, I look down at my menu, *Use Your Noodle*, and make notes in the margins. The large white bowl in front of her is half-filled with green noodles tossed with baby squash, rosemary, olive oil, garlic and something called umeboshi vinegar; a delicate red vinegar made from pickled Japanese plums. I like the way she runs her fingers through the dressed noodles, with relish, with authority, her nails glistening with oil and tiny black droplets of tamari. She smiles. 'Use your hands. Let your fingers flow through the noodles. Enjoy the sensuous feel of it. Let your energy harmonise with that of the food.' Now she is leaning over the pot on the stove which seems to boil with a complacent boil, neither frantic and surging nor lame and flat. I never seem able to get my pots of salted water to boil in exactly this way. My energy in the kitchen is too rushed and indifferent. That's why I'm here, to improve my attitude. And for Camille.

Jo tells us that the quality of the energy we put into our cooking is everything, that in Buddhist monasteries only those considered the most spiritually advanced are allowed to cook. And that is why, in families, mothers do the cooking. Mothers, she says, are more spiritually advanced than fathers.

'Some of them.' It's a male voice. And I am aware, for the first time, of the only man in the room.

'*Most* of them.' Her eyes twinkle, but she is adamant. 'Women are responsible for nurturing, that is their fate. However they may choose to organise it, or delegate it, is their business, but if they refuse that responsibility entirely they destroy a part of their spiritual self. Of course,' she goes on, 'a part of this is that they must nurture themselves. That's where women traditionally have gone wrong, made martyrs of themselves, nurturing others at their own expense. And then their daughters have reacted in the other direction, and worked on nurturing themselves at the expense of others. Women have to find a way of doing both, looking after themselves *and* looking after their families.'

From in among the throng comes a faint female groan.

'Alright, alright, it's difficult,' she says, 'but to find that balance is the art of women's genius.'

At this point I feel that some of us are confused as to how we should respond: should we take issue now, as if in a seminar, or shut up and concentrate on our noodles?

Jo is standing over the pot, lifting a long strand of noodle from the water with chopsticks. She is very deft. 'For the Chinese, noodles are a symbol of longevity so they never break them,' she says, 'but I do.' And she breaks off the long noodle suspended above the pot, as if to say: we do it our way; we learn from them, but we are not in their thrall; we have our own smartness. Cooks are wilful.

'Marita,' she says, glancing at my name-tag, 'would you say this was cooked?'

I take the sticky noodle in my fingers, hold it high above my mouth, and nibble on the end. I feel self-conscious. I am aware that *he* is watching me, nibbling on my noodle. Him, the one at the back, tall, lean and very brown, with black hair pulled back in a ponytail. Before, when challenging Jo, he'd been very serious but now, staring at me, he seems faintly amused.

Already he seems to know a lot about this food: the pickled limes, the bonito flakes, the opaque blocks of agar agar, the buckwheat soba; kuzu noodles, fruit kanten, bunya nuts, bean-thread noodles, kombu strips, nori, shiitake and hijiki are clearly not mysteries to him.

Jo has completed her preparations for a kanten of strawberry jelly and is demonstrating the blending of a cream substitute made from cooked oats pureed in a blender with soy milk and maple syrup. 'Being a vegan doesn't mean you have to give up on all creamy foods,' she says. 'We have to have *some* creaminess in our diet, we have to acknowledge our need for food as consolation for the loss of mother's milk.' She laughs, but *he* is frowning, I notice, although he seems later to approve of her lecture on creative eclecticism. Tradition is a signpost not a straitjacket, she says; we can take Aboriginal bush food, like bunya nuts, and mix them with Ligurian olives. Japanese this, Chinese that — we make our own cuisine, our own synthesis.

'Exactly!' he says, softly but emphatically. I stare at him. His black eyes stare back.

Meanwhile as the jelly — sorry, kanten — sets, she instructs us in the daily ritual of sharpening the knife, and her words ring like an incantation. A poem.

> *immerse the sharpening stone in water*
> *whet the knife*
> *with small rhythmic movements*
> *pushing the blade away from you*
> *never looking at it.*
> *And then*
> *to test*
> *run along the thumbnail*
> *it ought to catch not slip*
> *— see*
> *perfect*

I stand next to him while we cut the carrot shapes for the salad: stars, flowers, wheels and straws. And I notice how expert he is with the knife, how quietly practised but unhurried. I pause and stare into the huge white bowl with red carrot shapes sprinkled with black strands of hijiki seaweed. I feel clumsy.

'Looks good, doesn't it?' he says. I smile, and while he bends his head to resume his chopping I study his broken nose — sort of splayed — which is the thing about him that I like best, a broken nose on a lean head and a lean brown body, and strong hands with square fingers.

'I don't like these shapes,' he says. 'They're kitsch. It's an unnatural look. Ornamental.'

His way of speaking is quiet but precise. A pedant, I think. While we, the women, are ever so polite, he has already challenged her twice. When she tosses the spiral pasta in Ligurian olive oil with torn basil leaves and tofu marinated in mustard and tamari, he gives his disapproving little frown.

'That's a lot of olive oil.'

'It's the best oil in the world,' she says, giving her sharp, mischievous smile. 'Low in cholesterol.'

'It's still a lot.'

Her eyes glint. 'Use to taste,' she says. 'I give no quantities on your menu sheet. You must learn to trust your own palates. Each time you make a dish, you re-invent it. Nothing is ever the same twice.'

At noon we move from the big kitchen with the gas jets to an adjoining room where we all sit around the big scrubbed pine table and drink bancha tea from small white porcelain bowls. 'Bancha tea,' she explains, 'is made from the leaf and twig of the Japanese bancha bush. It is not only free of tannin or caffeine but has more calcium per cup than milk.' It also has the advantage, I think, of tasting like real tea.

On the wall is an old black and white photograph, framed, of a 1938 Rolls Royce. Draped in shapeless fur coats its owners stand cheerlessly against the running board. Are these the original owners of the house? Despite the incense and this assembly of vegetarians there is still, in this kitchen, a feeling of the butcher shop. The whole house seems to breathe 'meat meat meat . . .' vast quantities of red beef and lamb and chicken and duck and rabbit and pig; stewed and stuffed and roasted and fried and gravied; black pudding, pig's trotters, calves' knuckles, beef tripe, ox hearts, lamb's liver and blood sausage . . .

The bowls of food are set before us and we begin to eat. I hear him speaking: is he addressing me? 'Hey,' he says quietly, and I realise he is reprimanding a girl opposite us for sticking her fingers in the sauces. She giggles. I suppress a smile.

I'm distracted by another girl who sits at the corner of the table and is, well, beautiful. She could be no more than twenty, with short black hair, creamy pale skin, thick black lashes, a red mouth. Snow-White as urban sophisticate. She wears refined black lace-up shoes on small narrow feet which she crosses daintily as she sits demurely in front of her empty white bowl, watching while we scoff appreciatively, gluttonously. She looks apprehensive; perhaps it's the thought of some wicked stepmother somewhere, waiting to dine off her daughter's liver. At this moment he notices her too, and pushes the bowl of black-bean noodle towards her. I wonder, with a pang, if this is a sexual feint. She looks up at him from under her black lashes and demurs quietly.

'I can't,' she says, 'I have a dance class in an hour.'

Maybe she does have a dance class in an hour but I would guess that she is anorexic as well. I've heard of anorexic girls who go to cooking classes and stare at the food all day and don't eat. They find ways to test their will.

He is smiling at her and I think: Mmmm, yes, she's probably his type. It occurs to me for the first time that I am older than any of these young purists, older even than Jo, and I am momentarily disconcerted by the idea that I have been a willing participant in an event in which I am older even than the presiding mother-figure.

After our glistening feast we are farewelled at the door by our sibyl. We put on our coats and walk in drizzling rain, down to the ferry. Deliberately, I walk behind him. He has a way of walking on the balls of his feet, leaning slightly forward, as if about to take off into a sprint, a run, a lope: there is something ascetic about him, fanatical, at once stubbornly grounded and poised for flight. I watch him unlock the door of a lumbering old Commodore and I must be staring too hard for he turns and catches me out. 'Want a lift?' he says. Just like that. It's as if something has registered in him, belatedly and he's made up his mind in an instant.

'I'm going to Leichhardt.'

'That's OK.'

So I walk over and let him open the door for me while I climb into his car. On the winding drive along Military Road I tell him why I came and after listening to me in silence he begins to talk quietly, insistently, about what I should feed Camille.

'Children don't know what they want,' he says, 'but they can be educated to eat the right food if they're given an appetising choice.'

It sounds like a line he's read in a book. The correct line. I don't ask if he has children; I sense that he hasn't and I don't want to defuse the pleasurable tension of the drive by challenging his certainty.

'I'll draw up a diet chart for you,' he says.

I smile. (Later he is to describe this smile as patronising.)

'Where do you work?'

'I don't work. I used to, but I've given it up for a while.'

'Lucky you.'

'I needed a break, and time with my daughter. I felt that I wasn't — I don't know — nourishing her properly. I was coming home at six every night, sometimes later, tired, cooking scratch meals. It bothered me.'

It bothered me that I had become a practitioner of hysterical extremes: one night, take-away pizza and a rush of queasy angst; the next, two hours preparing a proper meal, and washing up half the night, while Camille, bored and disgruntled, watched television alone. And Camille seemingly indifferent to either option. *Seemingly*, but underneath (on some unconscious or half-conscious plane) she must surely judge me. Was I nourishing my daughter? Was I nourishing myself?

'I wanted time to bake a proper cake,' I say. (I notice I'm using the word 'proper' a lot. And wonder why. Am I trying to make up for Mother, and her sublime indifference?)

'Cake is one thing she can do without,' he says. This is almost a reprimand and I don't like it.

'What about you?' I ask. 'Are you in a job?'

'I work in the Treasury Office,' he says, adding quickly, 'but I'm training to become a masseur.'

'Swedish?'

He gives a little smile: *his* turn to be patronising. 'Shiatsu. Swedish is just tinkering. Cosmetic really.'

'Oh.'

'I've been doing it for quite a while. I have my own clients now, on a Saturday. Why don't you come into the Shiatsu Institute in the Haymarket and I'll give you a treatment.'

'When?' I laugh. Is this a pass?

'Any Saturday, around four. That's a good time because it's quiet then. '

I look away, look out the window. We are approaching the bridge: the grey drizzle disappears soothingly into the flat, grey water; the white sails of the Opera House curve into low black cloud. I begin to notice small things: a rivulet of silver drops along the dirty windscreen; masking-tape around the steering wheel; dark hair on his forearms and wrists; a torn vinyl flap on my seat; a feeling that the car and we in it are held together by static, a kind of nervous, quivering strength.

The rain begins to beat heavily now against the roof.

When I get home I'm too tired to cook so Camille and I eat take-away vegetarian pizza and ice-cream. And dance the tango up and down the hallway. Camille likes to dance just before bedtime as a way of distracting the night demons, likes to glide up and down the fake Persian runner, in and out of rooms and back into the narrow hall. We take it in turns to play the male part and when it's Camille's turn she draws on an imaginary moustache, straightens her imaginary tie, coughs, and solemnly places her thin arm around my waist. 'Madam,' she says, 'may I have this dance?' or 'Allow me, won't you?' and we sashay, giggling, up and down the hall. Tonight, after she has danced us both into exhaustion, and herself into bed, I sit out in the courtyard and reflect on my intense and ponderous masseur, so dark and swarthy. So lean and hard in the body. And the incongruous vanity of the ponytail. Is it vanity? What does long hair mean to a man? Saturday afternoon, he said. But of course, until the day arrives, I can't know what my mood will be, can't say whether I will go or not. I have sworn, for this year of grace at least, not to make plans.

4

skinship

A week passes. Saturday morning, and it's hot, and Camille wants to go for a swim. I say, yes, we'll go. Camille butters toast to the mellow bop of 2WS and its Saturday morning fifties retrospective. She is in the first throes of infatuation: Jerry Lee Lewis. '*You shake my nerves and you rattle my brain*' (this is Camille singing) '*Too much love drives a man insane . . .*'

'*Woman*,' I interject.

She stops. 'No, *girl*,' she says.

'*Woman* scans better.'

'What do you mean, scans?'

'Fits in with the beat of the music.'

'Yeah, but *girl* sounds more right . . .' And she's off again: '*You broke my will, what a thrill . . .*'

We walk to the Petersham pool, already crowded and hectic. I sit under a tree and try to read while Camille thrashes her stiff freestyle in the shallow end and shouts, 'Look at this, Mum. Look. *Look.*' And I look. This is what I am here for, if not to play then to offer the maternal gaze. To reflect; to mirror. And I put my book down, and I *look*. At twelve I order her out and she dries herself and turbans her hair while I buy some hot chips from the kiosk. These are surprisingly good and we toss the black-pitted ones to the birds on the nature strip as we wander home, keeping to the shade of the trees. I ask her if she wants to stop at the nursery and buy a plant for her flower garden and she sighs and says no, she is too hot and too tired. As we turn the corner into Bright Street we see Basia waiting by the gate. 'Would you like to come in and play?' I ask, and she gives a solemn nod, and follows us down the side lane. Little Basia, plump and surly. How I wish I could like her more. Her father beats her and we hear her screams from the back of the house, and for this

I feel I should love her, but her anger and sullenness make it hard for me even to like her. The most I can do is offer her another space, a haven. Sometimes I think Basia has been sent to me as a test.

In the mid-afternoon Dona Maria comes in from next door to babysit. I kiss Camille goodbye and swear softly when I think I've mislaid the keys to the car I've borrowed from Zoe while she is away. My heart begins to pound in mild panic. Up until this moment, the moment with the keys, I have thought myself indifferent to the possibility of this encounter but there is nothing like the whiff of an empty afternoon and a risk that fizzes to make your heart flare and send you racing out into the street and into a hot stuffy car, a little yellow Volkswagon that barely turns over but will get you there somehow.

●

When eventually I arrive I find that the building has an almost derelict exterior. There are blackened pipes and charred windowsills; signs of a fire.

I push open the heavy metal fire door at the front and look around. Inside, the wooden ceiling beams, scorched black by the fire, remain untouched; the rest has been renovated with a brutal Japanese spareness. The downstairs room, wide and long, is empty. It's past four, the time he said to come, and a humid gloom is settling in over the city, a black cloud of electric potential that promises a storm. In the far corner I see a steep iron stairway and I walk across and begin, tentatively, to climb it, hesitating halfway up and calling 'Hello?' No response. I keep climbing and come out into a long white room, like a gallery. One half of the room is marked with two neat rows of dark blue massage mats, separated by white rice-paper screens, waist high, but the mats are unoccupied and this room too appears to be empty. And then I see him, or rather I see his reflection in a bamboo-framed mirror. His dark head is leaning over a table where he is absorbed in re-arranging leaflets. He looks unfamiliar, perhaps because he is barefoot and dressed in the loose white clothes of the masseur. A priest in the temple. And I'm struck again by how thin he is, except for that thick neck, so striking a dissent from the rest of him as if his body were once much larger, gross even, and this is its last column of stubborn resistance.

Before looking up he waits for a few moments, as if composing himself. When he is satisfied that the leaflets are neatly aligned, he raises his head. 'Hi,' he says, 'how are you?'

'Fine.' I'm nervous. I wait for him to say more. He seems subdued, distracted. Perhaps he's annoyed that I'm late. I am about to apologise, to explain that I had trouble parking, but no sooner do I frame the thought than the words fade from my head; something in his demeanour, and the ambience of the room itself, pre-empt speech. This is a room of ritual silence. I feel stalled, stunned almost, by his lack of welcome. Surely we ought to exchange more pleasantries than this? I am surprised that my heart is beating quickly; after all, I was in two minds about coming; this was no breathless, headlong rush to an object of unambiguous desire. More a desperate curiosity, a break from boredom.

'Did you have trouble parking?'

'Yes, I did.'

I find I am staring at his neck. There is something about the look of that neck and, I suspect, the smell of it, that could be my undoing.

'You can undress in there,' he says, gesturing at a cluster of bamboo screens in the corner.

So matter-of-fact! Feeling a little strange, I obey. His detachment is disconcerting. We are alone in the building; I hardly know him. I thought someone else would be here, a receptionist. Someone.

Behind the bamboo screen is an old hat stand hung with cotton kimonos in pale colours. I choose the white with a faint blue pattern in Japanese characters and tie the thin belt in a loose knot. I think: I'm dressing myself like a sacrificial lamb.

When I step out from behind the screen he is standing at the far end of the room at the head of a blue futon mat. 'Lie down,' he says.

He could at least smile. Perhaps he too is nervous. 'You want me to lie down here?' I ask tentatively.

He nods.

I lower myself on to the futon and stretch out like a docile child, pulling at my kimono so that one fold decorously overlays the other and only my bare feet are exposed.

What next?

He bends to the floor and picks up a folded sheet and waits, as if for me to become composed beneath him, and then he flaps the sheet out into the air above me, and I hold my breath and wait for it to settle over my body, like a shroud, so that I am entirely covered from chin to toe. Then he kneels on the floor beside me.

'Comfortable?'

'Hmmmm.'

'Want a pillow?'

'No. Thanks.'

'Are you going to solve my problems for me?' I ask. It comes out sounding arch and flirtatious.

'We're not counsellors,' he says, unsmiling. 'We don't treat on the level of the ego.'

How solemn he is!

'Did you think I'd come?'

'I had no idea.' He is resolute; he will not not flirt with me. Though he does, at least, smile briefly. Then his face goes blank as he places his large brown hand, palm down, on my stomach and pushes in, firmly, with the tips of his fingers. I can feel a tightness there across the wall of my abdomen, like the surface of a drum, as he moves his hand and presses in again, first on either side of my navel, then below the navel just above the pubic bone.

'What are you doing?'

'Feeling your *hara*. Your energy.'

Whatever I ask, he seems intent on withholding. Am I supposed not to talk? What are the protocols?

'What does it tell you?'

'Kidneys are up, heart is down.'

And is this some kind of shorthand? I feel a tic of irritation; I am impatient with people who use technical terms and don't explain them.

'Meaning?'

'In Shiatsu, each of the vital organs is in either a *kyo* or a *jitsu* state. In *kyo* you feel a kind of emptiness, a lack of the life force. In *jitsu* it's the reverse, too much fullness. The life force is in excess, or concentrated too much in the one spot instead of being spread throughout the body. The Shiatsu practitioner works to support the weak areas and disperse the energy in the strong areas to where it's needed.' He says all this without looking at me, still with his hand pressed firmly against the wall of my abdomen. 'Have you been irritable lately?'

'I'm always irritable. I'm famous for it.' Instantly I wish I could take this remark back; it sounds silly; affected. And he smiles; a brief, professional smile, like a doctor; a masculine smile of a particular kind. I hate that smile. I want to throw off the sheet, get up and walk away.

'Can you lie on your side?' he says. And the 'can' pacifies me; for the moment, anyway. This is less of an order than before, more of a polite request. I roll on to my side, lying on my left arm; from the corner of my eye I can see him, on his knees, bending over me. With one hand over the other he presses firmly into a point on my shoulder and then at other points, in slow succession, all the way down my arm.

'What are you doing now?'

'I'm treating your heart meridian.'

'What's wrong with it?'

No answer. Am I talking too much? He has that look in his eye, a kind of gaze into space look that doesn't want to talk, or be spoken to, a serious abstracted look that makes me feel childish and insignificant. I am uncomfortable with the silence. What is it about him that so annoys me? His air of clinical detachment? I hadn't known what to expect (and that, in the end, is why I came, since once I can imagine something I lose interest in it) but I hadn't expected this, this solemn distance between us. How quickly that insistent erotic flutter in my heart has been all but stilled by this formality. How dull! Oh well, I could slide into interview mode and fill up the time that way. I begin to wish I had my recorder here, had a tape running on him.

'How often do you work here?' Ask a man for information, ask him about himself, deflect his power, like light reflected off a mirror back to its source.

He is working down my thigh now, pressing on a series of points. One hand resting on the other he leans his weight into the invisible point in the flesh, my flesh, and he is answering my question, saying something in response (he is working down my calf now) but I am yawning, my eyes are watering,

I wipe them with the tips of my fingers, I feel suddenly tired, he is talking, yes, but what he says seems unimportant, he has just told me something and instantly I have forgotten it. Already my mind is wandering. What is it that I am surrendering to here? The exact character of this transaction is too unclear. There's a fuzziness within and without. I focus on a sign that hangs from the screen beside me: *Setsu — Shin.*

'What does that mean?'

He stops, looks up. 'Literally translated it means the principle of touching. Skinship.'

'Oh.'

'Actually, it means more than that,' he adds. 'It means touching without judgement.'

'And that photograph there? Who's that?'

'Todoroki *Sensei.*'

'Who's he?'

'A master of yoga.'

'Have you studied with him?'

'No. He has a *dojo* in Kyoto where practitioners can do advanced training.'

'And you want to go there, right?'

'Yes. Eventually.'

Did he answer? My mind is going fuzzy again, my limbs are like cotton wool and I have just stifled another yawn. So this is how it works, the body overtaken by a kind of mindless trance . . . surely I couldn't go to sleep here, here on this mat, in a strange room, beneath a strange man . . .

'OK. On to your right side now.'

Recalled to him by this command, I rally. 'So how long have you been doing this?' It's a feeble question: I can hardly be bothered asking it; that fierce impulse in me to interrogate, to barricade myself with words, is at last ebbing away, has ebbed away . . . here I am, prone on the mat, and I can't be bothered to open my mouth; can't be bothered, am sliding into vacancy . . . the process has taken me over; two dispassionate bodies, separated by a sheet . . . and yet there is something here; his will, his touch, the pressure of his hands, the ebb and flow of my resistance, the traffic sounds wafting in from the street, the black rafters of the charred ceiling receding above me. I feel the steady almost abrupt rhythm of his hands against my arm, my hip, my thigh. And now he is kneeling on one knee: with both arms he lifts my legs and drapes them over his other knee. Grasping my legs with his right arm he leans across me and extends his left arm fully downwards so that his palm presses hard against the wall of my abdomen. I gasp, softly, something in me released . . . and he lowers my legs on to the mat. He is kneeling at my feet now, pressing hard with his thumb into the sole of my foot. It's growing darker outside. He stands, bends over, takes my feet in his hands and lifts my legs, pulling them gently away from my torso for just a few seconds before lowering them, slowly, to the floor. Then he walks to the other end of the mat and kneels behind my head. For a few moments he massages my scalp. His hands are warm. He has good hands, warm hands full of energy.

'Sit up,' he says. 'Lock your hands behind your neck.'

He is squatting on his haunches now, immediately behind me. In a slow, trance-like state, I raise my body from the waist up, clasp my hands over the wisps of hair on my neck and wait for him to embrace me from behind. His arms wrap around my body and lock together just below my breasts. And I feel the insistent pressure of his knee, first at the soft pad of flesh just above the coccyx and then as it travels up my back I hear it, the slight, whispering click of my spine. He lets go, my arms drop to my sides, and I exhale in a long, silent sigh.

And he is kneeling beside me, looking at me, directly at me, into my eyes, for the first time since I got here. 'Lie back, lie still. Take as long as you like. Don't get up until you're ready.' And he gives a tight little smile.

I lie there, perhaps for a minute, perhaps three. Or is it ten? I want to get up, it's almost dark in the room now, he hasn't put the lights on, I hear him open a door at the end of the room and glimpse him from the corner of my eye as he steps out onto a concrete terrace. What is he doing? After a while I hear an old-fashioned cistern gush. The door squeaks.

I sit up, look around, the room is empty, my head is empty, is light. I am on my feet and gliding barefoot across the darkening room, down the space between the symmetrical rows of rice-paper screens, to the screen in the far corner where I left my clothes. Behind the screen I begin to dress, lifting first one item of clothing, then another, off the chair in the corner, in a daze, in what seems like slow motion. Though I am lightheaded, my hearing is acute. Hearing a rustle on the other side of the room, I pause; he is back in the room, then? I hear the sound of a zip; he too is dressing, changing from his loose white clothes into something else. I hear a light scuffing sound of leather against the floorboards and know that he is slipping on his shoes.

When I emerge from behind the screen he is standing at the head of the stairs, in jeans and a black T-shirt, leaning against the iron rail, waiting, no angel in white now but a dark figure in the dim light. What should I do? I am suddenly aware that we hadn't ever discussed money. I had assumed from the very first that this was an offering, but I do not want to presume. 'How much do I owe you?'

He lifts his hand in a half-wave. 'Nothing,' he says. There is something pregnant in that nothing, some hint of another transaction.

'Really?' This is provocative of me.

He smiles. 'If you decide you like it, come back. You can pay next time.'

'Well . . . thank you.'

I begin my descent down the perilous stairs and he walks behind me, our feet clomping noisily on the iron grilles. At the bottom I hesitate. What now? Is this it? And while I am hesitating he moves across to unlock the grey metal fire door that opens on to the warm, dusty street.

'Well,' I say, 'thanks again.'

'My pleasure.' He looks at me for a moment and I think that he might say something, but he doesn't, and I wish, as he shuts the door with a clang behind me, that he had at least spoken my name. I want to hear him say it: *Marita*.

That night I dream that someone, a hooded figure, is massaging my foot, my white foot, and drawing a long black tumour out of my sole, a long black sinewy thing that looks like a butcher's blood sausage. And as the hooded one stands there, holding the thing at arm's length, it turns — in a lightning arc — into a dancing illuminated snake. At that moment I wake, startled, to the sound of Camille in the next room, coughing in her sleep. I get up, walk out into the hallway and stand at the door of my daughter's room, and listen for the rise and fall of her breathing, gazing at the sweet fair head on the pillow, the small prim mouth, the perfect brow, the mousey curls. And wait until the coughing subsides.

Once again in my bed I drift back into sleep, eager to re-embrace my dream. It is mid-afternoon, and Camille and I are driving along a bare desert road in bright sunlight, past a big white billboard. The billboard has a message on it. Don't stop, says Camille, keep going. I'll have to stop and read it, I say, it won't take long. And I put my foot on the brake, and open the car door and walk barefoot in the warm red dust over to the monstrous rectangular sign, and look up at the black lettering, a metre high. And the message is? And the message is . . .

When I awake, I can't remember.

PART THREE

CONNEXION

1

Wednesday 6.40 p.m. 91 Bright Street, Leichhardt. Here is her small front garden; its tall lemon palm, its fragrant frangipani tree, a border of unruly flowers, two giant monstera plants darkening one corner of the fence. He opens the gate, knocks on the front door, waits, but no-one comes. Marita and Camille are arguing in the kitchen, Camille's resentful, childish shout escaping into the side lane.

He bangs on the door again, this time with his fist. The ornamental pane of red glass rattles in the door frame.

When Marita opens the door her black spiky hair is tufted up as if she has just this minute furrowed it with an exasperated hand. 'Hi,' she says. 'Have you been here long?'

He kisses her on the mouth, and receives a sweet warm kiss that has in it, nevertheless, a hint of resistance. She breaks away from him.

'I think it's time I gave you a key,' she says.

It has been raining again. Around four o'clock in the afternoon the charcoal sky lit up with fork lightning and the rain came down in sudden torrents. At five-thirty it just as suddenly stopped and within minutes steam began to rise from the roads and mist formed on the windows. In the hot damp evenings these inner-city houses are like stagnant pools. He follows her down the musty hallway, a miasma of mould spores, floating, invisible, and into the dark kitchen at the back where Camille awaits the unwelcome guest. *Him*. She is sitting bolt upright in a cane chair, arms folded, gazing resolutely up at the small portable television on top of the fridge.

'Hi, Stephen,' she says, tonelessly. This is the greeting of the vanquished. She does not look away from the flickering box.

The TV says: *You're too hard on yourself, Tracey. Why don't you just own up to your feelings?*

Camille is very thin, like her mother, who dresses her in an odd but charming way: tonight she is in an old-fashioned flower-print dress, dark green stockings with a hole just above the right knee and black lace-up school shoes. Her brown hair is pulled back in a French plait from which one large tendril wisps away to curl against her neck. She wears a suede thong around her bony arm and beaded bracelets on her wrists.

He's late, and they've been waiting for him. He pulls out a chair and sits at the kitchen table, feeling uncomfortably like a husband. Marita begins almost at once to serve dinner, banging pots and plates in that distracted way she has in the kitchen, like someone who has struck an uneven deal with a bad fairy. Soon, when Camille has accepted him here, he'll take over in the kitchen and then the energy in the house will begin to change for the better. He will bring calm. He is confident of this.

Camille glares at her plate. 'Yuk, brown rice again,' she says, and this he knows is directed at him. ' Why can't we have chips, we used to have chips.'

The TV says: *I just wanted to tell you that you don't have to do it on your own.*

●

Is it only a few weeks since he first came here, driven to her door by a single monochrome image, her dark head above the white massage sheet; an image that wouldn't leave him, day or night? How much control it had taken that day to say nothing, to do nothing, to discipline his will, to maintain the integrity of the treatment; that, and that alone. It was a test, and he had come through it well. But from the moment he had closed the iron door behind her he had been seized by disappointment and restlessness, a jittery, hollow feeling of loss. That very night he'd driven over to her house, on impulse, without ringing, but there had been no-one home, and he'd driven on to a party at Eva's and sulked in a corner, wishing, for once, that he still drank. The next night he'd returned, parking the green Commodore outside her dark little terrace. 'Oh,' she'd said, when she opened the door, startled, her eyes uncertain. She led him through to the dark kitchen and they sat for a while, sipping that pale herbal tea he abhors. Above the freezer hung a startling print in yellow and red and black of a Modigliani nude who looked not unlike Marita.

Camille came in just after six, a thin child with pale blue eyes.

'This is Stephen Eyenon,' Marita had said, very formally. Sitting with her chin cupped in her delicate hand she looked flushed and uneasy.

Camille gave him *the look* — that look he has come to know well. Shy, hostile, hopeful.

'Why don't we go up the road and have a meal,' he'd said, thinking how easy it was to proposition a woman with a child; having the child there made it seem no big deal, unromantic, nothing at stake; a few mates going out for a chat and a tofu burger.

'We could go to Nutters,' she replied, just as casually, 'it's in Marion Street.'

On the way there Camille was derisive about his car. 'This is a dag's car,' she whispered to her mother. He liked the way Marita wasn't fazed. She laughed, and looked at him, and he gave a wry smile back — their first smile of complicity. The significance of this had not been lost on Marita. She hoped Camille hadn't seen it. Holding her breath she stared ahead at the familiar shopfronts on Norton Street.

At Nutters they sat on uncomfortable iron chairs and scanned the blackboard. His instinct told him this wasn't the time to deliver a lecture on diet, on how it's pointless to give up meat if you're going to smother everything in solidified and oversalted dairy fat, i.e. cheese. At this stage the child was more of a problem. Camille. How should he behave with her? The temptation with children, as he knew from the past, is to ignore them, and wait patiently for bedtime. While pretending to study the menu he tried to get a feel for her response to him, to pick up some vibes. All he knew about children was this: they always fight on their own ground and within seconds they can make you doubt yourself. Whenever he attempted eye contact she avoided it and gazed around, for much of the time, at the walls. She seemed a remote, self-contained child.

So he gave in to what he wanted to do, which was to stare at Marita. Marita, spiky and soft, with puffy eyes, a cynical smile and a delicate, long white neck; alluring, swan-like. There are times now when he wonders why he's so attracted to her. Studying her that night he decided that she hadn't a single good feature and yet her face as a whole was mesmerising; the expression in her dark eyes, the way her lips pursed when she talked and the reluctant sympathy in her laugh. And the way her body moved, some indefinable grace, all the more seductive because she was unaware of it. Nothing willed. An unconscious poise that could make him feel lumpen.

•

It was the first time he'd ended up in bed with a woman without either of them having had something to drink, something to ease the passage of strange bodies, and it had taken them until two in the morning, after overlong conversation, and on the brink of nervous exhaustion, to lie together in her strange, untidy bed. From the moment he saw it he was enchanted by that bed, a heavy cedar piece from the turn of the century with high bedheads, like ramparts, ornately carved with waratahs and gumnuts. He ran his hands over the dark wooden protruberances that coiled and swathed and intertwined, and declared the whole thing hallucinatory. 'It's an heirloom,' she said, waiting for him to ask her how she came by it. He didn't. And she sensed that he was someone who resisted the past, who didn't want to talk about it. Not that she cared.

Afloat in that dark cedar ship, they were surprisingly at ease with one another. In bed, she decided, he was another person; the intensity melted away; he became playful, yielding. He, too, was content; she had opened herself to him and there was none of that cold self-containment that could ambush you in some women who seemed capable of experiencing pleasure from behind an impenetrable wall of self. Afterwards, as they lay together, she gave her reluctant laugh, poked him in the ribs and said he was too thin. He gripped her shoulder and moved towards her but at that moment Camille had groaned in her sleep. Marita's hand on his thigh stiffened. She sat up, alert, listening.

'You think she heard us?' he whispered.

'No,' she replied. And listened again. 'Camille has asthma. Often, in the night, she starts to wheeze.'

That was the first time he noticed the poetic cadence in her speech, and began his obsessive habit of echoing her phrases in his head, 'often in the night . . . often in the night . . .' She listened for another minute and then subsided onto his chest, sighing. 'There are some nights when I lie awake just listening to Camille breathe.'

He found this statement indescribably erotic; he felt his heart slipping into a slower rhythm; he folded his arms around her in a soft vice; he wanted to stay and cook for her, for them both, in the morning. But again Camille began to cough, a light rasping sound from somewhere on the other side of the hallway. Marita raised her head; her hair stood up in dark spikes; she looked, in silhouette, like a soft unsettled animal, listening. She said: 'I think you'd better go.'

In the morning he rang her from the office and she was warm in a remote, languid way. His own voice seemed to reverberate back to him in a nasal echo. Did he sound callow? He had planned to invite her over for dinner and then he thought: what about Camille, should he include Camille? And that complicated everything. After hesitating for a second too long he invited them both and she said fine, that would be nice.

For the rest of the day he could think about nothing but his menu. How many concessions should he make to an eight-year-old girl? Cooking for Marita would be easy but Camille was his real challenge. On the Friday night he made sour dough rolls for lentil hamburgers and for the grown-ups he decided on chick peas in tamarind, also a salad with green soba buckwheat noodles, dressed with rice wine and tamari, ginger, garlic and coriander, and fried tofu cubes and chili, and then for pudding, couscous cooked in apple juice and diced pears poached in spring water with cinnamon.

Camille ate hardly any of it.

'I don't like these noodles,' she whispered to her mother. 'They're gluggy. I like ordinary spaghetti.'

'Just eat a little,' her mother whispered back, but the look in her eyes said: Tough. No-one ever cooks for me and I'm enjoying it.

●

Tonight, as always, they eat with someone else's constant chatter in the background. He yearns to turn the television off. Marita and Camille have some frightful habits; a love of soap opera in the early evenings.

The TV says: *I know I was sucked in by Vanessa but that was then and right now all I want is for us to be friends again.*

After the first week of eating here, he'd risked an intervention. 'Marita,' he'd begun, softly. 'Do we have to have that thing on now?' Camille had gone on gazing at the box, as if in a trance, her fork finding its way to her mouth by invisible radar.

'It seems to help Camille eat,' she'd murmured in a low voice. 'It distracts her. She forgets to complain. She relaxes and just eats, automatically, what's on her plate.'

'She shouldn't eat automatically, like a zombie. She should give it her full attention. Pay the food the respect it's entitled to.' He might have added: 'It's a way of honouring life itself, of *paying attention.*' But he didn't want to risk sounding ponderous.

Marita had smiled, teasingly. 'If she gives it her full attention she'll find something to argue about. "These peas are cold. This ravioli is too floppy. This rice tastes spicy." You wait and see. It's called: Taking Mother On.'

Tonight Camille swings her feet rhythmically against the legs of her chair in a hollow, knocking sound. It unsettles him. It's important to be calm when eating but no-one told him how difficult this could be around children. To disguise his irritation he finds himself eating in a studied way, contemplating the glossy lacquered surface of his chopsticks.

Camille swivels her spoon back and forth, back and forth. 'What's for sweets?' she asks. 'I'm not eating any of that soy milk stuff.'

'You can have ice-cream if you like.'

'With chocolate sauce?'

'Plain.'

'*Great.*' The sarcasm in her voice is liquid. And she leans her elbows on the table with an affected, stagey sigh. For the first time tonight she looks at him, and he returns the look. Her eyes say: This is only a temporary defeat; don't think you've won yet.

The TV says: *I don't want you to feel, after what happened with Jason, that you can't trust me any more.*

●

On that second night it was hot and still, and they took a walk in Ashenby Park. Marita was in a good mood and stroked his arm while they loitered under the tall palms. A warm breeze blew her dark hair back from her forehead and for the first time he observed her in profile, and the sharp angry cast to her eyes that can make her look like a witch. Behind them, Camille hung by her legs from the monkey bars, her white pants like a beacon in the late evening dusk. From time to time Marita would glance over her shoulder; she had that distracted air mothers have, a part of them always watching the child; wanting to be separate, wanting too to draw the child back to them. He finds this erotic, this ambivalence of women; the co-existence of the loving heart alongside the evil eye, like two sides of a Picasso face; the nurturing smile that dips into the leer.

They strolled across the dry grass. He listened to her talk, or was it him talking? Inside, in the cavity of his chest, he could feel something beginning to shift, a tumescence in the heart. Half-listening he heard her say that her father was dead, that suddenly, one bright Saturday morning on the tennis court, his heart had stopped, and that her mother lived alone in a big rambling house at Darling Point, on the water. He got the feeling there was something odd about the mother but he had no desire to know any of this, in fact the opposite; he wanted to know only her warm body, not her past, he wanted only the present moment, and the strolling arm in arm and the euphoric fullness in his chest — dreamily unaware that Camille had crept up behind them. With a sudden movement she sprang out from behind a bush and slapped her mother hard on the bottom. Marita gasped, and began to chase Camille into the hedge, and together they ran away from him, windblown and laughing; disengaged, elusive, beyond his grasp. He felt for a moment that they might disappear and already, in that moment, he felt stranded.

•

That night she woke to a strange sound. The small luminous figures on the clock dial showed 12.05. The wind had dropped and the warmth of the day was seeping back into the night so that she woke in a clammy bed and pushed back the cotton covers. Through half-closed lids she looked up at the ceiling, at the blurred and shadowy movements of the fan blades that fluttered above her in a soft vibrating whirr. And then, some other sound, some strange, muffled noise, something weird.

It was him; it couldn't be anyone else. Hoisting herself up on to her pillow she peered at his face. His lips moved in a peculiar way and after a minute or so she realised that he was grinding his teeth. Gently she shook him by the shoulder. He groaned, insensible, stranded in some other world. 'Did you have a bad dream?' she whispered. He gave another kind of moan, a strange humming sound from between closed lips. Moving close into his back she put her arm over his ribcage (so thin) and brushed his long dark hair aside and lay her cheek against the back of his bare neck. Still asleep, he rolled over, facing her, and drew her hard against his chest with a kind of desperation. Breathing in the salty smell of his neck she kissed the hollow spaces above his collarbone, softly, over and over. After a while he sighed again, and the sigh came out as a low, shuddering moan.

And that's when he woke, in the dark, to find her nestling into his chest which was damp with a cold sweat . 'Are you OK?' she whispered, drowsily. 'Yes,' he answered, shivering slightly, and he was now, alright that is, now that he was awake, now that he had escaped the dream.

He rolled over onto his back. 'I had a dream,' he said.

'Do you want to talk about it?'

'No, not now.'

For a moment he was too fazed to touch her; then, recovering, he put his hand on her arm and said, 'It's OK.' He resisted women who demanded an explanation of everything, but she simply kissed him lightly on the shoulder and turned away on to her side and was almost instantly asleep, while he continued to lie on his back, stunned, with a feeling of having been, once again, ambushed by the past.

Why had this dream come back to haunt him now? Why tonight? It was a dream that hadn't come to him for years, but one that used to torment him in his early twenties. He dreamed that he was losing his teeth. He was sitting at the kitchen table with his mother, chatting away over a cup of coffee, and slowly he felt his teeth begin to crumble, like chalk; first the loosening in the gums and the sudden stab of panic, then a fractured, disintegrating tooth falls on to his tongue and sits there with the taste and texture of chalk. And he wants to gag. But he is afraid to vomit or even to open his mouth for fear his teeth will tumble out in a rush and be swept away irretrievably, and he presses his lips together and mutters through a small opening at the side of his mouth, 'Mother, my teeth are falling out.' And she says 'That's alright, dear,' and goes on talking about the weather. Or says nothing. He wants to cry 'Help me!' He wants his mother, in a very sensible and matter-of-fact way, to push his teeth back into place, firmly. But she goes on looking out the window at the hazy green vista of the hills, silently drinking her tea, and he feels the loosening and crumbling in his jaws and the little bits, the splinters and fragments clogging in his mouth like grit, and the feeling of desperation, of powerlessness . . .

And then he wakes, grinding his bite, and oh the strength of it, the fierce immutability of those molars! The relief after a nightmare is the purest of emotions.

●

Mornings are the best times. He has his rituals, they have theirs. He rises at six, needing no alarm to urge him into his day. At the back of her house is a little courtyard which gets the morning sun and he does his Chi Kung exercises there before meditating in the front parlour, and if he's lucky Camille will sleep late and the house will be quiet. Sometimes, if she wakes early, Camille will climb into her mother's bed and he will hear them play their favourite morning game, a guessing game they have invented, an odd game that makes no sense to him. They lie on their sides and each takes it in turn to inscribe a mystery word on the other's back. Marita lifts Camille's cotton nightdress up to her shoulders and with her index finger traces the mystery word across her skin. It is difficult to apprehend, blind, the skin-to-skin tracings, so they stick to short and simple words: *yes — too — me — I you*. Sometimes even this is too much for them and they can only guess at one letter, *m* or *s* or *x*. While he meditates in the front room he can hear them chattering and laughing behind the wall.

Forgetful of his presence Marita eases Camille's nightdress up to her neck and is overcome, as always, by an urge to kiss that delicate little back, the fine undulating ridge of the backbone all the way up to the fleshy hollow between the shoulder blades. And then to inhale the subtle scent of her daughter's skin, her little peach.

Camille's turn now. Roughly, she pushes up Marita's T-shirt exposing her white breasts. Marita feels a cool draught; she shudders. 'Keep still,' says Camille. 'How can you tell what I'm writing if you shiver!' Camille is always better at this game than her mother who this morning cannot decipher the last word, $b - r - e - a - d$. 'I'll do it again,' says Camille, and begins to repeat her inscription, just as Stephen comes in, saying: 'Get up, you two. I've got your breakfast ready. Camille will be late for school.'

Marita lies back on the pillow with her bare arms folded behind her head. 'Now what does it matter, Stephen,' she says, with a teasing smile, 'if she's late?' And something in her attitude is foreign to him, some indefinable assumption of privilege, of exemption, of immunity to the world. At moments like this it's as if she already has what he's working towards. Of course, she doesn't work; she is prepared to lead a spartan life to avoid this, to pay for her freedom, at least for a time. But it's deeper than that, some kind of otherworldliness, maybe. Or is it some ultimate worldliness? Freedom from will? Or an extreme assertion of it? It's the source of that peculiar poise of hers, the other side of hysteria; a sliding, a letting go. A quality he finds both seductive and alarming.

2

Slowly, then, he begins to settle into a life here, here in her small house in Leichhardt. From time to time he drops into his sister's palace of art in Glebe to collect the mail and check the alarm system but for the best part of each week he is bedded down here, in Bright Street.

It's Sunday morning and they lie in her cedar bed while Camille watches cartoons on television, turned up to a searing volume that for once he does not object to since it guarantees the privacy of their talk.

'You're so languid,' he tells her. 'So languid.'

Marita's body is small and slim. Her hair is short and dark, her breasts small with large, dark nipples; the hair under her arms and between her legs is obscenely lush. The quality of that languor mesmerises him. It is a graceful disinclination to movement, or action. There are days when this body wants only to sit and sleep and ride and drift. On other days there are outbursts of manic energy and she borrows his car and hoons off on excursions to God knows where, places she doesn't want to talk about. 'Oh, nowhere much,' she says, when he shows a more than polite interest. 'You know, just drove around.' Or she buzzes around in the kitchen with her slapdash mania for baking cakes. One afternoon, not long after he started sleeping here, Marita baked him a lavish torte. 'I left out the sugar,' she said, 'and used rice malt, and carob instead of chocolate' — thereby missing the point entirely, the point being that all baked flour is dead food. When he declined to try even a slice of it she became hurt and ceremoniously removed the plate from his end of the table, setting it down at the other end where Camille cast him a wide-eyed look of bafflement before carrying off a piece to eat in front of the television. Marita seemed able to accept everything in his diet except this — as if he had a choice in it. You were either on the diet or you weren't. And besides, ever since the dream about chocolate cake, any kind of cake makes him feel sick. 'Cakes don't have to be junk food, Stephen,' Marita said indignantly. 'It depends on how and why they're made.' And she lectured him on how ancient cultures used to mark special religious rituals by baking small cakes and inscribing them with sacred symbols and when these had been blessed or in some way consecrated, they were broken and consumed by the worshippers. 'Yes,' he replied, 'but only on special feast days, not routinely stuffed into the body, day after day.' 'This *is* a special feast day,' she said, eyes widening in a deadpan stare. 'I've made you a cake.'

She is pale, pale and hypersensitive to light; she wears her sunglasses, even in winter, to shield her eyes from brightness. She likes the dark. At first he finds this affected, kind of an inner-city cool, but then he observes her without her shades, squinting at the light, in retreat from the glare. Sometimes, when she is angry, her inner-city pallor takes on a crimson flush, and her eyes glitter with the flame of some deep affront, some unfocussed fear. That first time he'd treated her he had felt, almost the instant he put his hands on her, an electric hum of hysteria, something wired deep beneath the skin. And he'd wondered then why he found her pale languor so much more compelling than the energetic glow of more robust women, until he recalled Motoyana: *The latent, dark, unexpected aspect of things is the female, yin, while yang is the name given to the patent, the bright, the exposed.* God knows, he is yang enough for both of them.

'What do you mean by yang?' she'd asked once.

'Contracted, hard, stubborn.'

She laughed.

In truth he is a captive of that languid energy in bed. She is not athletic, no; instead she has an erotic sympathy that exudes like a perfume from her limpid white skin and from her brown eyes, and envelops him in a warm haze until he dissolves into it, into a warm unthinking fog, a long fugue of amnesia. Does this make any sense? No, of course not; if it made any 'sense' to him it would lose its power. Perhaps this is her hold over him: that she is not at all like his mother, or his sister; that she is uniquely foreign to him; that he cannot *explain* her. Love is supposed to be a recognition, some mirror image of the self, but then again, it is just as likely to be a recognition of the not-self. A distinctly other form of enchantment.

By the time they get up it is too late for breakfast and they eat lunch outside, in her tiny courtyard which is green and shady. This is Leichhardt, where the small dark terraces press together, separated by the narrowest of lanes; little houses with tiled steps and ornate Edwardian grilles and stained glass in the doors; some desecrated with brick veneer sunrooms and steel awnings and grey concrete patios with cheap concrete fountains in miniature and flaking grey cherubs and ragged pot plants in rusting iron planters. The charm of these houses is their small, subtropical courtyards which exist in defiance of the smog. The immigrants bring little packets of seeds from the homeland. Next door, the elderly Dona Maria sings wailing songs in Portuguese while she weeds her vegetable garden full of strange plants. One evening she gave Marita a green leafy vegetable called *grelos*. They cooked the *grelos* and it was bitter.

This morning they can hear Maria singing as she works in her garden behind the ivy-covered fence. 'Why don't you grow vegetables?' he asks Marita. 'What's the point?' she laughs. 'You wouldn't eat anything grown in this smog.' What about Dona Maria, he asks, and her flourishing vegetable bed, full of exotics? Maria is a peasant, she says, she would grow tomato plants anywhere. And what are you? he asks. She laughs: I'm an urban weed, one of those that spring up through the cracks in the pavement and are hardy. He smiles, and fondles her long white neck.

As it happens, there *is* a small garden in a corner of the courtyard, Camille's flower garden. Cosmos daisies, marigolds, zinnias and gold kangaroo paw. These cannot be picked for the house as Camille is allergic to many of them and they bring on her wheezing. Marita refers to them sardonically as Camille's 'petroleum blooms' growing, as they do, right under the belly of the flight path, thirteen kilometres due north of the Botany runway where the big white 747s ascend at a steep angle across a seagull-flecked horizon. Here in the hot still courtyard he can almost taste the high-octane fuel wafting down from the balmy sky, dumped from incoming jets as they prepare to land. Hearing the dull drone of their approach is enough to make him wince. Not so Marita and Camille who are shockingly indifferent to these mechanical beasts, roaring so loud and so low. They take these monsters for granted, as if they truly were birds that belonged in the sky and he is both impressed and appalled by what he thinks of as this very feminine form of acquiescence in the intolerable. Nor do they know the enemy. While Camille has memorised the botanical names of her flowers she is unable to identify even one of the major airlines whose white mammoths cast regular shadows over her small flower garden. Sitting here now, at the table, he is about to remark on this when he observes Marita gazing abstractedly into space. 'Hey, where are you?' he calls, but she does not respond. 'Hey?' he says again, but she appears not to have heard him.

Staring into the remains of the sweet and sour tofu dish on her plate, Marita is struck by a sudden restlessness. This morning she felt expansive and lightheaded, if a little tired, and she'd risen and prepared this food in a post-erotic trance in which conscious thought was beyond her and every movement had come instinctively and with ease. But now, in the vacant lull after lunch, that dull time that can seem like a shallow pit, it's as if she is swathed in an invisible blanket of encroachment. She is not accustomed to a man in the house, not, at least, for such prolonged periods. He presides at her table like a brooding phantom. Sometimes it is as if she is caught in his shadow, or as if she must measure her tread around some strange lumbering mass. And it seems, subtly, to change everything, as if all the particles in the air have been recharged in another way. The male scent, the male hormone. For that is what it is, that heavy charge. Testosterone.

On impulse she jumps up from the table. 'I need to go and talk to Zoe,' she says. 'I'd forgotten. She asked me to come around today. She wants to try some idea out on me. Could you mind Camille for two hours?'

'Sure,' he says, taken aback by the suddenness of this but anxious to please. 'Would you like a lift? Can I run you there?'

'No. It's walking distance. I'll be okay.'

And within minutes she is on her way to the front door, amazed at her own headlong rush. Camille will not be happy at being left alone, for the first time, with Stephen, but it will be good for both of them to have to work out some modus vivendi without the subtle warfare of their silent references to her. She finds Camille in her bedroom, playing with her school of trolls. Kissing her briefly on the forehead, she announces casually that

Stephen is babysitting and she is off to visit Zoe. 'When will you be back?' the child asks, not in surprise but as if she had been expecting this abandonment sooner or later.

'Around four.' And she is in the hallway again, with almost indecent haste, and on her way to the front door. In her black tote bag is her small tape-recorder.

Out in the courtyard Stephen begins to clear away the remnants of lunch. This is the first time he and Camille have been left alone and he contemplates the protocol. Should he attempt to amuse her? Left to herself she'll watch television — *I just don't know how to get him to see reason, Tania* — and that would be easy for him, all too easy, but they'd both feel sort of half-dead afterwards, she tired and empty, he guilty. Maybe they could cook. Kids like to cook, don't they? He could give her a cooking lesson: they could make some bread. She lives on the stuff; wanders to the fridge in a trance and plucks slices of it from the plastic bag, Tip Top, Ezy-Bake, Country Fresh, and chews on them, blank-eyed, in front of the soap operas; no butter, no jam or Vegemite, just mouthfuls of fermented sludge to clog up the pathways of the *chi*. He runs through a mental check-list of ingredients: though he doesn't eat bread any more there was a time when he'd learned how to make it and he can still remember the basic drill. But first they'd have to go shopping, and he ponders the psychology of this exercise: if he asks her if she wants to make bread she'll probably say no, or her favourite word, *yuk*, and the whole exercise is, when he thinks about it, too close to the source of their on-going disputes. No, better to try something else, to escape the house altogether. What do you do with children? You take them on an outing — in this case, maybe, somewhere unexpected. Intuitively he senses that to avoid demoralisation you should make up your mind quickly and not give them time to argue. And he puts his head around the door of her room and says, 'C'mon, we're going out.'

'Where?'

'To the airport.'

'Why?' She screws up her nose in mature disapproval.

'You'll see.'

And within minutes they are on their way to Mascot, out through the drab streets of Sydenham towards the bay. He clicks on the radio and turns it up loud on 2WS so that she can listen to retro hits and they don't have to make conversation. All the while Camille stares out the window, oblivious, it seems, to his occasional glances in her direction.

Once at the international air terminal she becomes animated. She has never been here before. She likes the long escalators and the even longer walkways. At the coffee shop she loiters by the entrance, casting a wanton eye at the hot chips and icy Coke (chilled to the point where it might deaden the digestive fires for good) and he realises the pitfalls of taking a child anywhere there is hot fat and Coca-Cola cabinets. It's like an obstacle course where you have to be alert for buried mines, silver and red striped canisters of gassy black poison. If Marita were here he would act the role of censor but since he is in sole charge it is incumbent on him to dispense some largesse and he compromises on a bag of low-salt chips and a fruit juice; a treat, he recognises ruefully, that is not a treat at all.

In the Panorama Lounge they stand at the curved and tinted windows and watch the jumbos glide in and glide out. Insulated from the noise they can contemplate form and colour, the bloated white curve of the nose, decorated with insignia. See how many you can memorise, he says to her, and she willingly enters into the game. I'll give you a dollar, he promises, for every one you can identify when we get home. See, Qantas: red tail, white kangaroo. That's an easy one. Cathay Pacific: thick green stripes. She nods. Sunday is a good day to initiate the game: it's a heavy day for international traffic and the skies are light until nine. When they get home, they'll wait for the familiar roar and see who can identify the first fat jumbo to momentarily block out the sky above the courtyard. British Airways: blue and white stripes, Union Jack on the nose. Singapore Airlines: maroon and gold and a festive lion's head on the tail. JAL: red mythological bird with wings spread in a circle. United Airlines: stars and stripes on the nose, grey body. The afternoon drifts on . . . he looks down at his watch and then at Camille who is gazing out at the shimmering tarmac. She has the same indefinable grace as her mother, he decides, but is nothing like Marita in either colouring or features. And for the first time, he wonders who her father might be.

●

On the drive home she is more talkative than before and wants to know if he has ever flown in a jumbo. 'No,' he says, 'but I'm saving up to go to Japan.' 'Why?' she asks. 'Because there might be something special for me there and I won't know until I go and see for myself.' Not surprisingly this answer is too oblique for her and her mind drifts off onto more practical things.

Just before the turn-off to Leichhardt he makes a sudden decision and swerves right, into Glebe. He will stop in at his sister's place to check that all is well. It's been a few days now and her many solemn injunctions to safeguard the place have left him with a niggling sense of responsibility. Outside her front door he is momentarily disconcerted to see an unruly pile of junk mail, a dead give away. 'Do you want to come in?' he asks Camille.

She shrugs. 'OK.'

Inside, the house is dark and still. 'You can look around if you like,' he says. 'There's a big four-poster bed upstairs.' She turns away from him, and looks inquiringly up the stairs.

As always, there is a pile of mail on the floor. No letter from his mother but another postcard from Helen, this one from Naples.

Dearest Stephen, he reads, *Europe is like a dream! We picnicked by the Danube this morning and somehow I felt at home, far far away from those scrawny eucalypts. The European trees are so sublimely symmetrical, and that symmetry is reassuring. And yet I feel a little sick this morning, sort of over-stimulated. My bag is crammed with souvenirs that seemed amusing at the time — a paper napkin from the Reichstag coffee shop, a Minnie Mouse pen from EuroDisney ('Mademoiselle Mouse'), a flyer in Hungarian advertising the latest crusade of American evangelists — such cultural flux, no wonder I feel disoriented. Ric and I arguing a lot I'm afraid. Love Helen.*

While he reads, Camille wanders around the salon, occasionally pausing to stroke a figurine.

'My grandma has a big house,' she says. 'But we hardly ever go there.' And then, 'Is your sister rich?'

'No, she's not rich. She and her husband both have jobs that pay a lot of money and my sister spends all her money on the house.'

'She's got a lot of ornaments and stuff.'

'Yes, she has.'

'Did you used to live here?'

'I still do, sort of. Sometimes it's nicer to stay at your place, though,' he adds, anticipating her next question and hoping she won't ask him why. She doesn't.

When they get home Marita is in the kitchen, brewing tea; the coarse brown twigs of bancha, simmering in a stoneware pot. This is one of his conversions: he had introduced her to the tea and immediately she loved it.

'Where did you two disappear to!' she exclaims, smiling.

He observes at once that the restlessness of the morning has eased out of her; she is calmer, more within herself.

That night they again eat outside in the courtyard. Camille relieves him of three dollars by correctly identifying three of the five jumbos to roar down their conversation. She seems pleased by this and he thinks maybe they might yet develop a rapport through the time-honoured method of bribery. Quietly he congratulates himself on not being too pure, on being human, flexible, able to compromise. It's one of those evenings where everything seems to flow effortlessly and the warm night bathes them in a sense of well-being, so much so that he is inclined to linger in the courtyard.

Around eight, while Camille and Marita bicker good-naturedly over bedtime, he sits alone and contemplates this small, unruly, smog-ridden patch of green, and the dense tangle of leaf that reflects each wave of immigrants to the city: figtree, lemon, grapevine, bluegum, banana palm, white frangipani and there, in a fraught clump by the fence, a climbing red rose entwined with a scarlet hibiscus, while at their base wild tomato plants run riot. The English, the Mediterranean, the tropical and the native bush entwined in a ceaseless tangle, and above them the sweet heady smell of frangipani floating on an acrid wave of gasoline. Soon, when it's dark, the cicadas will start their shrill, insistent warbling, invisible tribes vibrating in the trees; a sweet orchestration of the familiar and the exotic. Wherever there is some element of the exotic, of the strange, only then can he relax and feel at ease with himself. The last thing he wants is to feel 'at home' — that's precisely what he *doesn't* want to feel; tense and empty, as if something vital is missing.

Indoors Marita is reading the opening pages of Camille's new book, *The Big Friendly Giant*, a present from Zoe who had sent it over this afternoon. Though Marita thinks the story delightful, the child appears hardly to be listening; she stares at the muslin curtains at the window as if musing on something else.

'How long is Stephen going to live here?' she asks.

'I don't know. He isn't exactly living here. He's staying for a while.'

'Are you in love?'

Marita puts the book down. 'I'm not sure. It takes a long time to discover whether or not you're in love.' She waits for the next question but Camille simply yawns and turns over on to her side.

Marita has a question of her own. 'Do you like Stephen?' she asks, guiltily, possessed by the thought that this is somehow an unfair question to put to an eight-year-old child.

Camille turns her head back towards her. 'Well I sort of do and I sort of don't.' This is a good answer, one that displays an instinctive tact. She's about to follow up on the 'do' and the 'don't' parts when the devil himself appears at the door. He could almost be the devil, standing in the half-light of the hallway with his black hair loose on his shoulders, his dark cheeks unshaven.

'Goodnight, Camille,' he says, and the tone in his voice is particularly mellow. And then to Marita: 'I'm tired, and I want to get up a flex hour in the morning. I'm going to bed.'

'I'll be up for a while yet,' she says.

He raises his eyebrows and purses his lips in a kind of mock disappointment: he likes her to retire with him. Like most men of her experience he has the unconscious expectation that she will adopt his routine.

'I have some things I want to do,' she says.

He shrugs.

Yes, there is something she is eager to do. And it's luck that he should be tired — she is itching to get at the tape she made this afternoon with Zoe.

She busies herself in the kitchen, baking an orange cake for Camille's lunches and ironing Camille's clothes for the week. These are stalling manoeuvres to make sure he is asleep before she begins work on her tapes. Around ten-thirty, she walks softly into the bedroom: his arm is flung back in abandon and he snores gently on his back. Returning to the kitchen she takes the small tape-recorder down from the top shelf of the pantry (where it sits next to Camille's asthma medication) and sets it down on the kitchen table. Removing the tape from her bag she slides it into the sleek little box and listens to the discreet click of the Play button.

Appropriately, the first sound is of Zoe's droll, muted, sensual laughter. The afternoon had had all the charm of impulse. It was sometimes like that; easy, with a spontaneous flow. She had sat with Zoe in the back sunroom that faced the high brick wall of the chocolate factory and the faint aroma of sickliness that emanated from over the wall had wafted in through the flyscreen door. Zoe had woven her long tawny hair into a loose plait as she spoke, pulling the strands against her bare, freckled shoulder in a gesture of worldly ease. Zoe: her own age; divorced, childless, restless with need. Zoe is accustomed to the tape and free with it, indeed seems even to look forward to it as if conspiring in the creation of an archive of the ordinary. She had no particular reason to visit Zoe today, had not even expected to find her at home, had just wanted to get out of the house. Often when she visits, Camille is with her, a bored spectator, a semi-hostile eavesdropper, and they must censor their conversation or confine it to safe gossip which is difficult for Zoe who is nothing if not confessional.

This afternoon Zoe had been full of a pick-up she had made earlier in the week on the way back from a conference at Palm Beach. Two detectives had stopped her on the road and suggested she join them for a drink at a motel nearby. Mildly attracted to the younger of the two, she had agreed and driven on to the bar down the road while they followed on behind. 'I liked the fair one. I thought he looked terrifically fuckable,' she began, in her blunt, lascivious way, 'and I've never been propositioned by a man with a gun before. He was full-on from the start, kind of desperate in a controlled, almost hostile way. He tried to impress me by ordering the barman around and showing me his gun and I know it sounds crass but it was kind of endearing.' At this point Marita had raised her eyebrows. She did not think it sounded endearing.

'Then what happened?'

'We talked and talked. I began to get a sense that this wasn't for me. I started to feel a bit trapped — you know that feeling you get when you think maybe this is more complicated than you imagined? Let's face it,' she sighed, 'it's always more complicated than you imagined. All you want is a man who can fuck like a maniac for an afternoon, share a drink and be on his way — or see you off on yours — but where do you find one?'

For another twenty minutes she listens, now to her friend's voice on tape, allowing the words to skim across the surface of her consciousness until, suddenly, she stops . . . her attention arrested and caught . . . there's something in there . . . something about entrapment. Within one story there is always another, and another, like Chinese boxes. She stares at the recorder for a few moments and then gets up, quietly, to make herself some tea. This one is easy. Already she knows what she will do with it. She rummages in her tote bag for one of her thick nibbed pens and, putting the machine to one side, begins to write in her loose flowing script in which the individual letters barely connect to one another and seem to dance on the page with a life of their own.

After a while, she puts down her pen and contemplates the page. Yes, she's satisfied with it now; the necessary alchemy has taken place, the hook has caught; she has remade it in her own image. On another night she might run this tape over again, and make some new sense of it. She has trouble with men; she has trouble with the idea of romance: she looks at other peoples' romances and wonders why hers have been so unsatisfactory. If she keeps working the same story over and over again, in all its versions, one day there's a chance she might get it right.

It's 1.55 a.m. Walking softly and barefoot down the hallway she pauses at Camille's door and listens for the child's breathing. She counts ten breaths, enough to tell her whether or not there is any wheeze present. No, tonight there is none.

In her own room Stephen is in a deep sleep, sprawled across the bed, naked, his face turned to one side, his long black hair flowing out in thick strands against the white pillow. His lips are parted but he makes no sound. How deeply he sleeps. When he first began to sleep here she recalls him lamenting that he was an insomniac but in the nights since she has seen no sign of it. She is grateful for this. And now that she has put some distance between them she is ready to be close again. She slides into bed beside him and embraces him from behind, resting her small hand against the wide bone of his hip.

●

In the morning he is woken by the sound of screaming in the street, and then a frantic banging on the front door. Marita sits bolt upright in the bed. 'What is it?' he asks. She doesn't answer but swings her legs over the bed and reaches for her dressing-gown. 'Not again,' she mutters, as she heads for the door. Someone on the doorstep is sobbing, a young woman, gasping in half phrases . . . her boyfriend has locked her out again . . . he came home from the nightshift and flew into a rage because there was no milk . . . no, she does not want to come in for breakfast . . . can Marita lend her twenty dollars for a taxi to her sister's place in Concord . . . Marita returns to the bedroom, rummages in her purse and exits again. The front door closes and he hears her sigh and turn down the hallway towards the kitchen.

'Was that Melissa again?' he hears Camille yell from her bed.

Melissa, it appears, is a regular. Smiling to himself he gets out of bed, puts on some shorts and carries his meditation mat into the front room.

Programme completed he heads for the bathroom just as Marita emerges steamily from the shower. In the front parlour, Camille is sitting in front of the TV, sprawled on the old lounge, eating sliced white bread from the open packet.

Sunshine Wonderbread Hy Fibre

'Camille,' says her mother, 'don't eat from the packet, get yourself a plate.'

Why? he thinks. Might as well eat the plate for all the good it will do. He bites his tongue and goes into the kitchen to prepare his ground porridge.

But when, some minutes later, Camille comes out into the kitchen to swing the plastic bag of bread into the fridge, he can't help himself.

'Look,' he says. He takes the bag from the fridge, removes two of those pristine white slices, moves across to the sink, turns on the cold water tap and, letting the bread rest in his palm, runs the cold water across the bread until it is saturated.

'Look,' he says again, squeezing the water from the bread. 'See, it's like glue, isn't it? An over-processed paste that gums up your insides.'

She glances into the sink condescendingly. 'Yeah, but it tastes good,' she says, and saunters off into the living room.

He flips up the lid of the garbage bin and drops the gluey mush onto the leftovers from dinner.

Later, on the bus to work, he relives this little scene in his head. It may seem trivial to others but he knows better. This issue of bread is at the crux of things; it cannot but affect Camille's problem with her breathing: she eats so much of it. Bread for breakfast, bread in her lunchbox, bread for snacks, bread for supper and sometimes, most damagingly, as a substitute for dinner. And bread eaten completely without ceremony, plucked from the plastic packet and snacked on at odd hours, broken into ragged pieces, whenever and wherever, so that he is continually discovering small white crumbs in every corner of the house, once, even, on his meditation mat. This absence of ceremony is almost as lamentable as the bread itself. If life is constructed out of a series of oblique rituals, many of them are now so oblique that we are no longer conscious of them and hence unable to benefit from their energising focus, their subtle poetry. He of course is opposed to all bread: it clogs up the vital channels of the *chi*, but he has begun to sense that, ultimately, he may have to compromise on something, and if he could just get her to improve the quality of the bread she eats, he would have achieved something, brown rice or no brown rice. Perhaps if he gave her a bread-making lesson, took her to the Demeter Bakery in Glebe where they have special classes and where the baker explains to the assembled pilgrims how they plant their grain by the moon, how everything is done in accordance with nature. Perhaps then, for a child, this question of bread would take on the allure of a fairy story:

Cinderella learns how to make a biodynamic loaf; Sleeping Beauty is awakened by the aroma of freshly baked wholemeal damper prepared by the Prince in his portable camp oven.

3

Marita sits outside in her courtyard, wondering if she really wants a man under her roof. Who is this cuckoo in her garden? Who is this blackbird of desire? It's been six weeks and, mostly, Stephen has been on his best behaviour, yet in some subtle way he pervades the house with a masculine presence. Its symptoms are subtle, like a slight change in the air, a heaviness in the sky. She'd forgotten how invasive men are, how *there* they are, even when they're out. She had let him into her bed too suddenly, overwhelmed by desire, eager to feel the hot rush of it once again and to let go, yes, that's it, to just let go, and stop being in control for once, to stop being *responsible*. And now he wants to take over, to re-order the house in his own image. How provoking and inflexible he is in his personal routine, rigid about his meditation times which delay meals in the evenings and cause tension: twenty minutes of Chi Kung exercises followed by twenty minutes of meditation add up to a forty minute wait for dinner so that either they're ravenous by the time he makes it to the kitchen and have snacked out or they have eaten without him and he eats in sanctimonious silence on his own while she helps Camille with her homework or hears music practice.

'Do you have to do all your meditation when you come home from work? It holds up dinner.'

'Eat without me.'

'That's a bit antisocial.' Thinking: this is typical New Age selfishness, Stephen.

Camille: 'Eat without him, I'm starving.'

'See, children know what they want. They don't have set ideas about how things should be done.'

That's rich, coming from him! How like a man to complain that they have no proper observance of ritual and then expect the properly observed rituals to be at a time convenient to him! Or worse, casually abandon them if they don't happen to dovetail with his other needs. Look how he likes always to be in bed by ten, which would be fine by her except that he wants her to come with him and becomes irritable if she stays up late, reading or working on her tapes.

Sometimes he's smug in a way that provokes her, and she wants to slap him. He's like a schoolboy, naive in an unattractive way; moody and sulky one day, gauche and self-satisfied the next; ponderous about small things; infuriatingly simple-minded and at the same time, in his calm, self-regarding rituals, out of reach. He pontificates about the least little thing; even the smallest domestic detail can provoke some ponderous dissertation that leaves her feeling claustrophobic, shut-in, corralled by his certainties. But at other times he takes her by surprise; seems composed, powerful; full of inner certainty and a simple grace and she thinks: who is he? Who is he, really? There's something about him, something about the look of him, that suggests that he might once have had a drug habit; while he's asleep she has peered at the dark veins of his skin for signs of needle tracks and found no trace. He won't talk about his past, except in cryptic, unadorned statements that reveal almost nothing. His father is dead, his mother lives in Melbourne. She knows that he writes to his mother and that his mother's letters destroy his mood for a while. He has an older sister in Glebe who is overseas on an extended holiday and when she comes back no doubt they'll meet and she, Marita, will know more. As for baggage, he has brought very little of himself to her house; has stocked up her cupboards with his preferred food, hung a small quantity of clothes in her wardrobe — including his 'clerk's disguise', a pair of Country Road chinos, a white shirt and tan brogues — and installed one or two of his favourite cooking implements in her kitchen; a bamboo steamer, a ceramic ginger grater, a Japanese earthenware mortar and pestle. And, of course, his collection of cooking knives.

She is older than she looks (older than Stephen believes her to be) and she has seen enough of men and their conviction that they have discovered the secret programme of the world, the magic disk that brings up the thoughts of God, to be resistant to their need to turn her into a consort in the kingdom of the convinced. She has her own inner dramas to contend with. Then there's the question of Camille, who is not accustomed to male authority, never mind a universe as black and white as Stephen's. Children live through their stomachs and he challenges her at her primal point of pleasure . . . And then there is that other, larger question: she does not want to share her child with any man. Most of the time she doesn't even want to share Camille with her own mother.

But for all this there is her weakness, that magical aura around his neck. There is something about the way he sits on the edge of the bed after he's showered, the way his loose wet hair lies in a tangle on his shoulders, the damp tendrils curling into his neck. This, and other moments, have lulled her into believing that everything erotically significant about a man is around his neck, and more than anything, the smell of it . . . from a distance you can be beguiled by other things, but up close, it's the hands and the neck, and especially the neck . . . the line of it, the scent, the faint bristle just beneath the chin, the subtle, salty fragrance of its hollows, its invitation to rub your nose in it, to sigh into it, to raise your mouth at last to his ear-lobe and take it gently between your teeth and listen to the sudden gasp of breath caught up in his chest and feel his pulse slippery and warm, and your own voice is a liquid slur saying over and over — *You have a beautiful neck, you have a beautiful neck, you have a beautiful neck* . . . There are times in the middle of the day when he is at work and she is taken unawares, ambushed by a yearning for this one part of him . . .

And then, of course, he cooks for her! And here, undeniably, he is gifted. Though his diet is eccentric he is a magician in the kitchen. Elegant, unhurried, commanding. Even in her worst moods she likes to watch him cook. She likes the way he can make something out of nothing: baked carrots in rice wine; beancurd and Chinese cabbage braised in mustard. She likes the quality of his concentration; relaxed, assured; completely *there* with the snake beans, the wet tofu, the fragrant coriander. It's a performance, an expression of the ineffable, a moment of graceful authority that charms her, and in a way the food itself seems insignificant, though Stephen would be exasperated to hear her say this, being, as he is, so *material* in his thinking.

And perhaps he's right. Almost everything he cooks tastes exquisite. He has the touch. And yet there is the nagging thought, always, that she does not know him well.

4

One night, reading in bed and waiting for him to come home from a class, she falls asleep. And wakes, much later, to find that beside her the bed is still empty. The small luminous figures on the bedside clock glow 12.05. Where is he? It's so unlike him to be late. She gets up from her humid bed and wanders out towards the light. And there he is, sitting at the kitchen table. He has his back to her and is humming to himself, a low murmuring song, almost a mutter, like some foreign tongue. And it's as if she is seeing him for the first time; his black hair pulled back from his forehead in an oily ponytail, his sinewy arms poised against the marble edge. In the dim kitchen light he looks like a demonic angel, caught in repose. Or exile.

In front of him there is a bowl of water and a small rectangular stone, and along the stone, rhythmically, he is sliding the blade of a ten-inch knife.

She freezes.

Well, OK, the knife is alright, the knife she can handle: it's the sight of the cleaver, lying to one side, that instantly unnerves her so that she feels a sudden thump in the cavity of her chest and a coldness at the base of her spine.

He looks up. 'Hi,' he says. And then, 'What's the matter?'

'Where did you get the cleaver?'

'The cleaver? It's beautiful, isn't it? I've had it for ages. You must have noticed it.'

No, she hasn't noticed it. Not once, not anywhere. She moves closer to the edge of the table, picks it up, tentatively, and it feels coldly elegant in the palm of her hand. Her heart is pounding. Is she dreaming this? 'It's an unusual size and shape,' she says. And her voice surprises her in its steadiness. 'Is it Japanese?' She pretends to peer at the worn inscription. *Usuba Seki.*

'Is that a good brand?' she asks, trying to still the dangerous flutter in her chest. Thinking: *I always knew that one night I'd come into my kitchen and there would be a man here with a cleaver.*

'The brand isn't important,' he says.

'Oh, I would have thought it was.' She lays the cleaver down, gently, on to the table. There, that's better.

'No,' he says again. 'It's not the name that matters. It's the way it feels in your hand. Look.' And he picks the cleaver up from where she'd lain it a moment before and lets it rest in the palm of his hand, as if weighing it. Then, gripping it by the blade, he holds it out to her. 'Try it,' he says. 'Feel the weight. Does it feel right?'

She feels a little dizzy now, unsteady. 'Don't count on names,' he is saying, 'take nothing for granted.' The way he says this sounds ominous, and yet he seems unusually relaxed; playful with the stone, the water and his blades. 'How could names matter . . .' he says again, almost under his breath, and begins to drift into some sort of rave, something about the difference between carbonated and stainless steel, but she isn't listening, or rather she is hearing the words but not taking them in. She has entered her old dream. She can see her mother, running around the kitchen table, screaming, and behind her that man with his cleaver poised in the air. And she looks at Stephen, and at this moment he is so in command of himself, in her kitchen, so in harmony with his knives, that it is almost obscene. This is an intimate ritual in which there is no place for her.

And still he's talking, in that quiet voice, and from somewhere in the air she hears the word 'sharp' — and stirs from her frozen reverie.

'How sharp is "sharp"?' Had she said something? She must sound like a walking zombie.

He stops, interrupted in his flow, and picks up the long knife. 'Just the weight of it, drawn across a tomato, should slit the skin.' He pauses. 'Like this.' And with a slow gesture he draws the knife across an invisible object between them.

At that moment she can bear it no longer. This is juvenile, she thinks. I must get out of the kitchen. She turns and walks down the dark hallway, wondering if he will put the knife aside and follow her or whether he must, obsessive that he is, complete his task. And while she is thinking this she hears his step behind her and he is following her into the bedroom and he puts his hands on her shoulders, from behind, and eases her on to the mat on the floor and they lay on the floor in the dark and fuck. And it's a quick, hard, easy fuck, accelerated by the racing pulse of her fear.

Afterward, still slumped against her like heavy wood, he lifts his head and breathes hoarsely into her ear. 'Where did that come from?'

Speechless, she slides out from under him and climbs into her high bed, trembling. But as he hoists himself up from the floor and sits, almost tentatively, on the edge of the bed, she reaches her arm across and grasps him about the waist. Steadying himself with one hand he eases down onto his back and puts his arm around her shoulders, and she drapes her body across his, clinging to him with a tremor of childish panic that alarms him. 'What's the matter?' he asks.

'Nothing,' she says. 'Nothing.'

After some time, her breathing calmer, she slips off his chest and onto her back. Listening to his deep, regular breathing she realises that he is asleep. How angelic he looks, in his dark, fine honed, way. Of course he would not harm her, she knows this, knew it instinctively the moment she first observed him in that kitchen in Mosman, smiling to himself as he pared a radish into the shape of a flower. In the past she has been too wary of men. Fear can be disabling. Fear will isolate her. She must take him as a gift. She must embrace the animal whole.

You cannot have the cook without the knife.

The following night, when she is herself again, she tells him about her childhood dream. At the end of the telling she is trembling.

Ah, so that's what it was all about. He strokes her hair. Together they lie there in silence. A siren wails past their window. Yes, he knows what that dream means. He is not a fool. *He* is the knife man, domesticated, an ogre becalmed in the kitchen, putting his knife to some other, more nourishing use.

And he's relieved that she told him this: he recognises now the fever of desire and revulsion, of need and fear that made her gestures late last night so dizzyingly contradictory and confusing. And he's grateful for her confidences; she could just as easily have freaked out and turned away from him, and he'd have been left alone, stranded. Again. He leans across and kisses her forehead. A moment of danger has passed.

5

All is going well, more or less. Marita, he will tell himself, is a mystery to him and sometimes it seems to him that she is, well, a little aimless: he wonders what she does all day though something tells him not to ask, that something being a latent anger, ready to flare at any moment. He's always had a problem with anger; his father's, his mother's, his own, and now something he senses in Marita. 'What's your problem, Steve?' Isobel had said to him once. 'What's your problem?' It had been a long, long afternoon, a negotiation over something trivial and he'd lost his temper and made a fool of himself. *What's my problem?* he'd wanted to shout. Anger; frustration: that's my problem. His father was always angry, his mother, too; the family hearth quivered, at any moment, on the edge of meltdown. Whenever they shouted he became panic-stricken, engulfed in a wave of nausea. His sister retired to her bedroom to dust, and compulsively re-arrange her dainty ornaments but he, a fool for the moment, stayed on the scene and trembled, waiting for the first blow. For as long as he could remember every atom in that house had been charged with an irate current; a bad spell; a hangover that never went away. It was as if anger had become a habit, a blind curtain of habit.

Old habits are what he is determined to annul, although Marita teases him and says that he is a slave to his personal routine. How could anyone be a slave to routine in this house? It's too chaotic! Too irregular. Take this morning. Marita has read too late and is sluggish and pulls the sheet up over her head. As he settles on his mat in the front room he hears, mingling together, the brash warblings of the currawongs and Camille's early morning cough as she hawks the sticky mucus from her chest. And he finds that he's listening for the sound of Camille's feet padding along the dark hallway into the kitchen. Soon she'll return with the biscuit tin under her arm and he'll hear the sudden explosion of static through the wall that separates them, a crackling swish and roar and yes, here it comes, thunderous music, and the TV says: *Come with us now into the mysterious worlds of another galaxy and the stirring adventures of — The Galaxy Rangers!*

So here he is, halfway through his Chi Kung exercises, restless, his breathing unsettled. Soon he'll have to shave and get ready for work. On mornings like this he can begin to see why men choose to live in monasteries, why domesticity is not conducive to poise. He closes his eyes, draws his breath in through the top of his head and down into the spiral of his coccyx, holds for a moment, and waits for the white light to come simmering up from the base of his spine; but what comes instead is the echo of that word — *coccyx* — which he knows from his Shiatsu class is Greek for cuckoo. Is he the cuckoo in this nest? Can this be only a temporary haven?

There's a faint knock on the door. It's Camille, though Marita has told her never to interrupt him when he's doing his Chi Kung programme.

'Stephen?'

'Yes.' He keeps his eyes closed.

'It's okay. Sorry.'

'What's up?'

'Nothing. I just wanted to see if you were still here.'

He can tell that she's talking with her mouth half full of Milk Arrowroot or Cheezie Bits or Assorted Creams or Chicken Snacko and he wants to shout, *For God's sake, Camille stop eating that rubbish! Do you want to eat yourself to death?*

Instead, adjusting his pose, he closes his eyes. 'I'm still here,' he says.

Over breakfast she munches loudly on some tacky cereal, caramelised loops of junk that would kill a canary within days. When he offers her a freshly made chapati spread with tahini she takes one bite and gags histrionically, rushing to the bathroom to rinse out her mouth.

'Give up, Stephen,' Marita mutters at him, 'she's only a child.'

He stares down at his own half-eaten chapati feeling absurdly rebuffed. In his peripheral vision is the intrusively loud and chaotically designed cereal packet with its images of muscle-bound surfers, tiny yellow skullcaps strapped under their moronic chins. *Iron Man Food. Fill out a form and you can win a holiday in Fiji, a Surf Action windsurfer or 100 Fuji underwater cameras.* Iron men? He could tell them something about iron men, but not the kind that frolic in the water.

That night, for the first time in this house, he loses his temper.

It's just an ordinary night after work and he is cooking dinner for the three of them, as he more and more often does.

Marita is sitting at the table, watching him. He is standing at the sink, rinsing some fine yellow grains in the wire strainer, sluicing the water through the grains with his fingers. 'What are you making?' she asks because she knows he resents it if she doesn't take an interest, if she fails to show respect for his meticulous preparation.

'Millet burgers,' he says. 'I won't spice them, just put in some crushed peanuts and coconut milk to sweeten them. Camille won't notice the difference.'

'Uh-oh,' she murmurs, softly, under her breath.

And sure enough, when they are seated at the table, Camille does notice the difference. 'What are *these?*' she asks.

Marita can almost feel him stiffen. She watches his hands freeze, chopsticks poised above the bowl. There is something new here between him and Camille, some small moment of danger.

And she is right. Something has taken him by surprise, a sudden thump in the chest, something from a long way off, some warp in the heart, and he wants to fling his right arm out and send the whole table, his pretty food, smashing to the floor; send it flying in a demonstration of his power. He wants to hear that familiar sound, the loud smack of the plates as they crack against the tiles. He's heard that sound before. His father. His father pushed the table back into the fire — it was like an explosion from a gun, and he and his sister sat there, frozen to their chairs, gaping at an empty space where the table had been, half-chewed food congealing in their dry mouths while the chops charred in the fire and the red check tablecloth smouldered on the hearth — and before he can banish that thought from his head he has brought his right hand down on the table, hard, in a sudden slap, and the dishes rattle and Camille's bowl goes spinning off the edge and smashes onto the floor.

The child flinches back from him, her eyes wide, her mouth open.

And he finds he is clutching his chopsticks in his right fist. Slowly, very slowly, he lays the chopsticks down by the side of his bowl, and braces his palms against the smooth rounded edge of the table. The muscle in his upper right arm begins to twitch. *'Jesus*, Camille,' he hisses, scowling at her, with a sudden black ferocity in his eyes. It's a look, just a look, but it's a look he can't take back. For one sharp moment she's mesmerised by it, and then, jumping up, she flings her chair angrily from the table with a force out of all proportion to her small body.

'I'm going to live with Ros!' she sobs at her mother. 'She doesn't care *what* I eat!'

Marita stares hard at some empty point on the table. She is rigid.

Slowly, deliberately, he lifts his right hand from the table and attempts to pick up his chopsticks, but his hand is trembling. With equal deliberation he lays the chopsticks down again. 'I think it would be a good idea for everyone,' he says, looking up, 'if I went out for a while.'

•

On Toxteth hill his sister's house is invitingly still. Fazed for a moment, he finds that he cannot remember the combination for the alarm and when, after three attempts, he finally punches in the correct sequence, something in him gives. Exhaling in a deep sigh of anguish he turns his face to the wall and stands for some minutes with his forehead pressed against its cool immaculate surface. Alone in the semi-dark he hears his own voice speak out loud. 'Peace,' it murmurs, and then again, 'peace.'

On the floor, lying at his feet, is a small pile of mail. Can he bear to look at it right now? Nothing from his mother but a letter from Helen, this time from Vienna; another bulletin from her own special dream of unease. She would have received his letter by now, telling her about Marita, and he can guess at her response. Slowly, he opens the envelope and begins to read.

Really, Stephen, she begins, *How could you leave the house like that!*

Yes, as usual, running true to form. If he weren't so down he could almost laugh out loud.

> *I ask you particularly to mind the place and you just up and go. What if someone breaks in! It must have been my intuition that told me to increase the special insurance on the contents before we left. And what about you? Ric and I thought — had hoped — that the house might provide you with a haven. Given your troubled past you can't wonder at our desire to see you settled. Well, at least try to drop in regularly and turn the lights and radio on for a while. You owe me that.*

> *Helen*

> *P. S. Everything I see here makes me think that you need to re-assess your priorities. I know you plan eventually to go and live in Japan but I think you should come here first and get to know your own cultural heritage.*

Re-assess his priorities? What would she know about that? Not as much as she ought to, given how many times he's tried to explain it to her. The only certain thing in his future is that one day he *will* go and live in that *dojo* in Kyoto, and maybe the sooner the better! He tosses the postcard down on to the cedar chiffonier, the one with the white marble top and the small Grecian head, eyeless and smooth, relic from one of her earlier pilgrimages. There's more, he knows, than Eva can teach him, and if it's not here then it must be there. And things don't exactly seem to be working out in his love life. This time last week the thought of leaving the little house in Leichhardt would have brought on a dizzying sense of free-fall that he might almost, in a more negative frame of mind, have interpreted as panic, but now, once again, he feels like the cuckoo in the nest. And what is panic compared to anger? If one doesn't destroy him the other will. What a hopeless thought! His 'troubled past' — she would throw that up at him! As if he had no recollection of his own, as if he were anything other than a dark funnel of memory that tells him, constantly, that he is unable to trust himself. That voice speaks a language that he would become wilfully deaf to; in all his efforts he is bent on learning another language, so that the body speaks the present moment and everything else is purged. Not for a long time has he felt so bereft. Seven thousand dollars for six months in a *dojo* and where would he find it? At his present rate of saving, some bounty or other would have to fall out of the sky. Some chance! What is he but a minor clerk with no resources and only a little training? He aspires to some status of philosopher but he cannot even manage an eight-year-old child. Worse, he can't control himself. And how, without any savings, can he strike out into the unknown? Listen to him, thinking — thinking too much as usual — locked on the endless fast track circuitry of the brain, round and round the same old loops . . . he must empty his head, just empty it, chant it all away, every bit of it, until his mind is a blank like the white spaces of the desert. Maybe that's where he belongs ultimately; the desert.

And it's all so quiet now, here at least. Yes, it's quiet; if nothing else he can be grateful for that. Fighting an impulse to slump onto his sister's bed and brood, he takes off his shoes and socks, strips down to his underpants and assumes lotus position on the living room floor.

So quiet.

'Ah, peace,' he breathes again.

But on the second utterance it sounds a little stagey, if not absurd. Flexing his shoulders in a lithe manoeuvre of preparation he adjusts his purchase on the silky surface of the Persian rug and as he settles onto its exquisite tracery (the tree of the Koran, alive with singing birds) he is aware of something. . . something . . . *absent*. His vision blurring for a moment, the heavy drapes swirl out of focus: he brings his fingertips together and spins the mantra into his head. . . but that thought won't go away; the image of Camille rushes into his eye, spitting his food out in a jet of golden vomit . . . yes, golden, almost pretty . . . what an abject fool he is! He shakes his head and opens his eyes and stares for a moment into the carpet only to see that some coarse bush bird, a currawong, has taken up its perch in the sacred tree and warbles a shrill dissenting song. What are you doing here? it says. Something here is stifled, it says. This house is like a still life. Is it calm? Or is it dead? If calm, then it's a spiritless calm. This is not poise, the bird sings. Poise is the balance of dynamic forces; it has a random, unpredictable element in it, something organic and spontaneous. Well then, somewhere between the hysterical undertow of Marita's house and the fortified still life of his sister's there must be a middle point, some other kind of home. Right now he feels adrift between the two. And that *dojo* in Japan beckons. If only he had the money! He could leave Marita and Camille to their secret world, that tangled but radiant landscape in which, clearly, there is no place for a swarthy soul like his.

●

8.20 p.m. He bangs the gate loudly to let them know that he's back. The front door is still open, the lilting sound of some half-familiar music drifting out to meet him.

He stands in the doorway of the musty front room. Camille is playing some old tape of ballet music, waltzing around to its swooning romantic lilt. Seeing him, she stops dead.

'Hi,' he says, and before she can answer he walks on down the hallway. The music does not start up again. Is this his role then, he asks himself with a pang. The killjoy?

Marita is in the kitchen, on the phone. She looks at him with agitation in her eyes. 'I'll have to go now,' she says. 'I have a visitor.'

A *visitor!*

He allows himself a thin ironic smile. He doesn't want to talk; he doesn't trust himself to say anything useful; at times like these words are even more dangerous, a booby trap in every syllable. Nor will he risk putting his arms around her. How pretty she is, he thinks, knowing that she isn't pretty but that at this moment she is luminous, despite herself, with his desire for her.

'Hi,' he says.

'Hi,' she replies. She is cool. Fair enough. He is at a loss, he can be nothing other than casual. Instinct tells him to leave her in the kitchen and he goes into the living room and sits down on the old moquette couch that's as hard as dried earth and smells of mould and he picks up the Sunday paper from where it lies on the floor and tries to read. Something. Anything.

At that moment, in the front room, and without any preamble, Camille commences her piano practice. She is in thundering form. She makes clear what she thinks of his return with the inflection she gives to that urgent, worrisome old piece, *Für Elise*; the melody at first hesitant and then emphatic in its rippling ebb and flow, its compulsive repetition, over and over again; loudly, belabouring the house with a troubled resonance.

Suddenly he gets up and walks down the hallway to the door of the front room. Without turning her head, without even looking up from the music, she plays on, her face set in a slight frown, her fine dark eyebrows meeting; her chin tucked in, her mouth resolute. In the stiff arc of her arms and shoulders there is a grandiloquent poise that would be funny were it not so heartfelt. On and on, the notes rippling across the discoloured keys . . .

Marita comes in, casually, as if he'd never left, smiles at her daughter's defiant poise and raises her eyebrows at him in an expression of maternal mockery. He smiles back.

As abruptly as she began, Camille breaks off — in the middle of a phrase — and solemnly folding her sheet music, places it on top of the piano. Banging the lid shut, she sniffs loudly and putting her hand up under her skirt adjusts her pants in an unselfconscious gesture that shows her mind is already elsewhere. Without a word she wanders off into the living room to switch on the TV and turn up the volume. Loud.

Alright, he thinks, alright; I get the message. Later, when the right moment presents itself, he'll tell her he's sorry. But not now. Right now he can't see past Marita.

As she turns to leave the room he puts his arms around her, quickly, from behind, and locks her against his chest, pressing his mouth against her hair, drawing her into him, feeling, once again, that electric hum of resistance, that current of prickly desire. And she gasps, in a way that makes him think, again, that she might be frightened of him. No, not this; surely not! He hadn't behaved that badly. Had he? And he holds her there, in the dark little room;

imprisoned and still, locked in an uncertain truce. Outside the sirens wail, a 747 drones beneath a low cloud and down the hallway the TV blares: *If you shoot that dog, Ricky, then I swear to God I'll never forgive you.*

6

He likes the way that in eastern philosophies there is no space for anger, not even a righteous anger as in the Bible; he likes the way the Indian meditation teachers never say anything negative, their belief that any small task, no matter how menial, can be performed in the spirit of prayer and how this can transform the domestic. When he observes this to Marita, whose energy in the house is so careless and slapdash, she laughs scornfully and says, 'Well, they would think that, wouldn't they, they don't have to perform any *small tasks*, their followers do it all for them.' And he reminds her of Jo's point that in some monasteries the preparation of food is performed only by the most spiritually advanced, and that's when she becomes irritable and runs her hand through her spiky hair and he realises he has fallen into the trap of trying to change the energy around him by using words, mere words.

Marita is hooked on words. She's always reading. Not something useful like a cookbook or a yoga book or a gardening guide, but novels, serious ones like *Jane Eyre* by Charlotte Brönte. What's the point, he says, in all these stories? He's given them up. They're just intellectual constructs. Nothing real. You can't learn from reading, or at least not the truth. You just get caught up in the same old bad circuitry and never break out into the truth of the body. 'That's what you think,' she says, or, 'It's not that simple.' On some nights when she reads in bed, he tries to distract her by tickling her or nibbling on various parts of her body.

And then he discovers this: not only is Marita hooked on reading stories, sometimes she tries to write them. It is Camille who tells him. 'Mum writes stories,' she says, 'but she won't show them to *you*.' When he asks Marita about it she is evasive, then dismissive. It's no big deal, she says: all she does is make tapes of people, talking, and sometimes turns them into something else. Fragments. Fragments, maybe, of some larger picture. He is not sure how to react: 'What are you looking for?' he asks. She shrugs: 'I don't know.'

Her secret out, she is more open about her taping excursions, her sorties to acquire material. The impulse seems to come on her like some kind of mild fit, as if a small alarm has gone off in her head and sent her forth. On the Saturday following Camille's revelation, she goes out, carrying Camille's large, cumbersome tape-recorder. She borrows his car but refuses to say where she is going. When she comes home she laughs about her difficulties with the equipment: how long it took her to get it working; how she'd forgotten to take a tape and had to borrow one; how she has mental blanks about which hole the microphone plugs into; how she tunes in to the wrong band and fails to record. She doesn't seem to mind this chaos, indeed it seems to be part of the point of it all. 'Your work is completely irrational,' he says. He can't help himself, he has to say this, though he laughs, to appease her.

'I thought you didn't believe in the rational.'

He ignores this. 'Did you get what you wanted?' he asks.

'I don't know,' she says again. And then: 'I'm not sure what I want.'

She shows him the cardboard box under her bed, full of tapes, collecting dust. She says some tapes run for two hours and she might use one line. She calls it her 'oral project' and though she is being sardonic he thinks that use of the word 'oral' is significant. Words instead of food. He is sceptical. He can see no poise in writing; only disembodied thought and endless, unreliable words, the human nervous system abstracted out from itself. On the other hand, it's possible that there may be another form of energy at work here; that this is the yin principle; expansive, imaginative; so different from his own energy which is still too masculine, too yang and analytical, despite his efforts to change. Perhaps if she read him one of her stories he would see the point of it, some magic that has so far eluded him. Modestly he puts this to her.

'Read me something you've written,' he says.

'No, not tonight.'

This rebuff annoys him, though he can't say why.

'Which night, then?'

Hearing the quiet edge of hostility in his tone she looks up from her book and into his eyes. Is this sexual aggression, the playful preliminary to making love? Her instinct tells her it's something else.

'Another night.' She resumes her reading, or rather she tries to, aware that he is looking up at her with a frown.

'Why won't you read to me?'

Uh-oh. He's lapsed now into that obtuse male tone that is solemnly wounded and won't be denied.

'Because it's too personal. I'm not ready for it.'

Stephen stares at her for a moment and then rolls over on to his back. In some obscure way he feels cheated. So, you don't trust me, he thinks. She'll give him her body but not her words: surely the one is more intimate than the other, the material flesh more intimate than mere signs. Obviously she's hiding something from him. He sighs.

'C'mon,' she says, suddenly. 'I'll tape you.'

He looks at her askance, but good-humouredly. 'Is this the end?' he says. 'I'm about to end up under the bed instead of in it.'

She purses her lips, smiles. 'That's up to you.'

Meanwhile she is sliding a blank tape into the deck and rigging up the microphone, a black fuzzy thing that she holds to his lips. I am not, he thinks, the first person to be struck by how phallic this thing is. He hears a loud click.

'Talk,' she says, and nestles back into her pillow.

He holds the microphone limply against his chest, suddenly dumbstruck.

'Where did you grow up?' she asks, matter-of-factly.

He hesitates. 'In the suburbs.'

'Did you like it?'

'Your interviewing technique is pretty basic.'

'Did you *like* it?'

'I hated it.'

'Why?'

Why did he hate it? How to explain this? The long stretch of nature strip and the suffocating circle of sameness. The seething mother; the edgy father. No, this is a trap, a playful trap but a trap nevertheless. He leans across her, heavily, bearing down against her breasts, and presses the Stop button on the machine. He won't play this game. Marita thinks she can capture phantoms on tape and neutralise them in storage. *Her* phantoms, maybe, but not his. He has his own plans in store for them.

Observing that her bedside trolley is so cluttered that there is no room for the microphone he ceremoniously places it by her pillow. There it lies, like a large black phallus, close to her mouth: he looks at the microphone and then at her, knowingly. She smiles back, has divined his thinking. In a few deliciously blurred moments she has his cock in her mouth, is nibbling teasingly on the knob. He groans. Though often she can be vague and languid, at other times she is amazingly sudden, and swifter to arousal than any woman he has known. Their lovemaking on that first night had been shyly proper but they had soon discovered a mutual avidity for oral sex. Not surprisingly, she had remarked, given his finesse in the kitchen, he had demonstrated his gift for that other oral art, and the excruciating slowness of his tongue caresses could trigger something, first in her, then in him, a kind of shrill keening that one night had the dogs barking in the street — though, astonishingly, Camille had slept through it. The parental ear may awake to the merest snuffle but the child's ear is deaf to what it doesn't want to know.

. . . he is sinking now, sinking down into the dark catacombs of his body, into the foetid galleys of that cedar ship as she, oh so rhythmically, sucks and sucks on his long prick that seems to rear up like the arc of a bow, and he can feel her tongue lapping along the shaft and then jabbing insistently, wetly at the base and then the supreme moment, the exquisite pressure of her finger in his anus and oh . . .

Ah, but afterwards, the *let down!* Damn her! Damn her! It's unjust. Why won't she do it? He can feel her reaching across his body, almost blindly, to the tissue box on the trolley, and emptying her mouth into those white folds, spitting his seed out like so much rank refuse. She might just as well be blowing her nose!

Why?

Why won't she swallow?

He's wanted to ask her this before and hasn't been able to summon up the nerve, not at the time, anyway, and beyond a certain point, in the morning, say, it all seems like an irrecoverable dream, something that might be permanently spoiled by any attempt at recapitulation . . . but now, unexpectedly, he hears those soft words floating out from deep in his throat.

'Does it taste awful?'

She lifts her pert, dark head up suddenly from the edge of the bed.

'No. Not at all.'

'Then why . . .' he begins lamely.

'Why what? Why don't I swallow it?'

He all but winces. Sometimes she can be unbearably matter-of-fact.

'I'm not sure,' she says, as if this is the first time she's thought about it. 'It never bothered me before.'

It's just as he feared. It's him. Something repulsive in his essence. Dare he ask?

'Before what?'

'Before I had Camille.' She lies on her back now, beside him, her arms resting easily above her head. 'Before I had Camille I swallowed all the time, never gave it a thought. If anything I quite liked it. Some men are saltier than others, that's all.'

He can't think of anything to say. Damn Camille! Damn her, though it's nothing personal, it's not her especially, is it? It could be any child in her position; any child could rob a man of this . . . this privilege. This nipple in reverse.

'Why?' he asks again.

'I'm not sure,' she says again, her eyes turning cloudy. She twists away from him, snuggling down in under the sheet, showing him that this is as much as she wants to say. How can you explain to a man, a childless man, that once you have carried a child in your body then his sperm seems to belong in one orifice only. Beyond that, it's just a waste product and should be treated as such, spat out, with no ritual pretence.

And so he is left wondering: why does she refuse him this? In a prudish woman, or even a shy one, he could understand it. But Marita is neither of those things. Nor is she especially fastidious in matters of general hygiene (if it were up to him he would keep the house cleaner: though she is tidy enough she is blind to dust and fatalistically tolerant of cockroaches). Other women do it. Other men do it. Thousands of lovers are at some time nourished on swallows of semen. Could it be, then, that her reluctance goes beyond the physical? Could there be some symbolism in this? Some kind of payback? No, that's a crazy thought. Paranoid. Let it go, he thinks, just let it go. It's enough, he tells himself, that you're here. Six weeks ago you had nothing, now you have this.

Relax.

When she hears the regular breathing of his sleep, Marita gets up and tiptoes into Camille's room. Every time she makes love she must check Camille afterwards. In the fucking some vital connexion is momentarily severed and in that moment, one of them might die. Bending over the low bed, she listens for the child's breathing. She can't hear it.

This is absurd, of course. She folds back the white mosquito net and puts her ear closer to that delicate chin and watches the narrow chest rise and, ever so slightly, fall. Ah, yes. Her clear breathing, her sweet whispering breath. This is all that matters. There are other bodies, beautiful bodies, but none so lovely as this, so full of innocent grace: the curve of the chin, the tilt of the nose, the small freckle on the cheekbone, the perfect symmetry of the arms, the lingering sigh of the chest. It's been some time since they have shared one of those long, anguished nights with Camille gasping for breath, the smoky blue light of the respiratory machine glowing by the bed, the steady drone of the motor lulling them both into a kind of calm. On each of those endless nights of hoarse coughing, the rasping wheeze in her chest, Camille has slept with her mother, propped up on four pillows in the big cedar bed. But now she has been supplanted in the cedar ship. And no-one is more alert to this than Marita. Each time she lets a man into her bed she is afraid of impairing that connexion with her child, of dimming, even for a day, their blood rapport. But this is a foolish hysterical morbidity. After all, Camille is hers and hers alone: there is no father, and no interloper should be so foolish as to think he could become one.

7

Stephen hesitates on the threshold of the Shiatsu Institute in Harris Street. Something Sanjay said to him this morning unsettled him. They had been discussing the authority of the scriptures, a favourite study of Sanjay's. Like Marita, Sanjay is infatuated with the word and again, he, Stephen, had been sceptical of the value of any knowledge that comes from a book. Knowledge must come from a teacher, he'd argued, from a kindred body, otherwise it's useless.

'My mother would agree with you,' Sanjay had replied. 'She believed you could learn only to cook the food of your own culture, and that by watching your own mother and aunts. She had no time for cookbooks. But, my dear friend, when the body is dead, what then? How to pass on what the body knew?'

'Through followers, those who are trained and carry on the tradition.'

'But suppose something happens to these disciples — suppose they are wiped out by a plague? Or, more likely, put to death by a tyrant?'

This was another of those absurdly brief exchanges in the pause between processing files. In those moments Sanjay was always more eloquent than he. It was only afterwards, while he was on the bus, or most often when he was cooking, that the right phrases floated into his brain. What he wanted to say was that once they were compelled to stand alone, words became a problem; a kind of nightmare. Mere words, that is disembodied words, betray the senses; they are abstractions; the antithesis of Nature; a sad and impossible substitute for the body's own knowledge. Words are the traditional weapon of the joker, who neither has power nor wants it. He had been trying to explain to Sanjay why it was that he had chosen to train as a Shiatsu practitioner, why he must eventually give up his work as a clerk: he would be free of those false abstractions that, at best, can only approximate the truth. He wants to relate to the world through the senses, through touch. Skinship. No questions asked, since all that counts about a person is their body and he is determined on the discipline of reading this alone. History is a residue in the tissues, a weakness or excess in the organs, a knot in the muscles, a hump in the spine. It is his ambition to exist, ultimately, on a plane of silence. He would like to train himself to use fewer words on every occasion and to learn how to work in the world without having to speak at all, to achieve a state of poise that would speak for itself. What a state of grace, that the body could speak for itself! That one would have only to look into the eyes of another to say what one wanted to say, and to hear what one needed to hear.

Sanjay had listened with a bemused smile. 'Why, then, do you write in that journal of yours, Stephen?' he had asked.

'I don't, Sanjay. Not any more.'

He had almost forgotten the journal. It lay in his suitcase, abandoned; a red herring. He had begun his journal as a kind of purge, a way of writing himself out — of bad words, of all the old mad words that clogged his past — but then he had realised that the process was self-defeating and that putting words on paper did nothing but fossilise the anger. It was simpler, wiser, to jettison the lot. Before he had reached the age of thirty he had learned this: almost every category presented to him since childhood — history, morality — had proved to be a chimera, and re-arranging words on a page could not and would not change any of it. At the end of this outpouring Sanjay had shrugged his broad shoulders, smiled and said: 'You speak as if we are pilgrims in the desert for whom every oasis proves to be a mirage, and there is only the body. I understand this thinking, Stephen, but I have doubts. In the past you have been very disapproving — no? — of what you call pure rationalism. Well, this macrobiotics — you will forgive me, my friend, for saying this — seems to be a kind of pure materialism, perhaps equally rigid. Unmoderated, it could prove to be a little severe, a trifle harsh, don't you think?'

Because he had such respect for Sanjay he would not dismiss this reproof without examination. Has he fallen into the trap of dogmatism? How to apply what you know to be true and at the same time remain open? He might well raise this with Eva, tonight, after class, here in the heart of Chinatown, in the very building where he had once attended classes with Yuan Shen — which is how he had discovered Eva.

Tonight as always the acolytes sit on the floor in the long gallery room in

Harris Street, the one with the white walls and the high ceiling painted a deep blue. Five of the masseurs, in their whites, wander about performing perfunctory tasks, waiting for Eva. When she arrives, dressed in white cotton pants and a white shirt, she simply smiles, bows to everyone, and sits cross-legged on the floor in front of a long, low rockpool.

Eva Hrasky is a woman of around forty, born in Prague, with high cheek bones and tawny blond hair swept up in a no-nonsense roll. There is something in her demeanour that is intensely European with a quality both sensual and ascetic. She is nothing if not androgynous; in her broad-hipped body there is a hint of the earth mother but in her rolling walk there is a loose masculine swagger that draws the observer into an aroused complicity. So European is she that it is hard to imagine how she came to take on all the trappings of the Zen tradition. It's hard to imagine her living for some years in Kyoto.

As a mark of favour she has invited him to assist her with the beginners' class. By the time she is ready to deliver her introductory lecture, he too has changed into his whites. 'Why are you all here?' she begins, in her imperious voice with the light accent. Behind her, in the rockpool, thin, translucent goldfish quiver a path through the clear water. 'You are here because you want to unblock the life force, yes? Not just yours but that of others as well. And you think you can do this from the head, from your brain, because, maybe, you are clever and you think a lot, yes? Or maybe from your heart because you are a kind person, you are compassionate? Mmmm?'

He has never been able to guess Eva's age. The lines around her eyes say that she must be near forty though in every other way she looks younger.

'Shiatsu teaches us that everything comes from *here*,' and she places a fine, ascetic hand over her very flat abdomen. 'From the stomach. The stomach, not the brain or the heart is the centre of life. In Shiatsu we call the lower abdomen area, below the navel, the *hara*, and the life force the *ki*, both Japanese words. Some people prefer the Chinese word, *chi*. *Ki* or *chi*, either is fine. So, we begin here: control your stomach and you will control all else.' Pausing, she looks around her. 'This is a difficult idea for westerners to grasp, so accustomed to focussing their attention on the brain or the heart, neither of which can compare in complexity and subtlety to the workings of the gut.'

She smiles. 'This is the first thing everyone who comes here is surprised by. They think they are coming here to enter into some rarefied sphere but nothing could be further from the truth.' She shrugs. 'The small intestine has more nerve endings in it than the brain, and the heart, after all, is just a simple pump. We westerners are obsessed with the heart, are we not? But that is another story.

'So. What is Zen Shiatsu? Firstly, we throw away the mechanical model of the body, the western model.' At this point she stands up and points to a large wall chart hanging from an elegant Chinese screen. ' We explain the human body in terms of a network of meridians — the meridians are the true map of the body, yes? Because through these meridians flows this energy I have been speaking about, this *chi*. So, if you decide to train here you will learn to follow the meridian lines with your finger; you will feel the "echo" of life. You will discover that if the flow through the meridians is smooth, the person is healthy; if the flow becomes sluggish the person falls ill. The body is not a machine, it is a force field.'

Some of the newcomers uncross their legs, already cramped in the lotus position, and tuck their feet under their buttocks.

'How then to diagnose? In Shiatsu all diagnosis is done through the abdomen. We learn to feel the quality of the *hara*. Especially, you learn to feel for *kyo*, for emptiness. Where a person is empty, that is where they are least strong. Diagnosing the *kyo* is what Zen Shiatsu is all about. And it is very difficult. Why? Because it is difficult to locate what is empty, what isn't there, when fullness, or *jitsu* is more obvious. *Jitsu* covers up for *kyo*. We always present our strength to the world to protect our weakness. You will learn to locate that underlying weakness. You support or tonify the *kyo* and sedate the *jitsu* so that the experience for the client is one of wholeness, and after a treatment the energy feels just right. In this way balance is restored and then real healing can occur, rather than just focussing on some superficial symptom.

'So often, problems with diet are about this experience of emptiness. And it is difficult to change your diet until the *kyo* is supported. We have all had that experience of trying to change our diet on the intellectual level but until the body is supported change will prove to be too hard. We go on eating the very foods that aggravate our condition. And this is why we study diet here.

Macrobiotics is a beginning, a way of cleansing the body of its toxic past. After you've got yourself into a reasonable state then you can begin to find your own path, and that may include other things, perhaps spiritual.'

Though he has heard all this before Stephen experiences a kind of energising joy in listening to Eva. She is always calm and reasonable in her teaching even though her new clients are shocked by the drastic proscriptions she enunciates: no bread, no sugar, no dairy food, *ever*! Stop now! Bread and cake are dead food, as is all baked flour. Sugar is poison. There is an uncompromising purity at the heart of this that can bring on a catharsis of the body.

Yet what of Eva herself? At first he was bewildered by the paradoxes of her own behaviour, the fact that she had left her children to train in Kyoto, that she goes out to clubs and dance parties with her much younger lover, Keith, that she stays up until all hours and can look haggard from lack of sleep and that despite everything, and somehow this is particularly shocking, she still smokes! She is certainly not 'pure'. And yet she is a healer who achieves startling results in just one session, who moves energy through the body with a kind of mesmeric detachment. It is her ability to blank out her mind and read with her hands the map of the body, to *feel* the problem. Eva is an artist. He knew he wanted to learn from her that first night when he wandered up from Yuan Shen's class and watched her performing the corrections. Her body was so strong and flexible. She had extraordinary balance. When, in the culmination, she draped the client's back against her knees, she was poised like a magnificent bird. Watching her, that first time, he knew he wanted to be that bird; he wanted to recover the poetry of his own body which, somehow, has been mislaid. Working with Yuan Shen was not enough. It had to be a collective, or symbiotic enterprise. To restore your own body you somehow had to work on restoring the body of the other.

Later, when the demonstration treatment is over and the beginners are putting on their shoes, he approaches Eva and asks her if they could talk for a moment. She leads him out on to the wide concrete ledge above the fire-escape at the back, and leaning against the rusty iron steps, lights up a cigarette. 'Well,' she says.

'I'm not sure I'm dealing with all this in the right way.'

'How so?'

'I wonder about my approach. That maybe I'm becoming, well, a little over-focussed. That I might be hardening into another version of my father.'

She blows smoke out of the corner of her mouth, and looks at him with wry sympathy.

'You know what I mean? Different beliefs, same . . .' he searches for the right word, 'same certainty.'

'Meaning?'

'He always thought he was right. We could never discuss anything. He had his books he believed in, and every word was the gospel truth. *His* every word was the gospel truth.'

'Forget about fathers, Stephen, they get in the way.'

'I was thinking more about words.' And he tells Eva of his conversation with Sanjay.

After which she simply smiles, and pats his arm, tossing the dead butt of her cigarette down into the alley below. 'You know, Stephen, you think too much. We have talked about this in classes before; you know, that whole kidney and bladder anxiety, that insecurity. Referring to the self through past experience. None of that stuff is relevant anymore. You are way beyond that, beyond all those relationships. They only define your ego, who you think you are. Try not to mistake the self for the self-image. Through your training here you will learn to do everything effortlessly, from the *hara*, without desire. You must give yourself up to your technique. The worst thing is to *try*. We have faith in the process, not the idea. Abandon the idea. There is being which is subtle and words which are gross. Of course, we must use words to communicate, we are using words now, but as we get better at what we do we need them less and less. In the more advanced forms of Zen, almost nothing is said.' And she turns away from him, as if to go back inside. She has not alluded to Sanjay or his argument; each time she is queried she restates her own teaching, either repeating what she has said before in class or re-framing it in a new form. This is her way.

In the advanced forms of Zen almost nothing is said.

Easier said than done.

8

Another week passes. Nine weeks now, nine weeks in Marita's house and he has almost become accustomed to the raucousness of this street.

Someone is always calling at this house. Dona Maria, Melissa, the child, Basia, who lives across the street and, most troubling of all to Marita, the old woman, Estelle.

One night they are lazing in front of the television. It's hot: the front door is open. They are lethargic and damp with sweat. Marita, who until this minute has been dozing with her head on his shoulder, sits up with a jerk. 'What's that?' she says.

He listens. 'What's what?'

'Someone is out there, in the front garden.'

He looks at his watch. It's just after ten. He gets up from the couch but Marita is already ahead of him, walking, with slow deliberation, to the open doorway. Almost to the door she stops, stares out into the dark, and exclaims, 'Estelle!'

As he comes up behind her, a hot wave of jasmine wafts in through the iron grille. He looks out, over her shoulder. There, loitering in the garden, is a small, thin, woman in late middle age. She is wearing what looks like a long cotton nightdress and soft slippers. With one hand she clasps a pale grey cardigan around her bony shoulders; in the crook of her other arm she cradles a box of chocolates. Seeing Marita she has stopped, frozen to the spot, exposed in the harsh streetlight like a bewildered bird.

At the open window of the front bedroom is Camille, leaning against the sill in her nightdress, her hair loose on her shoulders, her chin cupped in her hands like a small Rapunzel.

Marita recovers from her surprise. 'Estelle! What are you doing here?'

The old woman blinks. 'Sweeties, dear, just sweeties. I thought Camille might like one.'

'For heaven's sake, Estelle, it's after ten o'clock. Camille should be asleep.'

Estelle gazes back at her with an odd, impersonal stare. 'Sorry, love, sorry.'

And she begins to back away and out through the rickety gate and onto the street, her hands clasped to her chest like a penitent.

Marita orders Camille back to bed and returns to the living room.

'Who was *that?*' he asks, with wry incredulity.

But Marita is not amused. Frowning and with a distracted look in her eye, she tells him the story of Estelle; how she lives in the little brown semi-detached on the brow of the hill, how until recently she was a nun in a convent and is now returned home to care for her father who is seventy-six and in a wheelchair. All day Estelle cares for her father behind drawn curtains but at night she has taken to walking the street, in her nightdress, proffering chocolates to the local children. Or she stands in her front garden and cries out that she is lonely, and that the old man beats her with his stick. Nuns from the convent come to visit and bring in their wake a surly priest who administers the sacred wafer of bread to the old man. But Estelle refuses it. All this they know from Dona Maria who attends the local church where she absorbs the tattle about Estelle.

Marita grimaces as she tells this story, as if it causes her some inexplicable pain. In this, as in other things, he suspects that she is prone to over-reacting, a symptom of that latent hysteria so close to the surface in women. Marita, especially, seems to suffer from a sense of encroachment. 'What is it about me?' she says. 'Why do I attract the mad? I'm like a sponge; moody children haunt my kitchen, deranged men talk to me on trains.' She shudders. 'No-one ever bothers my mother! Why me?'

He doesn't answer. He is disconcerted by that word. Mad. They used to say that about him once and it isn't true.

9

One day, out of the blue, Marita says that she would like to meet Gareth. 'Invite him to dinner,' she says, but when he suggests this to Gareth his friend is reluctant. Over the past few months he seems to have given up going out at night, perhaps because he is more and more fatigued and is having to call on whatever reserves of strength he has just to get to work. Instead he suggests that they come over to see him at Manly on the Sunday. Marita agrees. 'It's a long time since Camille has been on a ferry,' she says. 'The sea air will be good for her.'

The journey out of Leichhardt and across the harbour is a trip to another country. It's humid and stifling along Parramatta Road; exhaust fumes and flashy billboards and a fretwork of black overhead power lines. But down at the quay it's clean and clear with a light breeze coming off the water. Camille skips along the walkway, making little forays ahead to the buskers and returning to pester her mother for change. She stops in front of a slim, dishevelled Koori playing a huge didgeridoo and selling dusty, unmarked tapes of his own artistry. She stares at him, then drops a dull gold dollar coin into his hat. *Pock.* Wherever she wants to stop, they wait, smiling, humouring her: it's her first trip on the Manly ferry, a special ritual not to be rushed. When, finally, they arrive at Pier 3 they are relieved to step into the shade of the iron roof. Camille wants to work the new electronic ticket machines, to fathom it out herself, which takes ages. Or seems to. Stephen is beginning to get impatient when at last the *Narrabeen* chugs into the pier and the incoming crowd filters across the ramp and on to the quay.

Camille wafts on to the ferry, ahead of them, and makes purposefully for the front. She wants to sit outside on the white plastic seats in the cool wind. No way, says Marita, not with your chest, and points to a seat inside. Camille sits up front, alone, the window open, her hair blowing blindly across her face. Every now and then she looks back and smiles at them unselfconsciously. After a while she stops this and stares ahead in a seeming trance. They know she is lost in the child's fantasy of travelling alone.

Stephen begins to think about lunch. He hasn't brought any food with him and he doesn't know why. He could have packed a nourishing picnic lunch; some brown rice salad, rice crackers with tahini, fruit, masubi, a thermos of mu tea and some ginger cookies with rice malt. He didn't. Every now and then he has lapses of, for want of a better word, *address*. He finds himself just wanting to walk out of the house on impulse, without the lengthy premeditation that eating cleanly in a barbaric world calls for. He knows there will be nothing in Manly worth eating, that to put Gareth at ease he'll drink a cold beer on an empty stomach and feel querulous for the rest of the afternoon. No, he can do better than that: he can always buy some rice and stir fry vegetables from the Thai restaurant by the dock and fruit salad from the little canvas booth with the festive red and white striped awning.

At Manly Pier, it's lunchtime and the mall is congested with shoppers who mill around a jazz band that plays with a lazy even tempo. He hates jazz. They enter the cool dark lounge of the Blue Stag and look around for Gareth who, he knows, will have got there long before them and had two or three schooners to ease his shyness.

He spots him at a table near the far door, waves, ushers Marita and Camille over, makes quick introductions and leaves to order drinks at the bar, hoping that Marita will make an effort with Gareth. Sometimes she can be withdrawn, like him.

'Yeah?'

The barman is all of twenty, a bleach-blond surfer in a fluorescent pink and yellow singlet. The sort of person you never see in Leichhardt. Looking at the electric display of his Mambo shorts, Stephen feels a distinct presence: the Pacific Ocean. Outside, out there in that bright sunlight there are palm trees and the Corso and cake shops with sticky sugar bombs of pink icing and mock cream and matrons in bright pastels and young girls in tan moccasins, white socks and pale denim shorts and brown legs. And Marita and he look like a pair of pale, inner-city blackbirds.

Back at the table it's clear that Marita is in a cool mode, but friendly. She doesn't say much but she gives Gareth her attention. He hopes that she will respond to Gareth's shy irony but just now Gareth is inhibited by her presence and doesn't offer any remark that's dry or witty.

Camille sips on her lemonade quietly, but is restless. 'Can we go to the beach soon?' she whispers to her mother, swinging her legs, knocking her heels insistently against the chrome in a monotonous clatter. He's beginning to learn that even when children are quiet they have a way of being interventionist.

But for the moment he's glad to be in the bar where he can adjust to the shock of seeing Gareth out of the office, and what seems to be a sudden deterioration in his body. Today he looks even thinner and more sallow. His skin is papery and dry; his fine hair even wispier.

'I'm *hungry*,' says Camille.

'We'll have to eat soon, Stephen,' says Marita. And they agree to buy some chips and eat them on the Corso.

Fifty minutes later they are sitting on the beach, staring at the water. Pacific blue. Gareth is lying prone on the sand. He had agreed, in the office, to let Stephen give him a Shiatsu treatment and when reminded of this just minutes ago he had simply smiled, shrugged and lay back on to the sand with his head resting on his hands and his eyes shut against the glare.

Stephen kneels beside him. The hot sun makes his head feel expansive, infused with the power of white light and blue water. Marita has taken off her shirt and sits in her bikini top. She lifts her pale face and neck to the sun, eyes closed. Camille paddles at the water's edge, entranced by the big surging dumpers that roar in and dissolve into frantic white foam at her feet. Stephen is aware of the woman near them who lounges in a white bikini. She has a low forehead, bleached hair, an unusually prominent mons and *that look*; brazen, receptive. They're different on this side of the harbour; they have an *expectation* of the sun. For a moment he wonders what it would be like to make love to such a woman, to enter into a kind of delirium of vacancy where there is only the body and yet the space of this body is somehow empty. Isn't that what he wants? Only the body? And yet, in the dazzling whiteness of her bikini he has an intimation of absence, of slipping into some kind of vacant space, which is not what he wants at all. Shaking his head to clear it, he leans back on his heels, closes his eyes and begins to focus on Gareth. Resting the flat of his hand on Gareth's midriff he presses firmly into the *hara*. Ah, yes, he might have guessed: heart deficient; a sadness, the heart swamped in damp: moisture, un-shed tears. Heart deficient people are cut off from their connexion to the world. But they have to find it for themselves, you can't do it for them; all you can do is open them up to change, to possibility. He works on, tracing the meridians with care. Gareth appears to be half-asleep. Soon even the roar of the surf begins to recede in his head until the line of Norfolk pines along the Corso throws lengthening shadows across the sand.

Marita shivers. The blue of the Pacific no longer shimmers; is a dull, late afternoon glint of grey-green. He feels Gareth's *hara* and there has been some change, a little. Perhaps this is what is reflected in his droll abstracted gaze as he stands now and brushes the sand from his clothes.

'How was that?' asks Marita.

'Good,' he says. And gives a little laugh. 'Yes, quite good.'

'Gareth,' she begins, 'I was wondering if you'd mind if I talked to you for a little bit on tape?'

He looks puzzled, taken aback. 'Why? What about?'

'Just a general chat. I'm making a collection of tapes, of voices.'

He hesitates for a moment. 'Okay. Where?'

'We could do it just here, on the beach. Wouldn't take long.'

He looks slowly around. 'The wind's coming up a bit. What about over there?' He nods in the direction of the Blue Stag.

Stephen frowns at them both. 'Not the pub,' he says. Another drink, or several, and all his work on the body undone by words, by Marita and her selfish, pointless obsession. 'Why don't we do this another day?'

'No, let's get it over with now,' says Gareth, in his slow drawl, smiling, colluding with her against his own body. Compliant.

'I'll take Camille for a walk. C'mon, mate.' He takes her by the hand and turns coldly away from the other two.

Forty minutes later he stands at the door of the pub. Gareth and Marita are intent in conversation, as if they could talk only in his absence. Watching them he feels a tight knot of anger rising in his chest. Talk, talk, talk. From the doorway he lets out a low street whistle and when Marita looks up he beckons her over in a peremptory gesture, pointing at his watch. She frowns at him: how dare he summon her like this? Beside him, Camille shivers. 'I'm cold,' she says. 'Let's go home.'

On the ferry home they say little to one another and stare out the window. Behind them Manly recedes like a picture postcard slowly bobbing out of focus. Ahead, black clouds loom over the water. Marita frowns up at the sky. 'It's going to rain,' she says.

10

When the rain comes, it comes in an unrelenting torrent. Around one in the morning the first flash of lightning opens up the night sky. Marita dozes . . . wakes. Through half-closed lids she can see the curtain at the window lit up from behind by a bright flash of light, and sure enough, some few seconds later, the first explosion of thunder rumbles above her head. And subsides, like some rolling war train receding into the west. In the next room Camille is in the throes of a violent sneezing fit; one after another they come in a paroxysm of gasps and convulsively expelled air. Marita is alert, uneasy. For some time she lies in the dark, fretful, waiting for the first wheeze. 'These storms,' she had said to him on the ferry. 'Often they bring on her asthma.'

In the morning Camille is tired. She yawns over breakfast, and lays her head on the table beside her un-eaten cereal. The rain teems down into the courtyard garden, already sodden and bedraggled. Camille gets up, and slouches over to the kitchen window where she presses her nose against the steamy pane and gazes out at her flowers that sit forlornly in little round pools of water.

'Come here.' Her mother beckons her over to the kitchen table. She puts her arms around Camille's waist and lays her head against the child's chest, listening. 'I think you'd better take your puffer,' she says.

He watches while Marita fossicks on the top shelf of her pantry cupboard where the medicines are kept. From here she extracts 'the puffer', a small blue and white gadget which she hands to Camille. With a practised air Camille removes the cap, puts the nozzle into her mouth and inhales.

'What's in that?'

'Don't ask,' says Marita, curtly.

The rain beats steadily against the tin roof.

Later, while Marita walks Camille to school, he examines this unmentionable, this bronchodilator, as it's called: Terbutaline Sulphate, 500 mcg. Removing the cap he places it in his mouth and sucks in, as he had seen Camille do earlier. A fine film of powder enters his lungs. Then comes the bitter after-taste.

All day it rains. From time to time he lifts his head from the console screen and looks out through the panoramic plate glass, and can see only grey black cumulo nimbus cloud lumbering over the harbour. When the storms come again the show of lightning over the water will be spectacular; the great renting forks of yellow light will fracture the sky and yoke the heavens to the water and the clerks will stand at the windows and grin like awed children.

Evening comes, and it's still raining. After work he has a six o'clock class with Eva, and does not see Camille over dinner, but as soon as he unlocks the door and enters the hallway, dripping from his long coat and permeated with an uncomfortable feeling of damp, he becomes aware of a light but persistent cough coming from her room. He pauses in her doorway, long enough to judge that she is coughing in her sleep.

3 a.m. The rain pelts against the tin roof. Camille is in the next room, coughing. She sits up in bed, in the dark, her narrow shoulders quivering. She coughs and coughs and coughs and yells out, '*Muuuuum*.'

He wakes, watches as Marita's shadowy figure fumbles for her dressing-gown, hears her soft footfall in the hallway, her whispered words to Camille. Then he hears her rummaging noisily in the kitchen, a cupboard door bangs, she is back in Camille's bedroom, the lights are on, he hears a loud click and then a strange noise, a low humming sound. Alarmed by some sense of imminent crisis he gets up, puts on some shorts and a T-shirt and walks to the door of Camille's room.

And there it is. The machine. All set up on a stool bedside her bed, long tubes of transparent plastic, the little red light, the buzzing sound of the motor, the rising mist of steam and the thick plastic mask that Camille, sitting back against her propped-up pillows, holds to her face, her mousey ringlets framing its hi-tech contours, her small hand clasping the green tube.

The machine begins to make a hissing, spluttering sound. Marita peers into the plastic capsule at the base of the mask. 'I think it's empty,' she says to Camille. Camille nods her head and says something stifled from behind the mask.

He feels superfluous, in the way, and leaves them to it, backing away, down the hall, appalled by the apparition of the green mask.

Day after day the city is bathed in torrents of humid rain, day after day, night after night, a subtropical deluge of monsoonal duration, relentless, drenching rain that soaks through your jacket and shoes within minutes and cascades from your umbrella in fine running streams. All sporting fixtures are abandoned, picnics are cancelled, the outer suburbs in the west are flooded; on the North Shore lightning rents the trees in Turramurra. Then suddenly it stops. The sky clears. And it's warm, and a fine, humid steam rises from the roads and begins to permeate everything. You can smell the seeping eruption of dank growth everywhere. Another week of this, says Marita, and the mould will begin to grow; mould on old shoes and leather bags stored at the back of wardrobes, a blue-grey film of spores that gives off the odour of must, of nature perverse. Already, mould has begun to grow on the walls beneath the windowsills. The smell of must is everywhere. The house smells like a fen. I should move to the south coast, she says, to the desert, to the Blue Mountains; anywhere but this foetid city. Marita is beginning to panic.

The next night. More coughing. Broken sleep. The hum of the nebuliser machine, the milky green apparition of the mask. Marita is racked by something she can't express. Somewhere around three in the morning he wakes to the low tenor of a male voice and realises that she is in the kitchen, working on her tapes. In the morning, over breakfast, he looks the other way as Camille sucks the vile steroid into her lungs. Marita stands at the kitchen bench, sallow from lack of sleep, cutting sandwiches for Camille's lunch: she is offhand, and seems to perform every small task as if in an anxious fog.

On the bus he extracts his Kushi book from his bag and looks up the index on 'asthma'. Asthma, it says, is a yin condition, often induced or aggravated by the intake of too many fluids and quite commonly by wet weather. Diet is critical. Eliminate yin foods such as sugary sweets, fruit, ice-creams, sugared drinks, etc. Yes, he thinks, some chance of that!

3 a.m. Camille is in the next room coughing in her sleep. In his sleep. That cough bothers him. It has bothered him for the last five nights, ever since the rain came. He tries to think of something else . . . nothing comes.

Marita gives a long, weary sigh.

He sits up, listening. 'I'll go,' he says, 'let me work on the meridians.'

'If she'll let you.'

He pushes the sheet down, stands, pulls on his shorts, goes into Camille's dark stuffy room. Her night lamp is a lurid clown face in black, yellow and red. It's alarming. It grins.

'Where's Mum?' she says.

'In bed.'

'It woke me up,' she says.

'It' is the cough that won't go away.

'I might be able to do something for that cough,' he says.

She yawns, sleepily.

'Turn over on your stomach.'

He waits for her to resist him but she twists her body over onto its front and settles her cheek into the pillow. He knows that he should leave her on her back and press her abdomen to diagnose her *hara* but, there in the dark, it seems too intimate. She doesn't know him all that well yet. She might think he is trying to molest her. He guesses at her condition. Colon, he thinks. Too much sugar, too many sweets, too much bread and flour, milk and cheese; cloying, clogging, squeezing the cloudy mucous into the airways of the spirit, blocking the path of the *chi*. 'Tell me if it hurts,' he says.

She lies very still.

He kneels by her bed and leans his body into the line of the colon meridian, trying to judge the weight of his palm against her small frame. Though he has treated Marita several times he has been wary of laying a hand on Camille, but she is compliant now, she does not murmur or complain, she begins to drift, and eventually she is asleep, a slight rasping rattle in her chest. He listens to her breath, its steady wheeze and sigh, he counts ten breaths, he waits for the cough, it doesn't come.

He creeps from the room; the floor creaks.

In the front room Marita flaps testily at the sheets, sighs, flicks on the light.

'Did you give her the puffer?'

'No.'

'Then she'll start coughing again.' She slumps back against the massive bedhead.

'Maybe she will.' He is offended.

'I can't sleep,' she says. 'I'll work for a while.'

He knows what this means. She'll work on her tapes and he hates this. He'll feel marooned in her bed, her words between them. He puts his hand on her arm and says, for the first time, 'No'. He says it urgently, emphatically. She looks at him askance. She knows he means it.

'Alright,' she sighs.

'Read to me. Something you've written.'

'No,' she says. 'Another time.' And flicks off the light.

'Why won't you trust me?'

Why won't you trust *me*? she thinks. You don't tell me anything about your past.

Together they listen for Camille's cough; she listens and he listens to her listening. But the house is quiet; no cough, no words, and now for a while at least, no rain, just the incoming roar of a jet engine low over the roof. Marita pounds the bed with her fist. 'They break that bloody curfew!' she hisses.

In the dark they lie, side by side, each alert to the other's restlessness; something uncertain hanging there; a low-level irritability; each waiting for the other to fall asleep first so that the one who remains awake can subside into a silent musing, a state of dream-like wakefulness.

And then it begins again, that faint rasping sound from down the hall.

'See, I told you,' she says wearily, and sits up. 'I'll get the machine.'

This can't go on, he thinks. Something must change. There is not enough connexion. But inside his head the small voice says: It could be that all this is beyond your grasp. You are powerless.

●

The following night Marita sits on the edge of her daughter's bed, reading, in a subdued voice, from *The Big Friendly Giant*. At the point where the BFG is boasting of his dream collection Camille lifts her head from the pillow, as if struck by a sudden thought. 'We haven't seen Ros for a long time,' she says.

Marita doesn't answer. She's been expecting this.

'Why can't we go and see Ros?'

'Would you like to?'

The child nods her head solemnly.

'Well, we can if you like.' She is determined not to make an issue of this. She had decided, long ago, that while she would not initiate visits to her mother, she would take Camille whenever the child asked to go. And especially now, with a strange man in the house, she may feel the need of reassurance from her grandmother. And it could be that a day of sea-air, away from the inner-city smog, might help to relieve her lungs.

'Alright,' she says, 'we'll go soon.'

'How soon?'

'As soon as you like.'

'Tomorrow?'

'No, not tomorrow. What about Sunday?'

First a weary sigh of resignation, and then: 'Will Stephen come?'

'I don't know. How would you feel about that?'

Camille shrugs; a shrug that says: 'I'd rather he didn't but it's up to you.'

'We'll see,' says Marita, putting the book down by the hollow clown's face that glows in the dark. And as she begins to unloop the white mosquito net that hangs in a giant knot from the ceiling she smiles down at her daughter who lies on her back and nods her head in a way that is both sullen and knowing.

For some time Marita sits on the edge of the bed, holding Camille's hand, waiting for her to drift off into sleep. How long is it since she visited Mother? Not since Stephen came. There have been phone conversations and promises to call in but no actual visit. And for part of that time Ros has been in Mittagong, visiting a friend.

Now, perhaps, it's time to humour Camille.

PART FOUR

MOTHER

1

Darling Point

Mother, of course, lives in another world. Marita puts on her dark glasses and braces herself for the light.

On a day like this the combination of exposed headland and glare off the water creates a light so bright you could cut it. Under this pure sky, old mansions look like embassies, facades decked out in lustrous columns of sun-struck marble. Down by the water, white apartment blocks glitter with a diamond-sharp edge.

As a child she can remember her mother gazing out at the water with a kind of rapture. 'Just look at it,' she would say. 'Look at the play of light on the horizon.' And sighing: 'I couldn't live anywhere else. Remember, Marita, the derivation of the word, luxury. From the Latin, *lux*, meaning light.'

Stephen is besotted. 'It's beautiful here,' he says. 'It must be the most. . .' he hesitates, laughs, 'the most *civilised* part of the city.'

Mother opens the door.

'Hello, you must be Stephen. I'm Ros. I'm so glad you could come.'

She is barefoot and wearing her pearls: nature and culture in perfect harmony.

Camille waits to be welcomed. 'Hello, my pet,' says Mother. 'I hear you haven't been well.'

'I've had asthma. Since the rain came.'

'That's no good, is it? No good at all.' She places her slim hand on her grand-daughter's head, smoothing her hair, absent-mindedly, for a moment.

At Darling Point the sun shines in a blinding white light, an ecstatic glare that comes from the sky and reflects off the water. Marita's aunt has a house nearby that was once featured in a magazine and everything in this house is white like the light, and there is the photographer, William De La Manze, who set up his lens here in a series of living rooms, his camera pointing at the windows that framed the sea, and he exposed these sunlit rooms until they had the same glaring light as the water on the other side of the frame, white glare to white glare, but this is only art and many of these rooms are, in real life, dark, shaded, so that the Persian carpets will not fade, and those who have always had the light can have too much of the light. This, at least, is what her aunt used to say. In this country, she would say, with her cynical laugh, we have too much light — it can be exhausting.

Stephen follows Ros into the dim living room and sits, in what appears to be a relaxed way, on the edge of the tapestried chaise, leaning forward, his arms resting lightly on his bony thighs. Next to him, on a side table, is a large, glossy picture book, *Medicine Men of the South Pacific*.

Ros nods in its direction. 'That's a very interesting book,' she says, 'you might like to look at it sometime.'

'Yes, I would,' he says, politely.

And so they begin to talk. He calls her 'Mrs Black' in a stiff, gauche way that almost unsettles her since it pre-empts any display of elegant girlishness on her part and might move her regressively into the posture of *grande dame* or matriarch, but she adjusts to this with her usual quicksilver elan, says 'Please, "Ros",' and invites him out on to the terrace to look at the water, this purely so they can re-enter the room later on more comfortable terms, as equals.

He is oblivious of these manoeuvres, pushed cumbersomely forward by her graciousness which is of an order that makes little sense to him. Camille takes her grandmother's hand which Ros allows to rest in hers and Marita stands against the window with her hands in her pockets, leaving Stephen to negotiate his way alone. After all, it doesn't matter to her whether Mother likes him. It was Camille who wanted to come.

Stephen is faintly amused by Ros, she can tell. The fact that he comes from somewhere else, that these are not the *haut bourgeois* manners that patronised him in his childhood may give him a certain detachment.

'You're interested in forms of consciousness,' she hears her mother say, 'in what we can learn from native peoples.'

This isn't exactly how she, Marita, had described him, but Ros has her own way of phrasing things so as to draw them into her orbit.

'I'm interested in that myself. I was in the New Guinea highlands recently where I met up again with dear old Aui Tongu — do you know him?'

Marita rolls her eyes. Of course Stephen wouldn't know him but it's typical of Mother to ask.

'— and he explained to me about spirits in rocks . . .'

'In *our* medicine,' she hears him say, 'we believe there's a spirit in everything . . .'

As an attempt to fend off Mother's colonising empathy (no 'special' sensibility is entirely foreign to *her*) this sounds, at first, rather lame, except that she's struck by the use of the possessive 'we' that she hasn't heard him deploy before.

Camille looks up at them both, studiously on her best behaviour, though she will tire of this soon. Both Stephen and Ros have one hand to their eyes to shade their faces from the glare that flares off the water: they look for a moment as if they are standing to attention, each offering an absent-minded salute to the other. Mother's ruse is working, Stephen is more relaxed, beginning to unwind. Soon the words will flow and Ros will have what she wants, a contest of equals, and if that goes well then out will come the journal and she'll read to them.

But first she will serve them afternoon tea and all the little observances of class that might unsettle him in lesser households will not be apparent here because Ros is beyond them and will make tea carelessly, perhaps too weak, perhaps too strong, it is impossible to predict which, since she never bothers to notice how many spoons she is ladling into the porcelain teapot (chipped) and she will rummage around under her scattered books and papers for an open packet of Arnott's biscuits, perhaps stale, perhaps recently opened, and wait for him to comment on both the tea and the biscuits, as Marita is wont to do.

But whether from an absent-mindedness akin to her own or a shrewd playful withholding, he merely accepts the tea (despite the fact that it's made from unfiltered water) and says nothing about the biscuits and while she is explaining some point about highland vegetation he moves blithely to the cluttered sink and pours half his tea down the sink, reaching, assertively, for the kettle from which he slowly and studiedly fills his cup with hot water.

Ros observes all of this, barely pausing in her monologue. She simply smiles to acknowledge his fastidiousness, his preference, his correction.

'Too strong?'

'Just a bit.'

And Marita observes how subtle a refusal of the other's power is the rejection of their ritual offer of nourishment.

If only I had been less ravenous as a child, she thinks. Then I might have become one of those wan but fiercely powerful girls who exasperate their mothers and starve themselves.

Camille intervenes. 'Is this all you've got, Ros?' she asks, peering into a packet of shortbread. 'I don't like these.'

'Don't you, my love? Let me see what else I can find.' She opens the cupboard, which is revealed as more than half empty, and Stephen smiles at Marita but she finds it an idiotic smile and can only stare back.

'I do believe I have some ice-cream,' says Ros, rummaging scratchily in the freezer.

'I wouldn't give her any of that just now,' he says, almost peremptorily. 'It won't do her cough any good.'

Ros hesitates, her arm still raised to the freezer, the merest look of haughty offence in her eyes. She looks to Marita. For once, and it pains her, she has to appeal to her daughter's authority.

Marita gazes into the sink.

Ros changes tack. 'Her asthma, you mean,' she says.

'Her cough,' he corrects her. 'We don't see any point in giving it a name other than what it is. To name it generically separates out the symptom from the body, fetishising the symptom and isolating it from the whole.'

His little speech, his pedantry, has let her off the hook and the contest over the ice-cream is diffused, unless Marita intervenes as the one true maternal voice and says 'Yes' or 'No', and she prefers to leave this unresolved. Camille looks to her mother who tells her with her eyes that she is not to persist and the child lowers her gaze and sulks and fiddles sullenly with the papers spilling over the edge of the kitchen bench. Marita knows that it's one of those moments when the *petit abyss* begins to open up and Ros is at a loss and you can see her eyes emptying and her thoughts wandering to the water, or to her journal . . . It's time, thinks Marita, for me to rescue all three of them.

'Let's sit out on the verandah,' she says.

Let's go out into the light.

'I'm hungry,' whispers Camille and Marita puts her hand stealthily into her pocket as the other two walk ahead and she gives her some chocolate-coated licorice sticks, and Camille smiles. They collude, happily, against Ros, who doesn't care, and against Stephen, who cares too much. And Marita is content in this, thinking: she's *my* daughter, after all.

Out on the verandah Ros sits cross-legged on the old Georgian oak settle and you can see where her white cotton pants meet her slim brown thighs. Stephen gazes at the horizon, as if mesmerised by the glare.

In the company of mothers the lineaments of a lover become transformed, are exaggerated; they seem somehow larger, or smaller; duller or more charming. You detect for the first time a slight, shameful gaucherie, or observe as you haven't before a dismaying slickness of response. That wart on the upper right cheek becomes suddenly more prominent; that soft chin seems a fraction weaker, that light, pleasant voice reveals a hitherto undetected whine; perhaps because we see for a moment through the maternal gaze of the critical parent instead of that cloudy eye of neediness that Mother created in us in the first place.

But watching Mother and Stephen on the terrace Marita is shocked to discover, not that one makes the other look foolish but that there is a curious resemblance between them. She realises how alike they are in their stainless self-absorption, their metallic glare of certainty, and how, in conversation, they simply glance off one another. Is there nothing at stake here between them, she wonders? And she begins to fear that each thing she loves will blur into every other thing she loves and all will be absorbed into the fear. In their own way both Stephen and Ros have found a way of staving off the fear — their own little self-contained bubble of enlightenment.

Camille bends over the fine tracery of the iron balcony, her arms swinging almost to her toes, her body poised at the fulcrum of her narrow waist, four storeys above the ground, high on this densely populated cliff-face that runs down to the silver bay. Watching her, Marita feels the usual rush of vertigo, the sick lurch in the chest: don't fall, my darling, don't fall. And she snaps at her, 'Camille, don't *do* that!' And what she means is, don't summon up the fear.

Mother looks across. 'She's perfectly alright, aren't you darling?'

Of course.

As a child she'd stand out here for a long time, gazing at the water until she felt dizzy; unable, ever, to feel at ease in it, to take it for granted as other children in this privileged enclave took it for granted; trundling down to the water's edge with dutiful mothers in tow, like well brought-up beasts of burden laden down with beach bags, towels, buckets, picnic rugs and hats. Ros was sublimely free of such disabling encumbrance. Ros, upstairs at her *escritoire*; Marita on the balcony, staring down into the water until a sudden, blind rush of vertigo made her tilt and sway and hurled her back inside. She is waiting, now, for the journal to appear but it seems that today Ros is not in the mood, inhibited perhaps by that abrupt exchange over the ice-cream. A reading might be risky.

She can hear her mother's voice. 'And then, when Nick and I were in Somaliland . . .'

Oh, no, not Africa. Her friend, the village shaman, the photograph of her with Amamu; Mother and her rapport with the pagan healer, the natural man. Always the natural man, not the natural wise woman, the earth mother; the witch drying her herbs. Ros never seems to feel much rapport with other women. Perhaps, instead of the journal, she will show Stephen her prized photograph of herself with Einstein.

'This is an amazing light,' he says.

'Isn't it? Such a great expanse of it,' and she gestures elegantly at the silvery blue shimmer of the bay. 'It gives one such a sense of limitless possibility . . . In this country we are so privileged in the quality of our light. We can believe whatever we like . . . It makes us less timid, more expansive.'

Does it? Marita grimaces. It can also give you vertigo. When Camille was born, she had left and gone to live in the inner city, in the dark damp terraces and the narrow lanes and the smog; away from the water, away from the reflected light. She found a small dark house where she could stock up her cupboards and learn to be a mother. Away from the vertiginous glare.

Stephen, she thinks, you're receding from me. After the confrontation in the kitchen Ros is recovering ground, getting the better of you. Say something. She hears him laugh, inanely. She looks at that strong neck, that part of him she likes best. That stubborn neck is a surprise on a tall, lean body. It should look out of proportion, like a deformation, but it doesn't. Perhaps that laugh means he's charmed, or it may be that he's humouring her.

'Yes, Ros . . . yes.'

And then she hears her mother say: 'And what is the aim of all this? Where does it take you?'

'Hopefully to achieving balance, or harmony, a kind of . . . well, a kind of poise.'

'Poise?' She holds the word up for examination. 'I see. And is this some sort of state of grace?'

'Well, that's the Christian view of it. Zen would talk about the balance between yin and yang when the body is unobstructed and you can achieve a state of flow.'

'Ah, yes, well the Zen view is very convenient nowadays, isn't it, because of course one doesn't have to bother about the difficult question of sin . . .'

'I don't think that sin is a very helpful idea,' he says quietly, 'not when it's taken on its own. You have to ask where sin comes from, what creates the conditions for it. Sin is a fixed idea, it's static. We should be talking about process. Sin isn't just that you break some rule somewhere, it's poisoned consciousness and poisoned consciousness grows out of a poisoned body. Bad air, bad water, bad food. . .'

Marita sighs. This could go on forever.

Camille, who has been skipping around and around the terrace, stops. 'Ros, Ros . . .' she interrupts, insistently. 'I'm hungry.'

Marita smiles. Ah, yes, she thinks. This is the best way to intervene. Feed me. Feed me.

And with Camille's intervention, suddenly the male disappears, the male recedes into a silver shimmer, and there's just the three of them, the women.

She wants her mother to stop talking now, to turn her gaze away from the light, to rush up and hug her grand-daughter, to be infatuated with her, to coo and smooch and stroke and smooth so that she, Marita, can rest for a while from her cherished psychic burden, her maternal heaviness. She can switch off her red alert button for just a time and be, again, a vague, libidinal child, lost in herself; lost, light, floating out in the glare. And the men in this world are all out there, way out there, pale glimmering figures on the horizon, like silver beacons or Easter Island buoys . . .

But Mother will never play this game. Mother does not want to be a grandmother: Mother wants to be a philosopher, out there on the water, out with the lost boys on the burning horizon . . .

For much of the drive home, Stephen is silent. 'You're very quiet,' she says, at last. She is still trying to figure out who got the best of this encounter, Mother or Stephen.

'Hmmm,' he says, staring ahead at the road. And then: 'I couldn't live there.'

'Where?'

'Darling Point.'

'No? Really? Everyone always says how beautiful it is.' Trust Stephen to be different.

'It's stifled.' He takes his right hand off the wheel and waves it dismissively. What he wants to say is that it's stifled beneath a blanket of sameness. Everyone looks like everyone else. There is no sense of the other, of the exotic, of life beyond the bay. A beautifully packaged sameness that others might find reassuring but he finds stifling. 'Have you ever noticed,' he says, 'in these affluent suburbs, that you hardly ever see a public building? ' He smiles to himself as he hears the tone of this remark. This is his old self, his resentful self, traces of which still surface at odd times if only to remind him of what a dead end resentment is.

'So if someone died and left you one of these houses you'd sell it and move on?'

'Maybe. Maybe I'd keep it and turn it into a *dojo*.'

Camille pipes up from the back. 'What's a *dojo?*'

A home away from home for angry young men, thinks Marita, but says nothing, leaving Stephen to make his explanation. At this moment she is scarcely interested in what he has to say because she has begun to feel sorry for herself. 'I am feeling sorry for myself,' she says, over and over in her head as if this incantation will effect a cure. Will there ever be a time when she leaves her mother's house feeling the better for it, or at least free of self-pity?

●

That night Camille sits at her white plywood desk in the corner of the kitchen and writes three letters.

> Dear Stephen,
>
> How are you? Please do not cook me any more brown rice. And
> because I am a child I should be allowed to eat ice-cream sometimes.
> I like you.
>
> Camille
>
> Dear Ros,
>
> How are you? Please buy some Choc-Mallow biscuits for when I visit
> next time. A Mars Bar would do also.
> Hugs and kisses,
>
> Camille
>
> Dear Mum,
>
> How are you? Thank you for the licorice sticks.
> I love you.
>
> Camille

While she scrawls officiously at her table Stephen sets to work with his knives. Tonight he prepares a particularly delicate meal of sliced shiitake mushrooms and silken tofu in a lemongrass sauce. As always at the chopping board he is methodical and precise: he slices the mushrooms with a calculated finesse that is mesmerising; his tofu pieces are perfect cubes; the two pale sticks of lemongrass are severed into even pieces, neatly shaped on the diagonal. Chop, chop, chop. Marita observes him from the kitchen table. Look at him: the philosopher in the kitchen. He is calm, powerful. He wields the knife with a slow, chopping rhythm that is sedative; every cut a proposition, every ingredient a verse from the sacred text of the Zen cookbook. Nevertheless, though she mocks it, the meal is delicious. It's not his fault that she has no appetite. Stephen puts Camille's plate in front of her and says nothing. She eats a few mouthfuls of the noodles, politely, and then, pushing her chair back, walks somewhat self-consciously over to the fridge where she extracts the white sliced bread from the bottom shelf. As if to spare his sensitivities she disappears into the living room, the transparent plastic bag of Wonderbread swinging from one hand. Stephen says nothing. He has read the little note she left on his plate and folded it into his pocket.

As the night moves on Marita becomes more and more restless. There's an agitation in her chest, a tightness around the heart. What is it? It can only be that old vertigo, that vertigo has followed her back, that flat fear, that lack of connexion that she always feels with Mother; the gaze down into the drop that leaves you startled, speechless, agape, and all your atoms prepare to fly out over the precipice before you make that sudden move and gather them in, back into the cyclonic funnel of the aorta. You feel your heart beating behind your eyes. Wings of blood. Panic.

11.50 p.m. Stephen, as usual, has gone to bed early and is already asleep. Lying next to him, she has read three chapters from the middle section of *Jane Eyre* waiting for his sleep to deepen. Lying on his back now he has begun, lightly, to snore. She gets up, puts on her red silk kimono and walks barefoot into the hallway. There she pauses in the doorway of Camille's bedroom and listens for her breathing; rise and fall, rise and fall. She counts up to ten breaths and then continues on out into the dark kitchen. There is something she wants to do. What is it? Read? Work on her tapes? No, she isn't in the mood. And then she thinks, yes; yes, she'll make a cake. She'll make chocolate cake. She hasn't made a chocolate cake for a long time. It's not yet midnight, after all, and there's something soothing in chocolate, watching it melt, slowly, in the shiny curve of the bain marie; watching the little squares seep and merge into a dark pool, the warm steam rising to the ceiling. And there's a new method she wants to try. Zoe has given her a book, *The Cake Bible* by Rose Levy Beranbaum. A woman of inexhaustible patience, Rose has scientifically researched one of the sacred tenets of cake making — the sifting of flour — and pronounced it unnecessary. As she recalls Rose's basic recipe there is an initial problem, the beating together of the dry ingredients. She does not want to risk waking Stephen or Camille with the sound of electric mixing, but that's OK, she'll do it by hand, so much the better; in this heat the butter, left out all day, will be at exactly the right temperature and the rhythmic circling motion of the whisk is a sure way to slow the adrenalin and soothe the heart. In an hour, a soothing hour of near silence, the cake will sit cooling above the white marble slab, and then, if she is still restless she will get out her pen and, in the bad habit she has acquired from Mother, she will write up her journal.

Stephen wakes with a sudden jolt. He listens for disturbing noises outside in the street but for once it is quiet. Why is he awake? Ah, yes, he's been dreaming. Oddly enough he's had that chocolate cake dream again, the one he hasn't had for two years, not since he reformed. And how vivid it was! Lying here in the dark, the miasma of cake is palpable; he can almost *smell* it. Instinctively he knows that the bed beside him is empty and he knows why. She's out there again, working secretively in the kitchen. Working on her words; often, at this time of night, a sign that she's upset about something. Her mother, perhaps? He can see now why she resists her mother, a woman who keeps an empty pantry. But Marita over-compensates. At Darling Point he'd observed her palming sweets to Camille. She didn't think he'd notice but he had, and at once he'd recognised the syndrome; a reliance on what Eva calls heart food, a sudden rush of sugar joy, the quick fix of 'love'. There was something here in women, some hysteria associated with nurturing. Eva was very clear on this: food is an area in which men are abject, women are hysterical. Rarely are either able to adequately nurture themselves. If, like him, they approached it philosophically, they could be free of whatever it was that plagued them.

1.35 a.m. The cake sits on its wire cooler, modest in its perfection. It is true, as Rose Beranbaum promises, that when the flour is beaten in rather than folded the cake neither sinks nor domes in the middle but maintains a perfect surface. Satisfied with its seductive form, she takes down her occasional journal from the kitchen shelf where she keeps it concealed among her recipe books, but after gazing at a blank page for some minutes she finds she is not in the mood for scribbling and reaches instead for her book, *Jane Eyre*. Every few years, or whenever moved, she takes up the old plot of romance and ponders it anew. Especially Mr Rochester. Mr Rochester is the problem. There is always a problem with this demon lover, this man who will and won't be tamed, who will or won't be domesticated, or only at a terrible cost . . .

Contemplating this now, she is suddenly aware of a presence and looks up. A large black cockroach has scurried out from under the bench and is poised beside the cooling rack. Rising quietly from the table she takes hold of a wooden spoon and flicks the beetle on to the floor where her first impulse is to stamp on it, but her feet are bare. With cold repugnance she stares down at its red-brown carapace, its black legs crooked at right angles, its long wavering antennae, fine and spidery. No matter what she does she is never rid of them and now she accepts that they will always be there; big, brutish, ugly and omnipresent. At least this one isn't flying about the kitchen like a small, haphazard bat. As she gazes down at it, the beetle rouses itself from its torpor and with a sudden start, scurries away into a crevice between the cupboards. When she is certain that it has gone, she picks up a clean tea towel and folds it around the cake.

PART FIVE

THE
FATHER

1

the client

Meanwhile, in his bed, the investment banker dreams about his daughter. He has never seen her face or any part of her, indeed, he could not tell you the date of her birth, but he knows that she is out there somewhere and he means to claim her soon, for surely she is, in some essential sense, his.

It's not his fault that her mother (a difficult woman) didn't press her claim, those nine years ago, when his seed had strayed (seed is blind, that's the bloody trouble!) without any thought on his part. This is the oddest thing about it, really, that he didn't plan it, since he's always been, first and foremost, a planner, always had his goals mapped out and in place, more or less, and if he failed he at least knew the reason why and could redefine the field, draft a new mission statement. Whatever. Whatever it takes.

But what's that? What was that noise? He has become jumpy lately, for no reason at all and of course he finds it difficult to sleep, he always has, but now something else, some insidious change. In the past few months he has developed an arrhythmia, an irregular heartbeat. 'It comes,' he likes to tell people, 'from going flat out all the time.' He's now on double doses of medication but still he can't sleep. 'The problem is,' he explains, 'I don't sleep! Three to four hours a night and that's it!' When they ask, tentatively, in a kind of code, whether it's life threatening, he gives his big-shouldered shrug. 'Could be, could be not. It's a bit of a mystery,' he tells his friends, 'and they [meaning doctors] know less about it than they'd like you to think.' He rouses himself now from his bed and, sitting on the edge, begins to take his pulse. On the luminous dial of his watch the fine spidery second hand counts down the slippery beat of his blood . . . twenty-six, twenty-seven, twenty-eight . . . It's alright now, he says to himself, and repeats this reassuring phrase. It's alright now. But he can never predict it.

'An electrical derangement,' his cardiac physician had called it. His cardiac physician is a guy called Ross whom he'd gone to boarding school with. He was a withdrawn, studious little runt then and he doesn't seem to have changed much. He has that dry neutral way of explaining how a man in the prime of life, a big, basically strong type like himself, might short-circuit in a sudden drop into death. 'The electrical wiring system that regulates the heartbeat,' he explained, 'induces the cardiac muscle to contract and thus push blood into the arterial circulation some seventy-two times a minute. The muscle begins to receive much more frequent signals, leading to abnormally fast pumping. If the heart beats too rapidly, its interior chambers don't have time to fill with blood. Because the organ cannot eject something it does not receive, delivery of blood to the body's tissues, including to the cardiac muscle itself, can drop precipitously, causing the heart to stop.'

'What does that mean exactly?' he'd asked; asked belligerently. (He couldn't help it, he couldn't believe this little runt with a terrible name like Ross might be going to outlive him, Adrian, who was three times his size and a better colour.)

'Cases vary. In all probability you'll respond well to medication. Everyone has their own metaphysical line of credit and yours may be one of the long ones that extend out for years.'

Metaphysical line of credit? Extend out for years? What kind of talk was that? Was puny little Ross making fun of him, of his profession? Did he detect a note of implied criticism? Maybe Ross was some kind of closet socialist. You couldn't tell with doctors. They always looked straight but half of them were fucking mad. Or was he just trying to be droll? Surely he didn't expect a man to continue on with his sense of humour unimpaired when he'd just been told that he had an 'electrical derangement'? It made him sound like some kind of unanticipated storm.

But, Jesus, he has to stop doing this, constant re-caps of the problem in his head, especially late at night. Besides, he's got other problems. He'll have to talk to his lawyer soon, about the child, about his chances of making a claim. Find out his rights, and how much he'll be up for, and all of that, and he's not as well-heeled as some of his friends think, some of his investments haven't worked out as well as they might have and he's a man to spend money, one way and another, and he's always thought that this was one of his better points, unlike Ross who, no doubt, is a little tight-arse with a safe investment portfolio that he, Adrian, wouldn't condescend to sell to somebody's maiden aunt.

Night has a weird quality, doesn't it? It's like another world. Not if you're busy, not if you're at a club, or hanging out in a Japanese bar with some visiting banker who's pissed and wants to make a fool of himself on the karaoke machine or, more likely, get you to fix him up with one of the expensive girls from Simone's agency. No, not on those nights. On nights like this, when you can't get any shut-eye and you're waiting for your heart to jump-start itself in the wrong direction.

He gets up and walks over to the sofa by the window where he sits in his silk pyjamas (a gift from an old flame) and looks down on to the street. It's a very pretty street, he thinks. Yes, it's a very pretty street, a facade of tarted-up terraces with pretty trees and art galleries on the corner and a new shop selling super-expensive marmalade with bits of twig wound around the lid. But looking out on to a dark street at three in the morning can be a bit depressing to say the least and he's not one to read, although occasionally his personal assistant, Fiona, will leave some best-seller or other on his desk. But they're always long, aren't they, and after a few pages he's restless again. Women seem to read more than men. He's known a few readers in his time though there's something about a woman lying in bed next to him reading that gets on his nerves. Speaking of which, *she* was always reading . . . but no, he won't dwell on that.

He wonders what she looks like now, the kid that is. Has she got his mother's red hair (his own has a reddish tinge) or his father's ominous black locks? The old man was proud of his hair, a little vain right up to the end, and why not? He hopes she isn't thickset like him: perfect for a boy but no good on a girl, but then again, have you noticed how thickset people often have a lot of commonsense? Unlike the child's mother and grandmother, both as thin as reeds and hopelessly neurotic. What if she takes after them? Never mind, he'll jolly her out of it. She'll come over for weekends, whatever, and they'll go off and have fun. Wonderland, the zoo, that sort of thing. Only last week he'd been at dinner with a barrister who complained about his custody problems. His eleven-year-old daughter flew across from Adelaide for the school holidays and he had to work until eight most nights, had to hire a student to take her around and often, by the time he got home, his daughter was tired and sullen and didn't seem interested in dining out. He hadn't thought much of that. He wouldn't be like that. His own father had always made time for him, kept the weekends free when he came home from boarding school. And when, finally, *he* becomes a father to his daughter, he'll be the same.

He'd like to talk to someone about this, though not his friends, not yet, it's too soon, and if it doesn't work out he'll lose face. Lately he's been thinking of asking Fiona out for a drink, though he doesn't approve of bonking the talent at work. It can get very messy, as he knows from experience, and a man of the world shouldn't be so strapped for resources. But she's an intelligent girl, and a good listener, and he could at least talk to her about this. On the sofa beside him are two embroidered cushions that she's made for him, and he suspects that she just might have a crush on him. It's a reasonable assumption when a girl starts to sew for you. Did young girls still learn embroidery? he had asked her when she presented him with the first of the cushions (he didn't know what else to say). 'They remind me of those things they used to hang on walls in the old days . . .'

'Samplers?'

'That's right, samplers. You know, with little mottoes.'

'I'll make you one with a motto,' she'd said, super-brightly.

Oh no, he thought, but when eventually she produced it, he liked it immediately. He liked her little joke. It was one of the favourite sayings of the company chairman, Grice, who likes to deliver rambling pep talks over dinner, little sermons on his personal philosophy of life. High on the list of these is his belief in change, change for its own sake. The importance of change and the power of dynamic thought. Dynamism as a principle (principle of what? some weird kind of conference room physics?). In his filofax Grice keeps a list of quotations and references to support his arguments. Especially his favourite argument: *Only change has meaning*. Only the man who understands change, who seeks change, who rides the back of the tiger, can achieve anything, let alone maximise his potential. Grice likes to talk about the 'quicksilver of life' *ad nauseam*. *Ad nauseam*. What a great expression that is. Must have been invented by someone with a delicate digestion who had to listen to a lot of bollocks over corporate dinners. There are no laws of capital accumulation (this is Grice talking), there is only change, and an instinct for it. Only the money men who throw off their attachments make real money, real gains in the market. They sniff out the new, the shifting, the emergent, the risky synthesis, heeding always the words of the great American industrialist, G. W. Woodward. And then he gets out his damned filofax and flicks through the index at the back and reads from his beloved list. '*We live to embrace the new,*' he reads, smacking his lips against the banality of the words as if they were prime beluga . . . Damn it, he can feel that twinge in his left shoulder starting to move again, just there in under the shoulder blade. An old squash injury. He'll take a Valium now to stop it seizing up altogether and laying him low for days.

And tomorrow he'll ring his lawyer; he has to make a move, he can't keep putting it off forever. He might die. And then she'd never know who she was. His daughter. And why would that matter? Why does it matter to him? He would never have seen her. He would not know what it feels like to be a father.

Looking down, he realises that he is cradling one of Fiona's cushions against his hip. This is the joke cushion, his favourite. She'd made it in the week after they'd come back from some ponderous lunch in the midst of which Grice had made a wide expansive gesture and quoted them 'G. W.'s favourite maxim' — the one, according to Grice, he had hung on the walls of his offices and factories to encourage a system overview and the renunciation of petty grievance in workers and management alike. And this is the one Fiona has, in a droll impulse, embroidered on the silk cushion nuzzling his hip: *In the face of eternity the mountains are as transient as the clouds.*

How true. And how pretty the handiwork. He is surprised that anyone with an MBA, like Fiona, would carry these anomalous feminine skills into the world of finance. But then her cushions are a kind of joke, he suspects, and the joke is always on them, the boys. Women always have something up their sleeve; an embroidery hook, a wedding ring, a child . . .

2

the coat

Another hot, humid day. Enclosed in the steel-grey lift of the Treasury Office Stephen closes his eyes and imagines the three of them, he, Marita and Camille, under a striped beach umbrella. And they just lie, side by side, a set of heartbeats in the sand, until he stands up and strolls down to the water and wades out beyond the frolicking children and the foam, and feels the first chill surge of the surf against his body . . .

Level 9, and the lift doors open with a hesitant hiss, on to the wide panorama of the floor. He looks out over the sea of consoles and maybe it's because the scent of Marita is still on his body that he's in a good mood this morning and it seems as if all the clerks are in white shirt-sleeves and that there is a kind of beauty in this. It's one of those moments of subtle joy that occasionally settle on him when he's least expecting it. It's only when he reaches his desk that he becomes aware of something odd.

And it's Freda, Freda who this morning is dressed peculiarly, even for her. It's not the black beret, which she wears all day every day; no, *it's the coat*. Outside it's hot and humid but in here Freda is wrapped in a huge black overcoat, the type of coat you almost never see in Sydney, the heavy wool kind with an ominous fur collar that suggests imminent exile to Siberia. Is this it? Has she finally flipped? Maybe she's just arrived, has forgotten, momentarily, to take it off? But no, as he settles to his desk, she rises, collects her bundle of forms, returns to her console and begins to work. A black bear in a bright field. Is Freda, always a little eccentric, moving that much closer to the edge?

She broods in this coat, all morning, and there's something unsettling about it. The office is a finely balanced constellation of wavering minds, a hum of social ecology that cannot bear too much distraction, too much overt or unexplained deviation. From time to time one of the clerks in the vicinity gives him a look: Sanjay frowns with concern; Bruce twirls his right index finger at his temple; Gareth raises a pale eyebrow, and at some point, no doubt, will scan the desk calendar for an epigraph. Stephen looks to Isobel, the Supervisor, who nervously adjusts her glasses and looks away.

And then, at 11.40, Freda shakes her head vehemently, shivers, and utters a low groan. In her slow, cumbersome way she pushes back her chair, stands up and begins to move toward him like some black ambling vision. The monstrous coat is buttoned to the neck, its fur collar nudging the leather rim of her beret.

'Can I talk to you a minute, Stephen?'

'Sure.'

She looks around her guardedly, and then leans her black bulk across his desk. 'Is it just me,' she says, her dark eyes chill, 'or could there be some fault in the air-conditioning?'

'The what?'

'The air-conditioning. Can't you feel it? It's freezing.'

He hesitates. She must have noticed that he, like everyone else, is in shirt-sleeves. He decides to play it straight.

'Do you want to have it checked?' he says.

'Yes.' She nods solemnly.

'Go back to your desk and I'll see what I can do.'

Without giving it much thought (could it be that domesticity is blunting his edge?) he crosses the floor to make representations to The Dwarf, to stare once again into those cloudy eyes. The Dwarf shifts irritably in his seat. 'Don't be ridiculous,' he mutters out of the side of his mouth, mutters in his furtive, grudging way. 'She's probably imagining it.' He leans into the desk. 'She's got a mental problem, remember?'

This is an unsatisfactory exchange but then again he's been caught off guard. He returns to Freda with the intention of uttering a few appeasing words on the wisdom of eating a substantial breakfast to generate more body heat . . . but then, the instant he reaches her desk, he can feel it. *It*. A funnel of icy air emanating from a vent in the wall. Freda looks up at him. 'You feel it, don't you, Stephen? I'm chilled to the bone.'

He returns to The Dwarf, this time insistent.

Late in the afternoon the dapper little engineer from Maintenance emerges from the lift, accompanied by his technician. The engineer introduces himself as Col and his offsider as Darren. Col is wearing one of those pale, check shirts with fine green lines that look like a graph sheet. His dark wool tie is tucked in neatly above the third button of his shirt and his glasses hang from a cord around his neck. Darren is in a white boilersuit and wears a jet earstud engraved with a silver peace sign. He stands with his arms folded and his feet apart, as if braced for a lot of nonsense from white-collar types.

Stephen introduces himself. 'This office,' he tells them, 'has developed its own climate.'

'Yeah,' says Col, casting an officious eye over the ceiling, 'some of 'em are like that.'

The Dwarf explains Freda's predicament.

'Not a problem,' says Col.

'Happens all the time,' says Darren.

Sanjay is standing behind them. 'Well, well, well,' he asks, in his heavy Indian accent, 'and what, pray, is this?'

They all look down at the square object that Darren has placed on the floor, a big silver box, a tacky looking contraption like something kids build in primary school for the Christmas nativity.

'That,' says Col, 'is the air meter.' He nods brusquely at Darren. Ceremoniously they hold the box up to the wall above Freda's desk, and since Darren is a good deal taller, Col has to stand on his toes. The clerks in the immediate vicinity gather round while Col, craning his neck, explains that the box is supposed to measure air flow.

'The key,' he says, 'is not the temperature of the air, but velocity.' They all nod, recalling those oppressive little gusts of icy air that assail you in the eyes from above your plane seat. 'Variations in velocity create a sort of horseshoe effect so that each of us exists in a different pocket of air and several climates co-exist in the one space, rather like your average day in Melbourne.' He pauses for effect and they all titter. Melbourne jokes always get a laugh. 'This is aggravated,' he continues, 'by unilateral efforts to modify the individual environment, such as clerks covering a vent with paper and sticky tape if their desk happens to be directly beside one. This,' he intones officiously, 'throws it out for everyone.'

Stephen listens to this sermon impassively. Why can't they just fix the bloody thing? Col is a man who enjoys his authority and hence can't forbear to moralise. He reminds Stephen of a teacher of technical drawing he once had in that boys' school, shaped like a prison, that had finally suspended him for 'silent insolence'. It's all part of management's control mechanism; they want no worker's input, no individual initiative or remedies.

'What can you do for Freda?' he asks bluntly.

'Not a problem,' says Col. He takes Darren aside and they confer for a minute and then begin to move in the direction of the lifts. 'Back in a tick,' says Col, and they disappear.

Later, they return with yet another makeshift cardboard contraption they've rigged up to redirect the flow of air— in effect, Freda's own vent.

This they fix to the wall with thumbtacks!

The union rep is not impressed, especially with the thumbtacks. 'How long,' he asks, 'before that thing drops to the floor and one of *them*,' he points in the direction of a thumbtack, 'spears her in the eye?'

'No need to take that tone,' says Col. They both look at him, affronted. He glares back. They are all mutually affronted.

It's Freda who breaks the silence. 'Thank you, gentlemen,' she says, in a solemn tone, and slowly, with almost ceremonious formality, she removes her black coat, a gesture that Stephen considers, under the circumstances, to be an act of faith.

'Our pleasure,' says Col frostily.

'Could be worse,' says Darren, exiting, with a larrikin leer, into the lift.

Reliving the event while walking to the carpark, Stephen is annoyed with himself. He ought to have seen the funny side of this; instead, he'd been peevish and hostile. The whole episode had had a farcical character, like a sequence from a Chaplin film. Once he would have enjoyed it, tongue in cheek, winking across at Gareth. Gareth had sent over a leaf from the desk calendar: *Here we are again with both feet planted firmly in the air* — Baron Scanlon, but in response he had managed only a dull grin. It's all so remote now from where he wants to be, what he wants to do. Increasingly he plays his role like an actor impersonating a former self, waiting for the day of escape. He could give it all up now, just walk out; he already has two regular Shiatsu clients, one of them tonight. Others would be bound to follow. He remembers when his sister had been given a gift of Viking runes, a small canvas bag with stones inside, each with a black squiggle engraved on it. She had closed her eyes and pulled out one at random. 'Let go', it had read. 'Do not be afraid to leap into the abyss empty handed.' She had gasped with scorn and tossed the bag across to him. 'This sort of mumbo jumbo is more in your line,' she'd said, which was unfair, since he's never been interested in any kind of fortune-telling, although just this once he'd have to say he was impressed. For a woman obsessed with her antiques and her security alarm it had seemed like good advice. Contemplating it now, for himself, it was a little harder to take. He has no money, and he thinks about this constantly. Last night, at his Shiatsu class, Eva had asked him if he wanted to rent a mat at the centre; there was one coming vacant in the next month, one of the practitioners was going to live at the Mother Divine retreat in Amsterdam, and he could have it if he wished. This was her way of telling him that he was ready to set up as a practitioner, ready, that is, at the level of skill. But he had grimaced, told her he was broke, had no savings and was afraid to strike out into the unknown. Eva had grinned and cited the teaching of some Indian guru she listens to: 'Trust in Nature to be supportive,' she said, 'and the universe will look after the details.' He knows she is right. He also knows what his sister would say to this: 'The universe will look after the details? She must be joking!' Methodically, his sister looks after her own details and prides herself on leaving nothing to chance.

Before clocking off he had rung Marita to remind her that he would be late tonight, that he has his regular Thursday night client in Woollahra. Camille, he knows, will be delighted. He won't be there when they eat; she can inveigle her mother into a vegetarian pizza and a can of Solo (having ruefully accepted that her mother draws the line at Coke). Marita was in one of her vague moods, the ones that make him uneasy, and seem to intimate that in the past few hours, unknowingly and through no fault of his own, he might somehow have come adrift, unmoored from her cedar bed. For much of the time he is ambivalent: if she clings to him he begins to think of that *dojo* in Kyoto; if she is remote he wants to enfold her in a tight knot of possession. Tonight he had had an impulse to panic, to ring his client and say that he was ill, that he could not make the treatment, but he steadied himself and breathed deeply into his *hara* while staring out the window at the facade opposite: something in the way the pedimented windows framed perfect rectangles of blue sky reminded him of the landscape of his dreams in which mildly apocalyptic elements blended in unexpected harmony to suggest unending possibility. A utopia of light. A new order. And as he exhaled, slowly, the panic blew away.

Entering the cool gloom of the underground carpark he catches sight of a white Alfa Sud and is reminded, with a pang, of his sister. He should stop in on his way and collect her mail. Lately he's been neglecting the place. Glancing at his watch he realises that he hasn't time. Perhaps later.

3

Jersey Road

Above the stream of late peak-hour traffic the heat rises in a shimmering haze. It's early evening now as he pilots the green Commodore away from the smog-ridden inner west and across to the designer groves of the eastern suburbs and the terraced hills of Paddington; lush, dandified, bathed in an excess of mellow amber light.

His client's house is a wide elegant terrace in lavender and grey that sits on the brow of the hill on Jersey Road and looks across to the city. Brushing aside the wisteria and the jasmine he unlatches the iron gate and walks to the front door, admiring the delicate tracery of the Japanese maple that all but obscures some French doors. He raps the brass knocker, a stolid lion that glares vacantly out into the street, and when no-one comes he plays a tune on the electronic chimes. On the window is a sign: WARNING *Advar Security System installed here*.

No answer. His client the investment banker is not at home, and this is customary, that he's late, and he'll pay extra for the time that his masseur loiters here watching the sky redden and darken swiftly into a subtropical twilight.

There is nothing to do but sit on the marble step and look out from the verandah, inhaling the luxuriant scents of the garden. It's so beautiful here, where the rich live. Here he could almost begin to believe in himself as a calm soul. Resting his head against the verandah post he closes his eyes and lets his mind drift . . . and drift and drift . . . into a space a long way from here, into that *dojo* in Kyoto: he can see the bare wooden floor, the high roof, the rice-paper doors, the bamboo rods. Last night, at Eva's class, Roger had spoken about his time there some years ago; the simplicity, the austerity, getting up at five in the morning, hours spent on the bare wooden floor doing yoga or meditation, with the *sensei* observing you closely, advising you, admonishing you; walking about with his bamboo staff and pausing, if he sensed some need in you, to strike you over the shoulders with it. Doesn't it hurt? someone had asked. Depends on how it's done, said Roger. With Todoroki *Sensei* I found I resented it, there was a hardness there, but Mitsuyu *Sensei* struck with compassion, and the effect was difficult to describe, like brushing away the cobwebs, like an opaque window shattering and the clean air suddenly blowing through. Listening, he had felt more drawn to this than ever. How vividly he can see himself there, on the bare *dojo* floor, in white pyjamas, his head shaved. But then again there are moments over the past year when he has had doubts. Could he follow a master? Wholeheartedly, without reservation, a complete yielding of the self? Could he give up his will in this way? His will is too powerful, he knows this; there are times when he has experienced it almost as another limb, a third arm, with a separate consciousness of its own and in the great Fatalist traditions (Greek, Romantic, Hindu), anyone with too strong a will must suffer some form of mutilation — eyes put out, limb lopped off — until the spiritual lesson is learned. Or the lesser penalty; a crack across the shoulders with a stout staff . . .

'*You stupid prick!*' His reverie is broken by a hoarse shout from up the street. He opens his eyes and looks out onto the pavement and at that moment, from around the top corner, Adrian's dark red BMW noses into the street, wheeling out of one of those hasty, casual, distracted turns that say everything about his driving and a lot about him. And here he is, climbing out of his car, red faced and puffing; heavy-shouldered with sandy receding hair. The young investment banker; thirty-eight going on fifty.

'Kept you waiting, mate.' This is both a question and a statement; a greeting, a challenge, an irritable unfocussed reproach of something out there, nothing in particular; a diffuse anger: everything Adrian says is all of these things at once.

He lumbers past the gate and stabs his key in the lock. In this thick air, he's wheezing slightly. The door flings back and he charges into the house knowing his masseur will follow, at a perversely slow pace, behind. 'Jesus, you're languid,' he'd said once and Stephen had laughed.

'What's funny?'

'Nothing.' It was just that he'd never thought of himself as languid, and at that moment he'd had a flash of insight into languor as one of the more subtle forms of resistance to another's power.

'Back in a tick, mate,' says Adrian, flinging his briefcase on to the leather couch. 'I'll just grab a shower.'

Adrian's house is almost dark now, the shadows blackening on the windowsill, the paintings on the walls receding into murkier visions. 'They're collector's pieces,' he'd boasted to Stephen. 'See this one. A very similar one from the same exhibition was bought by the National Gallery.' He laughs, and calls them his 'scalps'.

Stephen prepares the room, moving two halogen lamps into a corner and pushing the white leather couches back to create a space for his thin blue futon.

Adrian thumps downstairs, barefoot, wrapped in his black and white silk kimono with the red spots. Adrian has the fortified barrel chest of those who feel the need to defend the heart, encase it in armoury, the burden of this effort bringing on ultimately, a hump in the shoulders. For a big man he has small feet, small and white, and small hands. He lowers himself onto the mat and lies, prostrate, looking up at the ceiling.

They work in silence at first. In the early visits Adrian would say nothing for the whole hour, holding himself taut beneath the skin, grunting coarsely as his huge thighs pressed down against the floor. Then, as the treatments wrought their effect, he began to loosen up.

'You're getting through to me, Steve, old son. Last couple of times I've been out to dinner I've just had the fish. And I don't seem to want to drink as much any more. I got stirred at Rogue's last night. You're turnin' into a hippie, they said. '

Adrian is a frequenter of nightclubs: The Edge of Destruction, The Ice Cage and his favourite, Checkpoint Charlie where the walls are covered in *trompe l'oeil* murals of the Winter Palace in St Petersburg; plaster peeling from the brickwork, gilt cornices torn away (all fake of course) and portraits of Lenin and Stalin creating an effect of the barbarians taking control. 'It's a fantasy environment,' says Adrian, 'but full of reality, if you know what I mean.' He keeps offering to take Stephen along for a night on the town but they never set a date.

The masseur doesn't like to talk when he's treating so he laughs, and presses into his client's thigh. Adrian is still a driven man, a driven man with an irregular heartbeat for which he takes pills; some bizarre syndrome that makes your heart race for no reason at all — no *known* reason — because your heart has 'aberrant pathways' that create a cardiac flutter, as if some winged creature had been let loose in your chest. Lately he claims that he is becoming dissatisfied with his job. 'I'm bored,' he says, 'you know, *bored*. After all, what *is* money, Steve?' He is lying face down on the mat, his florid cheek curving over the edge of a silk cushion, his eyes gazing wistfully into the glossy surface of the parquet floor. 'The more you have the more you spend. Last night I went out to this new Japanese restaurant up the Cross where they do a special lobster sashimi. Paid a fucking fortune for it. You should see it. Little mounds of translucent flesh, still alive, and it sits there pulsating on your plate.'

The masseur says nothing. It is pointless, here, to be judgemental. As long as he keeps on with his treatments something in Adrian will begin to shift.

In the far corner of this room is a grand piano. Once, when Stephen had asked Adrian if he could play it, the client had sighed his overweight, overwrought sigh and said, 'Not any more.' On another day, apropos of nothing, he mentioned that his mother was a concert pianist. 'She taught me to play herself, until I was nine.'

'What happened then?'

'Then? Then she left us to marry a Swiss banker.'

'Oh,' he said.

'That's when I went to boarding school. What else could Dad do? It was alright, though. Makes you independent, toughens you up.'

'Mmmm,' he said, not wanting to buy into the client's history, which is, after all, only a set of conceptualisations, nothing as tangible as the body.

'Then just last year, out of the blue, I started to have dreams about Mother playing the piano. She'd play but I couldn't hear anything. Like a silent movie, no sound. I'd wake up feeling . . . I dunno, *off*. So I hired a student from the Con to come and play for me, one hour a week.'

'Turn over on your right side.'

'What?'

'Your right side.'

'Sorry, I'm daydreaming. This student was Korean. His English was atrocious which suited me. The first time he came, I told him: Play what you like, old son, it doesn't matter. Just don't talk, and don't ever ask me what I want to hear. I'd sit on the couch, that one over by the window, and listen to him . . . ouch!'

'That sore?'

'You bet.'

'Sorry.'

'It's the sound, the sound of those little hammers against the strings . . . the vibrations seem to massage your chest . . .' And while he spoke he rubbed the area over his heart with the palm of his hand.

The masseur paused and sat back on his heels and waited for him to lie still again. ' . . . at the end of an hour I'd sling him a hundred in cash and he'd give a little bow and go. Then a friend said to me, why don't you try a real massage, instead. So I found Eva and she sent me to you.'

Lucky for me, he thinks, because Adrian is one of his regular clients, once a week without fail, and that money is reliable money, money that in time will buy him out of the office and into his own day, but he does not want to think of this because money is one of his obsessions, he thinks of it incessantly; it eats away at his struggle to achieve poise, and yet to his fury and dismay it is the *sine qua non* of his liberation since how else can he leave his clerical prison and be free to work at his apprenticeship as a priest of the body. 'You have to trust in nature to be supportive,' says Eva. 'Something will turn up when you're ready for it' . . . but then he hears his father's voice, that squeaky, pompous little voice that spoke endlessly of thrift, and careful returns, and a steady job . . .

He's wandering. He stops, rests his hands against Adrian's back, counts to ten, empties himself into his arms, his hands . . . if he thinks too much he'll lose the thread of the client's energy, the echo of the life force along the meridians, the path of the *chi*. But as if to taunt him, his client lies there, murmuring, 'What is money, what is money, Steve?'

Don't do this, Adrian, don't stir me on this subject or you'll ruin your treatment.

' . . . is it really just so much shit?'

Adrian has a very vulgar turn of phrase; perhaps he learned it at that exclusive school of his. He speaks to his masseur as one man to another: how is he to know that since Stephen began his meditation he no longer feels the impulse to swear; the words are ugly, abrasive, they lacerate the very air; they are part of that unfocussed anger that Adrian and the rest of us shout into the void.

' . . . does it mean everything?' He addresses this question now to the ceiling as, gently, his masseur pushes his knee up into the curve of his chest. 'What other measure is there?'

Stephen leans in lightly, using the weight of his body. Money is love, he wants to say; food is love, aerobics is love, macrobiotics is love. Instead, he murmurs, almost to himself, 'It won't give you poise.'

'Poise?' Adrian lifts his head from the futon, his chin straining upwards. 'What the fuck's that?'

He could say: it's the reason you summon me here for a treatment once a week; the reason why you paid someone to play the piano for you: equilibrium. But this reminds him of scales and the weighing up of measures, and he's back to money in a perverse loop that baffles his intention so he says nothing.

'Poise . . .' says Adrian, exhaling the word in a slow hiss. 'Sounds to me like a static thing, Steve. What we have to deal with is change. Change is the thing. Learn to love it or go under.'

Yes, but what kind of change? The endless movement of money? Where does that get you?

'Eva says that change can only be dealt with from some stable centre of the self.'

'Stable, eh? She's probably referring to family life. Sooner or later women always get back to that.'

'Mmm.' He wants his client to stop talking now, to just be, but today Adrian's fire is stronger than ever and the energy is harder to shift.

'You ever been married?'

'No.'

'Good man. Me neither. But I've got a daughter somewhere.'

'Yeah?'

'Yeah. And I find I'm thinking about her lately. You think you won't think about it but you do. Not that I even know what she looks like.'

He has no curiosity about this. He wants to say: stop talking, Adrian, let it all go. But he knows he should be non-directive, say nothing, so he continues to blank out and lean his body into the other man's flesh.

'A girlfriend of mine got herself knocked up just as I was about to leave for a stint with the Bank of Hong Kong. I wrote when I got there but she never answered. When I got back I rang her mother but her ma's a strange old bird. She gushed at me like a silver sprinkler but wouldn't tell me where her daughter was.'

Stephen is holding him now, his arms around the burly chest. Something, a dim recognition, flickers across his mind like an errant homing pigeon but he blinks it out of sight.

'Yeah, now I'm thinking of having a search done for her, well, not for her, for the kid. A private dick, maybe. Something like that.'

'OK. Sit up and lock your fingers behind your neck.'

It's a gentle dance, between two male bodies, one knowing, the other trusting, all other things suspended in that moment of preparation for the final corrections. Knees wide apart, the masseur is balanced on his haunches. With a gentle manoeuvre of his right knee, he cracks his client's back, a loud click, click, click in the thoracic vertebrae. There's a moment's silence, while the masseur listens for unspoken messages, and then he lowers the client, smoothly, onto the mat. 'OK, just relax.' And taking the client's balding head in his hands he twists it, gently from side to side, releasing the neck. This is a good result. This is the first time the neck has released at all. 'Just rest quietly now,' he says. 'Take your time.'

Adrian's wallet lies on the floor, at arm's length. Soon, languorously, he will slide his fingers into the expensive doeskin and extract a single black and white note, and then, without turning his head, or opening his eyes, he will raise his arm and offer it aloft to his masseur, who will take it and slip it into his pocket. And leave his client, in the dark, resting on the floor, light-headed, light-bodied, in a kind of trance, a drifting half-sleep, so that when the client wakes, at midnight, he'll forget, momentarily, who he is.

●

9.40 p.m. Down William Street the whores prop on littered corners, their gothic reflections ghosting in the windows of the luxury car salons that line the street. *Porsche Daimler BMW Jaguar.* Black leather shorts and strappy platform sandals and black kohl under the eyes and glitter bras that expose their navels and the temperature has dropped in one of those sudden changes that herald an early autumn storm and they shiver and fold their arms over their breasts and look up and down the street for the comfort of a cruising car. The street is lined with ageing, high-rise hotels that suffer from concrete fatigue. Adrian would never come here: he would patronise one of the more exclusive houses in Riley Street where the women are *gorgeous* (quoting Adrian) and wear designer clothes and speak three languages and ask the client for advice on their share portfolios.

It's still not completely dark, the last traces of orange glow lingering in a charcoal sky. Driving slowly now down the blackening hill of Bright Street, Stephen thinks he sees a furtive figure flit from one bush to another in one of the gardens. As he cranes his neck to look back, the shadowy figure moves again. It's a woman, not quite old but beyond middle age, little and thin and wearing something odd, something long, down to her ankles. A nightdress?

Could this be the madwoman, Estelle? Out tonight to tap on a window and poke some chocolates under the chin of a drowsy child? He turns away, disturbed by something in her demeanour, something abject and yet predatory.

As he turns his key in the lock he hears the sound of a male voice coming from the kitchen, a voice which is abruptly terminated as his footsteps echo in the hall. The tape clicks off. So, she's working on her tapes tonight, transcribing some poor fool who has leapt willingly into the cannibal's pot; been lured into patronising her with the vanity of his thoughts. Who are these people? And why does this practice continue to annoy him?

Bending to give her a kiss, he ignores the tape-recorder sitting on the table between them. She returns his kiss, distractedly. How are you? he asks, but before she can answer, the phone rings. Knowing that there is only one person who ever rings this late — her mother — he wanders off to take a shower. When he returns the kitchen is empty.

Padding softly down the hall he pauses to look in on Camille who is breathing hoarsely through her open mouth but is otherwise undisturbed. In the next room Marita is sitting up in bed, reading.

'That was Ros on the phone,' she says. 'She wanted to talk about our visit.'

'Oh.'

'Yeah. She thinks you seem like a bit of a dark horse.'

He sits on the edge of the bed, strands of wet hair falling into his eyes. 'What's that supposed to mean?'

'If I know Mother it means that she thinks you mightn't prove to be very manageable, by her. She said: "Someone like Stephen is always a bit of a risk." ' Imitating the energetic, patrician tones of her mother and raising one eyebrow in a sardonic arc.

'I suppose she'll be dropping in soon to keep an eye on me.'

'You don't have to worry about that. She hates coming here. This area is "dismal", this house is "too dark". And anyway, I don't ask her.'

Stephen doesn't respond. 'I saw that woman, tonight,' he says. 'The one that prowls the street. What's her name?'

'Estelle.'

'Yeah, Estelle.'

'What was she doing?'

'It was hard to see. She was in someone's front garden, at least I think it was her. There was someone there. Whoever it was was lurking behind a bush.'

Marita frowns. 'I don't know what to do about her,' she says.

'What do you mean, "do" about her? It's not your problem.'

She stares up at him with one of her black, troubled looks. 'I could end up like that.'

'A bag lady?'

'She's not a bag lady, Stephen. She has a home. And that awful old man who sits on the verandah and grunts at her. Have you seen him? I think she's desperate to get away from him. She does her Christian duty as a daughter by day and breaks out at night . . .' Her voice trails off.

'How could you possibly end up like that?' he says.

'How do any of us know how we'll end up?' she says quietly, almost to herself.

He smiles at her, indulgently. 'Not all old women are eccentric. And besides, you don't know what Estelle has had to deal with.'

'I don't know what *I* might have to deal with. What if something happened to Camille? Then it would be easy to go mad, abandon the house, walk the streets all night . . .'

He changes the subject. 'How *was* Camille today?'

'So-so. A little tired. How was your client?'

'OK.' He doesn't like to gossip about his clients; it could break an important spell.

Marita takes the hint and picks up her book to resume her reading.

'What's the book? Still *Jane Eyre*, eh? I wouldn't have picked you for a slow reader.'

She pulls a face at him.

'You've been reading it ever since I came here.'

'I've read it before. More than once. I dip into it. Pick it up, put it down.'

'Why? What's the fascination?'

'Well . . .' she begins, and then stops. 'What's that?'

'What's what?'

'I heard a noise.'

'Where?'

'The front garden.'

He gets up and walks, naked, to the window and peers through a chink in the curtains. It's Estelle, standing at the gate with her hand on the latch, but as he watches she seems to have second thoughts; she turns, shuffles across the road and unlatches the gate of the house opposite. There, hovering beneath the grim steel awning, she taps on a front window.

'Basia? Basia? Are you asleep, love? Are you asleep? I've got some chocolates for you.'

A harsh male voice swears in a foreign tongue. Estelle starts, and clutching her box of chocolates to her chest she scurries over to the gate and out into the street.

'Who was it?'

'Estelle.'

'Estelle!' The name comes out somewhere between a sigh and a groan.

Something in the tone of her voice unsettles him. Soon she'll begin to toss in the bed. After a while she'll say that she can't sleep and get up and go out into the kitchen and leave him.

'Read to me,' he says.

'Why?'

'I don't know. Take your mind off things. Show me why this *Jane Eyre* is so fantastic.'

Jane Eyre lies open on the bed. She gazes at him for a moment, semi-distracted, and then picks up the book. 'You'll be surprised,' she says, 'it's quite gripping.' As she begins to read, he climbs into bed beside her and rests his arm across her bare thigh.

'*It was yet night, but July nights are short: soon after midnight, dawn comes.*'

'July nights are short?'

'We're in the Northern Hemisphere, you loon.'

'Oh, of course. This is *English* literature.'

She ignores him, and picks up where she left off. '"*It cannot be too early to commence the task I have to fulfil,*" thought I. I rose: I was dressed; for I had taken off nothing but my shoes. I knew where to find in my drawers some linen, a locket, a ring. In seeking these articles I encountered the beads of a pearl necklace Mr.*'

Rochester had forced me to accept a few days ago. I left that; it was not mine: it was the visionary bride's who had melted in air. The other articles I made up in a parcel; my purse, containing twenty shillings (it was all I had), I put in my pocket: I tied on my straw bonnet, pinned my shawl, took the parcel and my slippers, which I would not put on yet, and stole from my room.'

She stops, and looks up, as if listening for someone. After a minute's silence she resumes. 'I would have got past Mr. Rochester's chamber without a pause; but my heart momentarily stopping its beat at that threshhold, my foot was forced to do also. No sleep was there: the inmate was walking restlessly from wall to wall; and again and again he sighed while I listened. There was a heaven — a temporary heaven — in this room for me, if I chose: but I had to go in and to say, "Mr. Rochester, I will love and live with you through life till death," and a fount of rapture would spring to my lips. I thought of this.

'That kind master, who could not sleep now, was waiting with impatience for day. He would send for me in the morning: I should be gone. He would have me sought for: vainly. He would feel himself forsaken; his love rejected: he would suffer; perhaps grow desperate. I thought of this too. My hand moved towards the lock: I caught it back and glided on.'

At this point she pauses in her reading. 'Well?' she asks, softly. And receiving no reply looks down at the dark head resting on the pillow beside her. Stephen is fast asleep.

4

Estelle

Sunday afternoon. It's just on four and the Shiatsu Centre is almost empty. Stephen and a few of the other masseurs are tidying up; folding sheets, straightening futons, re-arranging brochures into neat piles. Eva is standing at the window in her loose white cotton pants and white cotton shirt, her blonde hair pulled back in a smooth knot. Today has been the first Open Day of the year and Eva has finally signalled her approval of him by inviting him to join the more experienced practitioners in demonstrating their skills to the public.

'Stephen.'

He looks up. She is beckoning him over and he joins her at the window where they look out over the city, hazy today with yellow smog.

'We're having a farewell party for Brigid tomorrow. Did you know?'

Yes, he did. 'I've been thinking about the mat,' he says, adding, 'a lot.' In case she thinks him too casual.

'But? You have a problem?'

'I have no money saved, well, some, but not enough. I'm not sure what I would live on while I built up a clientele.'

'Well, you will have to tell me soon, or someone else will take it.' She is, as always, a little abrupt.

'Fair enough.'

'Is there something else, some other problem besides money?'

'I'd like . . .' He stops. What is he presuming here?

'Yes?'

'I'd always planned, sometime, on going to study in Kyoto.'

'Well, yes, that is a good idea.' She looks at him appraisingly.

'But it costs money. And I'm likely to earn more money as a clerk than as a practitioner here. I think.'

'How do you know? You may do very well. You know, you should approach this with more confidence, more optimism.' She pauses. 'Does a clerk earn very much?'

'No.'

'Well, then, it could take you a very long time to save the money for Kyoto and meanwhile,' she shrugs, 'your skills are not developing as they might. You will not develop as a practitioner.'

'I realise that,' he says.

Then again, how strong is his desire? How badly does he want to go to Kyoto? It would mean leaving Marita (and Camille) for an indefinite period. When he was living alone, like a monk, everything seemed simple. Now that he's living with a woman and a child, he's confused.

'You don't like this clerk's job, do you?'

He shakes his head, and stares at his feet. 'No.'

'Being in too much of a hurry is not good, of course,' he hears her say, 'but equally, too much delay is not good either.' When he looks up she has turned away from him and is staring out the window. 'You know, Stephen,' she says, with an air of dismissive finality, 'you cannot afford to let anything stand in the way of your personal evolution.'

●

4.35 p.m. Hot bitumen and the air thick with diesel. He is in a good mood now as he turns the corner into Bright Street. Despite his wariness about the mat he is elated at Eva's inclusion of him in the Open Day and at the subtle change in her demeanour; she treats him now more as an assistant rather than as a student. He feels a light buzzing sensation in his chest, a sense that things are beginning to change, but that there is no real urgency; if he doesn't take this mat, another will come up soon; the important thing is that change is underway, and his life is coming together; his destiny, at first wayward and perverse, and then latterly, stalled, is coming into clearer focus. And he is looking forward to a quiet meditation and a peaceful meal outside in the courtyard with Marita and Camille. He'll try out some corn burgers on Camille, and he'll fry them, in deference to her love of fried food, omitting the eggs of course, and binding them with chickpea flour which absorbs hardly any of the oil but leaves a crisp coating on the outer, and for dessert . . . well, dessert is always more of a problem. Since sugar in any form is out of the question it remains a major site of confrontation and though he tries dish after dish, and any quantity of rice malt as a sweetener, Camille is not seduced.

Approaching Marita's house now he observes a small figure sitting outside the gate. It's little Basia, who has set up a scratched plywood card-table and is selling things to a hot, empty street. There is a big paper sign stuck to the picket fence which says, in crude lettering, S H O P. A fat toothless woman stares across from the garden opposite. 'You can't do that!' she shouts at Basia. 'You need a license. Wait and see, the cops'll come and take you away!'

Basia scowls. She is eleven, twelve maybe, with dark hair pulled back in an old-fashioned clip. Unsettled by her persecutor she shifts on her packing-case stool and glances down at the paint-speckled bitumen. On her stall is a cheap harlequin statue, a pink plastic piggy-bank, a brass alarm clock, a plastic spanner and some glass beads.

Last week Basia locked herself in the house for three days. An only child, her parents leave her alone at seven in the morning, six days a week, returning from the factory at six-thirty in the evening. Basia wakes to an empty house and prepares her own breakfast. Who knows if she goes to school? One day, walking up the street, they saw her peering out at them through the slatted blinds.

Staring at Basia's stall he decides to buy something, a red plastic nutcracker. Basia looks at a point just to the side of him, as if focussing on something in the distance, clouds maybe, an impending storm. 'That's forty cents,' she says. In her shape, her air, she reminds him of a photograph he'd seen once, of those little old women who sell from rough wooden tables in small towns by the Danube, a long way from the pink hibiscus, the narrow terraces, the white light and the hot sun.

While he is shuffling his change, Camille comes out of the house. She smiles at him; a frank, welcoming smile that takes him by surprise. This has been a good day and still, evidently, has some pleasures in store for him. Basia looks up, briefly, then back at her wares. Back to business.

'What are you doing, Basia?' asks Camille.

'What's it look like?' says Basia; hostile, matronly.

Camille is younger, and in that at least at a disadvantage. 'What have you got?' she asks him. He shows her the nutcracker.

'That's pretty, Basia,' she says. She wants to be kind, to not sneer.

'This your mum's boyfriend?' asks Basia.

Camille shrugs. 'Sort of.'

Stephen gives her a friendly shove. 'What do you mean, *sort of?*'

'You *know*,' she says, churlish, laughing.

As always in the inner west, the late afternoon is the hottest part of the day, the heat trapped in the narrow streets, too far from the harbour to be dispersed by breezes off the water. Marita is in the laundry, sorting the washing. She offers him some iced tea but he demurs. 'I'll meditate first,' he says, 'and then we can have an early dinner.' 'Fine,' she says, and he walks back down the hallway to the dark front room where, in his customary ritual, he re-arranges the furniture, unrolls his mat and assumes the lotus position. For a time he can hear splashing and yelling from the paddling pool in the courtyard. Then, silence. Suddenly a loud sob breaks into the house, and the hoarse, heaving sound of Camille crying in the kitchen. He would like to ignore this, but the sobbing persists and he can't hear Marita and wonders if she is over at Maria's.

He gets up and walks, hesitantly, into the hallway. Camille is whimpering. 'Basia says I'm not a good friend because I won't let her wear my new dress.' The back door is open; he can see out into the garden. Marita is in the doorway, her hand over her eyes against the glare. Basia is standing at the base of the steps, in wet shorts, trying to squeeze into Camille's favourite dress, a rare present from her grandmother, a hot pink and lime green tube of elasticised silk jersey, hand-painted in a pattern of gum leaves and wattle flowers and trimmed with a spectacular lizard's frill in shocking pink. Into this Basia has squashed her doughy shoulders and barrel trunk so forcefully, so uncompromisingly, that the seams of the dress have begun to tear and the lime-green gum leaves are a blur.

Marita's face is livid. In a few strides she reaches Basia and with a sudden jerk lifts the hem of the gum-leaf dress and yanks it over her head with a violent wrench.

'Go home! Go home, Basia! Get out of my house at once and don't come back! Go home *now*.'

Stephen looks on, curious. There is an unexpected ferocity in this.

Basia stands her ground impassively. 'There are some things, Marita,' she says, in an oddly mature voice, 'that I need to talk to you about.'

But Marita is screaming, '*Get out, get out, get out!*' The dress hangs limply by her side, a flashy rag.

Camille watches from the doorway, warily.

Basia looks for a moment disconsolate. Then, with a fat, surly dignity she walks, chin in the air, through the kitchen, dripping a trail of water down the dark hallway and out the front door.

Camille is in two minds whether to whimper over her dress or console her mother who seems, suddenly, to have gone over on to some demented plane.

'Camille,' says Marita, in a low voice, 'go inside and practise your piano.'

'What's the matter?' he calls down the hallway.

'Look,' she says, 'look at it! Her grandmother never gives her anything. The first thing in ages and now it's ruined!' She tosses the dress into the laundry sink and flings a chair out from the kitchen table, subsiding there with her head in her hands.

This episode makes no sense to him. There is something here, a subtext, that baffles him. Is it the dress? The heat? Basia? At times like this he feels that he is invisible, that as a man he understands nothing, that this female hysteria is some secret mystery. It seems to gush from nowhere and to be about nothing he can recognise; another language, like hieroglyphics, and he feels the thick, viscous cling of it, a dull drag, as if he is back in his mother's house. There's something here that could get out of control, he thinks; it's like a virus. He puts his arm around her shoulder. 'What's the matter?'

She looks up at him, white-faced. 'I was mean to that child, ' she says. 'I behaved despicably. I try to like her but I can't. I want to give her a refuge but she's sullen and she resents Camille, she resents us and I understand that but . . .' her voice trails off, 'but she *provokes* me.'

'Why don't you take Camille for a walk,' he says, 'while I make dinner.'

It's 8.50 in the warm evening and the house has begun to mellow. Camille is in an appeasing mood and makes some effort with the fried corn burgers after eating two bowls of miso soup (which she has actually grown to like, probably, he guesses, because of its saltiness). Marita, on the other hand, is flushed and listless and complains that her body aches. After dinner, with the streetlights burnishing the small stained-glass windows, they sit in front of the television, all three on the one couch. This is the first time Camille has deigned to sit beside him and Marita and this small detail does not go unnoticed, at least by him. At nine, Camille goes obediently to bed, without the usual protests, sensing her mother's distress and wanting to play some role in maintaining calm.

He suggests an early night for all of them but Marita says no, she wants to watch a documentary on nature, something intriguingly entitled *Purity and*

Danger. It starts in a few minutes, she says, and when it's over they can go to bed. In that febrile way of hers that is both attentive and distracted, she curls her feet up tightly beneath her and stares at the small screen on which, at this moment, a camera is zooming in on an industrial wasteland somewhere in eastern Germany. As he puts his arm around her shoulders, her body slumps, is tired, but alert too, in its resistant way. The TV says: *With today's pollution there can be no clear-cut distinction between the special and the ordinary, the sacred and the secular.* Yes, he thinks, Nature is damaged, perhaps fatally, and he begins to stroke her neck. The TV says: *We cannot rely on tradition or the old rituals to tell us what is clean and unclean, nurturing and destructive.* Resting his chin against the top of her head he kisses her hair lightly; she gives a little, he strokes her breast and her chest rises and falls in a reluctant sigh. *A swim in the ocean is no longer cleansing; beneath that pretty hill there might be a toxic dump; in the sacred river are mercury and organo-chlorides and the fish are bloated . . .* Yes, he wants to make love now, here on the couch with the rough moquette abrasive against their skin . . .

Suddenly Marita stiffens, and jerks her head towards the door.

'What's that?'

'What?'

'Listen. That's Camille talking.'

He can hear Camille's voice. 'Yes, please,' it says, politely, 'yes, I would.'

Then a woman's voice, coming from the front garden. A muffled voice, indistinct.

Marita looks at her watch. 'Ten o'clock,' she whispers. And then: 'Estelle!' She jumps up, as if bitten, and strides down the hall.

Taut with desire he follows her to the front door. From the corner of his eye he can see Camille, in her nightdress, standing at the open window of her bedroom, her arms resting on the sill. And sure enough, out there, loitering in the garden, is Estelle, also in her nightdress and cradling in her arm her box of *Rose*'s chocolates. From behind her grey-framed spectacles, she blinks at Camille like some startled bird. 'Here you are, dear,' she says, opening her right palm to reveal a cluster of gaudily wrapped sweets, 'a present from the Blessed Virgin.'

'*Estelle!* Estelle, what are you doing here!'

Abruptly the old woman turns and blinks in their direction. 'Oh!' she starts. 'Sorry, dear. Sorry, love. Only skiting.'

'Estelle you mustn't come here at this time of night. I've *told* you before, it's too late. *It's too late!*'

'Sorry, love, sorry.' For a long moment she stares at them and then begins to shuffle backwards across the grass, and into the picket fence, oblivious of the tall monstera plants whose giant leaves brush against her hips in a quick swish of trespass. Edging sideways to the gate she backs out into the streetlight: there she stops and stares distractedly up the dark street as if looking for a sign.

They wait for a moment, and then, as they turn to go indoors they hear a rasping croak from behind the fence. 'It's Dad,' she moans, 'it's Dad. He beats me with his stick!' The fence shudders, as if someone is shaking it in a rage. '*He beats me with his stick,*' she groans, '*he beats me with his stick!*'

Marita stands, frozen in the doorway, looking out into the dark street. Together they listen, as the shuffling steps begin to recede. Not until she is satisfied that Estelle has gone does Marita close the door.

'What was she saying to Camille?' he asks.

'God knows! That's what she was talking about, God! The Blessed Virgin!' Her eyes are a black flare of alarm. 'I could hear her saying, "The Blessed Virgin watches over you." That's what she said. "Don't worry about evil, pet, evil is all around us, but the Blessed Virgin watches over you." *I heard her say that!*' Marita is hissing at him in the dark hallway. 'Evil! *Evil!*' Her eyes glitter.

She turns and snaps on the light in Camille's room. 'And you, Miss, into bed!'

The child wanders, insouciant, away from the window, and yawns. 'Why does Estelle want to give me some chocolates?' she asks.

'Because she's mad!' says her mother, tucking the bedsheet in with a wrench that sends the mattress askew. And flicking off the light she thumps down the hallway into the bathroom. And turns both bath taps on at full bore. 'It's pathetic!' she shouts, 'it's so pathetic I can't stand it! I'm sick of this street, sick of it! I'm going to wash all this psychic dreck off me!'

Two outbursts of hysteria in the one day. And it began so well. He sits outside in the courtyard, on the broken plastic recliner, while Marita floats on the surface of her bath. Closing his eyes on the heavy scent of the frangipani and the whirr of the mosquitoes he lets his head empty out into the swimming dark of unconscious night until a thought summons him inside; the image of Marita; her white body, hot and steaming.

Inside she is lying on the couch, flushed and apathetic. He puts his hand on her forehead and her skin gives off a kind of febrile charge. She writhes irritably, flinching from him, and complains that her back is sore. He feels a sudden impulse to leave, to just walk out the door. Instead, he sits behind her and, resting her shoulders against his chest, he begins to massage her neck. She is rigid, shivering. 'Come to bed,' he says. While her body trembles like this he wants to make love to her, to annihilate all this hysteria in a rush of blood.

At one in the morning she wakes and complains of raking pains in her limbs, a throbbing in her lower back: her neck aches, a hot pain jabs inside her ear.

Some exorcism needs to be performed here, he thinks, and I'll have to do it.

Out in the kitchen he closes his eyes and summons up Oshawa's book on macrobiotic home remedies. He can visualise each page, knows it almost by heart. She thinks she might have the flu, in which case he should make something pungent, a hot drink of miso and chopped spring onion. But though flushed, she has no fever, though clearly she has muscle spasm in her back, and possibly acute inflammation, and the remedy for this is equally simple: a ginger compress. Of course. A ginger compress! He looks around for the ginger. Damn, they are almost out of it. He buys only small quantities of late since Camille can't abide it in anything. Where would he get some at this time of night? It's almost two in the morning, and there aren't any all-night Chinese supermarkets. Would there be some left from his old store at Glebe?

He bends over Marita who appears to be asleep on the couch, then he walks softly down the hall and out the front door. On the way up the street he keeps an eye out for Estelle but the street is deserted. On the drive over to his sister's house he is distracted but not unhappy, though he is tired, very tired, he realises, becoming for the first time aware of dry eyes and fatigue in the muscles of his arms. Yet in a curious way he is looking forward to this. The

Toxteth Estate is empty and, as always at night, possessed of a gothic gloom. Once inside the house he becomes impatient, flicking on the kitchen light and rummaging in the fridge. Nothing. Ah, but there's one medium length stick — knotty and a little shrivelled from age — in the fruit bowl. He shoves it in his pocket, flicks off the light, deadlocks the door, pulls it to as quietly as is possible and, mentally rehearsing the various stages in making a ginger compress, walks quickly to the car.

Marita looks up at him from her restless disarray on the couch, flushed and black-eyed. 'I thought you'd gone again,' she says.

'Really,' he says drily, and then relents. 'I went to get some ginger. For a compress.'

'Oh no, Stephen, not one of your quack remedies! Not at this time of night!' She groans, but her protest is half-hearted and he will ignore it; he will soothe her with his patience. When she's like this she reminds him of his mother and he will meet her anger with the same mute detachment with which he once weathered *her* scorn. The sooner he gets this compress applied the better: he's never done one before and he's curious to see if it works.

In the kitchen he puts a large pot of water on the stove to boil. After grating the ginger into a pile he ties it into the corner of a tea towel, then dunks the towel into the water and waits for the pale cloudy juice to stream out into a brew. As it does he lowers a flannel into the simmering water, lets it soak for a few seconds, lifts it out with tongs and, holding it gingerly (he smiles at his own joke) between the merest tip of his finger and thumb, squeezes as much water out of it as he can, using the tongs. Then he drops the cloth into another tea towel and shapes it into a roll. This he carries into the living room.

For a moment he thinks that Marita is asleep but she opens her eyes and gives him that angry reproachful glare of the sick.

'Turn over onto your stomach.'

'Why?'

'I've made you a ginger compress. I'm going to lay it across your lower back.'

Her shoulders heave in a long sigh but offer no further resistance. She moves listlessly onto her midriff and rests her head on her arms. He eases her old silk kimono down to her waist so that it sits in folds at the base of her slender white back.

'Tell me if it burns.'

She shakes her head to indicate that it's OK.

Knowing the heat will disperse quickly he keeps the pot on just below simmer and for the next half hour lays compresses on her pale, prickly skin, at two minute intervals, until she is flushed with the heat.

Standing in her dim kitchen, to the wail of early morning sirens and the occasional sound of glass smashing on the road outside the pub, a block away, he keeps the big pot simmering and drops his towels, one after the other, into the steaming brew.

Twelve compresses later she kisses his hand, limply, and says that she is soothed, but that she does not want to move, that she wants to stay and sleep on the couch.

Sitting on her bed, alone, he sets the alarm for six, undresses, and lies on top of the sheets. Why is he exhausted? Something here is unresolved, something baffling. He should find a soothing image and meditate on it. Dead fish floating on the surface of the sacred river? No, no. Must all landscapes be inflected with menace? This afternoon he had been in his favourite place, Chinatown; he had trod, barefoot, like a priest, on the polished boards of Eva's room in Chinatown, that golden floor the colour of honey, the sunlight through the open window, the practitioners in white, and outside, on the street, the Chinese grocers and piles of exotic greens. Closing his eyes he thinks of mustard greens, of making a poultice with greens bought fresh from the wide wooden boxes on the street, and he has a vivid flash of a bunch of limp greens arranged on the white flesh of her spine, nestling in the curve, the steam rising in delicate trails of mist, the whole beautifully composed, like a giant surreal sashimi. A succulent dish of white flesh and limp steaming greens.

In the morning he finds her asleep on the couch with her mouth open. Her face is pale and wasted. He carries her into bed where she wakes and writhes, fretfully. 'I want some Panadol,' she pleads. 'I can't stand this throbbing in my back. Please get me some Panadol.'

'It'll only put a strain on your kidneys and take longer for you to get better. Try and do without it.' She starts to cry. He feels momentarily defeated. The Panadol looms large in his mind's eye. Camille comes in. 'What's the matter, Mum?' she says.

'She's sick,' he says.

Camille goes off to her room and returns with an armful of books. 'I'll read to her,' she says, 'that always cheers her up.' She pauses, thoughtfully. 'And after that I'll take her in a tray.'

'A tray?'

'When you're sick, you always have a tray.' And she climbs into bed beside her mother, props her agile body against the wall and begins matter-of-factly to read.

In the kitchen he makes Camille's breakfast, buckwheat pancakes, the dish he knows she is least likely to argue with as long as he allows her to drench it in maple syrup. Camille is on her best behaviour; she seems to have made up her mind, as children sometimes do, to be a third force, wise and co-operative.

After breakfast he walks her up the hill to school. She is quiet and seems to be thinking. He waits for her to comment on this troubled night, waits for enquiries re the Blessed Virgin. None come. 'Why is Mum sick?' she asks. In a way this is a harder question to answer than one about the Virgin. It's not often she asks him a question; hitherto her energy has been spent on resisting his unsolicited answers to questions she never intends to frame, that have never even crossed her mind. It's a rare opening for him to give her his whole philosophy of life but she is, of course, too young, and it's only another fifty metres before they reach the iron gates of the school.

'She's just got a backache,' he says. 'She'll be alright in a few days. When the body, or the mind, gets too tired or too stressed it gives itself a holiday by getting sick. It forces you to stop, to rest. You eliminate all the toxins that have built up for a while and that stops you getting really sick, seriously sick, later on. We have to see illness as positive, instead of negative. And we have to treat the illness by supporting it, not denying it by taking lots of drugs . . .' He can feel himself winding up but it's only ten metres to the iron gates.

Camille looks thoughtful, abstracted. Perhaps she's ruminating on the Blessed Virgin. Someday he'll have to talk to her about the Spirit of the Universe and how it doesn't have a mother (and why some people feel they have to invent one for it). But at that moment she sees one of her friends and her face breaks out of its trance. 'Flora!' she cries and darts forward, her luminous pink nylon schoolbag bouncing on her back. 'See ya, Stephen.'

She stops, looks back. 'Thanks for walking me to school,' she says politely. And runs off into the yard.

He continues on, down the hill and across the road to Petersham station and the clapped-out red rattler that will carry him, sharp-eyed and wide-awake with fatigue, to work.

5

cake

Marita opens the front door, walks out into the sunstruck street and instantly feels lightheaded in the glare. It's a steep walk up the hill, especially as she is lugging her tape-recorder, the big black ghetto-blaster that she means to replace but never does. When at last she reaches Estelle's house she stops and leans against the gate, feeling a little giddy in the glare: the white tiled steps, the red tin on the roofs; in this heat everything seems almost to vibrate in a shimmering haze.

She knocks on Estelle's door, several times, and finally a thin voice, muffled from behind the wood, calls out: 'Who's there?' The door opens. 'Yes?'

Estelle's house: she is reluctant, almost, to enter it. In the dark hallway hangs a picture of the bleeding heart of Jesus, that small patch of blood and fire, obscenely neat; two precise drops of blood, like comic book tears, drip, drip; nothing messy, like suburban murder.

She stares at the portrait: Estelle stares at her. Up close, her small, pointed face has a look less of timidity than of baffled disdain.

Shuffling in her slippers, Estelle ushers her into the tiny front parlour, crammed with statuary of the Virgin Mary. On a blackwood planter in the near corner stands a large plaster figure, four feet high, in blue and gold with lilies strewn across the bare virgin feet. Next to it, the Edwardian mantelpiece is crowded with various effigies in garishly painted plaster, and little plastic grottoes, pale blue and white, that open and close onto painted paper images. Marita thinks of her mother who would wince at the sight of them, she who loves the *natural* religions of *earthy* peoples, with images that are *fierce* or *ecstatic* — the giant totems of the Sepik River people, say, with their glaring eyes and bared teeth — these plaster virgins are so passive, so melancholy, so *suburban*.

Estelle is staring at her. 'How are you, dear?' she says, and blinks. She is standing with her hands clasped together on her chest. Marita observes that for a small woman she has large feet. 'I'm well, thank you,' she says, perhaps too loudly because Estelle puts her fingers to her lips and says: 'Shhhh, dear. Dad's asleep. We mustn't disturb him.'

'About last night. . .' she whispers.

Estelle closes her eyes and begins, piously, to nod. And nod, and nod and nod and nod. This goes on for some time. How do I stop her? thinks Marita.

She puts her large, black machine down on the floor which is covered in frenetic red whorls of floral carpet.

'Estelle?'

Estelle opens her eyes, blinks, and looks down.

'Estelle, I'd like to talk to you about the Blessed Virgin.'

'Why, dear?' She sounds so sane, so reasonable.

'Because I'm interested. It's just that last night it was late, and Camille . . .' Camille gets very tired. And when she's tired she has trouble with her breathing.'

'I know, dear.'

Does she? How does she know?

'So, do you think we could talk a little, now?'

Estelle blinks again, with her hands still clasped in front of her chest like a child about to give a recitation. 'I don't think so, dear. Not now. Do you have any cake? I'd like a little cake if you have some. A nice slice of cake, that would be lovely.'

'Um . . . I thought you might like to explain . . .'

'Not today, dear. No thank you. Just a little cake. That would do nicely.'

'I don't have any cake at the moment,' she says, taken aback, 'but I could help you make some, if you like. Can I go to the shop for you?'

'Oh no, dear, no, I never make cake, never. Never learned how. I could give you a chocolate, though, if you'd like one. Would you like a chocolate?'

Noon. Outside the air is heavier and the street quivers in a film of heat. Marita walks down the hill, her eyes half closed to the glare, to the hot shimmer of russet and gold shrimp bushes, the overhanging red gum, scarlet hibiscus, wild tomato plants and white tiles that reflect the light.

In her kitchen cupboard she probes an open packet of white flour looking for weevils. It's an old purchase that she made before Stephen arrived in her kitchen with his many prohibitions. She doesn't imagine Estelle would like his heavy stoneground wholemeal that refuses to rise to satisfying heights and so she picks at the crushed flap of the white flour packet and looks for clinging threads of moth nest but no, it's fine, *superfine*, and she carries it to the bench and begins to measure it into a sifter.

Creaming the butter and sugar is the tedious part, especially when done by hand, and her wrists are fine and tend to ache after a short time. The best part is beating in the eggs and the perfect yellow gloss of the batter, the seamless fusion of elements, like an alchemist's meld, made ordinary again by the lumbering quality of the flour, no matter how fine. It drifts through the sifter and sits on the surface like a miniature sandhill until swept into the batter by the curve of a rubber spatula, the raisins swept up like black jewels, uncut. While she's mixing (she has decided, glancing at the blackspotted bananas in the bowl, on banana and raisin cake) she listens to an old tape she made of Mother, recalling her childhood memory of Einstein. ' . . . though he was a high-priest of reason, and seemed at first, grey and diffident, he had a wonderful male smell, and a magical aura, like that of certain witchdoctors I later met in Africa . . .'

At times she thinks there is some kind of code in here and it's simple, really, she just hasn't learned to decipher it. What she has deciphered is the shorthand of cookbooks. It's astonishing how easily you can reproduce a perfect cake simply by following the words on the page. Of many other things in the kitchen this isn't true; you need to have it shown to you, need to have demonstrated what the right 'texture' is, or the necessary degree of 'elasticity', but one of her first sources of gratification once she'd moved here had been discovering this, the reliability of cake. No matter how cryptic the recipe or erratic the oven, it always seemed to turn out right. As a child she had sat at the David Jones Christmas show for children and watched the magician pour all sorts of rubbish into his top hat — then, with a flourish of the magic rod, the incantation of the magic words and a puff of smoke, he had turned the hat upside down to produce a perfect cake. Year after year, it had been her favourite trick. How ironic that Stephen should be so disapproving of the one thing in the kitchen that seems to come naturally to her, to cause her no angst . . .

A shrill bell rings out from above the oven door. Could forty minutes have passed already? She lifts the cake from the oven, raps the base of the tin lightly with a knife and the steamy yellow mound flops obligingly onto the cooling rack. At that moment raucous shouts break in from the yard. It's Camille, racketing down the side lane and into the kitchen. Behind her is another child who Marita hasn't seen before, a robust girl with a short black bob and black, gleeful eyes. Camille leans into the doorway giggling while the dark one drops her school bag onto the floor without ceremony and says, 'Hi, I'm Flora.'

So this is the new friend.

'Hello,' says Marita, 'do you live around here?'

'Over in Waratah Street. Number 35. We've been here four weeks.'

'Flora's just come from London,' says Camille, twisting on one thin leg. She is clearly impressed by this.

'Oh, so you're English,' says Marita.

'Sort of.' Flora flicks her short black hair out of her eyes and takes on the solemn look children wear when imparting important information. 'One of my mothers is English, the other one's Australian.'

'You have *two* mothers?' Marita asks, absent-mindedly sifting some icing sugar into a cream bowl.

'Of course.' Flora is almost scornful.

It could take Marita a while to unravel this, this riddle of the sphinx, were it not for the fact that Flora is nothing if not a forthcoming child.

'Kay and Lizzie, that's my two mothers, are lesbians. I grew in Lizzie's tummy and my sperm donor, his name's Ron, well, he's Jewish, and he and his family had a narrow escape from the Nazis.'

All this tumbles out in her light husky child's voice and Camille, well, Camille is floored. She looks at Flora with a kind of naive wonder. It's not that she doesn't already know about the two mothers, it's Flora's boldness in the telling that impresses her.

'Oh,' says Marita, whisking the melted butter into the icing sugar. 'Just as well he did escape from the Nazis.'

'Why?'

'Well, otherwise you wouldn't be here, would you?'

'Oh, they'd have found someone else,' says Flora. Looking about her with a confident, curious gaze, her eyes come to rest on the red and black Modigliani print of a reclining nude, Blu-tacked above the freezer. She points: 'That painting's sexist,' she says. Camille titters nervously.

Marita is beginning to enjoy Flora. She has a sturdy waist, graceful, rounded arms and a confident tilt to the chin like a certain kind of European woman in her prime. She stands with her legs apart and her stomach thrust forward and when she smiles she has an engaging air of demonic glee.

'You think so, do you? Well, just because she hasn't got any clothes on doesn't mean it's sexist.'

'Yes, it does.'

'It could be a celebration of the female form . . .'

'You shouldn't use the word female, that's for classifying animals, you should say woman . . .' here Flora stumbles and nods her head in self-correction, 'you should say *womanly*.' Camille looks to her mother to see how she takes this rebuke. It's one thing for her to answer back, another for a visitor to take these liberties.

'Well,' says Marita, grating some lemon rind onto a plate, 'it's what we bring to the nude that counts. Just because some men have exploited the image of the nude in the past doesn't mean that women must give up forever the possibility of celebrating their own bodies.'

She waits for Flora's practised riposte but at this point the child falters. There's a silence. Marita looks up and sees that Flora is staring at the cake.

'Can I have a piece of that cake?' she asks, shyly.

'I cooked that for someone else. A neighbour. A woman who lives up the street who's very thin. I don't think she eats properly.'

'Who's that?' asks Camille.

'Estelle.'

'Estelle! But she's got heaps of chocolates!' she protests, and turns to Flora. 'You should see them.'

But Flora is not to be distracted.

'Couldn't we just have a bit?' she persists, her eyes never straying from the plump golden mound on the cooling tray.

'I can't give someone a cake with a piece out of it, now can I?'

'Give them half. That would be fair.'

'What about a glass of milk and some fruit?' she offers, 'it would be much healthier. Sugar isn't good for you.' She can't resist resuming their ideological debate, albeit on another domain.

'Yes, well, some of it's alright, isn't it? As long as you don't have too much.'

'Stephen says sugar is a form of poison,' blurts out Camille.

'Who's Stephen?'

Camille hesitates. 'Oh, a friend,' she says airily.

'Well . . .' Flora begins, and trails off. In the face of cake, argument deserts her.

'Please can we have a piece of cake?' She looks up at Marita, still combative but not wholly sure of herself, and beginning to deflate in the face of resistance.

Marita hesitates. Flora has already presumed too much. She is a child who knows no boundaries, or pushes hard wherever she finds them.

Sensing Marita's displeasure Flora retreats into jokey parody. 'I'm *starving*,' she growls, and raises her arms and snaps her jaws in imitation of some predatory beast.

Marita laughs. How vital this child looks; shiny, full-bodied, cossetted, cocky and robust. Thinking, 'She has no need of nurturing from me,' she cuts into the still warm cake and hands Flora a slice.

And instantly regrets this generous impulse. Too late, the damage is done. Flora almost drops the warm cake, juggling it clownishly in her hands. 'Gee, thanks,' she says, and 'Mmmm, yum,' as the warm crumbs spill greedily onto her chin.

Stephen yawns into the stuffy air of the foetid bus. On one side of him an old man exudes a rank sickly sweat of alcoholic perspiration and on the other a woman sighs listlessly into the window, her head resting on her palm, her limp hair clinging to her neck in damp little curls. He'd rung the Institute tonight and said that he would not be coming in to class, that his girlfriend was sick and he wanted to get home early and see that she was alright. Is she still in bed, he wonders. He'd rung in the morning, no-one had answered and he had assumed that she was sleeping, and in the afternoon he'd had to attend a training session in Personnel under the beady eye of The Dwarf and without access to a phone.

Walking up the steep hill of Bright Street he pauses by Basia's house which this evening is closed and shuttered with no trace of life. He hopes that Basia is not at Marita's. After his all-night ministrations he is tired; he does not feel like cooking, he does not feel like a gloomy house in which two raucous girls run amok and Marita aches in her sullen bed.

But no! Here she is now, in the kitchen, relaxed and cheerful! She kisses him on the lips, lightly, and rubs the small of his back in that affectionate way she has when she is in a good mood.

'You look a lot brighter!'

'I am. I'm fine.'

The ginger compress, he thinks. Eva said it would work miracles.

'We're having a cold meal,' she says. 'It's too hot to cook. Go and meditate, and then we'll eat.'

Too relieved to argue and for once too tired to cook himself, he retires to the front parlour and unfolds his mat.

After dinner they linger at the kitchen table and she tells him of her strange visit to Estelle. 'I took my tape-recorder,' she says, as if this explains everything.

Jesus, her tape-recorder. 'Your tape-recorder?'

'Yes.'

'Why?'

'So we could talk.'

He yawns, wearily. 'Couldn't you talk *without* the tape-recorder?'

'It's not the same.'

'I give up. What did you talk about?'

'I wanted to talk about the Blessed Virgin.'

'I thought you were opposed to that kind of conversation.'

'*I* am immune to the Blessed Virgin. It's Camille I'm worried about.'

'What sort of cake?'

'Banana.'

Banana, eh? Not so bad. 'Did you put icing on it?'

'Yes, Stephen,' she sighs, 'I put icing on it.'

'Sugar will only make her worse. Stoke up her bad dreams.'

'For God's sake, Stephen, what's *in* the cake is irrelevant. It's a gesture.'

It's his turn to sigh. That's where she's wrong. What's in the cake is everything. Until we recognise that we will be unable to console one another. Will he ever get this message through to her?

Camille says: 'Ssshhh, you two. Can't you argue in the bedroom? I can't hear the TV.'

●

In bed that night, Stephen ponders the question of cake. It's that nurturing hysteria again. Eve took the apple from the Serpent and she's been making up for it ever since by feeding everyone cake. But when we bake flour it becomes oxidised and oxidisation is the *Ling* process, the beginning of death . . . of rust, and breaking down. Once again this is a strongly materialist position, of the kind Sanjay had warned him against. Of late, he has modified his thinking on this and is inclined to argue now that it's not the cake as such but what goes into it, the quality of the energy, which includes not only the character of the ingredients but the energy of the cook as well. Marita believes it to be the other way around — what is important is not the reality but the idea. The idea of transformation. This is an argument that has the potential, if he dwells on it, to confuse him. Because it's undeniable, when you think about it, that cake, like bread, is one of the most persistent symbols we have of transformation through unity, or is it unity through transformation? Alchemy. The Last Supper, and all that. And as Marita had once reminded him, many pre-industrial peoples included some kind of baked dough in their religious rites, and when this had been blessed or in some way consecrated it was broken and consumed by the worshippers, consumed in the fiery furnace of the *hara* where the cake nurtured the life force. And it is significant, he thinks, that sacred food was always cooked food, because heat was needed to create a new kind of energy, to bring about metamorphosis, the transformation that stood in for the transformation of the flesh into spirit . . . the macrobiotic tradition is right in its emphasis on the efficacy of cooked food, not raw: the food must be invested with human energy, must enter into the social, must be eaten warm to stoke up the digestive fires which are the source of the life force and everything that means, both physical and spiritual, which is why all iced food is pernicious and why he is still fighting the battle with Camille over ice-cream. Ice-cream *especially* is pernicious. He makes a mental note to explain the principle of the cooked to Camille in the morning. Perhaps he'll walk her to school again; it seems to be a natural occasion on which to have an unforced discussion of things . . .

Marita is thinking about Flora, whose commitment to being ideologically sound had wavered in the face of the cake, such that she, Marita, had warmed to her, and had cut prematurely into her peace offering and now, alas, is left with only half a cake. Still, it looks pretty, with its rich caramel crumbs and its little crests of white icing. She'll put it on a festive plate and offer it up to Estelle in the morning.

●

Hoping for better things this time, she carries her tape-recorder with her in one hand; in her other hand is the white-iced cake. But at Estelle's gate she hesitates, her smug feelings evaporating in the face of the apparition on the verandah. For this morning *he* is there, the father, looking down on her from the verandah where he presides in his wheelchair, wrapped, despite the heat, in a heavy tweed jacket. His white, close-clipped hair is almost covered by a coarse woollen cap which does not conceal his enormous ears and their long pendulous lobes. Unshaven and morose he sits with his hands clasped around the top of his stick.

'Good morning,' she says brightly and opens the gate, but he won't acknowledge her and stares out into the street. The door is ajar and before she can call out, Estelle's birdlike head appears from behind the door.

'I've brought you some cake,' she says. For some reason her words sound gauche and what before she had been pleased with now seems like a hollow gesture, not such a good idea after all.

Estelle accepts it with her thin arms outstretched. 'Oh, thank you, dear,' she says, 'how kind of you.'

Marita glances at the old man.

'Dad's not feeling himself today,' says Estelle. 'He's brooding a bit. Look Dad,' she says, holding the cake out to him as one would to a child. 'Look what Marita's brought us.'

Stiff-necked he turns his head, slowly, toward her.

'Look,' she says again, as if he's deaf and may not have heard the first time, or is senile and has to have everything repeated.

Slowly his eyes fix unfocussedly upon the cake, glowering at it as if it were some object of disgust and danger. And then, with a casual deftness Marita, trying to recall this later, cannot believe how quickly, how unexpectedly, it was done — he flicks his stick upward from the tiled floor, up beneath the plate which flips, like a frisbee, out of Estelle's hands. The women watch as the plate clatters to the floor and fractures into two equal pieces, but the cake lands, miraculously, face up, in one perfect piece.

Estelle doesn't move.

Marita blinks. Did the stick connect with the plate or did Estelle see the stick coming and drop it?

For a moment she is mesmerised by the fact that the plate has broken but the cake is intact. Then, instinctively, she takes a small step forward to retrieve the cake and at this instant, seeing her approach, the old man jabs his stick down onto the white-iced surface, splaying it into a formless mush.

Half-bent to the floor, she flinches from shock. And then, 'How dare you!' she gasps. 'How dare you!'

Estelle's face is expressionless. For a moment she gazes distractedly at the stick. Then, kneeling on the floor of the verandah, she gathers up a lump of the mush which clings to her bony fingers. Still kneeling, she nibbles like a small animal at the morsel in her hands. 'Very nice, dear. Very moist.' She extends her thin sticky fingers to her father. 'Would you like some, Dad?'

For a moment Marita is fearful that the old man will take to Estelle with his stick — kneeling, she is so vulnerable, it would take so little strength to crack it across her back — but his hands seem only to clench more tightly around the brass knob. Scowling, and biting his gums, he stares mutely out into the street.

Marita's heart is racing. The blue of the sky, the glare of the sun, the red flowers on the trellis, all are absurd, absurd, *absurd*. She should stop and say, 'Estelle, are you alright?' but she is too angry, too angry, the street has defeated her again, and she strides out through the gate and down the hill, so incensed that for a long time she must hold her breath. And then, at last at her gate, she lets go, and gasps in a sudden, heaving relief. And she could almost laugh! At least he didn't get it all! It wasn't *all* wasted. Thank God for Flora.

That night Marita takes the tape she had planned for Estelle out of the machine and throws it, yet another discard, into the dusty box under the bed. Stephen listens to the sharp crack of the plastic casing as it hits the pile. Such a harsh sound. And where on earth did she get this idea that she could capture phantoms and neutralise them in storage?

For a while they lie together in silence, listening to the noises from the street. But Marita cannot let the idea of the cake go. Perhaps her gift was flawed. 'Perhaps if I'd taken the whole cake,' she says to him . . .

He puts his arm around her. Estelle has to learn to nurture herself, he thinks, instead of prowling the street with chocolates in her demented charade of motherhood.

'It wouldn't have made any difference,' he says. And then: 'I'll bet Ros has never made a cake.'

'Never!' And they both laugh.

For a long time they lie in silence, listening to the noises from the street. Five minutes before curfew and a big 747 roars unusually low, rattling the windows. Tonight, for some reason, the street is particularly raucous. Somewhere near, glass is being smashed against a wall; they hear swearing, groaning, fists banging on a door. 'Come out, you bastard, Ray!' someone shouts, and then the inevitable sirens begin their insidious wail. The sirens, always the sirens.

Then, oddly, above it all, the sound of someone singing, a raw tenor voice, a powerful disembodied song. And suddenly the street is quiet, this voice alone pouring out into the darkness.

'Who's that?' he asks. 'He's pretty good.'

'Basia's father,' she says. 'Sometimes, on his way off to the nightshift, he sings.'

As the lingering bravura of the song fades she can hear Stephen's breathing change. He is drifting into sleep. The universe has flown inwards to the small cosmos of her bed, this cedar ship that floats on the night tides of the street. And in the black sky over the tiled rooftops a solid mooncake glows with mellow light. And tomorrow, tomorrow she will try again. She *will* make a cake for Estelle; she won't be defeated by *him*.

●

Noon again, and a second cake (sultana and walnut with orange icing). Ah, but her expedition is aborted almost before it begins. As she closes her own gate she sees a car pull up outside Estelle's house and a young priest gets out and carries his small black bag to the door. Another visit from the spiritual doctor. And it occurs to her: why should she go *there*? What good could come of it? She should invite Estelle to *her* house, not to loiter at the windows at night but to share in the sanctioned rite of afternoon tea.

In the early afternoon, when the priest's car has gone, she slips a note under Estelle's front door. I'm crazy, she thinks. I am at home too much. I am alone too much. Since I gave up work I've become a little mad.

●

Estelle sits daintily at the kitchen table, sipping her tea and eating her third slice of cake. The black tape-recorder sits at one end of the table, an unlikely accompaniment to a sanctioned rite. The tape is running. Estelle seems entirely at home, almost disconcertingly composed.

'Why did you leave the convent, Estelle?'

'Well, dear, I don't know if I should talk about that.'

'Why not?' Once the tape is running, Marita is inclined to be blunt.

Estelle stares at her, as if assessing some irregularity of feature, some significant point of asymmetry. 'Mother Superior suggested that it might be a good idea not to talk about it for a time, not until I'd prayed to the Blessed Virgin every day for guidance.'

'Oh.'

'She thought I might like to go home for a while and look after Dad.'

Silence. Estelle sips her tea.

'Because he was sick.'

'Yes, dear. And because . . .' Her voice trails off and she sighs.

'Yes?'

'And because they didn't like me in the chapel.'

In the chapel? Weren't the nuns allowed in the chapel?

'Oh, yes, they were allowed in, dear, of course they were. They were allowed in to pray. And to sing. And to clean, of course. But they weren't allowed . . . they weren't allowed . . .' Here her voice trails off in mild exasperation as if the right words simply are not available to her. 'They weren't allowed to do other things.'

'Other things?'

'Yes, dear.' Estelle sighs again, and looks around her; at the cobweb in a corner of the sloping ceiling; at the crack in the pane of red glass by the door. She looks down at her hands, brushes the crumbs from her lap, looks up again. Suddenly she becomes matter-of-fact. 'They weren't allowed to say Mass, dear.'

Mass? What is she talking about? 'Surely only the priests can say Mass?'

'That's what they said, dear.' Having decided to spill the beans, Estelle's appetite is renewed. She picks up her cake and takes a large mouthful. Since they began she has eaten heartily, there is nothing at all birdlike in her demeanour today. Again, she flicks the crumbs briskly from her lap onto the floor.

'So what happened then?'

'What happened when, dear?'

'When they . . . um, found you in the chapel?'

'They made a bit of a fuss, dear. I suppose it was late, it was late at night I think, I can't say. I lost track of time.'

'And what were you doing there, Estelle?'

'Doing there? Oh, I was saying Mass, dear. Giving communion. I was giving out the host, the holy communion wafer . . .' She pauses. 'Are you a Christian, dear?'

'No, no I'm not.'

'Never been to a communion service?'

'No.'

'Not even an ecumenical service?'

'No.'

Estelle pauses. Is that look in her eye one of mild reproof at the irreligious history of the young? 'Well,' she resumes, 'there's a part in the middle, the most important part really, where you raise the wafer in the air, like this — ' she holds up a small portion of cake, 'and you say, "this is my body, this is my blood". And so on. And then it becomes the spiritual host, the body of Our Lord Jesus Christ.'

Marita nods, slowly. 'I see. And that's what you were doing?'

'Yes.'

'And that was wrong?'

'Yes, yes. Women are not allowed to touch the body of Our Lord. Their hands haven't been consecrated.'

'So why did you do it, Estelle?'

Estelle is silent. She begins to look glum and deflated, like a naughty child grown weary of chastisement. 'Well, to tell you the truth, I didn't like Father Croker, didn't care for him at all . . . he was the nuns' chaplain. I didn't like his manner. And you couldn't hear him, he mumbled. It's very important not to mumble. My mother had a beautiful speaking voice, every word clear as a bell. You couldn't hear Father Croker past the first row. And it's important to hear the words. I thought: I could do it better myself.' Estelle's delivery is suddenly offhand, brusque even.

Apprehending this, Marita experiences a quiet bloom of elation. The questions that a moment ago hovered on her tongue now seem fatuous, beside the point. The point has been reached. Is done with. Over. And it's not so much what Estelle has said about her reasons, or about Father Croker, as the fact that, in this last little speech she hasn't once called Marita 'dear'. She has abandoned her womanly courtesy, and spoken directly from the force of her will.

Footsteps in the lane. The flyscreen door bangs with a metallic thud. It's Camille. She stands in the doorway, her face flushed, her hair in damp wisps against her skin, her bag slouched over one slumped shoulder. 'It's so hot . . .' she begins, and then breaks off at the sight of Estelle.

'Hello, dear,' says Estelle, unfazed.

'Hello.' Camille has become shy, her voice a murmur.

'Come and sit down,' says her mother.

'I'm desperate for a drink.' She moves across to the fridge door and drinks from the neck of a plastic bottle that Stephen has filled with filtered water boiled for twenty minutes and steeped with a sliver of ginger. She swallows, gasps, drinks again and turns towards the table.

'Can I have a piece of cake?' she asks.

Marita is about to lift the knife when a quiet voice intervenes. 'No, dear,' says Estelle, 'you have a biscuit. Your mother made this cake for me. There's not much left and I have to save some for Dad.'

Camille, bemused, gazes at the cake. There is a good deal left, just over half. She looks across to her mother, waiting for a sign. Marita returns her gaze: 'There are some chocolate brownies in the koala tin,' she says, and her lips curve in an enigmatic smile. Camille hesitates, and then, looking slightly stunned, she walks to the pantry cupboard. Marita stands and begins to clear the table. 'I'll wrap the rest of the cake for you, Estelle,' she says.

Estelle sits with her hands folded neatly, serenely, in her lap. 'Thank you, dear,' she says. 'Dad *will* be pleased.'

With the remains of the cake wrapped in silver foil, she walks with Estelle to the front door. 'You must come again,' she says.

Estelle gives her curious little smile and nods. 'I will, dear,' she says. She blinks into the sunlight, walks briskly to the gate and out into the street where she pauses, and turns back to Marita. 'It's been very nice, dear. Thank you.'

As soon as she is out of earshot Marita returns to the kitchen where, hugging Camille to her breast, she lets out a loud whoop of laughter.

'What is it?' asks Camille, pleased at her mother's elation but baffled by it as well. 'What's so funny?'

'Nothing,' she says, 'nothing. I'll explain it to you one day when you're older, and — ' giving her a loud, emphatic kiss '— when you've learned to cook.'

'Do you think she'll come round again at night?'

'We'll have to wait and see.'

She will not tell Stephen about this visit, or anything to do with the second gift of cake. There are intractable paradoxes here, she believes, that are not accessible to a man.

Humming a tune she begins to busy herself in the kitchen, preparing dinner, slicing a small cabbage into delicate strips for a coleslaw, one of the few dishes the three of them like in common. Camille is practising her piano in the front room, the tinkling sound of her scales wafting down the hall. How pure are these simple moments of domestic joy!

That night she dreams that she and Camille are sitting on the couch watching their favourite soap opera. They are calm and content. Suddenly, in the rectangular frame of the television screen, there appears a dazzling image of the Holy Trinity — Marita, Camille and Estelle — standing on a small hillock in the desert, the bright sun behind them. At their feet, dressed like a Grecian maiden, is Flora, playing on a small, pink-stringed harp. Above their heads a shimmering vision of the cake hovers in a blazing aureole of light.

When she wakes from the dream she lies in the dark, drifting in a half sleep, suffused with a drowsy sense of elation. The important thing was this: they had defeated him. He was irrelevant. *Him*. The old man. The Father.

PART SIX

CHANGE

1

the city

'It can all change for you, Steve, old son, it can all change,' says Adrian over lunch. They are sitting in Borgia's, one of the more exclusive eating places in the city. In the morning he had received an unexpected call from Adrian, saying that he needed to see him 'urgently'. 'What's up?' he'd asked, taken aback at hearing from one of his clients at work. Adrian, as usual, was peremptory: 'Don't want to talk about it over the blower,' he had said. 'Do you know Borgia's in York Street? I'll see you there at one. If I'm late, tell the head waiter, Bertie, that I'm coming. And don't let the old bastard patronise you. He can smell a public servant at a hundred metres and he's a terrible snob.'

But when he arrives Adrian is already seated. At first he doesn't notice Stephen's entrance because he is gazing out the window and fiddling distractedly with the crystal salt cellar, rocking it back and forth between his finger and thumb like a bored baby with a valueless toy. Stephen observes that his shoulders are even more taut than usual and his cheeks more flushed. On the table by his glass of red wine is a small bottle of yellow pills.

He rises to shake Stephen's hand in a rather formal way and as they are seated Stephen glances at the pills. Perhaps the client wants to discuss his health?

'So,' says Adrian, 'how's work?'

'The same.'

'Looking for a step up?'

'Not really.' He's looking for a step out, not up; out into his own life. Has Adrian brought him here to offer him a job in the private sector?

'Not ambitious?'

'Depends on what you mean by ambition.' Perhaps this is the psychological moment to ask Adrian for sponsorship. How would you like, old son, to cough up seven thousand dollars to send me to a *dojo* in Japan for six months? But that's not why he's come here, to talk about his painfully slow-moving path.

'What's up?'

The client is full of unease, looking hard at him. He looks back at the client, at the light of irritable menace that flickers in his eye. This is something he hasn't noticed before, this menace, and it's why he doesn't like to meet clients 'outside'; outside the communion of skinship where each offers up his best, his undefended self.

'Let's deal with that after the main course. What'll you have?'

Stephen scans the list of specials. There is nothing suitable, of course. 'I'll have linguine tossed in olive oil with herbs and lemon juice.'

'Nothing else?'

'Nothing else.'

'Well, that's a bit pure for me, old son. I'll have the Napolitana. See, I'm learning. No meat or eggs.' At that moment, he turns away, responding to a shout of 'Ade!' Three businessmen at another table are smiling, in that taunting, almost jeering way that certain men greet another of their kind. They beckon him over. 'Sorry, mate,' says Adrian, rising from his chair. 'Just give me a minute with these pricks and I'll be back.'

Stephen looks around him. This place is absurd; full of suits and a stagey male pomposity. The man behind him is saying: 'Ian's alright. Ian's an OK guy. Ian's a one-two guy . . .'

A one-two guy? In a bent kind of way he is beginning to enjoy this place; it's like a big playpen for executives, with a few women, mostly young and in power suits, and he recognises a politician at the far table sitting beneath a huge black and white photograph of himself fixed to the wall.

When Adrian returns he is flushed with the effort of aping the heaving bonhomie of the other table, but still he is ill at ease. Stephen begins to wind the glistening linguine (too much oil) around his fork. The large clock above the bar is ticking on; no long lunches for him. Soon he will have to leave. He decides to deploy silence for the rest of the time he is here. He will not probe. If the client wants to tell him something, he will tell him. Sometimes he feels a certain deference towards Adrian, as the older, and worldlier, man. On his bad days, when the office is stifling and casts a coarse blanket over his heart, when he feels powerless and insignificant, Adrian looms above him as the smart financier: *he* is just a clerk. At other times, Adrian seems like a shallow fool, a bluff and overweight child.

The minutes pass. They eat in silence. It's only a few minutes but it seems longer. Adrian looks up at the clock and seeing the time, appears to make a decision. He sighs deeply, puts his fork down and picks up the bottle of pills by his untouched glass. 'Had a bit of a scare over the weekend,' he says. 'My heart started racing again. The old ticker. I dropped into St Vincent's and they gave me these until I see my own cardiologist. Which is tomorrow.' He fiddles with the bottle. 'It's nothing new, basically the same arrhythmia as before, it's just that for some reason the old pills don't seem to be working so they've given me these.' He pauses. 'What do *you* think?'

Stephen stares at him for a moment. 'You know I'm not expert enough to comment on this,' he says. 'Maybe you should talk to Eva.'

'I wanted to talk to you.'

Neither man is eating now. Stephen gazes into the roseate pattern of the damask tablecloth. Something in this conversation doesn't ring true. There's something here he's not telling me, he thinks. Adrian knows Eva: he knows he should talk to her if he has a life-threatening condition. He knows that he, Stephen, is still an assistant, and not at a level to diagnose or treat serious illness. Does he want to tempt me into hubris, he wonders. Adrian breathes a kind of generalised aggression, all of the time, every minute of his waking day and probably in his dreams as well. In the dim salon of his elegant terrace it's muted, not so apparent but here, in this high-priced feeding trough, it's like a black radiance. Is he trying to trap me in some way? No, this is a ridiculous thought; and Adrian is clearly distressed. He is gazing out the window now, at the feet of office workers walking briskly back to their high-rise batteries. As if he is trying to make up his mind about something. About what? About why he has asked Stephen to come here? Stephen feels the hairs rising on the back of his neck, a prickly sensation of resistance and it occurs to him, with a small stab of shock, that he doesn't particularly like Adrian, that despite having handled his body for several weeks, skinship has not transpired to bond them, and this is such a disconcerting thought, so subversive of his calling, that he must assert himself against it. He reaches across the table to where Adrian's right hand is resting beside the wine glass and the bottle of pills and he takes the client's beefy wrist in his right hand.

'What are you doing?'

'Taking your pulse.'

'Jesus, not here. They'll think we're a pair of poofters.'

Yes, this is bizarre. With his forefinger and thumb he slides Adrian's expensive designer watch back along the gingery blond hairs on his wrist and feels against the artery for the familiar throb. Adrian starts to say something but he interrupts.

'Shhhhh.'

The client subsides in a heave of resignation. 'I'll tell 'em you're a doctor,' he says, nodding in the direction of his friends at the table on the other side of the room. 'An eccentric one with a ponytail.'

Stephen is counting. One, two, three, four . . . there's a slight boom in the pulse; it beats at an even pace for a few seconds and then jumps and races, fitfully, speedily . . .

'So?' Adrian looks up as he releases his hand.

'I don't know,' he says. 'Hundred and ten. Not good but not dangerous.'

He senses that Adrian already knows this, knows all about his pulse, does not need Stephen to tell him anything. He has the uncomfortable feeling of being lured into playing a part in some fake drama. If it were not for the fact that Adrian is so manifestly troubled he would feel angry, would feel used.

'I have to go.'

'What? Oh, sorry. '

'Why don't I book you in for a consultation with Eva on Friday?'

'No, no. The usual Thursday night with you will be fine.'

'It wouldn't do any harm to just talk to her. See what your cardiologist says.'

Adrian's eyes are cloudy; he is despondent, as if he has failed some test he set himself for today. Stephen finds himself disconcertingly detached. Today his empathy has failed him. He feels that Adrian has played some kind of minor trick on him. Or is it just that they have both made the mistake of trying to discuss symptoms using the blunt and inaccurate instruments of words? If he cannot touch the client's body then the circuit of skinship — of empathy —

is not activated; the flow of connexion is easily broken. One might look at one's client across a table, in this bear pit of main-chancers and ego-dancers, and see only an aggravating money-man, a man who says 'old son' or 'mate' like it's a dagger going into your heart; a man who could easily lure you into the pit of your old paranoia, a pit that could bury you. And, in a curious way, him.

'I must go,' he says again, politely, conscious of somehow abandoning Adrian.

'Yeah, sure. Well, thanks for coming at short notice.'

Stephen begins to extract some money from his hip pocket but Adrian waves him away. 'It's mine,' he says, 'you can't afford this place.' This is both a gift, and a putdown.

Stephen says nothing, merely nods. One of the lesser waiters escorts him to the door. Walking up the stairs to ground level, and daylight, he has the niggling, inexplicable, sense that somehow he and Adrian have crossed swords.

Four o'clock in the afternoon and the house is stifling. Marita sighs into the gloom of her little kitchen. After the rain the heat has returned in an unrelenting wave. At night she throws open the windows and sprinkles the sheets with cold water and they lie naked in her humid bed, assailed, as always, by noises from the street. From behind the wardrobe she has dragged out an old mobile fan and placed it on Camille's bookcase so that the child can sleep fitfully beside the fan's vibrating whirr. Camille's wheezing is under control, the Ventolin dose reduced — until the next time, that is.

Miraculously, some kind of peace has descended on the house. She and Stephen have arrived at a delicate modus vivendi. Does she imagine it or has he softened a little in his orthodoxy? Not in relation to his own diet of course but in the degree to which he insists on imposing it on her and Camille. Increasingly she adopts some of his recipes for main courses but insists still on 'lacing' (his word) certain dishes with cheese and cooking traditional puddings for Camille so that he is obliged to pursue a kind of separatism. On those nights when he is at home and not at Eva's he cooks his own dinner alongside of her, and she comments favourably on his dishes and tastes them willingly and appreciatively, though she might observe that a certain dish is too bland. 'Only to the blunted and dulled palate,' he says, and she simply laughs at him, rather than argue. Isn't he the one who preaches harmony in the kitchen, and what harmony will there be if she is to enter into a war of words with him every night over their respective chopping boards? As usual, she tells herself, it is the woman who conciliates.

Despite this, and on some ineffable plane, she senses that he is beginning to loosen up. He has a pet name for her now; calls her 'black eyes', and she likes the sound of it on his tongue, something in the timbre of his voice. And he is freer with Camille; touches her sometimes. And Camille is relaxed with this; seems, even, to welcome it. Last weekend they had gone away to Blackheath to stay with her friends, Jane and Mario, and it had all gone off well. Stephen had baked a superb silken tofu pie with asparagus: needless to say Camille hadn't liked it but the others had demolished it enthusiastically and with much praise, after which Stephen and Mario had spent a lot of time laughing and arm-wrestling, to Stephen's advantage. She wasn't surprised to see a fierce competitive streak bristle in him, however good-naturedly. Mario was big and easygoing, and remarked on how you never could underestimate the strength of these wiry types, and then he'd grasped Stephen from behind, around the waist, and lifted him off his feet for just a moment. Stephen had raised his elbow in a reflex action as if he would drive it into Mario's face — and then laughed and dropped it. But it was the quickness of that elbow and the momentary stare in his eyes that told her something, something she'd always sensed in him.

She was surprised at how the two men got on, at how easily they touched one another: perhaps it was because Mario was Italian and Stephen was a masseur. Then on Sunday, while Mario cooked his special pasta dish and Jane prepared dessert, the three of them had taken a long walk in the bush, and Camille and Stephen seemed at ease with one another at last, almost like father and daughter. It was as if the crisis had passed; they'd had their first real fight and gotten over it. Camille complained, as always, about having to walk far, and began to wheeze, and Stephen carried her along the track on his back for quite some time. To see Camille's arms around his broad neck had given Marita a stab of pleasure she had not known before.

Tonight is one of those nights when Stephen will go straight from work to Eva's advanced class. Marita prepares a simple meal of riceballs and salad and for afterwards, lemon pudding. When the soap operas are over — *You're strong, Fin, and I need you to help me be strong too* — she listens absentmindedly to Camille's piano practice while thinking about her *Jane Eyre*. Once she had been absorbed in the question of what would have happened if Rochester, and not his wife, had been killed in the fire at Thornfield Hall. But lately she has become possessed of another notion: what if Jane had not been an orphan? What if she had had a mother? Or a father? This is of course, ridiculous: as Zoe would say: You can't ask *what if* anything. This is only a story. It has no other life but the events its author gave it. If you change even one of the elements you change everything. But is this true . . .?

She realises with a start that Camille has finished her playing, has said something — asked her a question? — and she has not heard it, or rather heard it but failed to take it in. 'I'm sorry, Cam,' she says, 'what did you say?'

'I said, can we go back to Jane and Mario's again. I like it there.'

'Sure.'

'When?'

'When? I don't know. Soon.'

When Camille has had her bath she ushers her into bed, puts an ear to her chest to check her breathing and then, since she is in a good mood tonight, reads not one but three chapters of *The BFG*. She is feeling uncommonly happy, almost too at peace to bother with her tapes or her journal and she sits on the old couch in the living room and muses for a while about nothing. This is why she gave up work for a year. So she would have time to daydream. To cook and to daydream. And to dance with Camille. And she drifts into a reverie about Larry, a friend of Zoe's who arrived out of nowhere last year, to stay a few nights in her bed, and she has remembered something about that time, about how chaotic it was, as if everything were grubby and fraying about the edges and how she'd woken up one morning and hated the dusty mats and the unwashed curtains and the grime around the laundry basin and she had wanted time, time to pander to her nest, to prettify her hearth, to make it shine and glow so that she and Camille could shine and glow within it, instead of occupying it like harrassed vagrants — and she'd suddenly lost interest in Larry and jumped out of bed early and drafted her application for leave at the kitchen table . . . Recalling all of this now she stretches her arms expansively along the back of the couch and laughs. Yes, the house looks a lot better, it looks cared for, it feels loved, but that's not why she's laughing. It's the fact that in her reverie she has forgotten about him. That she can take her mind off Stephen for even an hour is a good sign, a sign that they're becoming settled.

And then the telephone rings.

And she looks at her watch and is surprised to see that she has been sitting here, lost in reverie, for almost two hours. It must be her mother — only Ros ever rings this late, usually to impart some piece of inconsequential news ('Edith Ubaldi is dead, dear, do you remember her?') or, occasionally, to read from her journal. She hopes it's the former (news) as the journal readings tend to go on and on and in a few minutes Stephen will be home.

She picks up the receiver. 'Hello,' she says.

'Is that Marita Black?' It's a man's voice.

'Yes.'

'Hello, my dear.'

'Who is this?' But already she knows.

'It's me, Marita. Adrian.'

'Adrian?' Just for a moment her mind has completely blanked out.

'Yes, Adrian. Adrian Vickers. Don't pretend you've forgotten me.' In his voice she can hear the old tone; nervous bonhomie, tinged with anger.

'Why are you ringing?'

'Why am I ringing? Well, you might at least ask how I am. Same old Marita, I see.' She hears his slight snort of exasperation. 'The fact is there's something I want to discuss with you.'

'Why now, Adrian?'

'Why now? Because I haven't known where you were for . . .' the voice at the other end of the line hesitates, 'for a very long time and now I've managed to track you down at last.'

To track her down? As if it would take all that long, if he'd ever really wanted to before this! She'd like to hang up, now, and leave him stranded on the end of the line. Except that she knows Adrian, and she knows that having made contact now, he'll ring again and again and again. Until she listens to him.

2

flight

Stephen finds her sitting in the back courtyard, in the dark, staring at the vines. She's quiet. Unnaturally so. God help us, he thinks, not another mood; not when they seemed to be getting on so well. Why does she have to be so moody? Tonight it's as if she can barely bring herself to speak to him.

Over supper, as they drink the last of their tea, she puts down her cup, in a considered way, as if preparing to make an announcement. 'Stephen, Camille and I are going to go away for a few days. To the Blue Mountains. To Mario and Jane's.'

'We've just come back from Mario and Jane's.'

'I need to go again. It's Camille. She's still wheezing. A few more days in the mountains might do her good.'

'When are you going?'

'Tomorrow. On the train.'

'Isn't this a bit sudden?'

She shrugs, and it's an infuriating shrug. In the three months since he came here he's only ever seen this shrug once, maybe twice, but when she does it he could grip her roughly by the shoulders and shake her.

'If you feel she isn't improving, that she's sort of stuck, why don't I give her a treatment every day, just a twenty minute one, work on the lung meridian . . .'

'When would you have the time? You leave early, you have classes three nights a week. And anyway,' she adds, quickly, 'I need a break from the city as well. I realised that this weekend. It was so lovely up there.'

Why isn't he convinced by this? Why does he feel a creeping tide of prickly unease travel along his arms and down the base of his spine? Marita is in a state of panic. Something has happened. Just when they were beginning to seem settled. Isn't this how it always goes?

'Right,' he says. 'I'll look after the place here. Give me a ring when you decide to come back and I'll drive up and bring you back, if you like.'

'Thanks.' She attempts a smile but doesn't look at him. Something in her, it seems to him, is stricken.

Later, in bed, he lies with his back to her: she puts her arm around his waist, but it's a limp arm, a distracted arm. He can almost see the interior of her head, see her brain creaking and grinding, and in there, a locked chamber, her habitual secretiveness. She is barely with him. Yet in the morning, as he leaves for work, she puts her slim white hands on his shoulders and looks at him with great tenderness. Then she hugs him hard, almost with desperation.

'I'll ring you in a day or two,' he says.

•

All day, at work, he is restless. On Level 9 time passes fitfully in short jagged bursts of distraction: his concentration is erratic, he is unproductive. It's almost 5 p.m. and he realises that he is resisting the idea of returning to an empty house. This is the first time they have been away from one another since they began to sleep in the same bed: how instantly they had fallen into living as a couple, fallen into a domestic routine, almost from the first day, as if each had been hungry for it, waiting for it to come along, and all their arguments had been domestic ones; food, the timing of meals, Camille's habits. Not that there wasn't ambivalence on both sides. There had been moments of claustrophobia in that little house, moments almost of suffocation that had reminded him of why, until now, he had spurned the humid hearth with its sweaty and choleric dramas, its turgid undertow, that cloying ideal of Home. At those moments he had wanted to escape, to be alone again, but in recent weeks those moments had been fewer and now, now that she's not in the house at all, it's as if a vacuum has opened up and all the air has rushed out. He breathes but doesn't breathe. Something goes into his lungs and something comes out, but the house is stale.

He reaches across to switch off his console and decides that, no, he will work on for another hour to improve his flextime. Over the next twenty minutes the office becomes quiet, with only a few clerks staying behind. Gareth, too, is working late. In the corner of his eye he can see that fine chiselled head above the desk by the window. In the past months he has seen less of Gareth, too absorbed in his Shiatsu training and his life with Marita to meet up after work or at the weekends with his occasional friend.

Around 6.50 Gareth stands back from his desk and begins to put on his jacket. And Stephen decides, abruptly, that he will catch Gareth on the way out and perhaps walk with him down to the quay where every night Gareth takes the ferry to his mother's apartment in Narrabeen. He signals to Gareth to wait, and catches up with him at the noticeboard where Gareth nods wryly in the direction of the latest poem pinned up by the office poet, Damian.

'Have we perused the latest outpouring of the poet laureate? Lamentable, isn't it?'

Stephen glances at the first two lines, but isn't in the mood for the rest. 'Practise improves all other skills,' he says, as they enter the lift. 'Why doesn't it work on Damian's poetry?'

'Because what we sing expresses our essential self, and that self is laid down at birth, in the genes, and in tribal memory. And re-inforced in childhood. And that's the end of it. We are our limitations. We do not ever, really, change.'

'Spoken like a true Welshman.'

As always, they enter easily into their ritual banter. Once out on to the street, in the mild autumn evening, they turn left and walk briskly along Hunter Street.

'They've stopped work on the facade,' says Stephen. 'Must be the recession.'

'The company is in difficulties,' says Gareth, drily.

'Surely the longer it has to stand alone like that, the more likely it is to fall down.'

'Not necessarily. It's fairly well buttressed from the back. I know, I had a good look at it one lunchtime. Told the foreman I was an architect and he let me hang around. I told him I sometimes saw the top of the facade tremble in the high winds. Of course it does, mate, he said, of course it does. I asked him how safe it felt up there. About as safe as it feels anywhere else, he said. '

'What would they do if it fell down?'

'You mean apart from counting the dead?'

'Never mind the dead, what about the facade?'

'They could get the original plans and build it from scratch.'

'A replica?'

'Yeah, a replica.'

'So the old is rebuilt anew?'

'Exactly. Don't smirk, that's what they did in parts of Europe after the war. Before my brother died, we went backpacking through Germany. In the main drag of what used to be East Berlin they'd rebuilt all the old Prussian mansions so that you had a boulevarde of eighteenth and nineteenth century palaces looking all shiny and new. Like a film set, only real. You could buy these little postcard sets of before and after the bombing. Before was rubble, after was a spanking new palace.'

'Why bother?'

'Why? It's obvious why. They didn't want to give up their history. Imagine if someone blitzed the Opera House. We'd rebuild it, wouldn't we?'

'I wouldn't.'

'You wouldn't, no. You'd probably erect some bloody great Japanese pagoda.'

Stephen throws his head back and laughs, but at the back of his eyes is that phrase, floating: 'Before my brother died . . .'

Gareth is still talking, ' . . . so the world is divided into two camps. Those who want to give up their history and those who don't.'

'Like you and me.'

'You could say that.'

Stephen laughs again, a sharp mirthless laugh. 'The madness of history,' he says. What he really wants to say is: 'What happened to your brother?' And he's thinking: why do we always talk like this? In taunting abstractions? Why don't I put my arm around Gareth, and offer to treat his heart? Why can't we talk about loss, and fear? Though he is confident that Gareth likes him, still he insists on maintaining his distance, as if the whole world, even those who would love him, can only be handled with gloves of irony.

Approaching the quay from the bottom of Young Street, they hear the throttle of the ferry engines and the febrile twang of an electric guitar, a busker operating beside the ticket office. Gareth has only a few minutes to make his regular ferry and maybe, if Stephen asked him, he'd wait and catch the next one, and they could talk about his brother, but then he would want to adjourn to one of the taverns over at The Rocks and have a drink, and this has no appeal for his lapsed friend; they can't drink together any more, they can only wander down the streets and make their abstracted conversation. So he simply says, 'You'll have to run for it, mate,' and waves at Gareth who breaks into a lanky run toward the gangplank of the ferry where, without looking, he raises his arm in a languid wave. Stephen watches as the *Narrabeen* chugs out from the wharf. Then he begins to stroll, aimlessly, along the quay, in the direction of the passenger terminal — that temple of departures, designed like the deck of a giant liner — and past the old Maritime Services Building which is now the Museum of Contemporary Art. Perhaps he'll go in. No, it's closed, and just as well. It would only lower his spirits further. He'd gone in there once but it reminded him, in the clinical stillness of its rooms, of his sister's house, and all of the exhibits had seemed more hapless and alienated even than the *objets d'art* of that other precious salon.

His sister's place! He could call in and collect the mail: that would delay the moment of arriving home to an empty house. But how would he get there? He hasn't got the car. Then again, he could take the bus and walk from Glebe to Leichhardt afterwards, a long walk but one that would do him good on this calm autumn evening. Does he have his sister's key on him? Yes, he does. And he turns and heads back for the bus terminal and the 433 bus.

His sister's house is as quiet and as still as ever. Wandering through the salon, sorting her mail, suddenly it occurs him that he has completely forgotten when she is due back. Upstairs, in the cedar drawers of her vast wardrobe, is a copy of her itinerary that she left there in case he should need to contact her. Curious now, he leaves the mail on the chiffonier and climbs the stairs to the master bedroom where he pauses in front of the grandiose wardrobe with its dazzling trinity of bevelled mirrors. There he is, reflected in the half light; a tall, thin, almost gaunt figure; in this light, disconcertingly hollow-eyed. Looking like someone else. An old self. To cancel that image he opens the mirrored door and with a sense of minor trespass fossicks in the first of the cedar drawers. There, neatly aligned and undisturbed since Helen showed it to him on the day of her departure, is a long envelope marked 'For Emergencies'. Unfolding the contents he scans the list of destinations and finds, somewhat to his relief, that it's still four weeks before her return. As he puts the envelope back in its corner of the drawer he cannot help noticing a handsome leather book, elongated and embossed, that seems vaguely familiar. Lifting it out and looking at it in the light he recognises his mother's old photo album, something that apparently she has already passed on to Helen. And he sits on the edge of the four-poster bed and lays the album down on the immaculate white quilt and begins to turn the thick, charcoal grey pages that are stuck with candid, badly framed photographs of him and his sister as children. The usual stuff: in the backyard, at the beach, sitting up to the table in dumb paper party hats. Him in a sandpit somewhere with a bucket on his head; Helen in a ballerina tutu posing with laughable coyness, her eyes squinting into the direct sun. And later, when they were older, perched on their bikes by the nature strip. They were tall, lanky kids but Helen, he sees now, had a natural grace. It wasn't something she had assumed later, in her expensive clothes and her obsessive house. It was always there. Perhaps that was why she had always wanted something better. Has she found it in her precious objects arrayed around her? Does she look into their glossy surfaces and see her own image, the distortion of which is as nothing when the reflecting object is so fine a thing in itself? All the while he has been turning the pages but stops now, his eye caught by a photo that he can't recall seeing before. It's a rural scene. He and Helen are in heavy sweaters, leaning against a fence somewhere, somewhere in the country, in front of a ti-tree hedge, and she has her arm around him, very protectively, and she looks at the camera with a gaze of anxious and mature sadness, though she can only be twelve, if that. There is something poignant in this photo, something both familiar and disturbing. And he remembers where it must have been taken. At the Malone's farm, just after they'd been sent away —

And he shuts the album, the covers of which come together with a sharp slap of noise. He stands, walks over to the wardrobe and slides the album back into its cedar drawer where it is better left, as far as he is concerned; left for as long as it takes for the contents to rot away.

Will he sleep the night here or won't he? Perhaps not. That photograph could haunt him; his sister's protective arm. When he'd first come to Sydney, the black sheep, she had embraced him and offered him this place as a haven. An elegant, controlled woman, she had nevertheless made allowances for him. And Ric, who had been wary of trouble at first, had softened and teased him about his new ways, and called him The Monk. And after her irate letter he had written and promised to spend at least some nights here, and now is an opportunity to keep his word. Maybe he'll take a shower, which will give him time to think about it: this might also work to wash away some lingering film of dark nostalgia that had risen up from the pages of the album and settled on his skin like so much marsh gas.

In the white-tiled shower bay of the en suite he stands under the wide spray for a long, long time, his shoulders slumped, his legs heavy, the water scalding his ears, and he imagines that the phone might be ringing in Marita's kitchen, that she might ring at this minute and want to speak to him, and it's time he stopped moping around and went back to Bright Street. But his sense of obligation to his sister remains with him, despite the shower. Damn it, if he hadn't looked in that album he might have remained his careless and condescending self. How unhappy she'd looked in that photograph — how unhappy they'd been together.

For some reason he can't bring himself to sleep in her bed and he doesn't want to sleep in his old haunt, the spare room. What's the matter with him? What is this low-grade fever that makes him febrile and unable to settle on anything? At 2 a.m. he is still awake, slumped naked on the leather couch in Ric's den, fiddling with the remote control of the television. This is the last night he'll spend in this house, *the last night,* promise or no promise, and he drops the remote on to the coffee table and walks out into the hallway and back up into the spare room. There, spreadeagled on the absurdly uncomfortable chaise longue, upholstered in pale green silk, and thinking of Marita, her small white breasts floating on the surface of her bath, he masturbates himself into a short, sharp dreamless sleep.

●

Morning. And it's a relief, at last, to push open that picket gate at 91 and enter the dark hallway. If only she were here to console him. Whatever else her moods and resistances, in her softness, and her wry empathy, she is a woman with a consoling touch. Looking around the kitchen he realises that the place is in uncharacteristic disarray, as if, when she left it, she was distracted and had neglected to tidy up. Well then, he will clean up for her. As luck would have it, today is a public holiday and after he has meditated and had breakfast he'll water the garden, trim back the ivy, nail up the hole in the plank fence, clean out the guttering and later, when all that is done, he'll make soup and damper.

And so he does, he works all day, in a slow but steady rhythm that denies his lack of sleep the night before, his sense of guilty dislocation. Yesterday, Adrian had rung the office and cancelled his appointment for this evening and he is glad of this. He would prefer just to be here, all day, in her house. Moreover, after their odd lunch meeting at Borgia's he feels a new resistance to Adrian; he finds himself imagining a time when Adrian is no longer his client, no longer a figure in his life. Is he training to become a practitioner simply to become a panderer to the rich? No, he thinks, dragging the ladder out from under the house and making it steady against the side wall so that he can climb up on to the roof and unclog from the guttering the first fall of autumn leaves.

Around 3.15 he stops, and lies on the old lounge in the garden and dozes off; there are leaves in his hair and his forearms are smudged with dirt and the autumn sun warms his legs beneath his faded and torn jeans. Just before five he wakes, sits up, lowers his head momentarily onto his knees then throws his head back and flexes his neck. The courtyard is still warm; he can feel the sun on his shoulders and he is reluctant to go inside, and he thinks, yes, before going in to make dinner he will do one last thing, he will water Camille's flower patch. Anything to prolong that mindless reverie of the body that has soothed and becalmed him. And he squats at the tap and begins to untangle the hose and the pale green grooves of the hose seem to have an almost translucent charm — at least until the moment when he is disturbed by Dona Maria. There she is, standing on her toes, just managing to peer over the fence he has mended earlier in the afternoon. 'Senor Stephen,' she calls, 'Senor

Stephen. You have a visitor at the front door. You cannot hear the doorbell here, no? I tell him this. I say I come and I get you.'

'Thanks, Maria.'

When he opens the front door no-one is there. He looks out into the mellow light of late afternoon, looks up and down the street. No-one. Then he looks around for Maria but she has gone inside, and he is reluctant to go next door and ask about this caller for fear of having to listen to one of her interminable monologues. Some salesman, perhaps? Break-in merchants, looking for empty houses? He turns inwards, hovering at the open door, and at this moment, taking him by surprise, a worn brown image of his sister's photo album steals into his thoughts. All day it has hovered on the edge of his vision as he worked, methodically, to erase it. He closes the door.

Around six, while the soup is simmering on the stove, he rings the Blue Mountains number. He had planned to ring at nine, when Camille was in bed and he might cajole Marita into speaking freely but staring into the steamy surface of the soup he is overcome by impatient need and reaches now for the phone. It's Jane who answers. 'I'll get Marita,' she says, almost too quickly, as if she doesn't want to talk to him.

Though he has wanted, for hours, to talk to her, once he hears her voice on the line, sounding so near, and yet remote, he is stalled by a sudden reticence.

'I thought I might stay on for a few extra days,' she says.

'What about Camille and school?'

'At this age it doesn't matter. She likes it up here. Jane makes a big fuss of her.'

'I'm missing you both.'

'I miss you, too, Stephen. Especially at night.'

'But not at mealtimes, eh?'

'You're a better cook than Mario. His sauces are too heavy.'

He sighs. And can't speak.

'What's the matter?' she says, after a silence. 'You sound tired.'

'No, I'm not tired. Well, a bit. I've been working all day. Fixed the fence, cleared the guttering.'

'Oh. What about the office?'

'It's a public holiday, Marita.' This is typical of her, she never quite knows what day it is, or cares. She might at least say thanks.

'Thanks. I was worried about that guttering. I think it might need replacing.'

How soothing her voice: since they began to talk about the house it has changed, lost its remoteness, become intimate again, consoling, like a flush of warmth in his ear that travels, slowly, down his neck and across his shoulders and he can feel her hands on his face, her fingers stroking his neck; he feels a warm flush in the pit of his stomach, he wants desperately to hold her.

'When are you coming back?' he says, hoarsely.

There's a pause. In an instant the remoteness is back in her voice. 'Sunday,' she says.

Sunday! Damn it. Damn her. He says nothing.

'Stephen? Are you there?'

'*I'm* here. Where are you?'

'Don't get belligerent. Nothing's changed between us, I just need a break.'

'I thought this was for Camille's benefit.'

'Stephen, you're being churlish.'

He changes the subject. 'How *is* Camille.'

'She's fine. Do you want to speak to her?'

No, he doesn't. He hears her calling: 'Camille! Come and say hello to Stephen!' And then a soft, high voice. 'Hi, Stephen.'

'Hi. What's it like up there?'

'OK. We've done some bushwalking but mostly Mum and Jane keep going to coffee shops. They want to sit around and talk all the time. It's boring.'

'How's your cough?'

'Um, OK. Well, sometimes I get a bit short of breath when we go for walks.'

'What's the food like?'

'OK.'

'No treats?'

'Not really. Well, well there's this bread up here. They call it Mountain Bread. It's really excellent. It's really thin and it's got none of that stuff, y'know, yeast. You might like it.'

'You'd better save me a piece.'
'OK. I'll ask Jane if we can buy some more.'
'I'll look forward to it. Can you put Marita back on now?'
'OK. Bye, Stephen.'
'Bye, Camille.'

So, his first night alone in the cedar ship. He's already fought off the impulse to rifle through her things, a kind of demonic seizure; a desire to open all her drawers, pry into her notebooks, bury his face in her clothes. He knows about the box of tapes under the bed but he is and always has been repelled by the idea of that; literally, a Pandora's box. Or worse, a crucible of the mundane; dull, aimless prattle; monologues of the inessential, psychic waste, the narcissism of the gulled. He couldn't listen to any of it without becoming judgemental, which is always the effect that words have on him and precisely what working on the body is designed to avoid. Does he want her secrets? He doesn't.

But after the first night this fever passes, and for the rest of the week he does what works best for him, sticking to his routine, maintaining his regimen, the carefully controlled structure of his day. Both structure and carapace. In the evenings he sits out in the garden, eating alone, the jumbos droning across his line of vision, their tail lights flickering in the early dusk.

On Friday night at the Institute, when class is over, Eva again asks him to stay behind. She leads him out on to the terrace at the back of the upstairs gallery, a rectangular ledge that juts out, without rails, above the garbage-strewn alley below. The night is balmy, one of the last mellow nights of the month, and they sit cross-legged on the warm concrete and look out at the darkening skyline of the city. Below, a group of vagrants has settled into the alley and lit a blazing fire from debris stacked against a concrete wall. While the others squat around the fire, one of them, young, with a long black beard, leaps to his feet and lurches about, brandishing what looks like a sword.

'What did you think of that man tonight? Russell?' Eva is referring to one of a group of clients, willing to be treated by her in front of students in return for paying a reduced fee.

Stephen is gazing at the derelict men below, and the fire. Could that be a sword? Surely not. Who would throw out a sword? But he is listening to Eva and has heard her question. 'Heart *jitsu*, spleen *kyo*.'

'Yes, good. And why is the heart in excess?'

'Too much sugar, alcohol and coffee. And because it's his strongest organ so that when he's under stress it does most of the work. Or,' he corrects himself, 'more and more of the work of the other organs. All the energy is going up into the chest and getting caught there and it weakens the lower back. So he comes in and complains about his back and thinks he's got a back problem.'

'But it is not structure, you think?'

'No, I think it's function. The spleen needed tonifying so you worked on the spleen meridian.'

'Exactly.' And she turns and casts her confronting gaze on him. 'Now, Stephen, what about the mat? Have you made your decision about the mat?'

'I can't take the mat, not just yet.' There, he's said it. 'But I'm almost ready. I think. I'm beginning to get settled. I'm in a new relationship that I think could . . .' he hesitates, 'could go somewhere.'

Except that she's run away from him for a week, without a convincing account of herself. All this week the thought has nagged away at him that she might be preparing to ask him to move out. But this is paranoia; after all, they've been getting along so well.

'Then I will have to give the mat to someone else.'

'I know.'

She sighs. 'Stephen, of all the students I have had here you are the most perplexing.'

'Me?'

'Yes, you. On the one hand you appear to have a most intense commitment. On the other, you have the greatest hesitation. It is as if you need to make some breakthrough.'

He nods, silently. And staring down at the ragged band of men crouched around the fire, an abandoned thought sparks in his head. He should make the break now. Give up his job, take the mat and leap into the abyss empty-handed. Asking — no, demanding — that Nature support him. And he lifts his head, ready to mouth the necessary words. But the fire-escape door is open and the receptionist, Lucy, is calling Eva to the phone. And as Eva rises and turns away from him he feels that heady impulse begin to dissipate in his loins. And he thinks: no, not yet. I'll wait.

3

history

Saturday morning. A loud knocking at the front door. He opens it.

On the tiny verandah, in loose jeans and a cotton sweater, looking brushed and uptight, is Adrian.

'Adrian.'

'Stephen.'

This is not someone he expected to see in this garden, on this doorstep, ever. And he is immediately, viscerally resistant to it; he experiences it as an invasion, a transgression of boundaries. This is the wrong man in the wrong place: the client does not belong here in Bright Street, in *her* house. But, he won't formulate the question. He won't say: *What are you doing here?* Did you get my address from the Shiatsu Institute? Why didn't you ring me first? Is your heart racing again, Adrian? Are you panic-stricken? No, he won't say anything. For the moment.

'Is Marita here?'

Ah, now this really surprises him. So Adrian knows Marita. How is this possible? Who and what else does he know?

'No, she's away for the weekend.' Again, something, an instinct, tells him not to ask questions. Any display of curiosity will put him in a position of weakness. So he doesn't say it, doesn't ask why, though he is burning to know.

'Look, can I come in?'

'Sure.'

He leads Adrian down the dark hallway, and out into the dank kitchen at the back. Adrian stops, stands by the kitchen table and looks about him, chewing on his bottom lip, like some reluctant inspector. 'This place is damp,' he says, as if talking to himself, and then recovers. 'Sorry to just drop in like this, unannounced.' He waits for Stephen to utter some accommodating pleasantry or other but none is forthcoming.

'Mind if I sit down, old son?' Bravura rising, and a flare of the old belligerence in the face of this, well, this lack of breeding.

Stephen stares at him, and for the first time, smiles. If ever there was a bull in a china shop, it's Adrian. How odd, how out of place, he looks here.

'What's so funny?'

'I was just thinking of something. Would you like some tea, Adrian?'

'Bancha, I suppose.' There's a forced male jollity in his tone, something provoking.

'Of course.' Stephen finds he is very calm, stone cold calm with premonition. 'You can have a choice between leaf and twig.' So, he'll give a little here. In his chest he's begun to feel a massive shift. Slowly, in the hollow behind his ribs, something has begun to move; some dark, swinging pendulum of change. Already the room is taking on a different character, becoming a little strange to him.

'Leaf?'

'Leaf it is.'

'You must wonder what I'm doing here. As I said, I'm sorry to just front up like this.' Adrian is a little breathless.

For God's sake, Adrian, you're repeating yourself. Just get on with it.

'Marita comes back on Monday.'

'It isn't Marita I've come to see.'

'Somehow I got the impression it was.'

'She told you about me, then?'

In his chest his heart is swinging its wide, heavy burden, back and forth, back and forth, but his poise has not left him. 'What should she tell me, Adrian?'

Adrian stares at him. He is flushed and angry. 'What's going on here, Steve?'

Good. Another question. This will do. Adrian came here expecting that it would be him, Stephen, who would ask all the questions. He has manoeuvred Adrian into this with greater ease than he thought possible, and now he can say it.

'You're Camille's father, aren't you?'

Adrian leans forward into the table, his head resting on his hands. His shoulders begin to heave.

Stephen looks up from the steaming kettle. You big, pathetic animal, he thinks. Your heart races at night and you're frightened of dying and now you want to claim her. Claim her out of nowhere and with no right. But with this thought something in his own heart falls away and a sadness swamps his breathing and a voice in his head reproaches him: Where is your compassion for the client, it asks. Where is your skinship now? You've handled this man's body and he's paid you generously and Marita is yours, not his, and Camille never was yours, nor could be, nor at any stage have you wanted her to be.

He pulls a chair out from the table and sits opposite his client who lifts his ruddy face and stares achingly across at him. There is determination in his eyes. And those eyes are dry. It was his chest that heaved and broke, but his eyes are dry.

'I haven't come to make claims on Marita, if that's what you're wondering.'

Stephen nurses the bowl of tea with his fingers. The bowl is almost too hot to touch, almost but not quite. Slowly, distractingly, the large, delicate shreds of leaf float in a circuitous path to the bottom. He doesn't want to say anything, not one word. Now, more than ever, every word is loaded; a demand, a reproach, a judgement. And hence it is futile to speak. Adrian will say what he needs to say and that will be enough for both of them.

'Well? Haven't you got anything to say?'

'You need to talk to Marita, not me.'

'I wanted to talk to you first. I knew Marita wasn't here when I came. I'm not a bloody idiot, I wasn't going to just drop in on the child.'

And now, despite himself, he has to ask. 'How did you know they wouldn't be here?'

As he suspected he might, Adrian gains confidence from being asked something; anything. He stands up and begins to walk around, as if he has sucked the very life out of the question and fuelled his manic purpose with it. 'Same way I found them in the first place. I hired a private investigator.'

Stephen stares at him.

So.

Perhaps he should just get up and walk out. He doesn't want to hear any of this crass narrative; already he feels contaminated with the poisonous coincidence of it. The past is always a shoddy, sickly mess, a quicksand of circular thoughts that go round and round in the head, like a bad sentimental song. But he's locked in now. 'You could have found her yourself,' he says. 'Sydney's not that big.'

'Marita changed her name.'

And it occurs to him for the first time that — no, surely not — surely they couldn't have been married?

Adrian is roused now, has recovered the initiative, is full of his dreadful tale. He's had his moment of abasement, and release. Is free now to pursue his goal. 'Black is her mother's maiden name. Considering how she feels about the old bat, I'm surprised she took it. I rang the mother up but she wouldn't tell me a thing. It might have helped if we'd ever actually met but Marita kept me away from her.' He pauses. 'Have you met her?'

'Yes.'

'Well, good for you, eh? Look, mate, it was no big deal between me and Marita. It lasted less than a year. I just found that, for the last few months, I couldn't sleep at night thinking about the kid.'

'Who came first? Me or the detective?'

Adrian pauses in his pacing around the room. For the first time he seems abashed at his own revelations. ' *She* did,' he says, quietly.

'She?'

'The detective was a woman.'

'She told you about me, not Eva.'

'She told me about you, and Eva, and the whole set-up. I thought I'd try you out first and see what I could find out. I didn't want to come blundering in. For all I knew you might be married, might have adopted her. Whatever.'

'You never once asked me about them.'

'I meant to, gradually, after a while but it never seemed to happen.

You underestimate yourself, old son. You had an effect on me. I'd lie on that bloody futon and I'd keep drifting off into somewhere else, somewhere else I'd never thought about before, or not for a long time anyway.' His voice drops to a murmur, and he looks away. And then, recovering himself: 'Look, I've talked to a lawyer, all I want is the usual rights, y'know, take her out every second weekend, contribute to her education. I'm better off than Marita, that must be worth something.' He looks around him. 'This place is no palace, but so far Marita won't give an inch. She just wants to piss me off for good. But what about Camille? One day she'll want to know who her father is, won't she? Children do. God knows what Marita has told her.' He pauses. 'Do *you* know?'

'We've never discussed it.'

'*You've never discussed it?*' Adrian is incredulous. 'Come on, you must have been curious? Any man would be.'

Stephen is silent.

'Alright, alright.' Adrian gives one of his heavy sighs. 'I want you to tell Marita I came. I want you to put in a word for me. You've got to know me a bit over the past couple of months. I'm not such a bad guy, am I?'

And it's been alright up until now, it's been out *there*, at arm's length, with an isthmus between them. But the insinuating presumption of this gambit, the matey coyness of the request infuriates him. Here he is, the middle-aged investment banker, talking like a man who can get his secretary to do anything for him . . . a renewal of his car registration, a present for a colleague, a blow job in the tea-break . . . and what's a masseur but another flunkey!

'She's sick, you know.' He wants to sting, wants to needle jab. 'Camille is sick. She has asthma, gets it quite badly. That's why they've gone to the mountains for the weekend.'

Adrian's face doesn't change, it's as if he already knew this. 'I'm not surprised. I've had it all my life.' He sits down again, at the kitchen table, exhaling heavily into the damp air. 'I hope you've been treating her?'

And here it is at last, the hot rush of blood behind the eyes. 'No,' he says, between gritted teeth, 'I haven't been treating her. Her diet's a disaster . . .' And he's about to say: 'children are very stubborn in their desires . . .' But he stops, because we are all very stubborn in our desires and this is why the home is difficult, the hearth is fraught, littered with cindered chops and a smouldering tablecloth, and why he wanted in the first place to find a way out of the gluey swamp of the family, the angry father, and right now *he* is the angry father, for no reason at all, except habit, ingrained emotional habit, and this habit could suffocate him, leave him gasping on a suburban lawn somewhere, listening in fear to his child breathing at night, working by day as the lackey of some rich man, or some obstinate dwarf, propping up some big sook like Adrian while they collude in their hereditary male madness . . . and every night, like his father, that impulse to just up-end the table and throttle someone . . .

'Are they vegetarian?'

'What?' He blinks, recalling himself to the moment, to the dark little kitchen and the familiar, florid face opposite him.

'Marita and Camille. Are they vegetarian?'

He hears himself laughing, laughing out loud, a soft, derisive bark. Adrian is trying to appease him, offering him up some soft patter. 'I don't know anything about alternative approaches to asthma but I wouldn't want to interfere in any way with your regimen for her . . .' he hears him say. And somehow the absurdity of this breaks the spell. 'Look,' Stephen says, and stands up, in such a way as to indicate that for him at least, the encounter is over. 'It's pointless to say any of this to me. I've been here three months. Just three months. It's Marita you have to deal with. And you'll have to do that on your own.'

There's a moment silence. 'Fair enough. I appreciate your time.'

'Don't bullshit me, Adrian.'

It's a dangerous moment, the moment when one of them might let go. But it passes. And they walk in silence to the front door.

Out in the humid, overcast street he watches as Adrian wheezes into his car, watches while the red BMW makes one of its hasty, distracted U-turns, its owner's standard manoeuvre of arrogant retreat. From across the road, Basia's father raises his eyes from the pruning shears and stares blindly, enviously, after the car as it roars off down the hill.

So now it's a matter of waiting for her. Waiting for her to come home. He won't answer the phone when it rings in case it's her, and he doesn't want to talk about it at a distance. He wants her to be here.

When he hears her key in the lock on Sunday night, he is filled with immense relief, and tenderness. Striding to the front door he prepares to embrace her, but when he pulls back the door he is stunned by her pallor. Her hair is spiky and dishevelled; she is dark under the eyes. Camille is silent and uneasy. Everything is awkward. He kisses her lightly on the lips. 'Hi,' he says.

'Hi.'

He studies Camille for a moment, expecting to see some hitherto undetected likeness to Adrian but there's none. Not a flicker. He pats her head. 'Have a good time?' he asks.

'So-so,' she says, and clumps down the hall, dragging her overnight bag with exaggerated fatigue.

He carries Marita's bag into the bedroom and then follows her out into the kitchen.

'House looks nice,' she says, tonelessly.

'I cleaned it up. How was your week?'

'Wet.'

Of course, it had rained in the mountains for the past three days.

'Where were you? I rang several times and no-one ever answered.'

'I've been at the Institute a lot. And my sister's house.'

'Any calls?'

'No. Listen, have you eaten?'

She shakes her head.

'Want some soup?'

'That'd be nice.'

While she and Camille make the many small moves necessary to settle back into the house, he warms the chapatis and ladles out the soup. Marita eats in silence. Camille, however, has recovered her spirits and chatters on, describing for him her trip on the scenic railway.

'It was *so* steep,' she says, 'and some of the women screamed, but not the children.'

'Are children braver?'

She nods. 'Sometimes.'

'Where's my mountain bread?'

'Oops.' She covers her mouth with her hand and grins. 'Sorry. I forgot.'

'That's okay. Next time.'

Marita eats slowly, listlessly. He is tapping his foot under the table, impatient for the time to pass, for them to have a chance to speak. When Camille leaves the table and goes to her bedroom to unpack her bag, he lowers his voice and says. 'There are some things we need to talk about. Let's go for a walk.'

She looks up at him; gives him an odd, penetrating look. 'Not now, Stephen, I'm tired, really tired.'

'It has to be now. It won't take long. I'll go next door and ask Maria to come in for a while, or Camille can go over there.'

She begins to protest at this but he is insistent, almost fierce, and she appears to be too exhausted to resist. 'Ask Maria if she wouldn't mind coming here. I want Camille to have an early night.'

It's autumn now and the evenings are darker. As he closes the gate behind them he takes her hand and it's cold but that only makes him clasp it all the more firmly. They walk in silence in the direction of Memorial Park. Marita is too tired to say anything and he is too tense, so absorbed in rehearsing the moment that he is unable actually to precipitate it. When they reach the park she stops in her tracks and says: 'I'm tired. Let's sit on a bench.' And she heads for a bench near the old locomotive that has been painted in bright colours and cemented into its final resting place as a giant toy. Gazing at its massive iron funnel it is she, at last, who creates an opening.

'What's the matter?'

'I had a visit, yesterday morning. From Adrian.'

'Adrian came and saw *you*? The shit! What was he doing at my place? I told him I was going away for a while.'

'He wasn't looking for you, he was looking for me.'

'For you? What an arsehole!' Her face is white, and vehement. 'He told me he wouldn't come near you, that he'd stay away from the house — from Camille *and* from you — while I thought things over — ' She breaks off, sighs, and folding her arms disgustedly sits back against the bench, looking out with an angry glare at the slow traffic that cruises by the edge of the park. 'I don't know why I'm surprised,' she says at last. Her voice is low, and bitter.

'That's Adrian!'

'Did he tell you he's one of my clients?'

'Yes, he told me.'

She looks so unhappy that he can't bear it. He moves closer to her; he thinks he might put his arm around her shoulder. 'What are you going to do about it?' he begins to say, but she twists suddenly and turns to face him.

'Stephen,' she says, 'why didn't you tell me you'd been in gaol?'

'What?'

'Why didn't you tell me? That you'd done time?'

'Who told you that?' But he knows. Of course! Why hadn't this occurred to him before? Adrian and his private detective. His private detective who had evidently been very thorough and gone back way beyond the present, had dusted off his black pedigree in another time and another place. And he feels the old belligerence rising. 'Why should I tell you about that, Marita?' he says, coldly. But the look on her face is awful. He softens. 'I probably would have brought it up, eventually, in time. When we knew each other better.'

She gives him a look that is full of disappointment.

'Does it matter that much to you?'

'It might have done. It might have mattered a lot.'

What does she mean, it *might* have mattered? 'You mean, I might have been a murderer, or a rapist?'

She doesn't look at him, just nods her head.

'But I'm not, am I?'

'That's not the point, Stephen.'

'Well, what is the point? Why drag up the past? I never asked you who Camille's father was, or how you might have misspent *your* youth. None of my fucking business.'

'Don't be ridiculous, how can you say that? Everything about us is each other's business.'

That's an outdated notion, I reject it, he thinks. That's a romantic delusion, a woman's point of view. Possession. That's what that's all about. And maybe in time it might have become true, but she hadn't earned that right yet. Not in *his* mind.

'I don't believe that,' he says.

'Well, I do. Once you live with someone . . .' she begins, and her voice fades. She does not finish the sentence.

That was the problem, he thinks. They'd rushed into living together; fallen into it. Despite all their formidable resistances to it in the past, somehow they'd caught each other in an unguarded moment. If he hadn't offered her the Shiatsu treatment . . . if she hadn't come . . .

This conversation has winded him. He thought they were going to talk about Adrian, about the interloper on their hearth, about whether she still had feelings for him, about the fraught question of Camille, and how to tell her, how to accommodate the unwanted demons that search us out all the time and test our will. He had almost forgotten about himself, about the sullen young man who had been sentenced to two years while his sister stood in the public gallery, white-faced and in shock.

'Does it matter?'

'What?'

'Gaol.'

'Probably not.'

This, for a time, is all that either of them can manage, and they sit in silence, in what seems a trance, a dream. Some kids have come into the park and started up a game of soccer. Within minutes the ball cannons across their sightline, only a metre away. Normally he would get up and retrieve it for them, and warn them off, but he is unable to move. Finally he says: 'What are you going to do about Adrian?'

'I don't know.'

'Are you still fond of him?'

'*Fond?*' She looks up at him with a mixture of incredulity and scorn. 'I never was *fond* of him. '

'You must have liked something about him.' This is a challenge; a churlish, needling one.

'Must I? I don't know. It seems like something that happened to someone else, like a movie I once saw. A bit unreal. Anyway,' she sighs heavily, 'he pestered me a lot, and I was bored, and depressed. And he seemed . . .' she hesitates, searching for the right word, 'I don't know. Cheerful.' She laughs, derisively, and the derision is for herself. 'At that age, any man who wanted me badly enough could have me.' For the first time she looks him in the eye. 'That's not unusual, you know.'

He stares back at her, agitated by a flare of feeling that he would rather not acknowledge.

She looks away again. 'There's no question of renewing the relationship. He hasn't suggested it, and he'd get nowhere if he did.'

'So what, then?'

'So he wants Camille.'

'Is he threatening you?' He doesn't know why he asks this question; maybe because, at this moment, for reasons entirely obscure to him, *he'd* like to threaten her. Or someone.

'Not exactly.'

'What do you mean, *not exactly?*'

'He wants me to recognise Camille's paternity and give him certain rights. He says I should see a lawyer and we should do it all officially.' Her voice takes on a cutting matter-of-factness. 'He says he'll pay me any maintenance I want and I'll never have to work again.'

Buy an instant family, he thinks, money no object. 'How can he be sure he's Camille's father?'

'He can't. I know what you're saying, Stephen. I could say I'd slept with other men at the time and that there's no way of knowing, but the truth is that he *is* Camille's biological father.'

'So what? *He* doesn't know that. And he forfeited all his rights back then.'

'No, he didn't. Not exactly. I told him I didn't want him around. I pissed him off.' She says this softly, almost in a whisper. 'I did it all on my own, without help from anyone. Mother was useless. It's always been just us, me and Camille.'

No other men? He can't believe this.

'I had relationships,' she says, reading his mind. 'but no-one I allowed to move in. Until you.'

'Were you ever in love with him?'

She laughs. 'Stephen! What an old-fashioned question. Especially coming from you! Stephen the unsentimental! No, I wasn't in love with him, I told you that. Underneath, I don't think I even liked him. He's the most boring man I've ever been involved with. I wanted to have a child. And I wanted it to be mine, no-one else's. I didn't plan to get pregnant to Adrian but when it happened I didn't want an abortion either. I knew he was off to Hong Kong to work for a bank there, I thought he'd probably never come back, and even if he did, I didn't imagine he'd come looking for us. The world is full of children abandoned by their fathers! And full of women who are pissed off about it. But I have to have the one father who comes looking for his offspring. By now most other men would have had a wife and other children to distract them. It seemed a perfect scenario, really. Ironic, isn't it?'

He says nothing, just looks at her.

'I had no idea how hard it would be. You can't imagine, Stephen, what it's like to be alone with a small baby. And then to have to leave her behind with strangers when you go back to work. You can't imagine what it's like to be so tired that you could almost throttle your own child because you can't bear to hear her cry one more time. And there's no-one there to say, "I'll do it." If it hadn't been for Zoe, there would have been times when I might have packed up completely. And yet I love that child to distraction.' She is silent for a moment. 'And *now*, when all the hard part is over, he wants to swan in and have Sunday picnics in the park. Feel good days at the zoo, for Chrissake. But now, having come this far, I don't want to share her. Not with him, anyway.' She sighs. 'With you, maybe.'

He decides, for the moment, to ignore that. 'What about Camille? How's it going to affect her?'

'God knows.'

'What are you going to tell her?'

'I don't know. Adrian has agreed to a month's thinking time. I told him it was a shock and I needed time to think it over, not to mention prepare Camille for any consequences. "Oh, guess what, darling, your father's turned up." Or,' she adds, with a grimacing laugh, 'as Flora would say, your sperm donor.'

'What have you told her, all these years?'

'What I told her was more or less the truth. Her father went away to live in China and we've never heard from him since. Children accept things. I knew when she was older it might be different and she might want to know more.

It's not as if she has grandparents here, anyone who actually wanted to contribute something to her upbringing. Adrian's mother left him when he was young and went to live in the US. His father's dead. He's an only child.'

Stephen is listening, but only half-listening. Whatever this is, it's happened to him before: he stumbles into these force fields of anger and loss . . .

She has begun to speak again, but he isn't listening. Like a slow-burn, something in him is beginning to seethe. Why did Adrian have to tell her about his past? It has nothing to do with him, or Camille. What a mean, miserable calculation to make in all this! A power trip. It could only come from wanting to elbow him out of the picture, so that he doesn't have to put up with another man around the place. He thinks he can control everything, can move the pieces around on the chessboard, can buy and sell his way into and around the knight. And suddenly he feels a rush of possessiveness that floods him with annihilating force, and something in his head begins to throb, painfully, behind the eyes.

It's dark now. Side by side, without touching, they sit on the wooden bench, immobilised, like statues; staring ahead at the blurred trees. Finally she looks up. 'Let's go home,' she says. 'I don't want to talk anymore, not tonight, anyway.'

He waits for her — wants her — to move towards him, to put her hand on his. But she simply stands up, with her hands in the pockets of her jacket and, turning away from him, begins to walk home, leaving him on the bench. Then she stops, and looks back at him. 'Are you coming?' she says.

When he re-enters her house it is in an altered state of mind; restless; light in the head and limbs, too light, as if some reassuring weight at the centre of his chest has dropped out of him, on the walk home, and become mislaid. As soon as Maria is out the door he sinks into the couch in the living room and then thinks better of it; he needs to get up, move about, do something. 'Want some tea?' he asks her.

'OK,' she says, flatly, and disappears off down the hall.

And re-appears, some minutes later, in her kimono, hesitant in the doorway.

'Stephen?'

'Yes.'

'I don't want you to get the wrong idea about this, to get angry . . .'

'What?' Here it comes, he thinks.

'I know this might sound strange but I . . . I need to sleep on my own tonight. I feel really pressured, I feel like I need some space . . .' Her hands flap beside her helplessly. 'Please don't take it the wrong way.'

'You want me to sleep at Helen's.'

'I'd rather you stayed here. There's a camp bed in the cellar . . .'

'A camp bed?'

'Don't say it like that, it's just for tonight. My head . . . my head's all over the place.'

He puts down the cup he had been about to fill with hot spiced tea and reaches for his car keys that sit in their usual spot on top of her fridge.

'I think it would be better if I went.'

'Stephen, don't be angry — '

'Why not, why shouldn't I be angry?'

And at last she snaps at him. 'Because I'm the one under pressure here, that's why! I'm the one dealing with all the sudden revelations, I'm the one whose space is being invaded — '

'Not any more, you're not.' Thrusting the keys into his back pocket he brushes past her on his way to the door.

'I'm talking about him, not you!' She's shouting now.

'Look, you can have all the space you want, Marita!' he shouts back, and at that moment they both become aware of Camille, standing in the doorway of her bedroom, in her nightdress. Turning away from her he unhooks the chain on the front door and clicks open the lock. Camille follows him to the steps. 'Aren't you going to live here any more?' she says.

'No,' he says, spitefully, 'probably not.' And Christ, her face actually falls; her eyes cloud over and a look of, yes, disappointment, darkens her eyes. And he realises that he ought to say something to her, ought to pause at least and perhaps kiss her goodbye, or say he'll see her soon or tell her not to worry, but before he can summon any of these gestures he is already at the gate, full of a cold, dark, surly momentum; full of the worst kind of feeling, a black detachment; a sensation of being on automatic pilot, like a torpedo set off despite itself and with no sense of its mission. Jamming the car into reverse he backs out of the lane and drives off.

When he leaves the house he is intending to drive back to the Toxteth Estate but at the eastern outlet on the Ultimo freeway he finds himself taking the turn-off to the eastern suburbs and driving in the direction of Woollahra. When he pulls up outside Adrian's place the lights are on in the front room. Opening the gate he can hear muted voices, languid in late-night conversation. Poised for a moment on the verandah, he glances in through the French doors: behind the glass, suffused with mellow lighting, is a small group of men and women, the women in evening dress, the men in dinner suits. He steps up and rings the familiar doorbell. No-one comes. He rings it again.

Footsteps in the hall. Adrian's flushed and beaming face appears in the doorway. 'Stephen!' he exclaims, maintaining his outward appearance of jollity. 'A little late, isn't it?' Adrian is a bit drunk, a bit belligerent. 'Some other time, old son. I've got guests.'

Some other time? Did he say that? If only he hadn't said that. Stephen looks at him. A voice inside his head begins to speak. What are you doing here? it says. This is absurd. You are behaving unreasonably.

'Was it absolutely necessary to tell Marita about my prison record?' Is this someone else's voice talking? How formal those words — 'my prison record' — sound.

'Ah, that. Yes. Well, that was probably a mistake, old son, uttered in the heat of the moment. I didn't plan to tell her. She provoked me. Said that Camille didn't need me. That you could be a father to her. I got a bit stirred up.' Adrian is staring at him now, his guests forgotten. A woman's sleek blonde head appears around the living room doorway. 'Are you going to be long?' she asks.

'Not long,' he says, scarcely turning in her direction. 'Just give me a minute here.'

'You haven't exactly gone about this in a civilised way, have you?' Stephen can't help himself.

Adrian leans against the door jamb, his dinner jacket loose, one hand on his hip. 'You're a bit of a desperado, Steve, aren't you? I sensed it from the beginning, Zen pyjamas and all. Came out of a rough school, didn't you?'

Stephen is mute. Why is he baiting you like this? says the voice in his head. On Saturday morning he was all pathos and abject need. Now look at him, drunk on brandy with his friends and confident of his power.

'Ten months in Pentridge, eh? Can't have been much of a diet there.'

A car roars past in a frenzy of hoarse acceleration; somewhere, at the bottom of the hill, a woman is laughing with hysterical joy; from the living room comes the clink of metal on glass; in the hallway the light from the small chandelier blurs in a sudden, mesmeric flurry; the tessellation of the verandah tiles scuffs beneath his feet. He is breathless; his heart is pounding; he is looking down. Looking down at Adrian who is sitting, slumped, in an attitude of shock, fingering the blood from his broken nose that streams onto his fingers and down the front of his white shirt.

His voice is thick and furry. 'You bastard.'

'You're drunk.' He is quiet now. Calm. Speaking calmly to the client.

'You took advantage of me. You'll regret that.'

The two of them, winded. Stranded in the yellow glare of the street light. The aftermath is always like this, strangely anti-climactic.

'Ade?' A voice wafts out of the mellow living room and down the hallway. 'Ade? Are you okay?'

She's coming toward them. Now, now. It's time to go. Now.

And without being conscious of any movement, any intention, he is in his car and the engine is revving, and the car is moving, and he is driving down that softly curving road, and he is a cool, vacant body, shot out into space. Disconnected.

PART SEVEN

HOMECOMING

1

reprise (i)

Every night he rings her, every night after he has arrived home and after he has completed a turbulent meditation. And every night there is no answer, and he can only assume she has gone to the mountains. He drives over to Bright Street and knocks on Maria's door and asks where they've gone but Maria only sighs and shrugs and says: 'She did not say, Senor Stephen. She just go. One morning she is gone.' And he thinks Maria is foxing but he can't be sure. So he rings the mountains, and Mario answers and says, 'No, mate, haven't heard from her this week. Anything the matter?' 'Yeah, sort of,' he says, 'I'll talk to you later.'

The following morning a postcard arrives from his sister: *Cutting trip short. Arriving home Monday 16th. Qantas Fl. 1109, Helen.* So, she's coming back early. She doesn't trust him any longer to guard her precious house. Aroused by this news, he almost overlooks the letter that accompanies the postcard. When he opens the letter, he sees that it's from Marita.

•

The next day passes in a haze. It's unseasonally hot, a last flare of Indian summer and all day he breathes a kind of stifled breath. He has lost track of things, is careless; loses files on the console and makes more than one false beginning; finds that his pulse is racing in the morning and that he can barely stay awake in the afternoon. At one moment his senses are acute and everything, even the light, irritates him; and then, not so long after, he is dulled and unable even to taste the food in his mouth which congeals there like sodden chaff. In the mirror he looks sallow; at Eva's class he sits in a trance and hears only the odd word. He can't wait to escape, out into the streets of Chinatown, but when he does his nose is assailed by the smell of fried pork and his gorge rises and he thinks he might vomit into the trash in the alleyway. All he wants is to get home. No, no he doesn't. He doesn't want to go home at all, because it's stifling there, and he might as well stay on the streets where at least he can breathe, breathe in the smog, and he toys with the idea of playing the pin-ball machines in the blaring caverns of George Street. But no, the noise! The noise would unhinge him further. And he blanks out again and moves, like an automaton, to the bus shelter. And there in the shelter, among the motley night commuters and sitting on a scuffed wooden bench, is a woman carrying a baby. But he doesn't register this woman until he is on the bus and the woman has climbed aboard behind him and swung herself into the seat opposite. Ten o'clock at night and this woman is out with a baby. Is this right? Is this proper? He stares at her. She is the slatternly type, fat with unwashed hair, and she looks mildly retarded. She wears grey track pants stained with grease, a dirty pink T-shirt and rubber thongs that reveal her grimy feet and a thick rim of black dirt in her toenails. The odd thing about her is this: it's late at night and she is carrying a baby. The baby is barefoot and wearing a grubby white nightdress. From its downy head a single wisp of fair hair rises into an elfish point. Despite the hour, the baby is alert, and cheerful, and looks around with a kind of pert glee, smiling at the other passengers. Slumped in her seat the woman at first gazes ahead distractedly but after a while, lulled by the motion of the bus, her head begins to nod to one side, until finally she slumps against the window, dozing. They hear the clunk of her purse as it falls from her lap and rattles its small change against the floor. The baby, cradled precariously in the crook of her fat arm, continues to look around, still grinning, its little head bobbing with curiosity. He watches, holding his breath, and can feel the other passengers holding theirs, rigid with readiness to spring forward and catch the baby the moment the woman's arm relaxes — and the baby falls. But the baby does not fall. He catches the eye of the pubescent schoolboy next to the dozing woman. Before she had nodded off the woman had attempted to talk with the boy, had wanted to give him some money 'for an ice-cream' but he had turned away, flushed and taut with embarrassment.

The bus lurches on. The baby puts its finger in its mouth and then in the woman's mouth, and jabs, persistently. The woman wakes. The baby laughs.

The woman shouts: 'Geez, I've missed me stop!' She lurches out of her seat, her wide backside swaying unsteadily to the jolting rush of the bus, her dirty white thongs thumping down the aisle. Looking back at him, at all of them, still bright with a gleeful poise, the baby opens its small mouth wide and gives a silent laugh, before disappearing down the crowded stairs and out of sight. The other passengers exchange looks, as if to say: How can a creature like this have such an appealing baby? Is it hers? Did she steal it? Why are they out late? Stephen turns and smiles complicitly at the man next to him, a surly priest who smells of alcohol, but the man clears his sinuses and stares ahead.

Walking from the bus stop to the Toxteth Estate his head is beginning to clear and he is thinking about the baby. What was it about this baby? It had nothing; it was barefoot; it was grubby and cared for by an idiot. And yet it had a glow, as if it knew itself to be invulnerable. And it occurs to him that perhaps this baby has been sent to him, as a gift, to tell him something, and an apprehension of this creates in him, for the first time in days, a feeling of possibility.

But when he opens the door to the house, the still objects of his sister's salon rise up in the gloom like so many spectres and that brief utopian moment falls away. Slouching mindlessly to the phone in the kitchen, he dials Marita's number. Camille answers, and after hesitating for a moment too long, he hangs up.

●

It's 3 a.m. and he is banging on Marita's door. All of his being is in his hands and he can feel the skin on the side of his fist go numb as he thuds repeatedly against the wood.

He waits, can hear nothing. No movement inside. Breathing heavily he moves across to her window, trampling on the shrubs, and hissing through the bars: 'Marita! Open the door!'

When she opens the door to him her face is stern; she draws her kimono tightly around her, clutching it at the shoulders.

'I want to come in.' Surely she will see that he is desperate.

She stands to one side and waits for him to enter. As he makes to stride down the hall into the dark kitchen, an instinct moves her and she says, 'No', and takes his arm and begins to lead him awkwardly into the bedroom. Just over the threshhold he stops. 'I haven't come for a fuck!' he says, vehemently. His eyes are blazing. 'I know,' she says. 'Let's just sit on the bed.' He can see her in the bright glare of the streetlight. She is cold and white. He hears her voice, low, cautious.

She climbs up onto the bed and arranges the pillows against the high bedhead, then sits with her back against them, her knees drawn up to her chin. Watching her do this, a small figure, moving in shadow, a wave of dizziness and disorientation comes over him. He sinks onto the edge of the bed, with his back to her, looking down at the floor, his hands braced against the wood.

She waits for him to speak. For a long time he is silent. And so is she. She feels that anything she says, any *word*, might light the fuse. She hopes Camille is not awake and listening in the dark.

'I've made a mess of everything,' he says.

There's not as much self-pity in this as she might have expected, but she doesn't want to talk and simply closes her eyes, closes her eyes so that she does not have to look at him, at any part of him. And especially not at his neck, at the black ponytail coiled at the base of his shoulders. His neck; her undoing. Some special sanctuary, even now, that unravels any reasoned approach and leaves her prey to impulse, the impulse to throw herself on that neck and lose whatever guarded distance from him she might have achieved in the past days.

'I got your letter,' he says. His voice is a hostile whisper. 'Not a nice letter.' *I don't want to see either you or Adrian for a month,* she had written. *Men are like a dark, heavy wooden box that promises you comfort and ends by shutting you in.* And: *Neither Camille nor I are booty to be haggled over. I will think this through in my own way.*

'I was angry,' she says.

'I know what you're saying.'

'Do you? I'm not sure that I do.'

'And I accept what you say.'

Does he? Does he really? Then why is he here? She asked him not to come and he's here. What should she say now? What does she want to say? Whatever happens, she mustn't weaken.

'Has Adrian been pestering you?'

'He's not going to give up on wanting Camille, if that's what you mean. But it's OK, I can handle it. The last thing I want is for you to get involved.'

He continues to stare at the floor, trying to find the right words. He'll have to tell her.

'I know about the other night,' she adds. And saves him the trouble.

'No doubt he couldn't wait to tell you.'

In a sense, she reflects, that was probably true, because now, thanks to Stephen, Adrian has a weapon to bargain with. Should she tell him? What does she risk if he becomes angry again? Here, now? Will he go rushing off to Adrian a second time and make things even worse? 'He said he's thinking of pressing charges against you for assault.'

'He did, did he?'

Yes, he'd said that. With Stephen's record, he had told her, a magistrate might well send him back to gaol. And had then gone on to insinuate that he would drop the idea of charges in return for uncontested access to Camille. She had thought he might be bluffing, and rung her mother's solicitor for an opinion, which had not been encouraging. And she has to tell him all of this now, or he will find out later and think she has conspired against him. 'Somehow I don't think he will press charges,' she says, but he continues to stare blankly at the floor. Does he realise what she's saying? That she is willing to give over her precious Camille for some little time every week to keep this erratic man she doesn't know all that well out of gaol?

'What's it to you if he does?'

'Don't talk like that, Stephen.'

'Why not?' At last, self-pity has crept up on him.

'I think he wants to use this as a bargaining point with me. I give him access; he won't go to the police.'

For a while he's silent. '*Is* it a bargaining point?' he asks.

His hands rest against the edge of the bed. She stares at those hands. Such beautiful hands. Masculine hands. Large but beautifully made with fine dark hair leading the eye to the lower forearm, and the small, taut muscle just below the skin. 'You fool,' she says, softly, 'of course it is.'

For the first time he looks up. 'You give out very mixed messages, Marita.'

The heaviness in his sigh tells her that she can relax, that she needn't brace herself against him. 'No, I don't. You just don't know how to read them.'

'You think *that's* my problem?'

She thinks that words are becoming a burden, an exhausting aria of pain that cries out for its own demise. Her impatience overcomes her. I'll regret this, she thinks, and extending her arm, strokes his lower back with the tips of her fingers. And he shudders, and half turning to her, grabs her arm and stares at her, defiantly, with a look that says: It's your move, but don't complain later. And within seconds she is biting his shoulder, and he is locked into her, weeping, on the dishevelled bed.

But afterwards, as they lie in sweaty exhaustion, she makes it clear to him that nothing has changed. She still must have her month alone. Perhaps longer. And suddenly he doesn't want to be in this bed any more, and he gets up and stands by the window, contemplating the empty street outside. His long dark hair has worked loose and sits matted on his bare shoulders. She looks on as he dresses, slowly, clumsily, as if drugged. He thinks she is asleep but she isn't: she's lying still, and listening. She's seen these changes of mood before: one minute he's prostrate before her; the next, dismissive.

Some minutes after he has retreated into the rear of the house she gets up and wanders out into the moonlit kitchen and sees that he has unlocked the back door and is sitting in the courtyard. Seeing her, he looks back over his shoulder. 'Go to bed,' he says, 'I just want to sit here for a while.' She returns to the bedroom but does not sleep; simply lies in the dark, waiting for dawn. At five o'clock it comes, to her great relief. She can hear him in the kitchen and soon he appears bearing tea and toast which he offers to her in silence. And while she sips at the tea he opens the wardrobe and takes out his few clothes which he throws on the bed. Then, in an old bag that he brings in from the car, he packs his clothes and the few talismans of his short-lived occupation, his sharpening stone, his suribachi and his cooking knives.

Soon there will be no trace of him left in this house.

2

reprise (ii)

In the office he works in a scarified trance.

The others are gathered around Ralph's desk during the break having an earnest discussion about bushfires. Though it is autumn, for the past three days the city has been covered in an acrid pall. Out in the western suburbs the local councils have been burning off and the smoke from these man-made bushfires, trapped now in the wide, low-lying western basin, has drifted into the city. It's not our fault, opines the mayor: the Bureau of Meteorology predicted high winds blowing out to sea but the winds dropped without warning.

Sanjay is in a teasing mood. 'You people, you Australians, are obsessed with bush and bushfires. You are always burning off. Why don't you leave this bush alone?'

'It isn't that simple,' says Doug.

'You must understand,' says Ralph, 'the difference between backburning and protective burning. That's what we're on about here. A backburn is where you burn into or against the wind — '

' — but there was no wind — '

Gareth interjects: 'You might say this was a backburn that backfired,' Ralph ignores him.

' — to control a fire already raging — '

' — but there was no fire — '

'Exactly. This was protective burning. You want to avoid the situation, don't you, where summer comes, right? It's hot and dry, and you've got this massive undergrowth ready to go — ' Ralph throws up his arms in a mock flare — 'like that!'

'But surely,' says Sanjay, with dangerous persistence, 'if you burn off in early autumn, then by summer, this bush has already grown back, ready to —'

and he throws up *his* arms in a parody of Ralph — 'whoosh! Go up again!'

'Depends,' says Ralph, pausing to consider the obvious rejoinder, which for the moment eludes him.

'It's the eucalypt,' says Doug, drily. 'It's a tyrant. It burns and burns. Burns everything around it but the tree itself survives, see. You have to get to it first. Burn or be burned.'

'One of man's natural enemies,' says Gareth, completely deadpan.

Sanjay smiles. And turns to Stephen, who is still at his desk. 'This condition we observe, blanketing the city, is this smog or is this haze, Stephen?' he asks. 'Which is the correct English word? You used to keep a dictionary in your desk.'

'I gave it to Freda. Ask her.' He is abrupt.

'Freda is on psychiatric leave,' says Gareth. 'I'll look in her drawer.' Sure enough there is the dictionary. He flips over the pages until he finds the word 'haze' and then he looks up, smiling. '*Haze,*' he reads. '*Uncertainty.*'

They smile back at him, all of them, though they couldn't exactly say what it is they are smiling at.

Stephen goes on working.

3

Mascot

It's the last day of April, humid and overcast. In the wide, impersonal spaces of the Arrivals Lounge he waits for Helen, leaning against a steel column in front of the customs gates. Beyond the panoramic plate glass window a big white plane drones down out of a bank of low grey cloud.

When, finally, she emerges through the blue turnstile he is surprised at how pale she looks. She is very tall, his sister. Almost as tall as he. Her chestnut hair is shaped in a fashionable Italian cut and she wears the loose, flowing but tailored clothes of a woman who has shopped in Milan. But her narrow face is gaunt and her eyes are clouded with unfocussed resentment and he recognises with a small shock of familiarity that fierce, elegant will that is, and always has been, unfathomable to him.

He waves, walks unhurriedly toward her, kisses her lightly on the cheek and relieves her of a large, duty-free shopping bag.

'How are you?' he says.

'Tired.' Her eyes are glazed.

He looks over her shoulder to the turnstiles. 'Where's Ric?'

'Ric's staying behind in London for a while.'

'Oh.' He can't think of anything to say. As ever, small talk deserts him.

She looks around her, as if in a daze. 'I'm a bit disoriented. It's such a long flight, that one.'

Carrying the bags, they walk in silence to the main doors. She is no more or less cool to him than on any other occasion but there is some quality of distraction in her, some brooding distance. Maybe she is still resentful of him for not spending more time in the house; maybe it's just fatigue.

On the drive into the city the traffic is as frantic as ever and she is mostly silent, though she does tell him this. 'Ric and I have decided to separate,' she says. 'He'll move out and I'll keep the house.'

'Oh,' he says, 'I'm sorry to hear that.' The banality of his words! What else can he say? Oh, good. You'll be able to buy what you like now, all that stuff that Ric thought was a fetish. 'What brought this on?'

'Nothing special. It's been coming for a long while.' She looks up at him for the first time. 'You must have noticed we didn't get along awfully well.'

Well, yes and no. There seemed at times to be tension there, but then, what did he know about married couples? And besides, they were hardly ever home at the same time; careerists, always at work. Ric had been mildly scornful of her collecting, her *objets d'art*, and she'd had no interest in his addiction to football but that had seemed to him, Stephen, to be a fairly normal male–female split of interests and he could not recall ever having heard them argue.

'You're very quiet, Stephen,' she says to him, after a while. 'How's your new girlfriend? What's her name? Marita?'

'I'll tell you about that later,' he says.

As they turn into the Toxteth Estate he feels a heaviness descend from his chest into the pit of his stomach. Here they are driving home like some sort of couple; he without Marita, she without Ric. Thrown back on one another, like when they were children. Together they drag her heavy cases up the handsome Italianate steps. Then he inserts his key in the lock and turns. 'You aren't going to like this,' he says. 'It's pretty dusty.'

She steps in and looks about her, as if appraising an unfamiliar pensione. 'Well,' she says, setting her expensive leather carry-all down in the hallway. 'Well, I suppose I'm home.'

At this precise moment he realises how glad he is to see her. And feels an impulsive urge to put his arm around her and give her a hug, but it seems inappropriate, presumptuous somehow, if not self-serving. And he watches, respectfully, as she picks up the small Grecian head that sits on the chiffonier and gazes at it fondly.

'Everything's still here,' he says.

'Yes. Yes, it is.' And she runs her finger down the perfect nose of her eyeless God and sets it back on its plinth. 'I had a dream that it shattered,' she says, 'and thought it might be an omen or something. It's Apollo,' she adds.

'Is it? They all look alike to me.' Who on earth is Apollo? And how can this possibly matter to her?

In the kitchen he stands at the sink and fills the kettle. 'Vanilla tea?'

'Mmmm, yes.' She still seems distracted. There are dark smudges under her eyes. They remind him of Camille's. This is an unwanted thought and he stops, momentarily paralysed in the movement of lifting the tea scoop from out of the dark mass of tiny leaves. But she is too tired to notice.

He joins her at the table and pours the steaming tea into her cup. 'I'm sleeping here again,' he begins, 'if you're worried about being alone.'

She looks at him quizzically. 'I thought you were spending most of your nights with Marita.'

'I was.' He sighs. 'But things have changed.'

'Everything changes,' she says, 'and maybe that's not such a bad thing.' For a while she sips her tea in silence, and then: 'What happened to this Marita?'

Does she really want to know? He had thought she would be full of her own loss; but no, she is looking at him expectantly, with her austere, haughty gaze. So he tells her. Tells her, as baldly as he can, about the confrontation with Adrian, the aftermath with Marita. Adrian threatening to press charges. With this last information, her expression changes. 'Will he?' she asks, coldly. 'Probably not,' he says, wanting to pacify her, and shifts ground, telling her of Marita's desire to see neither of them for a month; the weakening of her resolve, though only for a night. He doesn't tell her about the agony of the next morning when he had taken his few clothes out of her wardrobe and shoved them into a small bag. And gathered up, in a clumsy, suppressed rage, his cookbooks and his cooking implements, the mortar and pestle, the suribachi, the sharpening stone. And his cooking knives, wrapping them carelessly in their green felt cloth so that the felt fell open in the bag and the knives worked their way into his clothes, disappearing like so many hidden daggers into the detritus of his abortive invasion. And worst of all, Camille had followed him to the door. A fleeting look not of triumph but of panic came into her eyes. And at that point, he'd almost lost it. He was just no good with things that took him by surprise. This most ordered life that he'd led for these past two years seemed to have left him essentially untouched, as molten and vulnerable and frantic as before. But he doesn't tell Helen any of that: it reeks of self-pity, and no doubt she has her own to contend with.

'What are you going to do?' she asks.

'I don't know.' Abruptly, he gets up from the table. 'It's getting late,' he says.

'Where are you going to live?'

'I don't know.' I have nowhere to live, he thinks. No mat at the Institute, no woman of my own, same old job, same old frustrations, same old anger; back where I was before, looking for a room, looking for a life, looking for a calling. For a few months he had begun to think that everything might change. Change! Huh! Here he was, back where he started, and not only had things not changed for the better but he had regressed into an old self, a ghost from his past had reared up and bitten a chunk out of his spirit.

There's a silence. No doubt she is running through her private litany of disapproval. He has been waiting, all this time, for her to utter some word of reproach but she seems unnaturally composed, her old bright-eyed, even febrile self becalmed at the kitchen table where her elbows rest against the white marble.

'Have you discussed this with anyone?'

'No.'

'What about Eva?'

He shakes his head.

'Ashamed?'

He laughs, despite himself. Laughs because it's a word that evokes childhood, as if he is still somehow a little boy. Shame? Is that what this sick feeling is? If only he knew. He doesn't answer her, just smiles and shakes his head, and looks down into his almost empty cup.

'You can stay here for a while, if you like. It might help me get used to the idea of living alone.'

How calm she is. It's so unlike her. This rift with Ric has obviously knocked her for six. Still, this is a relief to him. He had half expected her to lose her temper, to deliver a series of ultimatums, to express a desire that he leave shortly.

'Is it definite? About Ric?'

'Pretty definite.'

'He might change his mind once he's back in Sydney.'

At this she simply raises her eyebrows, and looks down at the table.

'Oh, well,' he says, 'at least you'll be able to buy what you like now, without any arguments from him.'

'Buy?'

'Yes.' He gestures in the direction of the front rooms. 'Your things.'

She simply nods her head, looking up at him distractedly, her mind elsewhere.

The afternoon is darkening. 'It's getting late,' he says. 'I'll go and buy some food.' She is still staring at him, oddly. Acutely. 'Alright,' she says. And then, as if talking to herself. 'Yes, yes, I *am* hungry.'

●

In the cramped aisle of the Macro shop in Newtown he rummages at the back of a pile of plastic-packed seaweeds for some dried kombu. How ironic that it is he, not Helen, who should take after their mother: she who, however else her life might be disintegrating around her, would always go on cooking. Helen on the other hand hates to cook, and hates shopping for food.

Last night he had intended preparing a homecoming meal for her, one or two of his special dishes, things he knew she liked from his diet (despite Ric's teasing) but when he'd arrived home from Eva's he had sunk on to the sofa in the den, twiddling with the remote control, angry with himself for not being able to capture Eva's attention so that he could tell her about his lapse with Adrian, the fiasco of his life. Lately she has been — not cool to him, but just slightly remote, as if he has failed some subtle test. And he knows it's because he had hesitated for too long about the vacant mat, and now Sarah has it. And the meal for Helen didn't happen, though it will tonight. He'll make an effort; he must always make that effort: when the day comes that he can't bring himself to cook then he'll know that his demoralisation is complete. But that day will never come. While ever he can use a knife that day will never come.

When he returns he finds her standing in the salon, like some mistress of Xanadu, gazing at her treasures. 'See that majolica lamp?' He follows her gaze to a dazzling white lamp base, ornately wrought in glossy cherubs who cavort beneath a shade of red silk. 'Ric bought that for me as a wedding present,' she says. 'At the time it was a bit Victorian for my taste. I was a purist for clean lines. But since then I've come to appreciate its baroque homeliness. You can't imagine the pleasure I get from it.' And absent-mindedly she fingers the cusped wing of an adoring cherub, its eyes upturned in playful ecstasy, its plump arms outstretched in carnal benediction.

She's mad, he thinks. Madder than I am.

'I know you can't see it, Stephen,' she says, 'but Art makes all the difference.'

All the difference to what? 'I'll make some dinner,' is all he says, and walks down the hallway and out into the kitchen. And after a moment's pause she follows on behind him. While he unpacks his purchases she stands at the

French windows contemplating, through the glass, the scarlet hibiscus in her courtyard. He glances over at her, and something in her stance affects him so that he moves across and puts his hand on her shoulder. 'It'll get better,' he says, mouthing a platitude that would offer no comfort to him. But he wants an excuse to touch her, to put his arm around her. Since he watched her walk through the customs gates at the airport, he cannot shake the image of that photograph in the album; he and Helen as children, she with her arm around his shoulder.

'I'm okay,' she says. 'If anything I feel heady. I feel a space opening up somewhere.'

'Good. I wish I could say the same.' He begins to move back to his work bench.

'Come here,' she says. 'I've got something for you.' And turning away from the window she reaches over to the fruit bowl and picks up an envelope that is propped beside it. 'Sit down,' she says.

Mechanically, he pulls out a chair and sits, without looking at her, or at anything in particular. Coming back to this house, seeing her again, like this, has flattened him, momentarily, like a psychic winding, but he doesn't want her to see this, and it won't last; it'll be alright once he gets going in the kitchen.

She lays the envelope down on the table in front of him. 'This is for you.'

He picks it up, opens the flap. Inside is a cheque. In her ragged, flowing hand the inscription is barely legible. He looks at it again. It appears to say this: '*Pay*: Stephen Eyenon *The sum of*: Seven thousand dollars.' He reads it again. Yes, that's what it says.

'What's this?'

'What's it look like? It's for you. It's for your precious *dojo* in Japan.'

'You're serious?'

'Yes, I am serious. I hope it's worth it.'

'You haven't got this kind of money. You've just been overseas for four months. I know you, you live off your credit cards.'

And for the first time since she came home she laughs. 'Stephen, don't ask where it comes from, just take it. And try to be gracious, for Christ's sake.'

He looks at her, the cheque like a light lethal weapon between his fingers, a booby prize that might go off any minute.

'You'll be in debt.'

'I'm always in debt. You worry too much about debt, you always have. It's one of the contradictions in your make-up. Careful about small things, reckless . . .' She does not complete the sentence but he knows what she was about to say: reckless in big things. The sudden move. The sudden strike. 'Debt's nothing.' She gets up and carries her empty cup to the sink where, in her usual methodical way, she begins to rinse and dry it, tossing the tea towel over her shoulder in a gesture of insouciance that floors him.

Oh, my God, he thinks, my God, and he lays his head on the table, against the white marble, and his eyes are wet and his damp cheek smudges against the cool, glossy surface.

She is opening the fridge. 'What have you got here?' she says, inspecting the contents in her imperious way.

He lifts his head. 'There's plenty of stuff there.' His voice is thick: it's an effort to speak. 'I'll cook something,' she says. Then hesitates. 'No,' turning to him, 'you cook. Some of that soup would be nice.'

'Which one?'

'That soup. What is it? Miso. That one.'

And with that word, 'miso', it comes to him. Change. It is possible, he thinks. Change is possible.

'You get on with it then.' She is walking away from him in the direction of the hallway. 'I'll start unpacking.'

'What about you?' he calls after her. 'You'll be living on your own.'

'That's alright,' she calls back, her voice echoing from the foot of the stairs. 'I've got plans for a new alarm.'

That night he dreams that he is walking along a fir-lined road across a white landscape, as if in some distant European outpost. And he realises that it's snowing: small white flakes fall onto his eyelids, catch in the black hair on his arms, and dissolve, leaving a cold wetness on the skin. And up ahead is a border crossing, and a dark figure waits for him there, clad in a uniform and a fur hat so large that his face is in shadow. As he approaches the figure, who must be some kind of border guard, he stops and the dark one advances towards him and says: Open your mouth. And he opens his mouth and the dark one says: Do you have all your teeth? And he runs the rim of his tongue around the inside surface of his teeth, upper and lower, and they're all there, intact, every one of them. He says: Yes, I have all my teeth. And the guard raises his torch and shines it into the hollow of his mouth, and he stands with his mouth gaping for what seems an age until the guard drops the torch to his side so that a circle of golden light is illumined on the snow.

And the guard says: Pass.

As he speaks his voice is no longer gruff, it has changed into a woman's voice, and he knows that voice, he's heard it before, somewhere, and as he trudges through the snow and across the border he realises that he has been talking to his mother.

PART EIGHT

BREAD

Demeter

Saturday afternoon. 1.45. 91 Bright Street, Leichhardt. Her small front garden. He opens the gate, knocks on the door, waits. Camille opens it.

'Hi, Stephen.'

He bends and kisses her on the top of the head. 'Hi. You ready?'

'Yep.'

Marita comes up behind Camille, her eyes widening in surprise. Almost brusquely, he kisses her on the cheek.

'You've cut your hair!'

Yes, he has. Cut off his long hair and had it cropped, all over, close to his head. 'What do you think?'

She gives a rueful smile. 'It makes you look hard.' And then: 'When are you going?'

'Thursday.'

'So soon?'

'Yes. The sooner the better. Eva has arranged it all for me. I'm staying with a friend of hers for the first week and then I'll be moving into the *dojo*.'

She nods. 'I see.'

It's the way she says it. 'I see.' He feels a sudden strong surge of yearning to cancel the outing he has planned for Camille, to stay here and sit with her, out in her small courtyard and drink tea. He looks at his watch. 'C'mon,' he says to Camille, 'we've got to be there by 2.15 sharp.'

On the corner of Mitchell and Derwent Streets, at the bottom end of Glebe, stands the Demeter Bakery. Once an old bakehouse of the conventional kind, it is owned and run now by the Helios group, anthroposophists of the Rudolf Steiner school who grow their own grain according to biodynamic principles and grind it weekly on the premises before baking it into many kinds of bread.

Once a month the bakers run a bread-making class for children and it's to this that Stephen is taking Camille this afternoon. A parting gift; a final injunction. Or, as Marita said laughingly, when he had issued the invitation: 'You don't give up, Stephen, do you? Still trying to have the last word.'

Not the last word, he might have said: the last *bite*.

They enter through a scrubbed pine door into the quaint little corner shop with its antique wooden counter and leadlight windows. On the counter are trays of freshly made fig pastries, apricot turnovers and cinnamon buns and the room is suffused with the smell of baking. The woman behind the counter indicates a side entrance and he ushers Camille through the door and down some steps to a small, open courtyard. There, a cluster of adults and children are already seated on wooden chairs, ranged in a semi-circle around two low tables. On each table is an antique grain grinder and ceramic pots of unhulled grain for the children to grind while they wait, and Stephen and Camille stand and look on as two energetic boys tackle the stone grinder, scattering grain all around them.

Soon a man appears from behind the steel door of the bakery and introduces himself as Gerry. He has bright red curly hair that seems to sit like an aura above his white baker's clothes; white shirt, white apron, white pants and black boots that are pale grey with flour dust. 'See that stone mill on the table,' he begins, 'that's an Indonesian rice mill and in that wooden bowl there is some of the flour that has been ground from this wheat. It's called golden flour, because it's golden treasure for our tummies.' Stephen looks around: he is not the only 'father' here, he notes, though most of the accompanying parents are women. 'So that's the first thing we have to do, we have to grind the grain in the right way. That way we preserve the life that is in the grain, the life that comes from the sun that nurtured it. We call this the life force, and if we grow our food in the right way, and cook it in the right way, then when we eat, this life force, this energy, goes into us and we're nurtured by it. Right?' He looks around at the small faces which stare back at him. They probably haven't followed a word of this, thinks Stephen. Already his own mind has begun to wander and he knows why. It's Marita. Today is the first time in ten days he has seen her and no less than ever, in fact more so, the mere sight of her unsettles him; activates a current that connects them across a deep crevice so that all his atoms rush to the precipice and look down. Meanwhile, beside him, two stocky boys are scuffing their feet and fisting each other furtively in the ribs. Gerry stares at them reprovingly.

'In the old days there used to be laws against bakers adding things to bread, things it shouldn't have. The ancient Romans used to add a thing called alum to whiten the bread. Alum was a powdered sulfate with aluminum in it. They used to do this in the Middle Ages too. But in Turkey, if the baker was caught doing that, they cut off his ear and nailed it to the baker's front door.' Suddenly he has the complete attention of the fidgeting boys. 'Right,' says Gerry, satisfied with his ploy. 'We'll go into the bakehouse now, and start preparing our dough.'

Inside, the bakehouse is warm and filled with the dusty wheat smell of milled flour. On four wooden tables a number of mixing bowls are set out, half-filled with a grainy flour. After a few minutes Gerry emerges from the rear with a bucket of liquid yeast which he proceeds to ladle out with an enamel mug, one mug into each bowl.

'OK,' he says, resuming his stance at the head of the room and in front of the iron doors of the old ovens, 'what we have here is our own special stoneground flour. Just flour, flour and salt, no extras, no chemicals, no add-ins. No preservatives, emulsifiers, no mould retardants to create 'shelf-life'. No short cuts either. This whole process is going to take us all afternoon. Right?'

Camille looks up at Stephen. 'All afternoon?' she whispers.

'Don't worry. It'll go quickly. There's a break for afternoon tea.'

'You right?' Gerry is looking at them. Stephen nods. 'OK. Start mixing your dough with your hands.'

As each of them sets to work Gerry walks between the tables, inspecting the dough for smoothness and consistency. Camille works her dough, at first tentatively, and then with an increasing earnestness which reminds Stephen of something Marita had once said: 'You make playful things serious, Stephen. You turn everyday stuff into a religion.' What was her term for him? A 'heavy customer'. This was rich, coming from Madame Angst!

'Right,' says Gerry, approvingly, having made his rounds, 'now we're going to knead it. Like this.' And he takes the dough of the small boy next to him and begins to demonstrate. 'When we knead we put our own energy, our own life force into the bread. In big bakeries they use machines for this and the result is never as good. Touching is very important. The human hand is a very special instrument, better than any substitute the brain can invent. OK, so away you go.'

Stephen looks down at his dough and smiles. Touching is a special thing. No kidding?

Beside him, Camille is working her dough with deft, graceful movements, every now and then looking over to see how he kneads his. On the other side of him a small boy is slamming his dough, banging it, and then punching it. Tiring of this he breaks it into two pieces and begins to shape them. 'This is a cat,' he says to Stephen, 'and this is a mouse,' and he crashes them together in one devouring movement so that the two segments collapse into one misshapen lump of dough. Camille screws up her face. 'Will that ruin the bread?' she murmurs discreetly to Stephen. 'Won't do it any good,' he murmurs back.

'Right,' says Gerry, patrolling the tables, 'how do you know when it's been kneaded enough? I'll tell you. There's an old German tradition that you feel the skin on the inside of your forearm, here, see? Nice and warm and loose and supple. That's how the dough should feel. Now, you try it.' They push up their sleeves and begin, self-consciously, to stroke the inside of their forearms. Then they finger the dough. Camille is absorbed now in the processes and follows obediently.

'Right!' says Gerry, clapping his hands together. 'What we're going to do next is let the dough ferment. Put the dough under your bowl so that it's completely covered. Like this.' And he demonstrates with the dough of the child nearest him. 'Now I'm going to explain to you about fermentation . . .'

Fermentation? Stephen knows all about fermentation, a word to describe the processes of his brain. And he's back in that night, that awful night when he'd driven around to her place at three in the morning and banged on her door and hissed her name through the barred window, terrified that she wouldn't open the door to him, and then what would he do? What could he trust himself not to do? But she had opened it and taken him wordlessly into her bed and stroked him patiently, endlessly, until he was coherent and they could begin to talk, whispering in the half light until morning. And he'd thought that it was all OK, that they were reconciled. But no, in the morning her resolve was unmoved. And yet, when he'd rung to tell her about his sister's gift, she had burst into tears! 'You want to punish me,' she said, and there was a tinge of bitterness in her voice. 'No,' he said, and for a long time couldn't say more. 'Then why do you have to go to this *dojo*?' she'd asked him. Because although she had wanted him to move out for a while she most definitely did not want him to move away altogether. And it was not as if Adrian was intent on pursuing him: once she had agreed to access to Camille all suggestion of charges had been abandoned. You want to punish me, she said again. No, he said, not any more, baffled at this outburst. I have to go because I've learnt nothing, or at least not enough. I thought things had changed and they haven't. I have to unlearn my old, bad habits.

'Any questions?' It's Gerry, breaking in on his reverie.

'Alright then, while we're waiting for the dough to rise I'll take you on a tour of the bakery. If you come out here with me I'll show you the big grain grinder.'

It's cold out in the courtyard now, at least it seems cold after the warmth of the bakehouse; the sky is overcast; the flagstones are chill. Camille shivers and stops to put on her green sweatshirt. By this time the others have taken up all the best vantage points around the massive electrical grinder. Stephen puts his hands on her shoulders and steers her through to the front row. 'This grinder,' begins Gerry, 'is a huge circle of stone that rotates against a second circle of stone. Now the usual method of milling requires roller mills which tear grains and separate out the endosperm, or starch, which is then bleached white to create what we call white flour. All the goodness and nutrients and fibre which are mostly in the outer husks of the grain are treated as waste, or sold separately as bran, sometimes to make chook food. So instead of going into our tummies it goes to the chooks. Does that make sense to you? Me neither. Now this is a big stone mill and one of the important things about it is that it's slow. It doesn't mangle the grain too much and it doesn't get too hot and heat up the flour which destroys nutrients. Now I'm going to press this switch and you'll see the fine flour begin to trickle out.' And the machine starts up with a whirr, maintaining a steady low vibration while fine curtains of flour waft down into the huge hessian bag at its mouth. The children come forward and congregate around the bag and rub their fingers in the drifting flour and before long all of them have the baker's badge, a white smudge on their face or clothing.

Then it's back to the bakehouse, with the brown wooden bowls, upended like turtle shells, dotted around the tables. 'Right,' says Gerry, with some dramatic flourish, 'lift up your bowls and see what's happened underneath.' There are smiles, low hubbub and exclamations of '*Cool!*' as the children examine the dough, now doubled in size, and seemingly possessed of a new energy; a dynamic plasticity, like a boulder come to life.

'We have to knead it a second time,' says Gerry, looking at his watch, 'and then we'll have afternoon tea. Knead it lightly this time, not too much, just enough to expel the air.'

Obediently, they all begin to knead.

After the second kneading they queue to wash their hands at the sink by the side wall and then they adjourn to the courtyard for afternoon tea. On the low tables are trays of warm cinnamon rolls and glasses of black grape juice. Camille bites into a cinnamon roll which is made with stoneground flour and is heavy compared to what she is accustomed to. 'What's it like?' Stephen asks. 'Nice,' she says, politely. He helps himself to one: just because this isn't really his sort of thing he shouldn't be stand-offish and remote. If he wants her to give a bit he'll have to do the same. Compromise on both sides. Unthinkable a few months ago, but then, a few months ago what did he know about children? Staring at the doughy rosette, studded with currents, it occurs to him: is it? Yes it is; it's the first time he's eaten anything like this since his black dream about the mound of chocolate cake. With an almost unnatural degree of focus, he lifts it to his mouth and permits his teeth, as if they had a life of their own, to take a bite of it. Yes, it's as he expected, a little sticky and cake-like for his taste, but it *is* an improvement on what he remembers of the commercial stuff. He wouldn't want to eat it every day, but for Camille, at least, it could be a first step.

Thus replenished they are ready for the final phase. Back in the bakehouse they take up their stations at the table. Camille looks up at Stephen and he winks at her. 'Nearly there,' he murmurs. She smiles complicitly. God, I'm tired, he thinks. I really am tired. This afternoon, after he drops her home, he'll go straight back to his sister's house and sleep.

'Right, now it's getting really interesting,' announces Gerry. 'Now we're at the artistic part. *You* have to choose a shape. Some people like to make just a basic round loaf, some like to do a plait — and I'll demonstrate one of those in a minute — and some of you children might like to make an animal shape, a lizard or a cat. OK, away you go.'

Deftly, Camille divides her dough in two. Stephen looks on while she pats one half into a small round loaf. Then she begins to break the other half into small pieces and roll them out into thin cylinders with the palm of her hand.

'What are you doing?'

'Making letters. I'm going to put my name along the top, see.' And she indicates the area of inscription with her finger. He smiles: the family obsession with words again.

But as she proceeds to shape the thin pieces into letters, C, A, M, I, L, she realises that she will not have enough dough. She looks up. 'Stephen,' she says, 'can I have a lend of some of yours?'

'A *lend* ?'

'Yeah. Do you mind? See, the problem is, my name's too long.'

'How do you propose paying it back?'

'Well . . .' she pauses, reflectively. 'I could give you some of my bread?'

'OK. It's a deal.' And he breaks off a piece and watches as she fashion the final letters: L, E.

Meanwhile the small boy next to him has been working his dough, trying to pinch and prod it into a vaguely recognisable shape.

What is it?' he asks

'Can't you guess?'

'No.'

'It's a sword.'

'Oh,' he says. Of course — what else? A sword. He himself fancies the intricate five star plait, a present for Marita, but he hasn't a clue how to weave it. Raising his hand, he beckons Gerry over.

And now for the final rites; spraying the loaves with water and sprinkling the surface with black poppy seeds. After which, they lay the many and diverse loaves on the table nearest the ovens where they can be admired, until the moment when Gerry produces a long wooden baker's ladle and begins to slide the loaves onto big black rectangular trays. And in through the high oven door they go. 'That'll take about twenty minutes,' he says, 'so come out into the courtyard. While we wait, I'm going to read you a story.'

Oh, no, thinks Stephen. Not a story.

So here they are, where they began, sitting in a half circle in the courtyard, only it's even colder now. A chill autumn wind gusts around their feet. Gerry emerges from the small office at the side carrying a candle in a brass candleholder which he sets down on one of the low tables. Cupping a hand around the wick to protect it from the wind he manages to get it alight on the third try. Then he squats on a stool and opens a thin picture book. 'I'm going to read you a story about the Goddess Demeter,' he begins. Clearing his throat he adjusts his purchase on the stool and adopting a solemn, almost reverent tone, commences on his narrative. 'Long, long, ago on Mount Olympus . . .'

Stephen closes his eyes. Suddenly he feels overcome. Fatigue. And more. The sad, sad drag in his stomach at the thought of seeing Marita soon, perhaps for the last time. The stress of the past few weeks seems all at once to sit in lead weights on his shoulders and in the muscles of his arms. His eyes are heavy. He yawns . . . and suddenly Camille is nudging him. He blinks, opens his eyes, blinks again, but a great wave of weariness is lowering him into the bench.

' . . . and Demeter takes her daughter out into the fields of Mount Olympus to show her which flowers she can pick, until they come to a flower that Persephone has never seen before, a flower with a purple centre and greyish white petals. This, says Demeter, is the narcissus and you should never, ever pick these. These are forbidden . . .'

Stephen yawns again. How dull these stories are. Folk culture and folk myth. He ought to find them moving, full of ancient wisdom, like Buddhist parables (which on the whole he likes) but instead they are merely soporific, childlike, and he is, alas, no longer a child, but the son of a corrupted culture, raised on speedier narratives, all of which he has tried to jettison.

'Well, back on Mount Olympus the sky begins to darken, and as Persephone plucks one of the narcissus flowers there's a mighty crash and the earth opens up beside her. She's a bit frightened now, and she can hear galloping coming up from the gloom of the earth and suddenly she sees four black war horses leading a chariot out of the earth and up into the sky. And in the chariot is the God of the underworld, Hades, and she knows he's come to get her . . .'

Stephen twists uncomfortably in his chair. These bare wooden chairs are hard, and too low for his long legs. He looks at his watch. Why couldn't Gerry just leave it at the bread? He glances down at Camille, who is gazing up at Gerry with a rapt expression.

' . . . When Demeter discovers what has happened to her beloved daughter, she is beside herself with fury. She puts out the torch she holds in her hand and takes off her robe of Goddess and from that night on Demeter wanders the earth, looking in all corners for her daughter, and so angry and upset is she that she neglects her most important jobs. The flowers die, the animals die. For the first time ever there is winter in the land, and snow falls on Mount Olympus . . .'

Ah! Jerking his chin up from his chest, he becomes aware that there, for a minute, he almost dozed off. He's not just tired, no, he's exhausted, wan from adrenalin burn-out. And now only this aching heaviness, this blurred buzzing in his head, these heavy, heavy lids. Sleep, if only he could let go, just for a moment, and sleep.

' . . . and despite famine in all the land Demeter will not be moved. Until, at last, in dismay Zeus orders Hades to release Persephone. And when, from a hilltop, Demeter sees her daughter approaching, she flies to her like a wild bird and they fall upon each other's neck, embracing. Long and long Demeter holds her dear child in her arms, gazing upon her. Then suddenly she has a thought. "My dear!" she cries out, "has any food passed your lips in all the time you have been in the underworld?" And Persephone remembers that she had been persuaded by Hades to eat the seeds of a pomegranate. When she tells her mother this, Demeter begins to weep. "Ah, my dearest," she cries, "now you have eaten from the underworld it will always have a claim on you . . ."'

If only he could, just for a few moments, lie down, or lean his head back against the wall. Yes, that's what he'll do, he'll lean his head back against the wall and look as if he is moved by the story and its eternal verities; lost in timeless contemplation. Adjusting his seat, quietly, noiselessly, he leans back into the circular cusp of the chair, and resting his head lightly against the cold brick of the old bakehouse he drifts, thoughtless at last, into sleep.

●

The front door is open, waiting for them to return. Camille skips down the passage, into the kitchen where her mother awaits them. 'Well, what was it like?' Marita asks.

'It was great.' Camille has her hands behind her back. 'Close your eyes.' Marita does as she is told and Camille flourishes her loaf from out of a large paper bag. 'Now open them.'

'Darling, that's wonderful!'

'*Oh, darling, that's wonderful!*' says Camille, mocking her mother in arch tones, and then squealing as Marita grabs her by the shoulders and tweaks her ear. All the while she clutches at her bread which, a moment before, she had proudly displayed, albeit minus a piece off the end.

'I see you've eaten a bit.'

'She ate some in the car on the way home,' says Stephen.

'I was starving.'

'What's it like?'

'OK. Quite nice, but I wouldn't want to eat it all the time.'

Marita looks at him, over Camille's head, and raises her eyebrows. He shrugs. It's alright, he thinks. I've sowed the seed. That's the best I can do.

'Stephen fell asleep. At the end, when the baker was reading a story!' says Camille.

'Dobber!' He grabs her playfully from behind and yanks on her plait.

'Did he now?' says Marita, staring him accusingly in the eye. 'He always falls asleep for the storytelling bit.' They look at one another, frankly, in silence. 'Would you like to stay for dinner?' she says.

'Yes, I would.' He says this without hesitation, though he had not for a moment anticipated the invitation.

'I've made a cake.'

'That's alright. I won't eat it.'

'What about your bread?'

'That's for you.'

And so they spend their last evening together, in her little courtyard that had for a time seemed like home. Camille waters her plants. When the planes fly over they play their old game of identifying them but he does not offer her money. Marita is quiet, and so is he. Neither of them is inclined to conversation. It's enough to sit here in peace together. If they began to say too much then one, or both, might crack, and the break might go either way; into anger and reproach, or sobbing and capitulation. Either way is too fraught. For now.

Maria is in her garden, singing to her pots as she waters her many herbs. Hearing his voice she comes to the fence — now, since he repaired it on that fateful Saturday, missing its gap where she was wont to poke her head through and make conversation. Since then, she has to stand on her toes. 'How are you, Senor Stephen?' she cries. 'You are going away?'

'Yes, Maria. I go on Thursday.'

'Ah,' she says, waving her hand, knowingly. 'Young people, always on the move!'

'I'll make some tea,' says Marita.

And in that moment he is seized by a sudden impulse. 'No,' he says, 'you talk to Maria. I'll make it.' He gets up, opens the screen door and walks into the kitchen, but instead of moving across to the sink to fill the kettle he continues walking, down the hall and out the front door to the car. Unlocking the boot, he lifts a green felt bundle out from under some loose newspaper. Closing the boot, he moves as quickly and silently as he can back in through the front door and into her bedroom. Crouching on the floor by the big cedar ship, he cannot resist a last look at what is underneath. Seeing the familiar cardboard box of dusty tapes, he feels a cold pricking at the base of his neck. No, he will not end up in that careless, motley pile, along with the others. Lifting his head, and squatting now beside the bed at sheet level, he lifts the bottom right-hand corner of the mattress. There, between foam underlay and antique iron springs, he conceals the green felt envelope of cooking knives. Then he gets up off his knees and goes out into the kitchen to make the tea.

•

It's some time after ten. Marita sits in her courtyard. Stephen has gone. He'd kissed her goodbye formally at the door and she'd taken a step back from him, overcoming a desire to lay her head on his chest and let it rest there for a very long time. They had already agreed, over dinner, to write to one another. That was enough. Is she relieved to see him go? She doesn't know. Yes, yes maybe that is what she's feeling now. On the other hand . . . there had been that terrible night, when he'd turned up on her doorstep at three in the morning, white-faced, and she'd been afraid of him. And after they'd talked, and wept, he'd become withdrawn. And got up and sat out in the courtyard on his own. Then, around five, when it was light, he came inside, opened the door of her wardrobe, lifted out his few clothes and threw them into an old bag. Camille must have heard him because she got up and followed him to the door. And they'd seen again that look of disappointment in her face. Camille wanted him to stay. From now on she would feel that something was missing. But only for a time. Children are adaptable, and part of their adaptation is knowing, instinctively, how to forget.

And now she has to get used to Adrian. Adrian. What a mess. Adrian, who annoys and repulses her. After the first shock of contact had subsided she had rummaged in the cardboard box under the bed. And listened again to the tapes she'd made of him, all those years ago. And they were as she remembered them, the most banal of any she had made. She'd been able to make nothing of them. No sense at all, no interesting story. No arresting detail here. . . no evocative phrase there. Nothing. How odd that Camille should be the outcome of the least interesting man she'd ever made love to. She winces at that phrase. Slept with. That was better. Perhaps Camille is Adrian's story? She turns this thought over in her mind to see if it disturbs her. Surprisingly, it doesn't. Perhaps Adrian's story is Camille? He obviously thinks so. And she sits, still a little stunned by this realisation: I'm going to have to put up with having this man around for the rest of my life.

And what of Stephen? Is he going because he wants an excuse to leave her? To opt out completely? All she'd asked for was some time, a moratorium while she sorted things out. But no, he has to go off altogether. One day he can't bear to be away from her, the next, he can't wait to get on the plane. She can understand him being upset about his loss of control, his losing it with Adrian, but his reaction since seems extreme. 'You don't understand,' he'd said to her on that horrible night. 'There was a moment when I could have throttled him. I thought I had it all down but I've learnt nothing. No, that's not true,' he'd said with vehemence. '*I haven't learned enough.* I have to go away, go somewhere where I can unlearn my bad habits.'

So here she is. Still alone. Still resisting. Though there are times when she feels unbearably alone in her responsibility to Camille, her need to be all things to her child, when she feels the burden of care wrap around her like a heavy blanket, there have been other times when they are ecstatic together, living in a dancing blur of impulse and light-headed freedom.

And now, Mother. Mother wants to intervene. You are not in a fit state emotionally or psychologically to negotiate anything with this man, she had said of Adrian. I will speak to my solicitor. And just when Marita had opened her mouth to say, Don't be ridiculous, I'm not a child, something unexpected had settled on her tongue and she had agreed, as if under a spell, to let her mother act as an intermediary. Her mother, she knows, will drive a hard bargain. Not that she, Marita, is interested in money . . . only in the boundaries of her time and space. And oddly enough, this is something, perhaps the one thing that Mother understands, the need for time and space!

However could she have let Stephen enter her house and occupy her hearth and bed so suddenly? Without any preamble, any struggle, any resistance . . . what had come over her? There was that aura about him. He had seemed like a black angel from another world . . . different. She laughs mockingly at that word. 'Different.' That's what women always think. Only this time it was true. He was — is — different.

She sighs. There are eight months left of her freedom. Eight months before she must go back to work. Already it has been an eventful year. Perhaps, with Adrian's maintenance money for Camille, she can string out her time even longer. In the three months since Stephen entered her life something has changed . . . something she cannot begin to express in words, although, perhaps, if she were to try and tease it out on paper . . . And she begins to compose a letter in her head. *Dearest Stephen* . . . it begins.

Coda

Kyoto

3 June

Dear Marita,

So how goes it, black eyes? I went for a long walk tonight during which I felt that I was ready at last to write to you. The first day I got here I wanted to write and say a whole lot of things, some good, some bad, but I held back. I told myself I was in another place now, and I should let go of what I'd left behind, at least for a while. Give myself a chance to get out of the old head space. Now I feel I'm ready to say something positive. You know how I feel about living in the past so I'm not going to dwell on the last few months, only on what's happening now.

I'm surprised at the dojo. Don't ask me why but it seems familiar. You think it's going to be exotic and it isn't. It wouldn't be the right scene for everyone (you'd hate it) but in crucial ways I fit into the Japanese scheme of things. The Japanese are very habitual, so that's what Todoroki Sensei focuses on. Habit is the first thing that has to go. He comes into our room in the middle of the night and says, 'Move your beds from this room to the room across the hall.' For no reason at all. And you never know when something like that is going to happen. In the morning he says: at 2 o'clock we're going for a hike, so when we turn up at the station he says, 'What are you doing here? We're not going for a hike, we're going to have a lecture.' And some people get angry, very angry, they aren't prepared for it. The next time he says we're going for a hike they think it's a trick and turn up without their kit, and then, disaster! They have to run back for their kit and miss the train. Or they walk all day in the wrong shoes. At this rate it doesn't take long for him to break you. After a while you start to think provisionally, as in, well, maybe we'll do this, maybe we won't. It's like being a bit on edge. Prepared for anything. Open to it. You begin to leave your habitual patterns behind. The hardest thing is learning how to sleep in a totally new way. Every morning they come around at 5.30 and play Japanese martial music. After about a month you can't help but wake up at 5.30 and then he goes, no, from now on you sleep in until seven. The moment you start getting used to getting up at 5.30 he orders you to stay in bed. And you're lying there, 5.30, wide awake, fidgeting, cursing and swearing about not being able to get up. And so you learn how to wake at 5.30 if you have to and also how to relax enough to sleep until 7 if that's OK too. You realise you have to be flexible. It's not surrendering yourself to the environment, rather you're in relationship to it, and sooner or later everything begins to heal. Master Todoroki says that all illness is based on habit, where you're just doing it because you're doing it, and it's the most comfortable way because you can't relate to the environment and so you're always going to be out of touch with what you actually need — brush your teeth with the opposite hand, walk backwards if you can't make a decision about something, run backwards down the beach, sleep on the other side of the bed for a while. Tough for us, very tough for us to do this in the West.

And then, if all this doesn't work, and you still don't loosen up, drastic measures. I'd heard about it from Eva and Keith and last Wednesday I saw it happen for the first time. Or rather I sensed it happening. We were all sitting in the great hall, meditating, as we normally do, and Todoroki is walking around with his bamboo staff, and we're supposed to ignore it, to be oblivious to it, although we know that at any moment we might get a crack across the shoulders. Anyway, I'm sitting there, in lotus position, and I hear it, a sort of dull thud, and this gasp, more like a grunt, and I don't open my eyes and I don't know who it is, and I feel relieved it isn't me— but at the same time I feel kind of envious, envious of the experience. How does it feel at that moment? What flows from it afterwards? And I pray soon that it will be me. Something in me craves that blow. This may seem crazy to you, it would probably seem crazy to all women, but if you were a man you'd understand.

Better go now. I've raved on a lot I know, or a lot for me, anyway. You always complained that I didn't talk enough. I won't tell you how often I think of you. You probably don't want to hear. Give Camille a hug from me.

My love,

Stephen

Sydney

29 June

Dearest Stephen,

It was lovely to get your letter. I know you said you would write but I thought that once you were in your monk's life you might think better of it. But as soon as I saw the blue airmail envelope and the Japanese stamps I got all excited again. I don't think I can begin to comment on what you're doing in Kyoto and I would only irritate you if I tried, which doesn't mean that I'm not interested. On the contrary, it sounds fascinating.

Things are kind of settling down here. I have almost come to an agreement with Adrian. I told him and his lawyer that I will accept only the legal minimum both in access terms and in child support — that should discourage him from believing that he can control the world with his money. At least he's accepted that he has to be patient. I'm not sure how I'm going to bring him and Camille together for the first time, I have to give that some thought.

After you left I became demoralised and depressed and Mother took over and negotiated the final terms. She never cared for Adrian, though funnily enough she continues to approve of you. I told her you'd been to gaol and she said: 'I'm not at all surprised' and didn't even ask why or how you got there. But that's Mother. She believes in essences. She makes up her mind and that's that. Do you remember that day we all went over to Darling Point? I could see then that you and she were in some way alike. I read her your letter — revenge on her for all the times I've had to listen to her journal.

You'll be pleased to know that Camille is teaching Flora to make bread. She's extremely bossy about it, too. Flora came over on Saturday afternoon and they threw flour around the kitchen for what seemed like hours. Flora lectured us on the story of Demeter and Persephone, pontificating at length, and loudly, as is her wont.

Camille kept trying to get a word in. 'That's not what happened,' she'd say, referring back to her day at the bakery and the story she heard there. They kept arguing over their respective versions until the bread was ready, then they really did tuck in — you wouldn't approve — lashings of butter and Vegemite! I had only a taste so that I could make approving noises. I've been sick, one of those viruses that come and decide they like it and they'll settle in, and I remember you saying that bread is bad for colds and flu. I lay in bed one night aching all over and then I thought of you and ginger compresses and that started me crying so I howled all night, on and off. I hope you get a good crack across the shoulders soon.

Yesterday Maria gave me a small figtree in a pot and I planted it in the corner near the loquat bush. Zoe came over and we ate outside in the courtyard for what will probably be the last time until spring comes. I've asked Zoe to be here on the first day that Adrian comes to collect Camille. Moral support.

So that's my news. See what a restrained letter I can write. Just like yours. How careful we are with our words. There are other things I could say, am tempted to say, things about your body. Sometimes I wake up in the middle of the night and I can smell the scent of you in my bed — but enough of that.

It's cold now, the leaves are cluttering up the yard, Maria is looking older and more weary, I'm missing you Stephen, and what else? Oh, yes. I almost forgot. I must be getting soft in the head or something because I actually invited Ros over tomorrow, perhaps because, since you left, the house sometimes feels a bit empty. She's coming to lunch here for the first time ever. I was tempted to serve up something execrable and see if she'd even notice but no, we're going to do it properly. I'm making your asparagus pie recipe. And Camille announced that as a 'special treat', she would be making us all some bread.

My love to you, Stephen

Marita

P.S. Yes, I found your knives under my mattress. I took them out and put them in the cutlery drawer next to mine. They're waiting for you.

'*You shake my nerves and you rattle my brain/ Too much love drives a man insane. . .*'
In the kitchen at 91 Bright Street, Camille is dancing to the rhythm of her new tape, *The Best of Jerry Lee*, another gift from Zoe. Beside her, Flora stamps her feet and flails her arms, giggling in self-conscious parody of a routine from their favourite film, *Grease*. 'You can be Danny and I'll be Sandy,' Camille had said as she'd slid the tape into her mother's big ghetto-blaster.

'No, we'll both be Danny and *then* we'll both be Sandy,' Flora had replied.

'But that doesn't make sense.'

'Yes, it does.'

'*You broke my will / But what a thrill . . .*' On the floor, strewn around their feet, are the coloured foil wrappers from a secret cache of chocolates and toffees that Camille has been hiding since Estelle's last visit.

'When will your mum be home?'

'What's the time?' Camille stops and looks at her watch. 'Soon,' she says.

'Doesn't your mum work? Mine do.'

'Not at the moment, she doesn't. She's at the lawyer's.'

'My uncle's a lawyer.'

'Yeah?' Camille stops in the middle of her gyrations. 'Did you know I've got a father now?'

'I thought he lived in China.'

'Yeah, well, he's come back.'

'Does he live here?'

'No. He isn't going to live here. I'm going to stay at his place sometimes.'

'What's he like?

'Don't know. Haven't met him yet. I'm seeing him on Saturday. I just hope he's good-looking. You know, not old or stuff.'

'Old and ugly! Old and ugly!' Flora begins to stomp in a grotesque dance around her friend.

'Don't, Flora! That's being mean!'

Flora stops, smiling her wide, gleeful smile. 'Have you got any more of Estelle's chocolates?' she asks.